TWELVE RED HERRINGS

Jeffrey Archer is a master storyteller, the author of eleven novels which have all been worldwide bestsellers. *Not a Penny More, Not a Penny Less* was his first book, and it achieved instant success. Next came the tense and terrifying thriller *Shall We Tell the President?*, followed by his triumphant bestseller *Kane & Abel*. His first collection of short stories, *A Quiver Full of Arrows*, came next, and then *The Prodigal Daughter*, the superb sequel to *Kane & Abel*. This was followed by *First Among Equals*, considered by the *Scotsman* to be the finest novel about parliament since Trollope, the thrilling chase story *A Matter of Honour*, his second collection of stories, *A Twist in the Tale*, and the novels *As the Crow Flies* and *Honour Among Thieves*. *Twelve Red Herrings*, his third collection of stories, was followed by the novels *The Fourth Estate* and *The Eleventh Commandment*. A collected edition of his short stories was published in 1997, followed by another collection, *To Cut a Long Story Short*. His latest novel, *False Impression*, was published by Macmillan in 2005.

Jeffrey Archer was born in 1940 and educated at Wellington School, Somerset, and Brasenose College, Oxford. He represented Great Britain in the 100 metres in the early sixties, and entered the House of Commons when he won the by-election at Louth in 1969. He wrote his first novel, *Not a Penny More, Not a Penny Less*, in 1974. From September 1985 to October 1986 he was deputy chairman of the Conservative Party, and he was created a life peer in the Queen's Birthday Honours of 1992. In 2001 he was sentenced to four years in prison for perjury and during that time wrote three volumes of prison diaries. He was released in July 2003 and since then has written his first screenplay, *Mallory: Walking off the Map*, and run the London Marathon (slowly). He is married with two children.

ALSO BY JEFFREY ARCHER

JEFFREY ARCHER

TWELVE RED HERRINGS

PAN BOOKS

First published 1994 by HarperCollins Publishers

This edition published 2004 by Pan Books
an imprint of Pan Macmillan Ltd
Pan Macmillan, 20 New Wharf Road, London N1 9RR
Basingstoke and Oxford
Associated companies throughout the world
www.panmacmillan.com

ISBN-13: 978-0-330-41906-2
ISBN-10: 0-330-41906-4

7 9 8

A CIP catalogue record for this book is available from
the British Library.

Printed and bound in Great Britain by
Mackays of Chatham plc, Chatham, Kent

To Chris, Carol . . . and Alyson

Contents

* The stories indicated with an asterisk are based on known incidents (some of them embellished with considerable licence). The others are the product of my own imagination.

J.A.
July 1994

TRIAL AND ERROR

I‍T'S HARD TO KNOW EXACTLY WHERE TO begin. But first, let me explain why I'm in jail.

The trial had lasted for eighteen days, and from the moment the judge had entered the courtroom the public benches had been filled to overflowing. The jury at Leeds Crown Court had been out for almost two days, and rumour had it that they were hopelessly divided. On the barristers' bench there was talk of hung juries and retrials, as it had been more than eight hours since Mr Justice Cartwright had told the foreman of the jury that their verdict need no longer be unanimous: a majority of ten to two would be acceptable.

Suddenly there was a buzz in the corridors, and the members of the jury filed quietly into their places. Press and public alike began to stampede back into court. All eyes were on the foreman of the jury, a fat, jolly-looking little man dressed in a double-breasted suit, striped shirt and a colourful bow tie, striving to appear solemn. He seemed the sort of fellow with whom, in normal circumstances, I would have enjoyed a pint at the local. But these were not normal circumstances.

As I climbed back up the steps into the dock, my eyes

settled on a pretty blonde who had been seated in the gallery every day of the trial. I wondered if she attended all the sensational murder trials, or if she was just fascinated by this one. She showed absolutely no interest in me, and like everyone else was concentrating her full attention on the foreman of the jury.

The clerk of the court, dressed in a wig and a long black gown, rose and read out from a card the words I suspect he knew by heart.

'Will the foreman of the jury please stand.'

The jolly little fat man rose slowly from his place.

'Please answer my next question yes or no. Members of the jury, have you reached a verdict on which at least ten of you are agreed?'

'Yes, we have.'

'Members of the jury, do you find the prisoner at the bar guilty or not guilty as charged?'

There was total silence in the courtroom.

My eyes were fixed on the foreman with the colourful bow tie. He cleared his throat and said, '. . .

I first met Jeremy Alexander in 1978, at a CBI training seminar in Bristol. Fifty-six British companies who were looking for ways to expand into Europe had come together for a briefing on Community Law. At the time that I signed up for the seminar Cooper's, the company of which I was chairman, ran 127 vehicles of varying weights and sizes, and was fast becoming one of the largest private road haulage companies in Britain.

My father had founded the firm in 1931, starting out with three vehicles – two of them pulled by horses – and an overdraft limit of ten pounds at his local Martins bank. By the time we became 'Cooper & Son' in 1967 the company had seventeen vehicles with four wheels or more, and delivered goods all over the north of England. But the old man still resolutely refused to exceed his ten-pound overdraft limit.

I once expressed the view, during a downturn in the market, that we should be looking further afield in search of new business – perhaps even as far as the Continent. But my father wouldn't hear of it. 'Not a risk worth taking,' he declared. He distrusted anyone born south of the Humber, let alone those who lived on the other side of the Channel. 'If God put a strip of water between us, he must have had good reasons for doing so,' were his final words on the subject. I would have laughed, if I hadn't realised he meant it.

When he retired in 1977 – reluctantly, at the age of seventy – I took over as chairman, and began to set in motion some ideas I'd been working on for the past decade, though I knew my father didn't approve of them. Europe was only the beginning of my plans for the company's expansion: within five years I wanted to go public. By then, I realised, we would require an overdraft facility of at least a million pounds, and would therefore have to move our account to a bank which recognised that the world stretched beyond the county boundaries of Yorkshire.

It was around this time that I heard about the CBI seminar at Bristol, and applied for a place.

The seminar began on the Friday, with an opening address from the Head of the European Directorate of the CBI. After that the delegates split into eight small working groups, each chaired by an expert on Community Law. My group was headed by Jeremy Alexander. I admired him from the moment he started speaking – in fact, it wouldn't be an exaggeration to say that I was overawed. He was totally self-assured, and as I was to learn, he could effortlessly present a convincing argument on any subject, from the superiority of the Code Napoléon to the inferiority of the English middle-order batting.

He lectured us for an hour on the fundamental differences in practice and procedure between the member states of the Community, then answered all our questions on Commercial and Company Law, even finding time to explain the significance of the Uruguay Round. Like me, the other members of our group never stopped taking notes.

We broke up for lunch a few minutes before one, and I managed to grab a place next to Jeremy. I was already beginning to think that he might be the ideal person to advise me on how to go about achieving my European ambitions.

Listening to him talk about his career over a meal of stargazy pie with red peppers, I kept thinking that, although we were about the same age, we couldn't have come from more different backgrounds. Jeremy's father, a banker by profession, had escaped from Eastern Europe only days before the outbreak of the Second World War.

He had settled in England, anglicised his name, and sent his son to Westminster. From there Jeremy had gone on to King's College, London, where he read Law, graduating with first-class honours.

My own father was a self-made man from the Yorkshire Dales who had insisted I leave school the moment I passed my O levels. 'I'll teach you more about the real world in a month than you'd learn from any of those university types in a lifetime,' he used to say. I accepted this philosophy without question, and left school a few weeks after my sixteenth birthday. The next morning I joined Cooper's as an apprentice, and spent my first three years at the depot under the watchful eye of Buster Jackson, the works manager, who taught me how to take the company's vehicles apart and, more importantly, how to put them back together again.

After graduating from the workshop, I spent two years in the invoicing department, learning how to calculate charges and collect bad debts. A few weeks after my twenty-first birthday I passed the test for my heavy goods vehicles licence, and for the next three years I zig-zagged across the north of England, delivering everything from poultry to pineapples to our far-flung customers. Jeremy spent the same period reading for a master's degree in Napoleonic Law at the Sorbonne.

When Buster Jackson retired I was moved back to the depot in Leeds to take over as works manager. Jeremy was in Hamburg, writing a doctoral thesis on international trade barriers. By the time he had finally left the world of academia and taken up his first real job, as a partner with a large firm of commercial solicitors in the City, I had been earning a working wage for eight years.

Although I was impressed by Jeremy at the seminar, I sensed, behind that surface affability, a powerful combination of ambition and intellectual snobbery that my father would have mistrusted. I felt he'd only agreed to give the lecture on the off-chance that, at some time in the future, we might be responsible for spreading some butter on his bread. I now realise that, even at our first meeting, he suspected that in my case it might be honey.

It didn't help my opinion of the man that he had a couple of inches on me in height, and a couple less around the waist. Not to mention the fact that the most attractive woman on the course that weekend ended up in his bed on the Saturday night.

We met up on the Sunday morning to play squash, when he ran me ragged, without even appearing to raise a sweat. 'We must get together again,' he said as we walked to the showers.' 'If you're really thinking of expanding into Europe, you might find I'm able to help.'

My father had taught me never to make the mistake of imagining that your friends and your colleagues were necessarily the same animals (he often cited the Cabinet as an example). So, although I didn't like him, I made sure that when I left Bristol at the end of the conference I was in possession of Jeremy's numerous telephone and telex numbers.

I drove back to Leeds on the Sunday evening, and when I reached home I ran upstairs and sat on the end of the bed regaling my sleepy wife with an account of why it had turned out to be such a worthwhile weekend.

Rosemary was my second wife. My first, Helen, had been at Leeds High School for Girls at the same time that I had attended the nearby grammar school. The two schools shared a gymnasium, and I fell in love with her at the age of thirteen, while watching her play netball. After that I would find any excuse to hang around the gym, hoping to catch a glimpse of her blue knickers as she leapt to send the ball unerringly into the net. As the schools took part in various joint activities, I began to take an active interest in theatrical productions, even though I couldn't act. I attended joint debates, and never opened my mouth. I enlisted in the combined schools orchestra and ended up playing the triangle. After I had left school and gone to work at the depot, I continued to see Helen, who was studying for her A levels. Despite my passion for her, we didn't make love until we were both eighteen, and even then I wasn't certain that we had consummated anything. Six weeks later she told me, in a flood of tears, that she was pregnant. Against the wishes of her parents, who had hoped that she would go on to university, a hasty wedding was arranged, but as I never wanted to look at another girl for the rest of my life, I was secretly delighted by the outcome of our youthful indiscretion.

Helen died on the night of 14 September 1964, giving birth to our son, Tom, who himself only survived a week. I thought I would never get over it, and I'm not sure I ever have. After her death I didn't so much as glance at another woman for years, putting all my energy into the company.

Following the funeral of my wife and son, my father, not a soft or sentimental man – you won't find many of those in Yorkshire – revealed a gentle side to his character that I had never seen before. He would often phone me in the evening to see how I was getting on, and insisted that I regularly joined him in the directors' box at Elland Road to watch Leeds United on Saturday afternoons. I began to understand, for the first time, why my mother still adored him after more than twenty years of marriage.

I met Rosemary about four years later at a ball given to launch the Leeds Music Festival. Not a natural habitat for me, but as Cooper's had taken a full-page advertisement in the programme, and Brigadier Kershaw, the High Sheriff of the county and Chairman of the Ball Committee, had invited us to join him as his guests, I had no choice but to dress up in my seldom-worn dinner jacket and accompany my parents to the ball.

I was placed on Table 17, next to a Miss Kershaw, who turned out to be the High Sheriff's daughter. She was elegantly dressed in a strapless blue gown that emphasised her comely figure, and had a mop of red hair and a smile that made me feel we had been friends for years. She told me over something described on the menu as 'avocado with dill' that she had just finished reading English at Durham University, and wasn't quite sure what she was going to do with her life.

'I don't want to be a teacher,' she said. 'And I'm

certainly not cut out to be a secretary.' We chatted through the second and third courses, ignoring the people seated on either side of us. After coffee she dragged me onto the dance floor, where she continued to explain the problems of contemplating any form of work while her diary was so packed with social engagements.

I felt rather flattered that the High Sheriff's daughter should show the slightest interest in me, and to be honest I didn't take it seriously when at the end of the evening, she whispered in my ear, 'Let's keep in touch.'

But a couple of days later she rang and invited me to join her and her parents for lunch that Sunday at their house in the country, 'And then perhaps we could play a little tennis afterwards. You do play tennis, I suppose?'

I drove over to Church Fenton on Sunday, and found that the Kershaws' residence was exactly what I would have expected – large and decaying, which, come to think of it, wasn't a bad description of Rosemary's father as well. But he seemed a nice enough chap. Her mother, however, wasn't quite so easy to please. She originated from somewhere in Hampshire, and was unable to mask her feeling that, although I might be good for the occasional charitable donation, I was not quite the sort of person with whom she expected to be sharing her Sunday lunch. Rosemary ignored the odd barbed comment from her, and continued to chat to me about my work.

As it rained all afternoon we never got round to playing tennis, so Rosemary used the time to seduce me in the little pavilion behind the court. At first I was nervous about making love to the High Sheriff's daughter, but I soon got used to the idea. However, as the weeks passed, I began to wonder if I was anything more to her than a 'lorry driver fantasy'. Until, that is, she started to talk about marriage. Mrs Kershaw was unable to hide her disgust at the very idea of someone like me becoming her son-in-law, but her opinion turned out to be irrelevant, as Rosemary remained implacable on the subject. We were married eighteen months later.

Over two hundred guests attended the rather grand county wedding in the parish church of St Mary's. But I confess that when I turned to watch Rosemary progressing up the aisle, my only thoughts were of my first wedding ceremony.

For a couple of years Rosemary made every effort to be a good wife. She took an interest in the company, learned the names of all the employees, even became friendly with the wives of some of the senior executives. But, as I worked all the hours God sent, I fear I may not always have given her as much attention as she needed. You see, Rosemary yearned for a life that was made up of regular visits to the Grand Theatre for Opera North, followed by dinner parties with her county friends that would run into the early hours, while I preferred to work at weekends, and to be tucked up in bed before eleven most nights. For Rosemary I wasn't turning out to be the husband in the title of the Oscar Wilde play she had recently taken me to – and it didn't help that I had fallen asleep during the second act.

After four years without producing any offspring – not that Rosemary wasn't very energetic in bed – we began to drift our separate ways. If she started having affairs (and I certainly did, when I could find the time), she was discreet about them. And then she met Jeremy Alexander.

It must have been about six weeks after the seminar in Bristol that I had occasion to phone Jeremy and seek his advice. I wanted to close a deal with a French cheese company to transport its wares to British supermarkets. The previous year I had made a large loss on a similar enterprise with a German beer company, and I couldn't afford to make the same mistake again.

'Send me all the details,' Jeremy had said. 'I'll look over the paperwork at the weekend and call you on Monday morning.'

He was as good as his word, and when he phoned me he mentioned that he had to be in York that Thursday to brief a client, and suggested we get together the following day to go over the contract. I agreed, and we spent most of that Friday closeted in the Cooper's boardroom checking over every dot and comma of the contract. It was a pleasure to watch such a professional at work, even if Jeremy did occasionally display an irritating habit of drumming his fingers on the table when I hadn't immediately understood what he was getting at.

Jeremy, it turned out, had already talked to the French

company's in-house lawyer in Toulouse about any reservations he might have. He assured me that, although Monsieur Sisley spoke no English, he had made him fully aware of our anxieties. I remember being struck by his use of the word 'our'.

After we had turned the last page of the contract, I realised that everyone else in the building had left for the weekend, so I suggested to Jeremy that he might like to join Rosemary and me for dinner. He checked his watch, considered the offer for a moment, and then said, 'Thank you, that's very kind of you. Could you drop me back at the Queen's Hotel so I can get changed?'

Rosemary, however, was not pleased to be told at the last minute that I had invited a complete stranger to dinner without warning her, even though I assured her that she would like him.

Jeremy rang our front doorbell a few minutes after eight. When I introduced him to Rosemary, he bowed slightly and kissed her hand. After that, they didn't take their eyes off each other all evening. Only a blind man could have missed what was likely to happen next, and although I might not have been blind, I certainly turned a blind eye.

Jeremy was soon finding excuses to spend more and more time in Leeds, and I am bound to admit that his sudden enthusiasm for the north of England enabled me to advance my ambitions for Cooper's far more quickly than I had originally dreamed possible. I had felt for some time that the company needed an in-house lawyer, and within a year of our first meeting I offered Jeremy a place on the board, with the remit to prepare the company for going public.

During that period I spent a great deal of my time in Madrid, Amsterdam and Brussels drumming up new contracts, and Rosemary certainly didn't discourage me. Meanwhile Jeremy skilfully guided the company through a thicket of legal and financial problems caused by our expansion. Thanks to his diligence and expertise, we were able to announce on 12 February 1980 that Cooper's would be applying for a listing on the Stock Exchange later that year. It was then that I made my first mistake: I invited Jeremy to become Deputy Chairman of the company.

Under the terms of the flotation, fifty-one per cent of the shares would be retained by Rosemary and myself. Jeremy explained to me that for tax reasons they should be divided equally between us. My accountants agreed, and at the time I didn't give it a second thought. The remaining 4,900,000 one pound shares were quickly taken up by institutions and the general public, and within days of the company being listed on the Stock Exchange their value had risen to £2.80.

My father, who had died the previous year, would never have accepted that it was possible to become worth several million pounds overnight. In fact I suspect he would have disapproved of the very idea, as he went to his deathbed still believing that a ten-pound overdraft was quite adequate to conduct a well-run business.

During the 1980s the British economy showed continual growth, and by March 1984 Cooper's shares had topped the five-pound mark, following press speculation about a possible takeover. Jeremy had advised me to accept one of the bids, but I told him that I would never allow Cooper's to be let out of the family's control. After that, we had to split the shares on three separate occasions, and by 1989 the *Sunday Times* was estimating that Rosemary and I were together worth around thirty million pounds.

I had never thought of myself as being wealthy – after all, as far as I was concerned the shares were simply pieces of paper held by Joe Ramsbottom, our company solicitor. I still lived in my father's house, drove a five-year-old Jaguar, and worked fourteen hours a day. I had never cared much for holidays, and wasn't by nature extravagant. Wealth seemed somehow irrelevant to me. I would have been happy to continue living much as I was, had I not arrived home unexpectedly one night.

I had caught the last plane back to Heathrow after a particularly long and arduous negotiation in Cologne, and had originally intended to stay overnight in London. But by then I'd had enough of hotels, and simply wanted to get home, despite the long drive. When I arrived back in Leeds a few minutes after one, I found Jeremy's white BMW parked in the driveway.

Had I phoned Rosemary earlier that day, I might never have ended up in jail.

I parked my car next to Jeremy's, and was walking towards the front door when I noticed that there was only one light on in the house – in the front room on the first floor. It wouldn't have taken Sherlock Holmes to deduce what might be taking place in that particular room.

I came to a halt, and stared up at the drawn curtains for some time. Nothing stirred, so clearly they hadn't heard the car, and were unaware of my presence. I retraced my steps and drove quietly off in the direction of the city centre. When I arrived at the Queen's Hotel I asked the duty manager if Mr Jeremy Alexander had booked a room for the night. He checked the register and confirmed that he had.

'Then I'll take his key,' I told him. 'Mr Alexander has booked himself in somewhere else for the night.' My father would have been proud of such thrifty use of the company's resources.

I lay on the hotel bed, quite unable to sleep, my anger rising as each hour passed. Although I no longer had a great deal of feeling for Rosemary, and even accepted that perhaps I never had, I now loathed Jeremy. But it wasn't until the next day that I discovered just how much I loathed him.

The following morning I rang my secretary, and told her I would be driving to the office straight from London. She reminded me that there was a board meeting scheduled for two o'clock, which Mr Alexander was pencilled in to chair. I was glad she couldn't see the smile of satisfaction that spread across my face. A quick glance at the agenda over breakfast and it had become abundantly clear why Jeremy had wanted to chair this particular meeting. But his plans didn't matter any more. I had already decided to let my fellow directors know exactly what he was up to, and to make sure that he was dismissed from the board as soon as was practicable.

I arrived at Cooper's just after 1.30, and parked in the space marked 'Chairman'. By the time the board meeting was scheduled to begin I'd had just enough time to check over my files, and became painfully aware of how many of the company's shares were now controlled by Jeremy, and what he and Rosemary must have been planning for some time.

Jeremy vacated the chairman's place without comment the moment I entered the boardroom, and showed no particular interest in the proceedings until we reached an item concerning a future share issue. It was at this point that he tried to push through a seemingly innocuous motion which could ultimately have resulted in Rosemary and myself losing overall control of the company, and therefore being unable to resist any future takeover bid. I might have fallen for it if I hadn't travelled up to Leeds the previous evening and found his car parked in my driveway, and the bedroom light on. Just when he thought he had succeeded in having the motion agreed without a vote, I asked the company accountants to prepare a full report for the next board meeting before we came to any decision. Jeremy showed no sign of emotion. He simply looked down at his notes and began drumming his fingers on the boardroom table. I was determined that the report would prove to be his downfall. If only it hadn't been for my short temper, I might, given time, have worked out a more sensible way of ridding myself of him.

As no one had 'any other business' to raise, I closed the meeting at 5.40, and suggested to Jeremy that he join Rosemary and me for dinner. I wanted to see them together. Jeremy didn't seem too keen, but after some bluffing from me about not fully understanding his new share proposal, and feeling that my wife ought to be brought in on it at some stage, he agreed. When I rang Rosemary to let her know that Jeremy would be coming to dinner, she seemed even less enthusiastic about the idea than he had been.

'Perhaps the two of you should go off to a restaurant together,' she suggested. 'Then Jeremy can bring you up to date on what's been going on while you've been away.' I tried not to laugh. 'We haven't got much food in at the moment,' she added. I told her that it wasn't the food I was worried about.

Jeremy was uncharacteristically late, but I had his usual whisky and soda ready the moment he walked through the door. I must say he put up a brilliant performance over dinner, though Rosemary was less convincing.

Over coffee in the sitting room, I managed to provoke the confrontation that Jeremy had so skilfully avoided at the board meeting.

'Why are you so keen to rush through this new share allocation?' I asked once he was on his second brandy. 'Surely you realise that it will take control of the company out of the hands of Rosemary and me. Can't you see that we could be taken over in no time?'

He tried a few well-rehearsed phrases. 'In the best

interests of the company, Richard. You must realise how quickly Cooper's is expanding. It's no longer a family firm. In the long term it has to be the most prudent course for both of you, not to mention the shareholders.' I wondered which particular shareholders he had in mind.

I was a little surprised to find Rosemary not only backing him up, but showing a remarkable grasp of the finer details of the share allocation, even after Jeremy had scowled rather too obviously at her. She seemed extremely well-versed in the arguments he had been putting forward, given the fact that she had never shown any interest in the company's transactions in the past. It was when she turned to me and said, 'We must consider our future, darling,' that I finally lost my temper.

Yorkshiremen are well known for being blunt, and my next question lived up to our county's reputation.

'Are you two having an affair, by any chance?'

Rosemary turned scarlet. Jeremy laughed a little too loudly, and then said, 'I think you've had one drink too many, Richard.'

'Not a drop,' I assured him. 'Sober as a judge. As I was when I came home late last night, and found your car parked in the driveway and the light on in the bedroom.'

For the first time since I'd met him, I had completely wrong-footed Jeremy, even if it was only for a moment. He began drumming his fingers on the glass table in front of him.

'I was simply explaining to Rosemary how the new

share issue would affect her,' he said, hardly missing a beat. 'Which is no more than is required under Stock Exchange regulations.'

'And is there a Stock Exchange regulation requiring that such explanations should take place in bed?'

'Oh, don't be absurd,' said Jeremy. 'I spent the night at the Queen's Hotel. Call the manager,' he added, picking up the telephone and offering it to me. 'He'll confirm that I was booked in to my usual room.'

'I'm sure he will,' I said. 'But he'll also confirm that it was I who spent the night in your usual bed.'

In the silence that followed I removed the hotel bedroom key from my jacket pocket, and dangled it in front of him. Jeremy immediately jumped to his feet.

I rose from my chair, rather more slowly, and faced him, wondering what his next line could possibly be.

'It's your own fault, you bloody fool,' he eventually stammered out. 'You should have taken more interest in Rosemary in the first place, and not gone off gallivanting around Europe all the time. It's no wonder you're in danger of losing the company.'

Funny, it wasn't the fact that Jeremy had been sleeping with my wife that caused me to snap, but that he had the arrogance to think he could take over my company as well. I didn't reply, but just took a pace forward and threw a punch at his clean-shaven jaw. I may have been a couple of inches shorter than he was, but after twenty years of hanging around with lorry drivers, I could still land a decent blow. Jeremy staggered first backwards and then forwards, before crumpling in front of me. As he fell, he cracked his right temple on the corner of the glass table, knocking his brandy all over the floor. He lay motionless in front of me, blood dripping onto the carpet.

I must admit I felt rather pleased with myself, especially when Rosemary rushed to his side and started screaming obscenities at me.

'Save your breath for the ex-Deputy Chairman,' I told her. 'And when he comes round, tell him not to bother with the Queen's Hotel, because I'll be sleeping in his bed again tonight.'

I strode out of the house and drove back into the city centre, leaving my Jaguar in the hotel carpark. When I walked into the Queen's the lobby was deserted, and I took the lift straight up to Jeremy's room. I lay on top of the bed, but was far too agitated to sleep.

I was just dozing off when four policemen burst into the room and pulled me off the bed. One of them told me that I was under arrest and read me my rights. Without further explanation I was marched out of the hotel and driven to Millgarth Police Station. A few minutes after five a.m., I was signed in by the custody officer and my personal possessions were taken from me and dropped into a bulky brown envelope. I was told that I had the right to make one telephone call, so I rang Joe Ramsbottom, woke his wife, and asked if Joe could join me at the station as quickly as possible. Then I was locked in a small cell and left alone.

I sat on the wooden bench and tried to fathom out why I had been arrested. I couldn't believe that Jeremy would have been foolish enough to charge me with assault. When Joe arrived about forty minutes later I told him exactly what had taken place earlier in the evening. He listened gravely, but didn't offer an opinion. When I had finished, he said he would try to find out what the police intended to charge me with.

After Joe left, I began to fear that Jeremy might have had a heart attack, or even that the blow to his head from the corner of the table might have killed him. My imagination ran riot as I considered all the worst possibilities, and I was becoming more and more desperate to learn what had happened when the cell door swung open and two plain-clothes detectives walked in. Joe was a pace behind them.

'I'm Chief Inspector Bainbridge,' said the taller of the two. 'And this is my colleague, Sergeant Harris.' Their eyes were tired and their suits crumpled. They looked as if they had been on duty all night, as both of them could have done with a shave. I felt my chin, and realised I needed one as well.

'We'd like to ask you some questions about what took place at your home earlier this evening,' said the Chief Inspector. I looked at Joe, who shook his head. 'It would help our enquiries, Mr Cooper, if you co-operated with us,' the Chief Inspector continued. 'Would you be prepared to give us a statement either in writing or as a tape recording?'

'I'm afraid my client has nothing to say at the moment, Chief Inspector,' said Joe. 'And he will have nothing to say until I have taken further instructions.'

I was rather impressed. I'd never seen Joe that firm with anyone other than his children.

'We would simply like to take a statement, Mr Ramsbottom,' Chief Inspector Bainbridge said to Joe, as if I didn't exist. 'We are quite happy for you to be present throughout.'

'No,' said Joe firmly. 'You either charge my client, or you leave us – and leave us immediately.'

The Chief Inspector hesitated for a moment, and then nodded to his colleague. They departed without another word.

'Charge me?' I said, once the cell door had been locked behind them. 'What with, for God's sake?'

'Murder, I suspect,' said Joe. 'After what Rosemary has been telling them.'

'Murder?' I said, almost unable to mouth the word. 'But . . .' I listened in disbelief as Joe told me what he'd been able to discover about the details of the statement my wife had given to the police during the early hours of the morning.

'But that's not what happened,' I protested. 'Surely no one would believe such an outrageous story.'

'They might when they learn the police have found a trail of blood leading from the sitting room to the spot where your car was parked in the drive,' said Joe.

'That's not possible,' I said. 'When I left Jeremy, he was still lying unconscious on the floor.'

'The police also found traces of blood in the boot of your car. They seem quite confident that it will match up with Jeremy's.'

'Oh, my God,' I said. 'He's clever. He's very clever. Can't you see what they've been up to?'

'No, to be honest, I can't,' Joe admitted. 'This isn't exactly all in a day's work for a company solicitor like me. But I managed to catch Sir Matthew Roberts QC on the phone before he left home this morning. He's the most eminent criminal silk on the north-eastern circuit. He's appearing in the York Crown Court today, and he's agreed to join us as soon as the court has risen. If you're innocent, Richard,' Joe said, 'with Sir Matthew defending you, there will be nothing to fear. Of that you can be certain.'

Later that afternoon I was charged with the murder of Jeremy Anatole Alexander; the police admitted to my solicitor that they still hadn't found the body, but they were confident that they would do so within a few hours. I knew they wouldn't. Joe told me the following day that they had done more digging in my garden during the past twenty-four hours than I had attempted in the past twenty-four years.

Around seven that evening the door of my cell swung open once again and Joe walked in, accompanied by a heavily-built, distinguished-looking man. Sir Matthew Roberts was about my height, but at least a couple of stone heavier. From his rubicund cheeks and warm smile he looked as if he regularly enjoyed a good bottle of wine and the company of amusing people. He had a full head of dark hair that remained modelled on the old Denis Compton Brylcreem advertisements, and he was attired in the garb of his profession, a dark three-piece suit and a silver-grey tie. I liked him from the moment he introduced himself. His first words were to express the wish that we had met in more pleasant circumstances.

I spent the rest of the evening with Sir Matthew, going over my story again and again. I could tell he didn't believe a word I was saying, but he still seemed quite happy to represent me. He and Joe left a few minutes after eleven, and I settled down to spend my first night behind bars.

I was remanded in custody until the police had processed and submitted all their evidence to the Department of Public Prosecutions. The following day a magistrate committed me to trial at Leeds Crown Court, and despite an eloquent plea from Sir Matthew, I was not granted bail.

Forty minutes later I was transferred to Armley Jail.

The hours turned into days, the days into weeks, and the weeks into months. I almost tired of telling anyone who would listen that they would never find Jeremy's body, because there was no body to find.

When the case finally reached Leeds Crown Court nine months later, the crime reporters turned up in their hordes, and followed every word of the trial with relish. A multi-millionaire, a possible adulterous affair and a missing body were too much for them to resist. The tabloids excelled themselves, describing Jeremy as the

Lord Lucan of Leeds and me as an oversexed lorry driver. I would have enjoyed every last syllable of it, if I hadn't been the accused.

In his opening address, Sir Matthew put up a magnificent fight on my behalf. Without a body, how could his client possibly be charged with murder? And how could I have disposed of the body, when I had spent the entire night in a bedroom at the Queen's Hotel? How I regretted not checking in the second time, but simply going straight up to Jeremy's room. It didn't help that the police had found me lying on the bed fully dressed.

I watched the faces of the jury at the end of the prosecution's opening speech. They were perplexed, and obviously in some doubt about my guilt. That doubt remained, until Rosemary entered the witness box. I couldn't bear to look at her, and diverted my eyes to a striking blonde who had been sitting in the front row of the public gallery on every day of the trial.

For an hour the counsel for the prosecution guided my wife gently through what had taken place that evening, up to the point when I had struck Jeremy. Until that moment, I couldn't have quarrelled with a word she had spoken.

'And then what happened, Mrs Cooper?' prodded counsel for the Crown.

'My husband bent down and checked Mr Alexander's pulse,' Rosemary whispered. 'Then he turned white, and all he said was, "He's dead. I've killed him."'

'And what did Mr Cooper do next?'

'He picked up the body, threw it over his shoulder,

and began walking towards the door. I shouted after him, "What do you think you're doing, Richard?"'

'And how did he respond?'

'He told me he intended to dispose of the body while it was still dark, and that I was to make sure that there was no sign that Jeremy had visited the house. As no one else had been in the office when they left, everyone would assume that Jeremy had returned to London earlier in the evening. "Be certain there are absolutely no traces of blood," were the last words I remember my husband saying as he left the room carrying Jeremy's body over his shoulder. That must have been when I fainted.'

Sir Matthew glanced quizzically up at me in the dock. I shook my head vigorously. He looked grim as counsel for the prosecution resumed his seat.

'Do you wish to question this witness, Sir Matthew?' the judge asked.

Sir Matthew rose slowly to his feet. 'I most certainly do, M'Lud,' he replied. He drew himself up to his full height, tugged at his gown and stared across at his adversary.

'Mrs Cooper, would you describe yourself as a friend of Mr Alexander?'

'Yes, but only in the sense that he was a colleague of my husband's,' replied Rosemary calmly.

'So you didn't ever see each other when your husband was away from Leeds, or even out of the country, on business?'

'Only at social events, when I was accompanied by

my husband, or if I dropped into the office to pick up his mail.'

'Are you certain that those were the only times you saw him, Mrs Cooper? Were there not other occasions when you spent a considerable amount of time alone with Mr Alexander? For example, on the night of 17 September 1989, before your husband returned unexpectedly from a European trip: did Mr Alexander not visit you then for several hours while you were alone in the house?'

'No. He dropped by after work to leave a document for my husband, but he didn't even have time to stay for a drink.'

'But your husband says . . .' began Sir Matthew.

'I know what my husband says,' Rosemary replied, as if she had rehearsed the line a hundred times.

'I see,' said Sir Matthew. 'Let's get to the point, shall we, Mrs Cooper? Were you having an affair with Jeremy Alexander at the time of his disappearance?'

'Is this relevant, Sir Matthew?' interrupted the judge.

'It most assuredly is, M'Lud. It goes to the very core of the case,' replied my QC in a quiet even tone.

Everyone's gaze was now fixed on Rosemary. I willed her to tell the truth.

She didn't hesitate. 'Certainly not,' she replied, 'although it wasn't the first time my husband had accused me unjustly.'

'I see,' said Sir Matthew. He paused. 'Do you love your husband, Mrs Cooper?'

'Really, Sir Matthew!' The judge was unable to

disguise his irritation. 'I must ask once again if this is relevant?'

Sir Matthew exploded. 'Relevant? It's absolutely vital, M'Lud, and I am not being assisted by your lordship's thinly veiled attempts to intervene on behalf of this witness.'

The judge was beginning to splutter with indignation when Rosemary said quietly, 'I have always been a good and faithful wife, but I cannot under any circumstances condone murder.'

The jury turned their eyes on me. Most of them looked as if they would be happy to bring back the death penalty.

'If that is the case, I am bound to ask why you waited two and a half hours to contact the police?' said Sir Matthew. 'Especially if, as you claim, you believed your husband had committed murder, and was about to dispose of the body.'

'As I explained, I fainted soon after he left the room. I phoned the police the moment I came to.'

'How convenient,' said Sir Matthew. 'Or perhaps the truth is that you made use of that time to set a trap for your husband, while allowing your lover to get clean away.' A murmur ran through the courtroom.

'Sir Matthew,' the judge said, jumping in once again. 'You are going too far.'

'Not so, M'Lud, with respect. In fact, not far enough.' He swung back round and faced my wife again.

'I put it to you, Mrs Cooper, that Jeremy Alexander was your lover, and still is, that you are perfectly aware he is alive and well, and that if you wished to, you could tell us exactly where he is now.'

Despite the judge's spluttering and the uproar in the court, Rosemary had her reply ready.

'I only wish he were,' she said, 'so that he could stand in this court and confirm that I am telling the truth.' Her voice was soft and gentle.

'But *you* already know the truth, Mrs Cooper,' said Sir Matthew, his voice gradually rising. 'The truth is that your husband left the house on his own. He then drove to the Queen's Hotel, where he spent the rest of the night, while you and your lover used that time to leave clues across the city of Leeds – clues, I might add, that were intended to incriminate your husband. But the one thing you couldn't leave was a body, because as you well know Mr Jeremy Alexander is still alive, and the two of you have together fabricated this entire bogus story, simply to further your own ends. Isn't that the truth, Mrs Cooper?'

'No, no!' Rosemary shouted, her voice cracking before she finally burst into tears.

'Oh, come, come, Mrs Cooper. Those are counterfeit tears, are they not?' said Sir Matthew quietly. 'Now you've been found out, the jury will decide if your distress is genuine.'

I glanced across at the jury. Not only had they fallen for Rosemary's performance, but they now despised me for allowing my insensitive bully of a counsel to attack such a gentle, long-suffering woman. To every one of Sir Matthew's probing questions, Rosemary proved well

31

capable of delivering a riposte that revealed to me all the hallmarks of Jeremy Alexander's expert tuition.

When it was my turn to enter the witness box, and Sir Matthew began questioning me, I felt my story sounded far less convincing than Rosemary's, despite its being the truth.

The closing speech for the Crown was deadly dull, but nevertheless deadly. Sir Matthew's was subtle and dramatic, but I feared less convincing.

After another night in Armley Jail I returned to the dock for the judge's summing up. It was clear that he was in no doubt as to my guilt. His selection of the evidence he chose to review was unbalanced and unfair, and when he ended by reminding the jury that his opinion of the evidence should ultimately carry no weight, he only added hypocrisy to bias.

After their first full day's deliberations, the jury had to be put up overnight in a hotel – ironically the Queen's – and when the jolly little fat man in the bow tie was finally asked: 'Members of the jury, do you find the prisoner at the bar guilty or not guilty as charged?' I wasn't surprised when he said clearly for all to hear, 'Guilty, my lord.'

In fact I was amazed that the jury had failed to reach a unanimous decision. I have often wondered which two members felt convinced enough to declare my innocence. I would have liked to thank them.

The judge stared down at me. 'Richard Wilfred Cooper, you have been found guilty of the murder of Jeremy Anatole Alexander . . .'

'I did not kill him, my lord,' I interrupted in a calm voice. 'In fact, he is not dead. I can only hope that you will live long enough to realise the truth.' Sir Matthew looked up anxiously as uproar broke out in the court.

The judge called for silence, and his voice became even more harsh as he pronounced, 'You will go to prison for life. That is the sentence prescribed by law. Take him down.'

Two prison officers stepped forward, gripped me firmly by the arms and led me down the steps at the back of the dock into the cell I had occupied every morning for the eighteen days of the trial.

'Sorry, old chum,' said the policeman who had been in charge of my welfare since the case had begun. 'It was that bitch of a wife who tipped the scales against you.' He slammed the cell door closed, and turned the key in the lock before I had a chance to agree with him. A few moments later the door was unlocked again, and Sir Matthew strode in.

He stared at me for some time before uttering a word. 'A terrible injustice has been done, Mr Cooper,' he eventually said, 'and we shall immediately lodge an appeal against your conviction. Be assured, I will not rest until we have found Jeremy Alexander and he has been brought to justice.'

For the first time I realised Sir Matthew knew that I was innocent.

*   *   *

I was put in a cell with a petty criminal called 'Fingers' Jenkins. Can you believe, as we approach the twenty-first century, that anyone could still be called 'Fingers'? Even so, the name had been well earned. Within moments of my entering the cell, Fingers was wearing my watch. He returned it immediately I noticed it had disappeared. 'Sorry,' he said. 'Just put it down to 'abit.'

Prison might have turned out to be far worse if it hadn't been known by my fellow inmates that I was a millionaire, and was quite happy to pay a little extra for certain privileges. Every morning the *Financial Times* was delivered to my bunk, which gave me the chance to keep up with what was happening in the City. I was nearly sick when I first read about the takeover bid for Cooper's. Sick not because of the offer of £12.50 a share, which made me even wealthier, but because it became painfully obvious what Jeremy and Rosemary had been up to. Jeremy's shares would now be worth several million pounds – money he could never have realised had I been around to prevent a takeover.

I spent hours each day lying on my bunk and scouring every word of the *Financial Times*. Whenever there was a mention of Cooper's, I went over the paragraph so often that I ended up knowing it by heart. The company was eventually taken over, but not before the share price had reached £13.43. I continued to follow its activities with great interest, and I became more and more anxious about the quality of the new management when they began to sack some of my most experienced staff, including Joe Ramsbottom. A week later, I wrote and instructed my stockbrokers to sell my shares as and when the opportunity arose.

It was at the beginning of my fourth month in prison that I asked for some writing paper. I had decided the time had come to keep a record of everything that had happened to me since that night I had returned home unexpectedly. Every day the prison officer on my landing would bring me fresh sheets of blue-lined paper, and I would write out in longhand the chronicle you're now reading. An added bonus was that it helped me to plan my next move.

At my request, Fingers took a straw poll among the prisoners as to who they believed was the best detective they had ever come up against. Three days later he told me the result: Chief Superintendent Donald Hackett, known as the Don, came out top on more than half the lists. More reliable than a Gallup Poll, I told Fingers.

'What puts Hackett ahead of all the others?' I asked him.

''e's honest, 'e's fair, you can't bribe 'im. And once the bastard knows you're a villain, 'e doesn't care 'ow long it takes to get you be'ind bars.'

Hackett, I was informed, hailed from Bradford. Rumour had it among the older cons that he had turned down the job of Assistant Chief Constable for West Yorkshire. Like a barrister who doesn't want to become a judge, he preferred to remain at the coalface.

'Arrestin' criminals is 'ow 'e gets his kicks,' Fingers said, with some feeling.

'Sounds just the man I'm looking for,' I said. 'How old is he?'

Fingers paused to consider. 'Must be past fifty by now,' he replied. 'After all, 'e 'ad me put in borstal for nickin' a toolset, and that was' – he paused again – 'more than twenty years ago.'

When Sir Matthew came to visit me the following Monday, I told him what I had in mind, and asked his opinion of the Don. I wanted a professional's view.

'He's a hell of a witness to cross-examine, that's one thing I can tell you,' replied my barrister.

'Why's that?'

'He doesn't exaggerate, he won't prevaricate, and I've never known him to lie, which makes him awfully hard to trap. No, I've rarely got the better of the Chief Superintendent. I have to say, though, that I doubt if he'd agree to become involved with a convicted criminal, whatever you offered him.'

'But I'm not . . .'

'I know, Mr Cooper,' said Sir Matthew, who still didn't seem able to call me by my first name. 'But Hackett will have to be convinced of that before he even agrees to see you.'

'But how can I convince him of my innocence while I'm stuck in jail?'

'I'll try to influence him on your behalf,' Sir Matthew said after some thought. Then he added, 'Come to think of it, he does owe me a favour.'

After Sir Matthew had left that night, I requested some more lined paper and began to compose a carefully worded letter to Chief Superintendent Hackett, several versions of which ended crumpled up on the floor of my cell. My final effort read as follows:

In replying to this letter, please write on the envelope:

Number A47283   Name COOPER, R.W.

ALL INCOMING MAIL MUST
HAVE SENDERS NAME AND
ADDRESS. ANONYMOUS
MAIL CANNOT BE ACCEPTED
NO NUMBER DELAYS MAIL

**H.M. PRISON
ARMLEY
LEEDS LS12 2TJ**

Dear Chief Superintendent,

As you can see I am currently detained at Her Majesty's pleasure. Nevertheless, I wonder if you would be kind enough to visit me, as I have a private matter I would like to discuss with you that could affect both our futures. I can assure you that my proposal is both legal and honest, and I am confident that it will also appeal to your sense of justice. It has the approval of my barrister, Sir Matthew Roberts QC, who I understand you have come across from time to time in your professional capacity. Naturally I will be happy to reimburse any expenses that this inconvenience may cause you.

I look forward to hearing from you.

Yours sincerely,

I reread the letter, corrected the spelling mistake, and scrawled my signature across the bottom.

At my request, Sir Matthew delivered the letter to Hackett by hand. The first thousand-pound-a-day postman in the history of the Royal Mail, I told him.

Sir Matthew reported back the following Monday that he had handed the letter to the Chief Superintendent in person. After Hackett had read it through a second time, his only comment was that he would have to speak to his superiors. He had promised he would let Sir Matthew know his decision within a week.

From the moment I had been sentenced, Sir Matthew had been preparing for my appeal, and although he had not at any time raised my hopes, he was unable to hide his delight at what he had discovered after paying a visit to the Probate Office.

It turned out that, in his will, Jeremy had left everything to Rosemary. This included over three million pounds' worth of Cooper's shares. But, Sir Matthew explained, the law did not allow her to dispose of them for seven years. 'An English jury may have pronounced on your guilt,' he declared, 'but the hard-headed taxmen are not so easily convinced. They won't hand over Jeremy Alexander's assets until either they have seen his body, or seven years have elapsed.'

'Do they think that Rosemary might have killed him for his money, and then disposed . . .'

'No, no,' said Sir Matthew, almost laughing at my

suggestion. 'It's simply that, as they're entitled to wait for seven years, they're going to sit on his assets and not take the risk that Alexander may still be alive. In any case, if your wife *had* killed him, she wouldn't have had a ready answer to every one of my questions when she was in the witness box, of that I'm sure.'

I smiled. For the first time in my life I was delighted to learn that the taxman had his nose in my affairs.

Sir Matthew promised he would report back if anything new came up. 'Goodnight, Richard,' he said as he left the interview room.

Another first.

It seemed that everyone else in the prison was aware that Chief Superintendent Hackett would be paying me a visit long before I was.

It was Dave Adams, an old lag from an adjoining cell, who explained why the inmates thought Hackett had agreed to see me. 'A good copper is never 'appy about anyone doin' time for somethin' 'e didn't do. 'ackett phoned the Governor last Tuesday, and 'ad a word with 'im on the Q.T., accordin' to Maurice,' Dave added mysteriously.

I would have been interested to learn how the Governor's trusty had managed to hear both sides of the conversation, but decided this was not the time for irrelevant questions.

'Even the 'ardest nuts in this place think you're innocent,' Dave continued. 'They can't wait for the day when Mr Jeremy Alexander takes over your cell. You can be sure the long termers'll give 'im a warm welcome.'

A letter from Bradford arrived the following morning. 'Dear Cooper,' the Chief Superintendent began, and went on to inform me that he intended to pay a visit to the jail at four o'clock the following Sunday. He made it clear that he would stay no longer than half an hour, and insisted on a witness being present throughout.

For the first time since I'd been locked up, I started counting the hours. Hours aren't that important when your room has been booked for a life sentence.

As I was taken from my cell that Sunday afternoon and escorted to the interview room, I received several messages from my fellow inmates to pass on to the Chief Superintendent.

'Give my best regards to the Don,' said Fingers. 'Tell 'im 'ow sorry I am not to bump into 'im this time.'

'When 'e's finished with you, ask 'im if 'e'd like to drop into my cell for a cup of char and a chat about old times.'

'Kick the bastard in the balls, and tell 'im I'll be 'appy to serve the extra time.'

One of the prisoners even suggested a question to which I already knew the answer: 'Ask 'im when 'e's going to retire, 'cause I'm not coming out till the day after.'

When I stepped into the interview room and saw the

Chief Superintendent for the first time, I thought there must have been some mistake. I had never asked Fingers what the Don looked like, and over the past few days I had built up in my mind the image of some sort of superman. But the man who stood before me was a couple of inches shorter than me, and I'm only five foot ten. He was as thin as the proverbial rake and wore pebble-lensed horn-rimmed glasses, which gave the impression that he was half-blind. All he needed was a grubby raincoat and he could have been mistaken for a debt collector.

Sir Matthew stepped forward to introduce us. I shook the policeman firmly by the hand. 'Thank you for coming to visit me, Chief Superintendent,' I began. 'Won't you have a seat?' I added, as if he had dropped into my home for a glass of sherry.

'Sir Matthew is very persuasive,' said Hackett, in a deep, gruff Yorkshire accent that didn't quite seem to go with his body. 'So tell me, Cooper, what do you imagine it is that I can do for you?' he asked as he took the chair opposite me. I detected an edge of cynicism in his voice.

He opened a notepad and placed it on the table as I was about to begin my story. 'For my use only,' he explained, 'should I need to remind myself of any relevant details at some time in the future.' Twenty minutes later, I had finished the abbreviated version of the life and times of Richard Cooper. I had already gone over the story on several occasions in my cell during the past week, to be certain I didn't take too long. I wanted to leave enough time for Hackett to ask any questions.

'If I believe your story,' he said, '– and I only say "if" – you still haven't explained what it is you think I can do for you.'

'You're due to leave the force in five months' time,' I said. 'I wondered if you had any plans once you've retired.'

He hesitated. I had obviously taken him by surprise.

'I've been offered a job with Group 4, as area manager for West Yorkshire.'

'And how much will they be paying you?' I asked bluntly.

'It won't be full time,' he said. 'Three days a week, to start with.' He hesitated again. 'Twenty thousand a year, guaranteed for three years.'

'I'll pay you a hundred thousand a year, but I'll expect you to be on the job seven days a week. I assume you'll be needing a secretary and an assistant – that Inspector Williams who's leaving at the same time as you might well fit the bill – so I'll also supply you with enough money for back-up staff, as well as the rent for an office.'

A flicker of respect appeared on the Chief Superintendent's face for the first time. He made some more notes on his pad.

'And what would you expect of me in return for such a large sum of money?' he asked.

'That's simple. I expect you to find Jeremy Alexander.'

This time he didn't hesitate. 'My God,' he said. 'You

really *are* innocent. Sir Matthew and the Governor both tried to convince me you were.'

'And if you find him within seven years,' I added, ignoring his comment, 'I'll pay a further five hundred thousand into any branch of any bank in the world that you stipulate.'

'The Midland, Bradford will suit me just fine,' he replied. 'It's only criminals who find it necessary to retire abroad. In any case, I have to be in Bradford every other Saturday afternoon, so I can be around to watch City lose.' Hackett rose from his place and looked hard at me for some time. 'One last question, Mr Cooper. Why seven years?'

'Because after that period, my wife can sell Alexander's shares, and he'll become a multi-millionaire overnight.'

The Chief Superintendent nodded his understanding. 'Thank you for asking to see me,' he said. 'It's been a long time since I enjoyed visiting anyone in jail, especially someone convicted of murder. I'll give your offer serious consideration, Mr Cooper, and let you know my decision by the end of the week.' He left without another word.

Hackett wrote to me three days later, accepting my offer.

I didn't have to wait five months for him to start working for me, because he handed in his resignation within a fortnight – though not before I had agreed to continue his pension contributions, and those of the two colleagues he wanted to leave the force and join him.

Having now disposed of all my Cooper's shares, the interest on my deposit account was earning me over four hundred thousand a year, and as I was living rent-free, Hackett's request was a minor consideration.

I would have shared with you in greater detail everything that happened to me over the following months, but during that time I was so preoccupied with briefing Hackett that I filled only three pages of my blue-lined prison paper. I should however mention that I studied several law books, to be sure that I fully understood the meaning of the legal term *'autrefois acquit'*.

The next important date in the diary was my appeal hearing.

Matthew — at his request I had long ago stopped calling him 'Sir' Matthew — tried valiantly not to show that he was becoming more and more confident of the outcome, but I was getting to know him so well that he was no longer able to disguise his true feelings. He told me how delighted he was with the make-up of the reviewing panel. 'Fair and just,' he kept repeating.

Later that night he told me with great sadness that his wife Victoria had died of cancer a few weeks before. 'A long illness and a blessed release,' he called it.

I felt guilty in his presence for the first time. Over the past eighteen months, we had only ever discussed my problems.

*   *   *

I must have been one of the few prisoners at Armley who ever had a bespoke tailor visit him in his cell. Matthew suggested that I should be fitted with a new suit before I faced the appeal tribunal, as I had lost over a stone since I had been in jail. When the tailor had finished measuring me and began rolling up his tape, I insisted that Fingers return his cigarette lighter, although I did allow him to keep the cigarettes.

Ten days later, I was escorted from my cell at five o'clock in the morning. My fellow inmates banged their tin mugs against their locked doors, the traditional way of indicating to the prison staff that they believed the man leaving for trial was innocent. Like some great symphony, it lifted my soul.

I was driven to London in a police car accompanied by two prison officers. We didn't stop once on the entire journey, and arrived in the capital a few minutes after nine; I remember looking out of the window and watching the commuters scurrying to their offices to begin the day's work. Any one of them who'd glanced at me sitting in the back of the car in my new suit, and was unable to spot the handcuffs, might have assumed I was a Chief Inspector at least.

Matthew was waiting for me at the entrance of the Old Bailey, a mountain of papers tucked under each arm. 'I like the suit,' he said, before leading me up some stone steps to the room where my fate would be decided.

Once again I sat impassively in the dock as Sir Matthew rose from his place to address the three appeal judges. His opening statement took him nearly an hour, and by now I felt I could have delivered it quite adequately myself, though not as eloquently, and certainly nowhere near as persuasively. He made great play of how Jeremy had left all his worldly goods to Rosemary, who in turn had sold our family house in Leeds, cashed in all her Cooper's shares within months of the takeover, pushed through a quickie divorce, and then disappeared off the face of the earth with an estimated seven million pounds. I couldn't help wondering just how much of that Jeremy had already got his hands on.

Sir Matthew repeatedly reminded the panel of the police's inability to produce a body, despite the fact they now seemed to have dug up half of Leeds.

I became more hopeful with each new fact Matthew placed before the judges. But after he had finished, I still had to wait another three days to learn the outcome of their deliberations.

Appeal dismissed. Reasons reserved.

Matthew travelled up to Armley on the Friday to tell me why he thought my appeal had been turned down without explanation. He felt that the judges must have been divided, and needed more time to make it appear as if they were not.

'How much time?' I asked.

'My hunch is that they'll let you out on licence within a few months. They were obviously influenced by the police's failure to produce a body, unimpressed by the trial judge's summing up, and impressed by the strength of your case.'

I thanked Matthew, who, for once, left the room with a smile on his face.

You may be wondering what Chief Superintendent Hackett – or rather ex-Chief Superintendent Hackett – had been up to while all this was going on.

He had not been idle. Inspector Williams and Constable Kenwright had left the force on the same day as he had. Within a week they had opened up a small office above the Constitutional Club in Bradford and begun their investigations. The Don reported to me at four o'clock every Sunday afternoon.

Within a month he had compiled a thick file on the case, with detailed dossiers on Rosemary, Jeremy, the company and me. I spent hours reading through the information he had gathered, and was even able to help by filling in a few gaps. I quickly came to appreciate why the Don was so respected by my fellow inmates. He followed up every clue, and went down every side road, however much it looked like a cul-de-sac, because once in a while it turned out to be a highway.

On the first Sunday in October, after Hackett had been working for four months, he told me that he thought he might have located Rosemary. A woman of her description was living on a small estate in the south of France called Villa Fleur.

'How did you manage to track her down?' I asked.

'Letter posted by her mother at her local pillarbox. The postman kindly allowed me to have a look at the

47

address on the envelope before it proceeded on its way,' Hackett said. 'Can't tell you how many hours we had to hang around, how many letters we've had to sift through, and how many doors we've knocked on in the past four months, just to get this one lead. Mrs Kershaw seems to be a compulsive letter writer, but this was the first time she's sent one to her daughter. By the way,' he added, 'your wife has reverted to her maiden name. Calls herself Ms Kershaw now.'

I nodded, not wishing to interrupt him.

'Williams flew out to Cannes on Wednesday, and he's holed up in the nearest village, posing as a tourist. He's already been able to tell us that Ms Kershaw's house is surrounded by a ten-foot stone wall, and she has more guard dogs than trees. It seems the locals know even less about her than we do. But at least it's a start.'

I felt for the first time that Jeremy Alexander might at last have met his match, but it was to be another five Sundays, and five more interim reports, before a thin smile appeared on Hackett's usually tight-lipped face.

'Ms Kershaw has placed an advertisement in the local paper,' he informed me. 'It seems she's in need of a new butler. At first I thought we should question the old butler at length as soon as he'd left, but as I couldn't risk anything getting back to her, I decided Inspector Williams would have to apply for his job instead.'

'But surely she'll realise within moments that he's totally unqualified to do the job.'

'Not necessarily,' said Hackett, his smile broadening. 'You see, Williams won't be able to leave his present

employment with the Countess of Rutland until he's
served a full month's notice, and in the meantime we've
signed him up for a special six-week course at Ivor
Spencer's School for Butlers. Williams has always been
a quick learner.'

'But what about references?'

'By the time Rosemary Kershaw interviews him, he'll
have a set of references that would impress a duchess.'

'I was told you never did anything underhand.'

'That is the case when I'm dealing with honest people,
Mr Cooper. Not when I'm up against a couple of crooks
like this. I'm going to get those two behind bars, if it's
the last thing I do.'

This was not the time to let Hackett know that the
final chapter of this story, as I plotted it, did not conclude
with Jeremy ending up in jail.

Once Williams had been put on the shortlist for the
position of Rosemary's butler, I played my own small
part in securing him the job. Rereading over the terms
of the proposed contract gave me the idea.

'Tell Williams to ask for 15,000 francs a month, and
five weeks' holiday,' I suggested to Hackett when he and
Matthew visited me the following Sunday.

'Why?' asked the ex-Chief Superintendent. 'She's
only offering 11,000, and three weeks' holiday.'

'She can well afford to pay the difference, and with
references like these,' I said, looking back down at my
file, 'she might become suspicious if he asked for anything less.'

Matthew smiled and nodded.

Rosemary finally offered Williams the job at 13,000 francs a month, with four weeks' holiday a year, which after forty-eight hours' consideration Williams accepted. But he did not join her for another month, by which time he had learnt how to iron newspapers, lay place settings with a ruler, and tell the difference between a port, sherry and liqueur glass.

I suppose that from the moment Williams took up the post as Rosemary's butler, I expected instant results. But as Hackett pointed out to me Sunday after Sunday, this was hardly realistic.

'Williams has to take his time,' explained the Don. 'He needs to gain her confidence, and avoid giving her any reason for the slightest suspicion. It once took me five years to nail a drug smuggler who was only living half a mile up the road from me.'

I wanted to remind him that it was me who was stuck in jail, and that five days was more like what I had in mind, but I knew how hard they were all working on my behalf, and tried not to show my impatience.

Within a month Williams had supplied us with photographs and life histories of all the staff working on the estate, along with descriptions of everyone who visited Rosemary – even the local priest, who came hoping to collect a donation for French aid workers in Somalia.

The cook: Gabrielle Pascal – no English, excellent cuisine, came from Marseilles, family checked out. The gardener: Jacques Reni – stupid and not particularly imaginative with the rosebeds, local and well known. Rosemary's personal maid: Charlotte Merieux – spoke

a little English, crafty, sexy, came from Paris, still checking her out. All the staff had been employed by Rosemary since her arrival in the south of France, and they
appeared to have no connection with each other, or with
her past life.

'Ah,' said Hackett as he studied the picture of Rosemary's personal maid. I raised an eyebrow. 'I was just
thinking about Williams being cooped up with Charlotte
Merieux day in and day out – and more important, night
in and night in,' he explained. 'He would have made
superintendent if he hadn't fooled around so much. Still,
let's hope this time it turns out to our advantage.'

I lay on my bunk studying the pictures of the staff
for hour after hour, but they revealed nothing. I read
and reread the notes on everyone who had ever visited
Villa Fleur, but as the weeks went by, it looked more
and more as if no one from Rosemary's past, other than
her mother, knew where she was – or if they did, they
were making no attempts to contact her. There was certainly no sign of Jeremy Alexander.

I was beginning to fear that she and Jeremy might
have split up, until Williams reported that there was a
picture of a dark, handsome man on a table by the side
of Rosemary's bed. It was inscribed: 'We'll always be
together – J'.

During the weeks following my appeal hearing I was
constantly interviewed by probation officers, social
workers and even the prison psychiatrist. I struggled

to maintain the warm, sincere smile that Matthew had warned me was so necessary to lubricate the wheels of the bureaucracy.

It must have been about eleven weeks after my appeal had been turned down that the cell door was thrown open, and the senior officer on my corridor announced, 'The Governor wants to see you, Cooper.' Fingers looked suspicious. Whenever he heard those words, it inevitably meant a dose of solitary.

I could hear my heart beating as I was led down the long corridor to the Governor's office. The prison officer knocked gently on the door before opening it. The Governor rose from behind his desk, thrust out his hand and said, 'I'm delighted to be the first person to tell you the good news.'

He ushered me into a comfortable chair on the other side of his desk, and went over the terms of my release. While he was doing this I was served coffee, as if we were old friends.

There was a knock on the door, and Matthew walked in, clutching a sheaf of papers that needed to be signed. I rose as he placed them on the desk, and without warning he turned round and gave me a bearhug. Not something I expect he did every day.

After I had signed the final document Matthew asked: 'What's the first thing you'll do once they release you?'

'I'm going to buy a gun,' I told him matter-of-factly.

Matthew and the Governor burst out laughing.

*　　*　　*

The great gate of Armley Prison was thrown open for me three days later. I walked away from the building carrying only the small leather suitcase I had arrived with. I didn't look back. I hailed a taxi and asked the driver to take me to the station, as I had no desire to remain in Leeds a moment longer than was necessary. I bought a first-class ticket, phoned Hackett to warn him I was on my way, and boarded the next train for Bradford. I savoured a British Rail breakfast that wasn't served on a tin plate, and read a copy of the *Financial Times* that had been handed to me by a pretty shop assistant and not a petty criminal. No one stared at me – but then, why should they, when I was sitting in a first-class carriage and dressed in my new suit? I glanced at every woman who passed by, however she was dressed, but they had no way of knowing why.

When the train pulled into Bradford, the Don and his secretary Jenny Kenwright were waiting for me on the platform. The Chief Superintendent had rented me a small furnished flat on the outskirts of the city, and after I had unpacked – not a long job – they took me out to lunch. The moment the small talk had been dispensed with and Jenny had poured me a glass of wine, the Don asked me a question I hadn't expected.

'Now that you're free, is it still your wish that we go on looking for Jeremy Alexander?'

'Yes,' I replied, without a moment's hesitation. 'I'm even more determined, now that I can taste the freedom he's enjoyed for the past three years. Never forget, that man stole my freedom from me, along with my wife, my company, and more than half my possessions. Oh yes, Donald, I won't rest until I come face to face with Jeremy Alexander.'

'Good,' said the Don. 'Because Williams thinks Rosemary is beginning to trust him, and might even, given time, start confiding in him. It seems he has made himself indispensable.'

I found a certain irony in the thought of Williams pocketing two wage packets simultaneously, and of my being responsible for one, while Rosemary paid the other. I asked if there was any news of Jeremy.

'Nothing to speak of,' said Donald. 'She certainly never phones him from the house, and we're fairly sure he never attempts to make any direct contact with her. But Williams has told us that every Friday at midday he has to drop her off at the Majestic, the only hotel in the village. She goes inside and doesn't reappear for at least forty minutes. He daren't follow her, because she's given specific instructions that he's to stay with the car. And he can't afford to lose this job by disobeying orders.'

I nodded my agreement.

'But that hasn't stopped him having the occasional drink in the hotel bar on his evening off, and he's managed to pick up a few snippets of information. He's convinced that Rosemary uses the time when she's in the hotel to make a long-distance phone call. She often drops in at the bank before going on to the Majestic, and comes out carrying a small packet of coins. The barman has told Williams that she always uses one of the two phone boxes in the corridor opposite the reception desk. She never allows the call to be put through the hotel switch-board, always dials direct.'

'So how do we discover who she's calling?' I asked.

'We wait for Williams to find an opportunity to use some of those skills he didn't learn at butlers' school.'

'But how long might that take?'

'No way of knowing, but Williams is due for a spot of leave in a couple of weeks, so he'll be able to bring us up to date.'

When Williams arrived back in Bradford at the end of the month I began asking him questions even before he had time to put his suitcase down. He was full of interesting information about Rosemary, and even the smallest detail fascinated me.

She had put on weight. I was pleased. She seemed lonely and depressed. I was delighted. She was spending my money fast. I wasn't exactly ecstatic. But, more to the point, Williams was convinced that if Rosemary had any contact with Jeremy Alexander, it had to be when she visited the hotel every Friday and placed that direct-dial call. But he still hadn't worked out how to discover who, or where, she was phoning.

By the time Williams returned to the south of France a fortnight later I knew more about my ex-wife than I had ever done when we were married.

As happens so often in the real world, the next move came when I least expected it. It must have been about 2.30 on a Monday afternoon when the phone rang.

Donald picked up the receiver, and was surprised to hear Williams's voice on the other end of the line. He switched him on to the squawk box and said, 'All three of us are listening, so you'd better begin by telling us why you're ringing when it's not your day off.'

'I've been sacked,' were Williams's opening words.

'Playing around with the maid, were you?' was Donald's first reaction.

'I only wish, chief, but I'm afraid it's far more stupid than that. I was driving Ms Kershaw into town this morning, when I had to stop at a red light. While I was waiting for the lights to change, a man crossed the road in front of the car. He stopped and stared at me. I recognised him immediately, and prayed the lights would turn to green before he could place me. But he walked back, looked at me again, and smiled. I shook my head at him, but he came over to the driver's side, tapped on the window, and said, "How are you, Inspector Williams?"'

'Who was it?' demanded Donald.

'Neil Case. Remember him, chief?'

'Could I ever forget him? "Never-on-the-Case Neil",' said Donald. 'I might have guessed.'

'I didn't acknowledge him, of course, and as Ms Kershaw said nothing, I thought I might have got away with it. But as soon as we arrived back at the house she told me to come and see her in the study, and without even asking for an explanation she dismissed me. She ordered me to be packed and off the premises within the hour, or she'd call the local police.'

'Damn. Back to square one,' said Donald.

'Not quite,' said Williams.

'What do you mean? If you're no longer in the house, we no longer have a point of contact. Worse, we can't play the butler card again, because she's bound to be on her guard from now on.'

'I know all that, chief,' said Williams, 'but suspecting that I was a policeman caused her to panic, and she went straight to her bedroom and made a phone call. As I wasn't afraid of being found out any longer, I picked up the extension in the corridor and listened in. All I heard was a woman's voice give a Cambridge number, and then the phone went dead. I assumed Rosemary had been expecting someone else to pick up the phone, and hung up when she heard a strange voice.'

'What was the number?' Donald asked.

'6407-something-7.'

'What do you mean, "something-7"?' barked Donald as he scribbled the numbers down.

'I didn't have anything to write with, chief, so I had to rely on my memory.' I was glad Williams couldn't see the expression on the Don's face.

'Then what happened?' he demanded.

'I found a pen in a drawer and wrote what I could remember of the number on my hand. I picked up the phone again a few moments later, and heard a different woman on the line, saying, "The Director's not in at the moment, but I'm expecting him back within the hour." Then I had to hang up quickly, because I could hear someone coming along the corridor. It was Charlotte, Rosemary's maid. She wanted to know why I'd been sacked. I couldn't think of a convincing reply, until she accused me of having made a pass at the mistress. I let her think that was it, and ended up getting a slapped face for my trouble.' I burst out laughing, but the Don and Jenny showed no reaction. Then Williams asked, 'So, what do I do now, chief? Come back to England?'

'No,' said Donald. 'Stay put for the moment. Book yourself into the Majestic and watch her round the clock. Let me know if she does anything out of character. Meanwhile, we're going to Cambridge. As soon as we've booked ourselves into a hotel there I'll call you.'

'Understood, sir,' said Williams, and rang off.

'When do we go?' I asked Donald once he had replaced the receiver.

'Tonight,' he replied. 'But not before I've made a few telephone calls.'

The Don dialled ten Cambridge numbers, using the digits Williams had been able to jot down, and inserting the numbers from nought to nine in the missing slot.

0223 640707 turned out to be a school. 'Sorry, wrong number,' said Donald. 717 was a chemist's shop; 727 was a garage; 737 was answered by an elderly male voice – 'Sorry, wrong number,' Donald repeated; 747 a newsagent; 757 a local policeman's wife (I tried not to laugh, but Donald only grunted); 767 a woman's voice – 'Sorry, wrong number,' yet again; 777 was St Catharine's College; 787 a woman's voice on an answering machine; 797 a hairdresser – 'Did you want a perm, or just a trim?'

Donald checked his list. 'It has to be either 737, 767 or 787. The time has come for me to pull a few strings.'

He dialled a Bradford number, and was told that the new Deputy Chief Constable of Cambridgeshire had been transferred from the West Yorkshire Constabulary the previous year.

'Leeke. Allan Leeke,' said Donald, without needing to be prompted. He turned to me. 'He was a sergeant when I was first made up to inspector.' He thanked his Bradford contact, then rang directory enquiries to find out the number of the Cambridge Police headquarters. He dialled another 0223 number.

'Cambridge Police. How can I help you?' asked a female voice.

'Can you put me through to the Deputy Chief Constable, please?' Donald asked.

'Who shall I say is calling?'

'Donald Hackett.'

The next voice that came on the line said, 'Don, this is a pleasant surprise. Or at least I hope it's a pleasant surprise, because knowing you, it won't be a social call. Are you looking for a job, by any chance? I heard you'd left the force.'

'Yes, it's true. I've resigned, but I'm not looking for a job, Allan. I don't think the Cambridge Constabulary could quite match my present salary.'

'So, what can I do for you, Don?'

'I need a trace done on three numbers in the Cambridge area.'

'Authorised?' asked the Deputy Chief Constable.

'No, but it might well lead to an arrest on your patch,' said Donald.

'That, and the fact that it's you who's asking, is good enough for me.'

Donald read out the three numbers, and Leeke asked him to hang on for a moment. While we waited, Donald told me, 'All they have to do is press a few buttons in the control room, and the numbers will appear on a screen in front of him. Things have changed since I first joined the force. In those days we had to let our legs do the walking.'

The Deputy Chief Constable's voice came back on the line. 'Right, the first number's come up. 640737 is a Wing Commander Danvers-Smith. He's the only person registered as living in the house.' He read out an address in Great Shelford, which he explained was just to the south of Cambridge. Jenny wrote the details down.

'767 is a Professor and Mrs Balcescu, also living in Great Shelford. 787 is Dame Julia Renaud, the opera singer. She lives in Grantchester. We know her quite well. She's hardly ever at home, because of her concert commitments all over the world. Her house has been burgled three times in the last year, always when she was abroad.'

'Thank you,' said Donald. 'You've been most helpful.'

'Anything you want to tell me?' asked the Deputy Chief Constable, sounding hopeful.

'Not at the moment,' replied Donald. 'But as soon as I've finished my investigation, I promise you'll be the first person to be informed.'

'Fair enough,' came back the reply, and the line went dead.

'Right,' Donald said, turning his attention back to us. 'We leave for Cambridge in a couple of hours. That will give us enough time to pack, and for Jenny to book us into a hotel near the city centre. We'll meet back here at' – he checked his watch – 'six o'clock.' He walked out of the room without uttering another word. I remember thinking that my father would have got on well with him.

Just over two hours later, Jenny was driving us at a steady sixty-nine miles per hour down the A1.

'Now the boring part of detective work begins,' said Donald. 'Intense research, followed by hours of surveillance. I think we can safely ignore Dame Julia. Jenny, you get to work on the wing commander. I want details of his career from the day he left school to the day he retired. First thing tomorrow you can begin by contacting RAF College Cranwell, and asking for details of his service record. I'll take the professor, and make a start in the university library.'

'What do I do?' I asked.

'For the time being, Mr Cooper, you keep yourself well out of sight. It's just possible that the wing commander or the professor might lead us to Alexander, so we don't need you trampling over any suspects and frightening them off.'

I reluctantly agreed.

Later that night I settled into a suite at the Garden House Hotel – a more refined sort of prison – but despite feather pillows and a comfortable mattress I was quite unable to sleep. I rose early the next morning and spent most of the day watching endless updates on Sky News, episodes of various Australian soaps, and a 'Film of the Week' every two hours. But my mind was continually switching between RAF Cranwell and the university library.

When we met up in Donald's room that evening, he and Jenny confirmed that their initial research suggested that both men were who they purported to be.

'I was sure one of them would turn out to be Jeremy,' I said, unable to hide my disappointment.

'It would be nice if it was always that easy, Mr Cooper,' said Donald. 'But it doesn't mean that one of them won't lead us to Jeremy.' He turned to Jenny. 'First, let's go over what you found out about the wing commander.'

'Wing Commander Danvers-Smith DFC graduated from Cranwell in 1938, served with Number Two Squadron at Binbrook in Lincolnshire during the Second World War, and flew several missions over Germany and occupied France. He was awarded the DFC for gallantry in 1943. He was grounded in 1958, and became an instructor at RAF Cottesmore in Gloucestershire. His final posting was as Deputy Commanding Officer at RAF Locking in Somerset. He retired in 1977, when he and his wife moved back to Great Shelford, where he had grown up.'

'Why's he living on his own now?' asked Donald.

'Wife died three years ago. He has two children, Sam

and Pamela, both married, but neither living in the area. They visit him occasionally.'

I wanted to ask Jenny how she had been able to find out so much information about the wing commander in such a short time, but said nothing, as I was more interested in hearing what the Don had discovered about Professor Balcescu.

Donald picked up a pile of notes that had been lying on the floor by his feet. 'So, let me tell you the results of my research into a very distinguished professor,' he began. 'Professor Balcescu escaped from Romania in 1989, after Ceausescu had had him placed under house arrest. He was smuggled out of the country by a group of dissident students, via Bulgaria and then on into Greece. His escape was well documented in the newspapers at the time. He applied for asylum in England, and was offered a teaching post at Gonville and Caius College, Cambridge, and three years later the Chair of Eastern European Studies. He advises the government on Romanian matters, and has written a scholarly book on the subject. Last year he was awarded a CBE in the Queen's Birthday Honours.'

'How could either of these men possibly know Rosemary?' I asked. 'Williams must have made a mistake when he wrote down the number.'

'Williams doesn't make mistakes, Mr Cooper,' said the Don. 'Otherwise I wouldn't have employed him. Your wife dialled one of those numbers, and we're just going to have to find out which one. This time we'll need your assistance.'

I mumbled an apology, but remained unconvinced.

Hackett nodded curtly, and turned back to Jenny. 'How long will it take us to get to the wing commander's home?'

'About fifteen minutes, sir. He lives in a cottage in Great Shelford, just south of Cambridge.'

'Right, we'll start with him. I'll see you both in the lobby at five o'clock tomorrow morning.'

I slept fitfully again that night, now convinced that we were embarked on a wild-goose chase. But at least I was going to be allowed to join them the following day, instead of being confined to my room and yet more Australian soaps.

I didn't need my 4.30 alarm call – I was already showering when the phone went. A few minutes after five, the three of us walked out of the hotel, trying not to look as if we were hoping to leave without paying our bill. It was a chilly morning, and I shivered as I climbed into the back of the car.

Jenny drove us out of the city and onto the London road. After a mile or so she turned left and took us into a charming little village with neat, well-kept houses on either side of the road. We passed a garden centre on the left and drove another half mile, then Jenny suddenly swung the car round and reversed into a layby. She switched off the engine and pointed to a small house with an RAF-blue door. 'That's where he lives,' she said. 'Number forty-seven.' Donald focused a tiny pair of binoculars on the house.

Some early-morning risers were already leaving their

homes, cars heading towards the station for the first commuter train to London. The paperboy turned out to be an old lady who pushed her heavily-laden bicycle slowly round the village, dropping off her deliveries. The milkman was next, clattering along in his electric van – two pints here, a pint there, the occasional half-dozen eggs or carton of orange juice left on front door-steps. Lights began to flick on all over the village. 'The wing commander has had one pint of red-top milk and a copy of the *Daily Telegraph* delivered to his front door,' said Donald.

People had emerged from the houses on either side of number forty-seven before a light appeared in an upstairs room of the wing commander's home. Once that light had been switched on Donald sat bolt upright, his eyes never leaving the house.

I became bored, and dozed off in the back at some point. When I woke up, I hoped we might at least be allowed a break for breakfast, but such mundane considerations didn't seem to worry the two professionals in the front. They continued to concentrate on any movement that took place around number forty-seven, and hardly exchanged a word.

At 10.19 a thin, elderly man, dressed in a Harris tweed jacket and grey flannels, emerged from number forty-seven and marched briskly down the path. All I could see at that distance was a huge, bushy white moustache. It looked almost as if his whole body had been designed around it. Donald kept the glasses trained on him.

'Ever seen him before?' he asked, passing the binoculars back to me.

I focused the glasses on the wing commander and studied him carefully. 'Never,' I said as he came to a halt by the side of a battered old Austin Allegro. 'How could anyone forget that moustache?'

'It certainly wasn't grown last week,' said Donald, as Danvers-Smith eased his car out onto the main road.

Jenny cursed. 'I thought that if he used his car, the odds would be on him heading into Cambridge.' She deftly performed a three-point turn and accelerated quickly after the wing commander. Within a few minutes she was only a couple of cars behind him.

Danvers-Smith was not proving to be the sort of fellow who habitually broke the speed limit. 'His days as a test pilot are obviously long behind him,' Donald said, as we trailed the Allegro at a safe distance into the next village. About half a mile later he pulled into a petrol station.

'Stay with him,' said Donald. Jenny followed the Allegro into the forecourt and came to a halt at the pump directly behind Danvers-Smith.

'Keep your head down, Mr Cooper,' said the Don, opening his door. 'We don't want him seeing you.'

'What are you going to do?' I asked, peeping between the front seats.

'Risk an old con's trick,' Donald replied.

He stepped out of the front seat, walked round to the back of the car, and unscrewed the petrol cap just as the wing commander slipped the nozzle of a petrol pump

into the tank of his Allegro. Donald began slowly topping up our already full tank, then suddenly turned to
face the old man.

'Wing Commander Danvers-Smith?' he asked in a
plummy voice.

The wing commander looked up immediately, and a
puzzled expression came over his weather-beaten face.

'Baker, sir,' said Donald. 'Flight Lieutenant Baker.
You lectured me at RAF Locking. Vulcans, if I
remember.'

'Bloody good memory, Baker. Good show,' said
Danvers-Smith. 'Delighted to see you, old chap,' he said,
taking the nozzle out of his car and replacing it in the
pump. 'What are you up to nowadays?'

Jenny stifled a laugh.

'Work for BA, sir. Grounded after I failed my eye
test. Bloody desk job, I'm afraid, but it was the only
offer I got.'

'Bad luck, old chap,' said the wing commander, as they
headed off towards the pay booth, and out of earshot.

When they came back a few minutes later, they were
chattering away like old chums, and the wing commander actually had his arm round Donald's shoulder.

When they reached his car they shook hands, and I
heard Donald say 'Goodbye, sir,' before Danvers-Smith
climbed into his Allegro. The old airman pulled out of
the forecourt and headed back towards his home. Donald
got in next to Jenny and pulled the passenger door
closed.

'I'm afraid *he* won't lead us to Alexander,' the Don

said with a sigh. 'Danvers-Smith is the genuine article
– misses his wife, doesn't see his children enough, and
feels a bit lonely. Even asked if I'd like to drop in for a
bite of lunch.'

'Why didn't you accept?' I asked.

Donald paused. 'I would have done, but when I mentioned that I was from Leeds, he told me he'd only been
there once in his life, to watch a test match. No, that
man has never heard of Rosemary Cooper or Jeremy
Alexander – I'd bet my pension on it. So, now it's the
turn of the professor. Let's head back towards Cambridge, Jenny. And drive slowly. I don't want to catch
up with the wing commander, or we'll all end up having
to join him for lunch.'

Jenny swung the car across the road and into the far
lane, then headed back towards the city. After a couple
of miles Donald told her to pull into the side of the
road just past a sign announcing the Shelford Rugby
Club.

'The professor and his wife live behind that hedge,'
Donald said, pointing across the road. 'Settle back, Mr
Cooper. This might take some time.'

At 12.30 Jenny went off to get some fish and chips
from the village. I devoured them hungrily. By three I
was bored stiff again, and was beginning to wonder just
how long Donald would hang around before we were
allowed to return to the hotel. I remembered 'Happy
Days' would be on at 6.30.

'We'll sit here all night, if necessary,' Donald said, as
if he were reading my thoughts. 'Forty-nine hours is

my record without sleep. What's yours, Jenny?' he asked, never taking his eyes off the house.

'Thirty-one, sir,' she replied.

'Then this may be your chance to break that record,' he said. A moment later, a woman in a white BMW nosed out of the driveway leading to the house and stopped at the edge of the pavement. She paused, looked both ways, then turned across the road and swung right, in the direction of Cambridge. As she passed us, I caught a glimpse of a blonde with a pretty face.

'I've seen her before,' I blurted out.

'Follow her, Jenny,' Donald said sharply. 'But keep your distance.' He turned round to face me.

'Where have you seen her?' he asked, passing over the binoculars.

'I can't remember,' I said, trying to focus on the back of a mop of fair, curly hair.

'Think, man. Think. It's our best chance yet,' said Donald, trying not to sound as if he was cross-examining an old lag.

I knew I had come across that face somewhere, though I felt certain we had never met. I had to rack my brains, because it was at least five years since I had seen any woman I recognised, let alone one that striking. But my mind remained blank.

'Keep on thinking,' said the Don, 'while I try to find out something a little more simple. And Jenny – don't get too close to her. Never forget she's got a rear-view mirror. Mr Cooper may not remember her, but she may remember him.'

Donald picked up the carphone and jabbed in ten numbers. 'Let's pray he doesn't realise I've retired,' he mumbled.

'DVLA Swansea. How can I help you?'

'Sergeant Crann, please,' said Donald.

'I'll put you through.'

'Dave Crann.'

'Donald Hackett.'

'Good afternoon, Chief Superintendent. How can I help you?'

'White BMW – K273 SCE,' said Donald, staring at the car in front of him.

'Hold on please, sir, I won't be a moment.'

Donald kept his eye fixed on the BMW while he waited. It was about thirty yards ahead of us, and heading towards a green light. Jenny accelerated to make sure she wouldn't get trapped if the lights changed, and as she shot through an amber light, Sergeant Crann came back on the line,

'We've identified the car, sir,' he said. 'Registered owner Mrs Susan Balcescu, The Kendalls, High Street, Great Shelford, Cambridge. One endorsement for speeding in a built-up area, 1991, a thirty-pound fine. Otherwise nothing known.'

'Thank you, sergeant. That's most helpful.'

'My pleasure, sir.'

'Why should Rosemary want to contact the Balcescus?' Donald said as he clipped the phone back into place. 'And is she contacting just one of them, or both?' Neither of us attempted to answer.

'I think it's time to let her go,' he said a moment later. 'I need to check out several more leads before we risk coming face to face with either of them. Let's head back to the hotel and consider our next move.'

'I know it's only a coincidence,' I ventured, 'but when I knew him, Jeremy had a white BMW.'

'F173 BZK,' said Jenny. 'I remember it from the file.'

Donald swung round. 'Some people can't give up smoking, you know, others drinking. But with some, it's a particular make of car,' he said. 'Although a lot of people must drive white BMWs,' he muttered almost to himself.

Once we were back in Donald's room, he began checking through the file he had put together on Professor Balcescu. The *Times* report of his escape from Romania, he told us, was the most detailed.

PROFESSOR BALCESCU first came to prominence while still a student at the University of Bucharest, where he called for the overthrow of the elected government. The authorities seemed relieved when he was offered a place at Oxford, and must have hoped that they had seen the last of him. But he returned to Bucharest University three years later, taking up the position of tutor in Politics. The following year he led a student revolt in support of Nicolae Ceausescu, and after he became president, Balcescu was rewarded with a Cabinet post, as Minister of Education. But he soon became disillusioned with the Ceausescu regime, and within eighteen months he had resigned and returned to the university as a humble

tutor. Three years later he was offered the Chair
of Politics and Economics.

Professor Balcescu's growing disillusionment
with the government finally turned to anger, and
in 1986 he began writing a series of pamphlets
denouncing Ceausescu and his puppet regime. A
few weeks after a particularly vitriolic attack on
the establishment, he was dismissed from his post
at the university, and later placed under house
arrest. A group of Oxford historians wrote a letter
of protest to *The Times*, but nothing more was
heard of the great scholar for several years. Then,
late in 1989, he was smuggled out of Romania by
a group of students, finally reaching Britain via
Bulgaria and Greece.

Cambridge won the battle of the universities to
tempt him with a teaching post, and he became a
fellow of Gonville and Caius in September 1990. In
November 1991, after the retirement of Sir Halford
McKay, Balcescu took over the Chair of Eastern
European Studies.

Donald looked up. 'There's a picture of him taken when
he was in Greece, but it's too blurred to be of much use.'

I studied the black-and-white photograph of a bearded
middle-aged man surrounded by students. He wasn't
anything like Jeremy. I frowned. 'Another blind alley,'
I said.

'It's beginning to look like it,' said Donald. 'Especially
after what I found out yesterday. According to his secretary, Balcescu delivers his weekly lecture every Friday
morning, from ten o'clock to eleven.'

'But that wouldn't stop him from taking a call from
Rosemary at midday,' interrupted Jenny.

'If you'll allow me to finish,' said Hackett sharply. Jenny bowed her head, and he continued. 'At twelve o'clock he chairs a full departmental meeting in his office, attended by all members of staff. I'm sure you'll agree, Jenny, that it would be quite difficult for him to take a personal call at that time every Friday, given the circumstances.'

Donald turned to me. 'I'm sorry to say we're back where we started, unless you can remember where you've seen Mrs Balcescu.' I shook my head. 'Perhaps I was mistaken,' I admitted.

Donald and Jenny spent the next few hours going over the files, even checking every one of the ten phone numbers a second time.

'Do you remember Rosemary's second call, sir,' said Jenny, in desperation. '"The Director's not in at the moment." Might that be the clue we're looking for?'

'Possibly,' said Donald. 'If we could find out who the Director is, we might be a step nearer to Jeremy Alexander.'

I remember Jenny's last words before I left for my room. 'I wonder how many directors there are in Britain, chief.'

Over breakfast in Donald's room the following morning, he reviewed all the intelligence that had been gathered to date, but none of us felt we were any nearer to a solution.

'What about Mrs Balcescu?' I said. '*She* may be the

person taking the call every Friday at midday, because that's the one time she knows exactly where her husband is.'

'I agree. But is she simply Rosemary's messenger, or is she a friend of Jeremy's?' asked Donald.

'Perhaps we'll have to tap her phone to find out,' said Jenny.

Donald ignored her comment, and checked his watch. 'It's time to go to Balcescu's lecture.'

'Why are we bothering?' I asked. 'Surely we ought to be concentrating on Mrs Balcescu.'

'You're probably right,' said Donald. 'But we can't afford to leave any stone unturned, and as his next lecture won't be for another week, we may as well get it over with. In any case, we'll be out by eleven, and if we find Mrs Balcescu's phone is engaged between twelve and twelve thirty . . .'

After Donald had asked Jenny to bring the car round to the front of the hotel, I slipped back into my room to pick up something that had been hidden in the bottom of my suitcase for several weeks. A few minutes later I joined them, and Jenny drove us out of the hotel carpark, turning right into the main road. Donald glanced at me suspiciously in the rear-view mirror as I sat silently in the back. Did I look guilty? I wondered.

Jenny spotted a parking meter a couple of hundred yards away from the Department of European Studies, and pulled in. We got out of the car and followed the flow of students along the pavement and up the steps. No one gave us a second look. Once we had entered the building, Donald whipped off his tie and slipped it in his jacket pocket. He looked more like a Marxist revolutionary than most of the people heading towards the lecture.

The lecture theatre was clearly signposted, and we entered it by a door on the ground floor, which turned out to be the only way in or out. Donald immediately walked up the raked auditorium to the back row of seats. Jenny and I followed, and Donald instructed me to sit behind a student who looked as if he spent his Saturday afternoons playing lock forward for his college rugby team.

While we waited for Balcescu to enter the room, I began to look around. The lecture theatre was a large semi-circle, not unlike a miniature Greek amphitheatre, and I estimated that it could hold around three hundred students. By the time the clock on the front wall read 9.55 there was hardly a seat to be found. No further proof was needed of the professor's reputation.

I felt a light sweat forming on my forehead as I waited for Balcescu to make his entrance. As the clock struck ten the door of the lecture theatre opened. I was so disappointed at the sight that greeted me that I groaned aloud. He couldn't have been less like Jeremy. I leaned across to Donald. 'Wrong-coloured hair, wrong-coloured eyes, about thirty pounds too light.' The Don showed no reaction.

'So the connection has to be with Mrs Balcescu,' whispered Jenny.

'Agreed,' said Donald under his breath. 'But we're stuck here for the next hour, because we certainly can't risk drawing attention to ourselves by walking out. We'll just have to make a dash for it as soon as the lecture is over. We'll still have time to see if she's at home to take the twelve o'clock call.' He paused. 'I should have checked the layout of the building earlier.' Jenny reddened slightly, because she knew I meant *you*.

And then I suddenly remembered where I had seen Mrs Balcescu. I was about to tell Donald, but the room fell silent as the professor began delivering his opening words.

'This is the sixth of eight lectures,' he began, 'on recent social and economic trends in Eastern Europe.' In a thick Central European accent he launched into a discourse that sounded as if he had given it many times before. The undergraduates began scribbling away on their pads, but I became increasingly irritated by the continual drone of the professor's nasal vowels, as I was impatient to tell Hackett about Mrs Balcescu and to get back to Great Shelford as quickly as possible. I found myself glancing up at the clock on the wall every few minutes. Not unlike my own schooldays, I thought. I touched my jacket pocket. It was still there, even though on this occasion it would serve no useful purpose.

Halfway through the lecture, the lights were dimmed so the professor could illustrate some of his points with slides. I glanced at the first few graphs as they appeared on the screen, showing different income groups across Eastern Europe related to their balance of payments and export figures, but I ended up none the wiser, and not just because I had missed the first five lectures.

The assistant in charge of the projector managed to get one of the slides upside down, showing Germany bottom of the export table and Romania top, which caused a light ripple of laughter throughout the theatre. The professor scowled, and began to deliver his lecture at a faster and faster pace, which only caused the assistant more difficulty in finding the right slides to coincide with the professor's statements.

Once again I became bored, and I was relieved when, at five to eleven, Balcescu called for the final graph. The previous one was replaced by a blank screen. Everyone began looking round at the assistant, who was searching desperately for the slide. The professor became irritable as the minute hand of the clock approached eleven. Still the assistant failed to locate the missing slide. He flicked the shutter back once again, but nothing appeared on the screen, leaving the professor brightly illuminated by a beam of light. Balcescu stepped forward, and began drumming his fingers impatiently on the wooden lectern. Then he turned sideways, and I caught his profile for the first time. There was a small scar above his right eye, which must have faded over the years, but in the bright light of the beam it was clear to see.

'It's him!' I whispered to Donald as the clock struck eleven. The lights came up, and the professor quickly left the lecture theatre without another word.

I leapt over the back of my bench seat, and began charging down the gangway, but my progress was impeded by students who were already sauntering out into the aisle. I pushed my way past them until I had reached ground level, and bolted through the door by which the professor had left so abruptly. I spotted him at the end of the corridor. He was opening another door, and disappeared out of sight. I ran after him, dodging in and out of the chattering students.

When I reached the door that had just been closed behind him I looked up at the sign:

PROFESSOR BALCESCU
Director of European Studies

I threw the door open, to discover a woman sitting behind a desk checking some papers. Another door was closing behind her.

'I need to see Professor Balcescu immediately,' I shouted, knowing that if I didn't get to him before Hackett caught up with me, I might lose my resolve.

The woman stopped what she was doing and looked up at me. 'The Director is expecting an overseas call at any moment, and cannot be disturbed,' she replied. 'I'm sorry, but . . .'

I ran straight past her, pulled open the door and rushed into the room, where I came face to face with Jeremy Alexander for the first time since I had left him lying on the floor of my drawing room. He was talking animatedly on the phone, but he looked up, and recognised me immediately. When I pulled the gun from my pocket, he dropped the receiver. As I took aim, the blood suddenly drained from his face.

'Are you there, Jeremy?' asked an agitated voice on

the other end of the line. Despite the passing of time, I had no difficulty in recognising Rosemary's strident tones.

Jeremy was shouting, 'No, Richard, no! I can explain! Believe me, I can explain!' as Donald came running in. He came to an abrupt halt by the professor's desk, but showed no interest in Jeremy.

'Don't do it, Richard,' he pleaded. 'You'll only spend the rest of your life regretting it.' I remember thinking it was the first time he had ever called me Richard.

'Wrong, for a change, Donald,' I told him. 'I won't regret killing Jeremy Alexander. You see, he's already been pronounced dead once. I know, because I was sentenced to life imprisonment for his murder. I'm sure you're aware of the meaning of "*autrefois acquit*", and will therefore know that I can't be charged a second time with a crime I've already been convicted of and sentenced for. Even though this time they will have a body.'

I moved the gun a few inches to the right, and aimed at Jeremy's heart. I squeezed the trigger just as Jenny came charging into the room. She dived at my legs.

Jeremy and I both hit the ground with a thud.

Well, as I pointed out to you at the beginning of this chronicle, I ought to explain why I'm in jail – or, to be more accurate, why I'm back in jail.

I *was* tried a second time; on this occasion for attempted murder – despite the fact that I had only grazed the bloody man's shoulder. I still blame Jenny for that.

Mind you, it was worth it just to hear Matthew's closing speech, because he certainly understood the meaning of 'autrefois acquit'. He surpassed himself with his description of Rosemary as a calculating, evil Jezebel, and Jeremy as a man motivated by malice and greed, quite willing to cynically pose as a national hero while his victim was rotting his life away in jail, put there by a wife's perjured testimony of which he had unquestionably been the mastermind. In another four years, a furious Matthew told the jury, they would have been able to pocket several more millions between them. This time the jury looked on me with considerable sympathy.

'Thou shalt not bear false witness against any man,' were Sir Matthew's closing words, his sonorous tones making him sound like an Old Testament prophet.

The tabloids always need a hero and a villain. This time they had got themselves a hero and two villains. They seemed to have forgotten everything they had printed during the previous trial about the oversexed lorry driver, and it would be foolish to suggest that the page after page devoted to every sordid detail of Jeremy and Rosemary's deception didn't influence the jury.

They found me guilty, of course, but only because they weren't given any choice. In his summing up the judge almost ordered them to do so. But the foreman expressed his fellow jurors' hope that, given the circumstances, the judge might consider a lenient sentence. Mr Justice Lampton obviously didn't read the tabloids, because he lectured me for several minutes, and then said I would be sent down for five years.

Matthew was on his feet immediately, appealing for clemency on the grounds that I had already served a long sentence. 'This man looks out on the world through a window of tears,' he told the judge. 'I beseech your lordship not to put bars across that window a second time.' The applause from the gallery was so thunderous that the judge had to instruct the bailiffs to clear the court before he could respond to Sir Matthew's plea.

'His lordship obviously needs a little time to think,' Matthew explained under his breath as he passed me in the dock. After much deliberation in his chambers, Mr Justice Lampton settled on three years. Later that day I was sent to Ford Open Prison.

After considerable press comment during the next few weeks, and what Sir Matthew described to the Court of Appeal as 'my client's unparalleled affliction and exemplary behaviour', I ended up only having to serve nine months.

Meanwhile, Jeremy had been arrested at Addenbrookes Hospital by Allan Leeke, Deputy Chief Constable of Cambridgeshire. After three days in a heavily guarded ward he was charged with conspiracy to pervert the course of public justice, and transferred to Armley Prison to await trial. He comes before the Leeds Crown Court next month, and you can be sure I'll be sitting in the gallery following the proceedings every day. By the way, Fingers and the boys gave him a very handsome welcome. I'm told he's lost even more weight than he did trooping backwards and forwards across Europe fixing up his new identity.

Rosemary has also been arrested and charged with perjury. They didn't grant her bail, and Donald informs me that French prisons, particularly the one in Marseilles, are less comfortable than Armley – one of the few disadvantages of living in the south of France. She's fighting the extradition order, of course, but I'm assured by Matthew that she has absolutely no chance of succeeding, now we've signed the Maastricht Treaty. I knew *something* good must come out of that.

As for Mrs Balcescu – I'm sure you worked out where I'd seen her long before I did.

In the case of Regina v. Alexander and Kershaw, I'm told, she will be giving evidence on behalf of the Crown. Jeremy made such a simple mistake for a normally calculating and shrewd man. In order to protect himself from being identified, he put all his worldly goods in his wife's name. So the striking blonde ended up with everything, and I have a feeling that when it comes to her cross-examination, Rosemary won't turn out to be all that helpful to Jeremy, because it slipped his mind to let her know that in between those weekly phone calls he was living with another woman.

It's been difficult to find out much more about the real Professor Balcescu, because since Ceausescu's downfall no one is quite sure what really happened to the distinguished academic. Even the Romanians believed he had escaped to Britain and begun a new life.

Bradford City have been relegated, so Donald has

bought a cottage in the West Country and settled down to watch Bath play rugby. Jenny has joined a private detective agency in London, but is already complaining about her salary and conditions. Williams has returned to Bradford and decided on an early retirement. It was he who pointed out the painfully obvious fact that when it's twelve o'clock in France, it's only eleven o'clock in Britain.

By the way, I've decided to go back to Leeds after all. Cooper's went into liquidation as I suspected they would, the new management team not proving all that effective when it came to riding out a recession. The official receiver was only too delighted to accept my offer of £250,000 for what remained of the company, because no one else was showing the slightest interest in it. Poor Jeremy will get almost nothing for his shares. Still, you should look up the new stock in the *F.T.* around the middle of next year, and buy yourself a few, because they'll be what my father would have called 'a risk worth taking'.

By the way, Matthew advises me that I've just given you what's termed as 'inside information', so please don't pass it on, as I have no desire to go back to jail for a third time.

CHEAP AT
HALF THE PRICE

WOMEN ARE NATURALLY SUPERIOR TO men, and Mrs Consuela Rosenheim was no exception.

Victor Rosenheim, an American banker, was Consuela's third husband, and the gossip columns on both sides of the Atlantic were suggesting that, like a chain smoker, the former Colombian model was already searching for her next spouse before she had extracted the last gasp from the old one. Her first two husbands – one an Arab, the other a Jew (Consuela showed no racial prejudice when it came to signing marriage contracts) – had not quite left her in a position that would guarantee her financial security once her natural beauty had faded. But two more divorce settlements would sort that out. With this in mind, Consuela estimated that she only had another five years before the final vow must be taken.

The Rosenheims flew into London from their home in New York – or, to be more accurate, from their homes in New York. Consuela had travelled to the airport by chauffeur-driven car from their mansion in the Hamptons, while her husband had been taken from his Wall Street office in a second chauffeur-driven car. They met up in the Concorde lounge at JFK. When they had landed at Heathrow another limousine transported them to the Ritz, where they were escorted to their usual suite without any suggestion of having to sign forms or book in.

The purpose of their trip was twofold. Mr Rosenheim was hoping to take over a small merchant bank that had not benefited from the recession, while Mrs Rosenheim intended to occupy her time looking for a suitable birthday present – for herself. Despite considerable research I have been unable to discover exactly which birthday Consuela would officially be celebrating.

After a sleepless night induced by jetlag, Victor Rosenheim was whisked away to an early-morning meeting in the City, while Consuela remained in bed toying with her breakfast. She managed one piece of thin unbuttered toast and a stab at a boiled egg.

Once the breakfast tray had been removed, Consuela made a couple of phone calls to confirm luncheon dates for the two days she would be in London. She then disappeared into the bathroom.

Fifty minutes later she emerged from her suite dressed in a pink Olaganie suit with a dark blue collar, her fair hair bouncing on her shoulders. Few of the men she passed between the elevator and the revolving doors failed to turn their heads, so Consuela judged that the previous fifty minutes had not been wasted. She stepped out of the hotel and into the morning sun to begin her search for the birthday present.

Consuela began her quest in New Bond Street. As in the past, she had no intention of straying more than a few blocks north, south, east or west from that comforting landmark, while a chauffeur-driven car hovered a few yards behind her.

She spent some time in Asprey's considering the latest slimline watches, a gold statue of a tiger with jade eyes, and a Fabergé egg, before moving on to Cartier, where she dismissed a crested silver salver, a platinum watch and a Louis XIV long-case clock. From there she walked another few yards to Tiffany's, which, despite a determined salesman who showed her almost everything the shop had to offer, she still left empty-handed.

Consuela stood on the pavement and checked her watch. It was 12.52, and she had to accept that it had been a fruitless morning. She instructed her chauffeur to drive her to Harry's Bar, where she found Mrs Stavros Kleanthis waiting for her at their usual table. Consuela greeted her friend with a kiss on both cheeks, and took the seat opposite her.

Mrs Kleanthis, the wife of a not unknown shipowner – the Greeks preferring one wife and several liaisons – had for the last few minutes been concentrating her attention on the menu to be sure that the restaurant served the few dishes that her latest diet would permit. Between them, the two women had read every book that had reached number one on the *New York Times* bestseller list which included the words 'youth', 'orgasm', 'slimming', 'fitness' or 'immortality' in its title.

'How's Victor?' asked Maria, once she and Consuela had ordered their meals.

Consuela paused to consider her response, and decided on the truth.

'Fast reaching his sell-by date,' she replied. 'And Stavros?'

'Well past his, I'm afraid,' said Maria. 'But as I have neither your looks nor your figure, not to mention the fact that I have three teenage children, I don't suppose I'll be returning to the market to select the latest brand.'

Consuela smiled as a salade niçoise was placed in front of her.

'So, what brings you to London – other than to have lunch with an old friend?' asked Maria.

'Victor has his eye on another bank,' replied Consuela, as if she were discussing a child who collected stamps. 'And I'm in search of a suitable birthday present.'

'And what are you expecting Victor to come up with this time?' asked Maria. 'A house in the country? A thoroughbred racehorse? Or perhaps your own Lear jet?'

'None of the above,' said Consuela, placing her fork by the half-finished salad. 'I need something that can't be bargained over at a future date, so my gift must be one that any court, in any state, will acknowledge is unquestionably mine.'

'Have you found anything appropriate yet?' asked Maria.

'Not yet,' admitted Consuela. 'Asprey's yielded nothing of interest, Cartier's cupboard was almost bare, and the only attractive thing in Tiffany's was the salesman, who was undoubtedly penniless. I shall have to continue my search this afternoon.'

The salad plates were deftly removed by a waiter whom Maria considered far too young and far too thin. Another waiter with the same problem poured them both a cup of fresh decaffeinated coffee. Consuela refused the proffered cream and sugar, though her companion was not quite so disciplined.

The two ladies grumbled on about the sacrifices they were having to make because of the recession until they were the only diners left in the room. At this point a fatter waiter presented them with the bill – an extraordinarily long ledger considering that neither of them had ordered a second course, or had requested more than Evian from the wine waiter.

On the pavement of South Audley Street they kissed again on both cheeks before going their separate ways, one to the east and the other to the west.

Consuela climbed into the back of her chauffeur-driven car in order to be returned to New Bond Street, a distance of no more than half a mile.

Once she was back on familiar territory, she began to work her way steadily down the other side of the street, stopping at Bentley's, where it appeared that they hadn't sold anything since last year, and moving rapidly on to Adler, who seemed to be suffering from much the same problem. She cursed the recession once again, and blamed it all on Bill Clinton, who Victor had assured her was the cause of most of the world's current problems.

Consuela was beginning to despair of finding anything worthwhile in Bond Street, and reluctantly began her

journey back towards the Ritz, feeling she might even
have to consider an expedition to Knightsbridge the following day, when she came to a sudden halt outside the
House of Graff. Consuela could not recall the shop from
her last visit to London some six months before, and as
she knew Bond Street better than she had ever known
any of her three husbands, she concluded that it must
be a new establishment.

She gazed at the stunning gems in their magnificent settings, heavily protected behind the bulletproof
windows. When she reached the third window her
mouth opened wide, like a newborn chick demanding to
be fed. From that moment she knew that no further
excursions would be necessary, for there, hanging round
a slender marble neck, was a peerless diamond and ruby
necklace. She felt that she had seen the magnificent piece
of jewellery somewhere before, but she quickly dismissed the thought from her mind, and continued to
study the exquisitely set rubies surrounded by perfectly
cut diamonds, making up a necklace of unparalleled
beauty. Without giving a moment's thought to how
much the object might cost, Consuela walked slowly
towards the thick glass door at the entrance to the shop,
and pressed a discreet ivory button on the wall. The
House of Graff obviously had no interest in passing
trade.

The door was unlocked by a security officer who
needed no more than a glance at Mrs Rosenheim to
know that he should usher her quickly through to the
inner portals, where a second door was opened and

Consuela came face to face with a tall, imposing man in a long black coat and pinstriped trousers.

'Good afternoon, madam,' he said, bowing slightly. Consuela noticed that he surreptitiously admired her rings as he did so. 'Can I be of assistance?'

Although the room was full of treasures that might in normal circumstances have deserved hours of her attention, Consuela's mind was focused on only one object.

'Yes. I would like to study more closely the diamond and ruby necklace on display in the third window.'

'Certainly, madam,' the manager replied, pulling back a chair for his customer. He nodded almost imperceptibly to an assistant, who silently walked over to the window, unlocked a little door and extracted the necklace. The manager slipped behind the counter and pressed a concealed button. Four floors above, a slight burr sounded in the private office of Mr Laurence Graff, warning the proprietor that a customer had enquired after a particularly expensive item, and that he might wish to deal with them personally.

Laurence Graff glanced up at the television screen on the wall to his left, which showed him what was taking place on the ground floor.

'Ah,' he said, once he saw the lady in the pink suit seated at the Louis XIV table. 'Mrs Consuela Rosenheim, if I'm not mistaken.' Just as the Speaker of the House of Commons can identify every one of its 650 members, so Laurence Graff recognised the 650 customers who might be able to afford the most extravagant of his treasures. He quickly stepped from behind his desk, walked out of his office and took the waiting lift to the ground floor.

Meanwhile, the manager had laid out a black velvet cloth on the table in front of Mrs Rosenheim, and the assistant placed the necklace delicately on top of it. Consuela stared down at the object of her desire, mesmerised.

'Good afternoon, Mrs Rosenheim,' said Laurence Graff as he stepped out of the lift and walked across the thick pile carpet towards his would-be customer. 'How nice to see you again.'

He had in truth only seen her once before – at a shoulder-to-shoulder cocktail party in Manhattan. But after that, he could have spotted her at a hundred paces on a moving escalator.

'Good afternoon, Mr . . .' Consuela hesitated, feeling unsure of herself for the first time that day.

'Laurence Graff,' he said, offering his hand. 'We met at Sotheby Parke Benett last year – a charity function in aid of the Red Cross, if I remember correctly.'

'Of course,' said Mrs Rosenheim, unable to recall him, or the occasion.

Mr Graff bowed reverently towards the diamond and ruby necklace.

'The Kanemarra heirloom,' he purred, then paused, before taking the manager's place at the table. 'Fashioned in 1936 by Silvio di Larchi,' he continued. 'All the rubies were extracted from a single mine in Burma, over a period of twenty years. The diamonds were purchased from De Beers by an Egyptian merchant who, after the necklace had been made up for him, offered the unique piece to King Farouk – for services rendered. When the monarch married Princess Farida he presented it to her on their wedding day, and she in return bore him four heirs, none of whom, alas, was destined to succeed to the throne.' Graff looked up from one object of beauty, and gazed on another.

'Since then it has passed through several hands before arriving at the House of Graff,' continued the proprietor. 'Its most recent owner was an actress, whose husband's oil wells unfortunately dried up.'

The flicker of a smile crossed the face of Consuela Rosenheim as she finally recalled where she had previously seen the necklace.

'Quite magnificent,' she said, giving it one final look. 'I will be back,' she added as she rose from her chair. Graff accompanied her to the door. Nine out of ten customers who make such a claim have no intention of returning, but he could always sense the tenth.

'May I ask the price?' Consuela asked indifferently as he held the door open for her.

'One million pounds, madam,' Graff replied, as casually as if she had enquired about the cost of a plastic keyring at a seaside gift shop.

Once she had reached the pavement, Consuela dismissed her chauffeur. Her mind was now working at a speed that would have impressed her husband. She slipped across the road, calling first at The White House, then Yves Saint Laurent, and finally at Chanel, emerging some two hours later with all the weapons she required for the battle that lay ahead. She did not arrive back at her suite at the Ritz until a few minutes before six.

Consuela was relieved to find that her husband had not yet returned from the bank. She used the time to take a long bath, and to contemplate how the trap should be set. Once she was dry and powdered, she dabbed a suggestion of a new scent on her neck, then slipped into some of her newly acquired clothes.

She was checking herself once again in the full-length mirror when Victor entered the room. He stopped on the spot, dropping his briefcase on the carpet. Consuela turned to face him.

'You look stunning,' he declared, with the same look of desire she had lavished on the Kanemarra heirloom a few hours before.

'Thank you, darling,' she replied. 'And how did your day go?'

'A triumph. The takeover has been agreed, and at half the price it would have cost me only a year ago.'

Consuela smiled. An unexpected bonus.

'Those of us who are still in possession of cash need have no fear of the recession,' Victor added with satisfaction.

Over a quiet supper in the Ritz's dining room, Victor described to his wife in great detail what had taken place at the bank that day. During the occasional break in this monologue Consuela indulged her husband by remarking 'How clever of you, Victor,' 'How amazing,' 'How you managed it I will never understand.' When he finally ordered a large brandy, lit a cigar and leaned back in his chair, she began to run her elegantly stockinged right foot gently along the inside of his thigh. For the first time that evening, Victor stopped thinking about the takeover.

As they left the dining room and strolled towards the lift, Victor placed an arm around his wife's slim waist. By the time the lift had reached the sixth floor he had already taken off his jacket, and his hand had slipped a few inches further down. Consuela giggled. Long before they had reached the door of their suite he had begun tugging off his tie.

When they entered the room, Consuela placed the 'Do Not Disturb' sign on the outside doorknob. For the next few minutes Victor was transfixed to the spot as he watched his slim wife slowly remove each garment she had purchased that afternoon. He quickly pulled off his own clothes, and wished once again that he had carried out his New Year's resolution.

Forty minutes later, Victor lay exhausted on the bed. After a few moments of sighing, he began to snore. Consuela pulled the sheet over their naked bodies, but her eyes remained wide open. She was already going over the next step in her plan.

Victor awoke the following morning to discover his wife's hand gently stroking the inside of his leg. He rolled over to face her, the memory of the previous night still vivid in his mind. They made love a second time, something they had not done for as long as he could recall.

It was not until he stepped out of the shower that Victor remembered it was his wife's birthday, and that he had promised to spend the morning with her selecting a gift. He only hoped that her eye had already settled on something she wanted, as he needed to spend most of the day closeted in the City with his lawyers, going over the offer document line by line.

'Happy birthday, darling,' he said as he padded back into the bedroom. 'By the way, did you have any luck finding a present?' he added as he scanned the front page of the *Financial Times*, which was already speculating on the possible takeover, describing it as a coup. A smile of satisfaction appeared on Victor's face for the second time that morning.

'Yes, my darling,' Consuela replied. 'I did come across one little bauble that I rather liked. I just hope it isn't too expensive.'

'And how much is this "little bauble"?' Victor asked. Consuela turned to face him. She was wearing only two garments, both of them black, and both of them remarkably skimpy.

Victor started to wonder if he still had the time, but then he remembered the lawyers, who had been up all night and would be waiting patiently for him at the bank.

'I didn't ask the price,' Consuela replied. 'You're so much cleverer than I am at that sort of thing,' she added, as she slipped into a navy silk blouse.

Victor glanced at his watch. 'How far away is it?' he asked.

'Just across the road, in Bond Street, my darling,' Consuela replied. 'I shouldn't have to delay you for too long.' She knew exactly what was going through her husband's mind.

'Good. Then let's go and look at this little bauble without delay,' he said as he did up the buttons on his shirt.

While Victor finished dressing, Consuela, with the help of the *Financial Times*, skilfully guided the conversation back to his triumph of the previous day. She listened once more to the details of the takeover as they left the hotel and strolled up Bond Street together arm in arm.

'Probably saved myself several million,' he told her yet again. Consuela smiled as she led him to the door of the House of Graff.

'Several million?' she gasped. 'How clever you are, Victor.'

The security guard quickly opened the door, and this time Consuela found that Mr Graff was already standing by the table waiting for her. He bowed low, then turned to Victor. 'May I offer my congratulations on your brilliant coup, Mr Rosenheim.' Victor smiled. 'How may I help you?'

'My husband would like to see the Kanemarra heirloom,' said Consuela, before Victor had a chance to reply.

'Of course, madam,' said the proprietor. He stepped behind the table and spread out the black velvet cloth. Once again the assistant removed the magnificent necklace from its stand in the third window, and carefully laid it out on the centre of the velvet cloth to show the jewels to their best advantage. Mr Graff was about to embark on the piece's history, when Victor simply said, 'How much is it?'

Mr Graff raised his head. 'This is no ordinary piece of jewellery. I feel . . .'

'How much?' repeated Victor.

'Its provenance alone warrants . . .'

'How much?'

'The sheer beauty, not to mention the craftsmanship involved . . .'

'How much?' asked Victor, his voice now rising.

'. . . the word unique would not be inappropriate.'

'You may be right, but I still need to know how much it's going to cost me,' said Victor, who was beginning to sound exasperated.

'One million pounds, sir,' Graff said in an even tone, aware that he could not risk another superlative.

'I'll settle at half a million, no more,' came back the immediate reply.

'I am sorry to say, sir,' said Graff, 'that with this particular piece, there is no room for bargaining.'

'There's always room for bargaining, whatever one is selling,' said Victor. 'I repeat my offer. Half a million.'

'I fear that in this case, sir . . .'

'I feel confident that you'll see things my way, given time,' said Victor. 'But I don't have that much time to spare this morning, so I'll write out a cheque for half a million, and leave *you* to decide whether you wish to cash it or not.'

'I fear you are wasting your time, sir,' said Graff. 'I cannot let the Kanemarra heirloom go for less than one million.'

Victor took out a chequebook from his inside pocket, unscrewed the top of his fountain pen, and wrote out the words 'Five Hundred Thousand Pounds Only' below the name of the bank that bore his name. His wife took a discreet pace backwards.

Graff was about to repeat his previous comment, when he glanced up, and observed Mrs Rosenheim silently pleading with him to accept the cheque.

A look of curiosity came over his face as Consuela continued her urgent mime.

Victor tore out the cheque and left it on the table. 'I'll give you twenty-four hours to decide,' he said. 'We return to New York tomorrow morning – with or without the Kanemarra heirloom. It's your decision.'

Graff left the cheque on the table as he accompanied Mr and Mrs Rosenheim to the front door and bowed them out onto Bond Street.

'You were brilliant, my darling,' said Consuela as the chauffeur opened the car door for his master.

'The bank,' Rosenheim instructed as he fell into the back seat. 'You'll have your little bauble, Consuela. He'll cash the cheque before the twenty-four hours are up, of that I'm sure.' The chauffeur closed the back door, and the window purred down as Victor added with a smile, 'Happy birthday, darling.'

Consuela returned his smile, and blew him a kiss as the car pulled out into the traffic and edged its way towards Piccadilly. The morning had not turned out quite as she had planned, because she felt unable to agree with her husband's judgement – but then, she still had twenty-four hours to play with.

Consuela returned to the suite at the Ritz, undressed, took a shower, opened another bottle of perfume, and slowly began to change into the second outfit she had purchased the previous day. Before she left the room she turned to the commodities section of the *Financial Times*, and checked the price of green coffee.

She emerged from the Arlington Street entrance of the Ritz wearing a double-breasted navy blue Yves Saint Laurent suit and a wide-brimmed red and white hat. Ignoring her chauffeur, she hailed a taxi, instructing the driver to take her to a small, discreet hotel in Knightsbridge. Fifteen minutes later she entered the foyer with her head bowed, and after giving the name of her host to the manager, was accompanied to a suite on the fourth floor. Her luncheon companion stood as she entered the room, walked forward, kissed her on both cheeks and wished her a happy birthday.

After an intimate lunch, and an even more intimate hour spent in the adjoining room, Consuela's companion listened to her request and, having first checked his watch, agreed to accompany her to Mayfair. He didn't mention to her that he would have to be back in his office by four o'clock to take an important call from South America. Since the downfall of the Brazilian president, coffee prices had gone through the roof.

As the car travelled down Brompton Road, Consuela's companion telephoned to check the latest spot price of green coffee in New York (only her skill in bed had managed to stop him from calling earlier). He was pleased to learn that it was up another two cents, but not as pleased as she was. Eleven minutes later, the car deposited them outside the House of Graff.

When they entered the shop together arm in arm, Mr Graff didn't so much as raise an eyebrow.

'Good afternoon, Mr Carvalho,' he said. 'I do hope that your estates yielded an abundant crop this year.'

Mr Carvalho smiled and replied, 'I cannot complain.'

'And how may I assist you?' enquired the proprietor.

'We would like to see the diamond necklace in the third window,' said Consuela, without a moment's hesitation.

'Of course, madam,' said Graff, as if he were addressing a complete stranger.

Once again the black velvet cloth was laid out on the table, and once again the assistant placed the Kanemarra heirloom in its centre.

This time Mr Graff was allowed to relate its history, before Carvalho politely enquired after the price.

'One million pounds,' said Graff.

After a moment's hesitation, Carvalho said, 'I'm willing to pay half a million.'

'This is no ordinary piece of jewellery,' replied the proprietor. 'I feel . . .'

'Possibly not, but half a million is my best offer,' said Carvalho.

'The sheer beauty, not to mention the craftsmanship involved . . .'

'Nevertheless, I am not willing to go above half a million.'

'. . . the word unique would not be inappropriate.'

'Half a million, and no more,' insisted Carvalho.

'I am sorry to say, sir,' said Graff, 'that with this particular piece there is no room for bargaining.'

'There's always room for bargaining, whatever one is selling,' the coffee grower insisted.

'I fear that is not true in this case, sir. You see . . .'

'I suspect you will come to your senses in time,' said Carvalho. 'But, regrettably, I do not have any time to spare this afternoon. I will write out a cheque for half a million pounds, and leave *you* to decide whether you wish to cash it.'

Carvalho took a chequebook from his inside pocket, unscrewed the top of his fountain pen, and wrote out the words 'Five Hundred Thousand Pounds Only'. Consuela looked silently on.

Carvalho tore out the cheque, and left it on the counter.

'I'll give you twenty-four hours to decide. I leave for Chicago on the early evening flight tomorrow. If the cheque has not been presented by the time I reach my office . . .'

Graff bowed his head slightly, and left the cheque on

the table. He accompanied them to the door, and bowed again when they stepped out onto the pavement.

'You were brilliant, my darling,' said Consuela as the chauffeur opened the car door for his employer.

'The Exchange,' said Carvalho. Turning back to face his mistress, he added, 'You'll have your necklace before the day is out, of that I'm certain, my darling.'

Consuela smiled and waved as the car disappeared in the direction of Piccadilly, and on this occasion she felt able to agree with her lover's judgement. Once the car had turned the corner, she slipped back into the House of Graff.

The proprietor smiled, and handed over the smartly wrapped gift. He bowed low and simply said, 'Happy birthday, Mrs Rosenheim.'

DOUGIE MORTIMER'S
RIGHT ARM

R<small>OBERT HENRY KEFFORD III</small>, KNOWN TO
his friends as Bob, was in bed with a girl called Helen
when he first heard about Dougie Mortimer's right arm.

Bob was sorry to be leaving Cambridge. He had spent
three glorious years at St John's, and although he hadn't
read as many books as he had done for his undergraduate
degree at the University of Chicago, he had striven every
bit as hard to come head of the river.

It wasn't unusual for an American to win a rowing
blue in the early 1970s, but to have stroked a victorious
Cambridge eight for three years in a row was acknowledged as a first.

Bob's father, Robert Henry Kefford II, known to his
friends as Robert, had travelled over to England to watch
his son take part in all three races from Putney to Mort-
lake. After Bob had stroked Cambridge to victory for
the third time, his father told him that he must not
return to his native Illinois without having presented a
memento to the University Boat Club that they would
remember him by.

'And don't forget, my boy,' declared Robert Henry
Kefford II, 'the gift must not be ostentatious. Better to

show that you have made an effort to present them with an object of historic value than give them something that obviously cost a great deal of money. The British appreciate that sort of thing.'

Bob spent many hours pondering his father's words, but completely failed to come up with any worthwhile ideas. After all, the Cambridge University Boat Club had more silver cups and trophies than they could possibly display.

It was on a Sunday morning that Helen first mentioned the name of Dougie Mortimer. She and Bob were lying in each other's arms, when she started prodding his biceps.

'Is this some form of ancient British foreplay that I ought to know about?' Bob asked, placing his free arm around Helen's shoulder.

'Certainly not,' Helen replied. 'I was simply trying to discover if your biceps are as big as Dougie Mortimer's.'

As Bob had never known a girl talk about another man while he was in bed with her, he was unable to think of an immediate response.

'And are they?' he eventually enquired, flexing his muscles.

'Hard to tell,' Helen replied. 'I've never actually touched Dougie's arm, only seen it at a distance.'

'And where did you come across this magnificent specimen of manhood?'

'It hangs over the bar at my dad's local, in Hull.'

'Doesn't Dougie Mortimer find that a little painful?' asked Bob, laughing.

'Doubt if he cares that much,' said Helen. 'After all, he's been dead for over sixty years.'

'And his arm still hangs above a bar?' asked Bob in disbelief. 'Hasn't it begun to smell a bit by now?'

This time it was Helen's turn to laugh. 'No, you Yankee fool. It's a bronze cast of his arm. In those days, if you were in the University crew for three years in a row, they made a cast of your arm to hang in the clubhouse. Not to mention a card with your picture on it in every packet of Player's cigarettes. I've never seen *your* picture in a cigarette packet, come to think of it,' said Helen as she pulled the sheet over his head.

'Did he row for Oxford or Cambridge?' asked Bob.

'No idea.'

'So, what's the name of this pub in Hull?'

'The King William,' Helen replied, as Bob took his arm from around her shoulder.

'Is this American foreplay?' she asked after a few moments.

Later that morning, after Helen had left for Newnham, Bob began searching his shelves for a book with a blue cover. He dug out his much-thumbed *History of the Boat Race* and flicked through the index, to discover that there were seven Mortimers listed. Five had rowed for Oxford, two for Cambridge. He began to pray as he checked their initials. Mortimer, A.J. (Westminster and Wadham, Oxon), Mortimer, C.K. (Uppingham and Oriel, Oxon), Mortimer, D.J.T. (Harrow and

St Catharine's, Cantab), Mortimer, E.L. (Oundle and
Magdalen, Oxon). Bob turned his attention to Mortimer,
D.J.T., biography page 129, and flicked the pages backwards until he reached the entry he sought. Douglas
John Townsend Mortimer (St Catharine's), Cambridge
1907, −08, −09, stroke. He then read the short summary
of Mortimer's rowing career.

> DOUGIE MORTIMER stroked the Cambridge boat to
> victory in 1907, a feat which he repeated in 1908. But
> in 1909, when the experts considered Cambridge to
> have one of the finest crews for years, the light blues
> lost to an Oxford boat that was regarded as the rank
> outsider. Although many explanations were sug-
> gested by the press at the time, the result of the race
> remains a mystery to this day. Mortimer died in 1914.

Bob closed the book and returned it to the shelf,
assuming the great oarsman must have been killed in
the First World War. He perched on the end of the
bed, considering the information he now possessed. If
he could bring Dougie Mortimer's right arm back to
Cambridge and present it to the Club at the annual Blues'
Dinner, it would surely be a prize that met his father's
demanding criterion.

He dressed quickly and went downstairs to the pay
phone in the corridor. Once directory enquiries had
given him the four numbers he required, he set about
trying to remove the next obstacle.

The first calls he made were to the King William −
or, to be precise, the King Williams, because the direc-

tory had supplied him with the numbers of three pubs in Hull which bore that name. When he was put through to the first, he asked, 'Does Dougie Mortimer's right arm hang above your counter?' He couldn't quite make out every word of the broad northern accent that replied, but he was left in no doubt that it didn't.

The second call was answered by a girl who said, 'Do you mean that thing that's nailed to the wall above the bar?'

'Yes, I guess that will be it,' said Bob.

'Well then, this is the pub you're looking for.'

After Bob had taken down the address and checked the pub's opening hours, he made a third call. 'Yes, that's possible,' he was told. 'You can take the 3.17 to Peterborough, where you'll have to change and catch the 4.09 for Doncaster, then change again. You'll arrive in Hull at 6.32.'

'What about the last train back?' asked Bob.

'8.52, change at Doncaster and Peterborough. You should be back in Cambridge just after midnight.'

'Thank you,' said Bob. He strolled off to his college for lunch and took a place at the large centre table, but proved unusually poor company for those around him.

He boarded the train to Peterborough later that afternoon, still thinking about how he could possibly relieve the pub owners of their prize possession. At Peterborough he jumped out, walked across to a waiting train on platform three and climbed aboard, still deep in thought. When his train pulled into Hull a couple of hours later he was no nearer to solving the problem. He asked the first taxi on the rank to take him to the King William.

'Market Place, Harold's Corner or Percy Street?' asked the cabbie.

'Percy Street, please,' replied Bob.

'They don't open until seven, lad,' the cabbie told him once he had dropped Bob outside the front door.

Bob checked the time. Twenty minutes to kill. He walked down a side street at the back of the pub, and stopped to watch some young lads playing football. They were using the front walls of two houses on either side of the street as goals, and showed amazing accuracy in never hitting any of the windows. Bob wondered if the game would ever catch on in America.

He became so captivated by the youngsters' skill that they stopped to ask him if he wanted to join in. He said, 'No thank you,' confident that if he did play with them, he would be the one person who ended up breaking a window.

He arrived back outside the King William a few minutes after seven, and strolled into the empty pub, hoping that no one would pay much attention to him. But at six feet four inches, and dressed in a double-breasted blue blazer, grey flannels, a blue shirt and college tie, the three people behind the bar might well have wondered if he had dropped in from another planet. He stopped himself from looking above the bar, as a young blonde barmaid stepped forward and asked him what he would like.

'A half a pint of your best bitter,' Bob said, trying to

sound like one of his English friends when they ordered a drink from the college buttery.

The landlord eyed Bob suspiciously as he took his half-pint glass over to a small round table in the corner and sat down quietly on a stool. He was pleased when two other men entered the pub, so that the landlord's attention was distracted.

Bob took a sip of the dark liquid and nearly choked. When he had recovered, he allowed his eyes to glance above the bar. He tried to hide his excitement when he saw the bronze cast of a massive arm embedded in a large piece of varnished wood. He thought the object both dreadful and inspiring at the same time. His eyes moved down to the bold lettering printed in gold beneath it:

D. J. T. MORTIMER
1907–08–09
(ST CATHARINE'S, STROKE)

Bob kept his eye on the landlord as the pub began to fill up, but he soon became aware that it was his wife — everyone called her Nora — who was not only in charge, but who did most of the serving.

When he had finished his drink, he made his way over to her end of the bar.

'What can I do for you, young man?' Nora asked.

'I'll have another, thank you,' said Bob.

'An American,' she said, as she pulled the pump and began to refill his glass. 'We don't get many of you lot up 'ere, at least not since the bases closed.' She placed his half-pint on the counter in front of him. 'So, what brings you to 'ull?'

'You do,' Bob replied, ignoring his drink.

Nora looked suspiciously at the stranger, who was young enough to be her son.

Bob smiled, 'Or, to be more accurate, Dougie Mortimer does.'

'Now I've figured you out,' said Nora. 'You phoned this morning, didn't you? My Christie told me. I should 'ave guessed.'

Bob nodded. 'How did the arm end up in Hull?' he asked.

'Now, that's a long story,' said Nora. 'It was my grandfather's, wasn't it. Born in Ely 'e was, and 'e used to spend his holidays fishin' the Cam. Said it was the only catch he managed that year, which I suppose is one better than sayin' it fell off the back of a lorry. Still, when 'e died a few years back, my father wanted to throw the bloody thing out with the rest of the rubbish, but I wouldn't 'ear of it, told 'im 'e should 'ang it in the pub, didn't I? I cleaned and polished it, it came up real nice, and then I 'ung it above the bar. Still, it's a long way for you to travel just to 'ave a look at that load of old cobblers.'

Bob looked up and admired the arm once again. He held his breath. 'I didn't come just to look.'

'Then why did you come?' she asked.

'I came to buy.'

'Get a move on, Nora,' said the landlord. 'Can't you see there are customers waitin' to be served?'

116

Nora swung round and said, 'Just 'old your tongue, Cyril Barnsworth. This young man's come all the way up to 'ull just to see Dougie Mortimer's arm, and what's more, 'e wants to buy it.' This caused a ripple of laughter from the regulars standing nearest to the bar, but as Nora didn't join in they quickly fell silent.

'Then it's been a wasted journey, 'asn't it?' said the landlord. 'Because it's not for sale.'

'It's not yours to sell,' said Nora, placing her hands on her hips. 'Mind you, lad, 'e's right,' she said, turning back to face Bob. 'I wouldn't part with it for a 'undred quid,' said Nora. Several others in the room were beginning to show an interest in the proceedings.

'How about two hundred,' said Bob quietly. This time Nora burst out laughing, but Bob didn't even smile.

When Nora had stopped laughing, she stared directly at the strange young man. 'My God, 'e means it,' she said.

'I certainly do,' said Bob. 'I would like to see the arm returned to its rightful home in Cambridge, and I'm willing to pay two hundred pounds for the privilege.'

The landlord looked across at his wife, as if he couldn't believe what he was hearing. 'We could buy that little second-hand car I've had my eye on,' he said.

'Not to mention a summer 'oliday and a new overcoat for next winter,' Nora added, staring at Bob as if she still needed to be convinced that he wasn't from another planet. Suddenly she thrust her hand over the counter and said, 'You've got yourself a deal, young man.'

Bob ended up having to supply several rounds of

drinks for those customers who claimed to have been close personal friends of Nora's grandfather, even if some of them looked rather obviously too young. He also had to stay overnight in a local hotel, because Nora wouldn't part with her grandfather's 'heirloom', as she now kept referring to it, until her bank manager had phoned Cambridge to check that Robert Henry Kefford III was good for two hundred pounds.

Bob clung onto his treasure all the way back to Cambridge that Monday morning, and then lugged the heavy object from the station to his digs in the Grange Road, where he hid it under the bed. The following day he handed it over to a local furniture restorer, who promised to return the arm to its former glory in time for the night of the Blues' Dinner.

When, three weeks later, Bob was allowed to see the results of the restorer's efforts, he immediately felt confident that he now possessed a prize not only worthy of the C.U.B.C., but that also complied with his father's wishes. He resolved not to share his secret with anyone – not even Helen – until the night of the Blues' Dinner, although he did warn the puzzled President that he was going to make a presentation, and that he required two hooks, eighteen inches apart and eight feet from the floor, to be screwed into the wall beforehand.

The University Blues' Dinner is an annual event held in the Boat House overlooking the Cam. Any former or current rowing blue is eligible to attend, and Bob was delighted to find when he arrived that night that it was a near-record turnout. He placed the carefully wrapped brown paper parcel under his chair, and put his camera on the table in front of him.

Because it was his last Blues' Dinner before returning to America, Bob had been seated at the top table, between the Honorary Secretary and the current President of Boats. Tom Adams, the Honorary Secretary, had gained his blue some twenty years before, and was recognised as the club's walking encyclopedia, because he could name not only everyone in the room, but all the great oarsmen of the past.

Tom pointed out to Bob three Olympic medallists dotted around the room. 'The oldest is sitting on the left of the President,' he said. 'Charles Forester. He rowed at number three for the club in 1908–09, so he must be over eighty.'

'Can it be possible?' said Bob, recalling Forester's youthful picture on the clubhouse wall.

'Certainly can,' said the Secretary. 'And what's more, young man,' he added, laughing, 'you'll look like that one day too.'

'What about the man at the far end of the table?' asked Bob. 'He looks even older.'

'He is,' said the Secretary. 'That's Sidney Fisk. He was boatman from 1912 to 1945, with only a break for the First World War. Took over from his uncle at short notice, if I remember correctly.'

'So he would have known Dougie Mortimer,' said Bob wistfully.

'Now, there's a great name from the past,' said Adams. 'Mortimer, D.J.T., 1907–08–09, St Catharine's, stroke. Oh, yes, Fisk would certainly have known Mortimer, that's for sure. Come to think of it, Charles Forester must have been in the same boat as Mortimer when he was stroke.'

During the meal, Bob continued to quiz Adams about Dougie Mortimer, but he was unable to add a great deal to the entry in Bob's *History of the Boat Race*, other than to confirm that Cambridge's defeat in 1909 still remained a mystery, as the light blues demonstrably had the superior crew.

When the last course had been cleared away, the President rose to welcome his guests and to make a short speech. Bob enjoyed the parts he was able to hear above the noise made by the rowdy undergraduates, and even joined in the frenzy whenever Oxford was mentioned. The President ended with the words, 'There will be a special presentation to the club this year, by our colonial stroke Bob Kefford, which I'm sure we're all going to appreciate.'

When Bob rose from his place the cheering became even more raucous, but he spoke so softly that the noise quickly died away. He told his fellow members how he had come to discover, and later retrieve, Dougie Mortimer's right arm, leaving out only his exact location when he first learned of its whereabouts.

With a flourish, he unwrapped the parcel that had been secreted under his chair, and revealed the newly restored bronze cast. The assembled members rose to their feet and cheered. A smile of satisfaction came over Bob's face as he looked around, only wishing his father could have been present to witness their reaction.

As his eyes swept the room, Bob couldn't help noticing that the oldest blue present, Charles Forester, had remained seated, and was not even joining in the applause. Bob's gaze then settled on Sidney Fisk, the only other person who had not risen to his feet. The old boatman's lips remained fixed in a straight line, and his hands didn't move from his knees.

Bob forgot about the two old men when the President, assisted by Tom Adams, hung the bronze arm on the wall, placing it between a blade that had been pulled by one of the Olympic crew of 1908, and a zephyr worn by the only blue ever to row in a Cambridge boat that had beaten Oxford four years in a row. Bob began to take photographs of the ceremony, so that he would have a record to show his father that he had carried out his wishes.

When the hanging was over, many of the members and old blues surrounded Bob to thank and congratulate him, leaving him in no doubt that all the trouble he had taken to track down the arm had been worthwhile.

Bob was among the last to leave that night, because so many members had wanted to wish him good luck for the future. He was strolling along the footpath back to his digs, humming as he went, when he suddenly remembered that he had left his camera on the table. He decided to collect it in the morning, as he was sure that the clubhouse would be locked and deserted by now, but when he turned round to check, he saw a single light coming from the ground floor.

He turned and began walking back towards the clubhouse, still humming. When he was a few paces away, he glanced through the window, and saw that there were two figures standing in the committee room. He strode over to take a closer look, and was surprised to see the elderly blue, Charles Forester, and Sidney Fisk, the retired boatman, trying to shift a heavy table. He would have gone in to assist them if Fisk hadn't suddenly pointed up towards Dougie Mortimer's arm. Bob remained motionless as he watched the two old men drag the table inch by inch nearer to the wall, until it was directly below the plaque.

Fisk picked up a chair and placed it against the wall, and Forester used it as a step to climb onto the table. Forester then bent down and took the arm of the older man, to help him up.

Once they were both safely on the table, they held a short conversation before reaching up to the bronze cast, easing it off its hooks and slowly lowering it until it rested between their feet. Forester, with the help of the chair, stepped back down onto the floor, then turned round to assist his companion again.

Bob still didn't move, as the two old men carried Dougie Mortimer's arm across the room and out of the boathouse. Having placed it on the ground outside the door, Forester returned to switch off the lights. When he stepped back outside into the cold night air, the boatman quickly padlocked the door.

Once again the two old men held a short conversation before lifting Bob's trophy up and stumbling off with it along the towpath. They had to stop, lower the arm to the ground, rest, and start again several times. Bob followed silently in their wake, using the broad-trunked trees to conceal himself, until the elderly pair suddenly turned and màde their way down the bank towards the river. They came to a halt at the water's edge, and lowered their bounty into a small rowing boat.

The old blue untied the rope, and the two men pushed the boat slowly out into the river, until the water was lapping around the knees of their evening dress trousers. Neither seemed at all concerned about the fact that they were getting soaked. Forester managed to clamber up into the little boat quite quickly, but it took Fisk several minutes to join him. Once they were both aboard, Forester took his place at the oars, while the boatman remained in the bow, clutching on to Dougie Mortimer's arm.

Forester began to row steadily towards the middle of the river. His progress was slow, but his easy rhythm revealed that he had rowed many times before. When the two men calculated that they had reached the centre of the Cam, at its deepest point, Forester stopped rowing and joined his companion in the bow. They picked up the bronze arm and, without ceremony, cast it over the side and into the river. Bob heard the splash and saw the boat rock dangerously from side to side. Fisk then took his turn at the oars; his progress back to the river-bank was even slower than Forester's. They eventually reached land, and both men stumbled out and shoved the boat up towards its mooring, the boatman finally securing the rope to a large ring.

Soaked and exhausted, their breath rising visibly in the clear night air, the two old men stood and faced each other. They shook hands like two business tycoons who had closed an important deal, before disappearing into the night.

Tom Adams, the Club's Honorary Secretary, rang Bob the following morning to tell him something he already knew. In fact he had lain awake all night thinking of little else.

Bob listened to Adams's account of the break-in. 'What's surprising is that they only took one thing.' He paused. 'Your arm – or rather, Dougie's arm. It's very strange, especially as someone had left an expensive camera on the top table.'

'Is there anything I can do to help?' asked Bob.

'No, I don't think so, old boy,' said Adams. 'The local police are making enquiries, but my bet is that whoever stole the arm will probably be halfway across the county by now.'

'I expect you're right,' said Bob. 'While you're on the line, Mr Adams, I wonder if I could ask you a question about the history of the club.'

'I'll do my best,' said Adams. 'But you must remember that it's only a hobby for me, old chap.'

'Do you by any chance know who is the oldest living

Oxford rowing blue?' There was a long silence the other end of the line. 'Are you still there?' Bob asked eventually.

'Yes. I was just trying to think if old Harold Deering is still alive. I can't remember seeing his obituary in *The Times*.'

'Deering?' said Bob.

'Yes. Radley and Keble, 1909–10–11. He became a bishop, if I remember correctly, but I'm damned if I can recall where.'

'Thank you,' said Bob, 'that's most helpful.'

'I could be wrong,' Adams pointed out. 'After all, I don't read the obituary columns every day. And I'm a bit rusty when it comes to Oxford.'

Bob thanked him once again before ringing off.

After a college lunch he didn't eat, Bob returned to his digs and rang the porter's lodge at Keble. He was answered by a curmudgeonly voice.

'Do you have any record of a Harold Deering, a former member of the college?' Bob asked.

'Deering . . . Deering . . .' said the voice. 'That's a new one on me. Let me see if he's in the college handbook.' Another long pause, during which Bob really did begin to think he'd been cut off, until the voice said, 'Good heavens, no wonder. It was just a bit before my time. Deering, Harold, 1909–11, BA 1911, MA 1916 (Theology). Became Bishop of Truro. Is that the one?'

'Yes, that's the man,' said Bob. 'Do you by any chance have an address for him?'

'I do,' said the voice. 'The Rt Revd Harold Deering,

The Stone House, Mill Road, Tewkesbury, Gloucestershire.'

'Thank you,' said Bob. 'You've been very helpful.'

Bob spent the rest of the afternoon composing a letter to the former bishop, in the hope that the old blue might agree to see him.

He was surprised to receive a call at his digs three days later from a Mrs Elliot, who turned out to be Mr Deering's daughter, with whom he was now living.

'The poor old chap can't see much beyond his nose these days,' she explained, 'so I had to read your letter out to him. But he'd be delighted to meet you, and wonders if you could call on him this Sunday at 11.30, after Matins – assuming that's not inconvenient for you.'

'That's fine,' said Bob. 'Please tell your father to expect me around 11.30.'

'It has to be in the morning,' Mrs Elliot went on to explain, 'because, you see, he has a tendency to fall asleep after lunch. I'm sure you understand. By the way, I'll send directions to your college.'

On the Sunday morning, Bob was up long before the sun rose, and started out on his journey to Tewkesbury in a car he had hired the previous day. He would have gone by train, but British Rail didn't seem willing to rise quite early enough for him to reach his destination on time. As he journeyed across the Cotswolds, he tried to remember to keep the car on the left, and couldn't help wondering how long it would be before the British started to build some highways with more than one lane.

He drove into Tewkesbury a few minutes after eleven, and thanks to Mrs Elliot's clear directions, quickly found The Stone House. He parked the car outside a little wicket gate.

A woman had opened the door of the house even before Bob was halfway up the scrub-covered path. 'It must be Mr Kefford,' she declared. 'I'm Susan Elliot.' Bob smiled and shook her hand. 'I should warn you,' Mrs Elliot explained as she led him towards the front door, 'that you'll have to speak up. Father's become rather deaf lately, and I'm afraid his memory isn't what it used to be. He can recall everything that happened to him at your age, but not even the most simple things that I told him yesterday. I've had to remind him what time you would be coming this morning,' she said as they walked through the open door. 'Three times.'

'I'm sorry to have put you to so much trouble, Mrs Elliot,' said Bob.

'No trouble at all,' said Mrs Elliot as she led him down the corridor. 'The truth is, my father's been rather excited by the thought of an American blue from Cambridge coming to visit him after all these years. He hasn't stopped talking about it for the past two days. He's also curious about why you wanted to see him in the first place,' she added conspiratorially.

She led Bob into the drawing room, where he immediately came face to face with an old man seated in a winged leather chair, wrapped in a warm plaid dressing gown and propped up on several cushions, his legs covered by a tartan blanket. Bob found it hard to believe that this frail figure had once been an Olympic oarsman.

'Is it him?' the old man asked in a loud voice.

'Yes, Father,' Mrs Elliot replied, equally loudly. 'It's Mr Kefford. He's driven over from Cambridge especially to see you.'

Bob walked forward and shook the old man's bony outstretched hand.

'Good of you to come all this way, Kefford,' said the former bishop, pulling his blanket up a little higher.

'I appreciate your seeing me, sir,' said Bob, as Mrs Elliot directed him to a comfortable chair opposite her father.

'Would you care for a cup of tea, Kefford?'

'No, thank you, sir,' said Bob. 'I really don't want anything.'

'As you wish,' said the old man. 'Now, I must warn you, Kefford, that my concentration span isn't quite what it used to be, so you'd better tell me straight away why you've come to see me.'

Bob attempted to marshal his thoughts. 'I'm doing a little research on a Cambridge blue who must have rowed around the same time as you, sir.'

'What's his name?' asked Deering. 'I can't remember them all, you know.'

Bob looked at him, fearing that this was going to turn out to be a wasted journey.

'Mortimer. Dougie Mortimer,' he said.

'D.J.T. Mortimer,' the old man responded without

hesitation. 'Now, there's someone you couldn't easily forget. One of the finest strokes Cambridge ever produced – as Oxford found out, to their cost.' The old man paused. 'You're not a journalist, by any chance?'

'No, sir. It's just a personal whim. I wanted to find out one or two things about him before I return to America.'

'Then I will certainly try to help if I can,' said the old man in a piping voice.

'Thank you,' said Bob. 'I'd actually like to begin at the end, if I may, by asking if you knew the circumstances of his death.'

There was no response for several moments. The old cleric's eyelids closed, and Bob began to wonder if he had fallen asleep.

'Not the sort of thing chaps talked about in my day,' he eventually replied. 'Especially with its being against the law at the time, don't you know.'

'Against the law?' said Bob, puzzled.

'Suicide. A bit silly, when you think about it,' the old priest continued, 'even if it is a mortal sin. Because you can't put someone in jail who's already dead, now can you? Not that it was ever confirmed, you understand.'

'Do you think it might have been connected with Cambridge losing the Boat Race in 1909, when they were such clear favourites?'

'It's possible, I suppose,' said Deering, hesitating once again. 'I must admit, the thought had crossed my mind. I took part in that race, as you may know.' He paused again, breathing heavily. 'Cambridge were the clear favourites, and we didn't give ourselves a chance. The result was never properly explained, I must admit. There were a lot of rumours doing the rounds at the time, but no proof – no proof, you understand.'

'What wasn't proved?' asked Bob. There was another long silence, during which Bob began to fear that the old man might have thought he'd gone too far.

'My turn to ask you a few questions, Kefford,' he said eventually.

'Of course, sir.'

'My daughter tells me that you've stroked the winning boat for Cambridge three years in a row.'

'That's correct, sir.'

'Congratulations, my boy. But tell me: if you had wanted to lose one of those races, could you have done so, without the rest of the crew being aware of it?'

It was Bob's turn to ponder. He realised for the first time since he had entered the room that he shouldn't assume that a frail body necessarily indicates a frail mind.

'Yes, I guess so,' he eventually said. 'You could always change the stroke rate without warning, or even catch a crab as you took the Surrey bend. Heaven knows, there's always enough flotsam on the river to make it appear unavoidable.' Bob looked the old man straight in the eye. 'But it would never have crossed my mind that anyone might do so deliberately.'

'Nor mine,' said the priest, 'had their cox not taken holy orders.'

'I'm not sure I understand, sir,' said Bob.

'No reason you should, young man. I find nowadays

that I think in non sequiturs. I'll try to be less obscure. The cox of the 1909 Cambridge boat was a chap called Bertie Partridge. He went on to become a parish priest in some outpost called Chersfield in Rutland. Probably the only place that would have him,' he chuckled. 'But when I became Bishop of Truro, he wrote and invited me to address his flock. It was such an arduous journey from Cornwall to Rutland in those days, that I could easily have made my excuses, but like you, I wanted the mystery of the 1909 race solved, and I thought this might be my only chance.'

Bob made no attempt to interrupt, fearing he might stop the old man's flow.

'Partridge was a bachelor, and bachelors get very lonely, don't you know. If you give them half a chance, they love to gossip. I stayed overnight, which gave him every chance. He told me, over a long dinner accompanied by a bottle of non-vintage wine, that it was well known that Mortimer had run up debts all over Cambridge. Not many undergraduates don't, you might say, but in Mortimer's case they far exceeded even his potential income. I think he rather hoped that his fame and popularity would stop his creditors from pressing their claims. Not unlike Disraeli when he was Prime Minister,' he added with another chuckle.

'But in Mortimer's case one particular shopkeeper, who had absolutely no interest in rowing, and even less in undergraduates, threatened to bankrupt him the week before the 1909 Boat Race. A few days after the race had been lost, Mortimer seemed, without explanation, to have cleared all his obligations, and nothing more was heard of the matter.'

Once again the old man paused as if in deep thought. Bob remained silent, still not wishing to distract him.

'The only other thing I can recall is that the bookies made a killing,' Deering said without warning. 'I know that to my personal cost, because my tutor lost a five-pound wager, and never let me forget that I had told him we didn't have a snowball's chance in hell. Mind you, I was always able to offer that as my excuse for not getting a First.' He looked up and smiled at his visitor.

Bob sat on the edge of his seat, mesmerised by the old man's recollections.

'I'm grateful for your candour, sir,' he said. 'And you can be assured of my discretion.'

'Thank you, Kefford,' said the old man, now almost whispering. 'I'm only too delighted to have been able to assist you. Is there anything else I can help you with?'

'No, thank you, sir,' said Bob. 'I think you've covered everything I needed to know.'

Bob rose from his chair, and as he turned to thank Mrs Elliot he noticed for the first time a bronze cast of an arm hanging on the far wall. Below it was printed in gold:

H. R. R. DEERING
1909–10–11
(KEBLE, BOW)

'You must have been a fine oarsman, sir.'

'No, not really,' said the old blue. 'But I was lucky enough to be in the winning boat three years in a row, which wouldn't please a Cambridge man like yourself.'

Bob laughed. 'Perhaps one last question before I leave, sir.'

'Of course, Kefford.'

'Did they ever make a bronze of Dougie Mortimer's arm?'

'They most certainly did,' replied the priest. 'But it mysteriously disappeared from your boathouse in 1912. A few weeks later the boatman was sacked without explanation – caused quite a stir at the time.'

'Was it known why he was sacked?' asked Bob.

'Partridge claimed that when the old boatman got drunk one night, he confessed to having dumped Mortimer's arm in the middle of the Cam.' The old man paused, smiled, and added, 'Best place for it, wouldn't you say, Kefford?'

Bob thought about the question for some time, wondering how his father would have reacted. He then replied simply, 'Yes, sir. Best place for it.'

DO NOT PASS GO

May 1986

HAMID ZEBARI SMILED AT THE THOUGHT
of his wife Shereen driving him to the airport. Neither
of them would have believed it possible five years before,
when they had first arrived in America as political refugees. But since he had begun a new life in the States,
Hamid was beginning to think anything might be
possible.

'When will you be coming home, Papa?' asked Nadim,
who was strapped safely in the back seat next to his
sister May. She was too young to understand why Papa
was going away.

'Just a fortnight, I promise. No more,' their father
replied. 'And when I get back, we'll all go on holiday.'

'How long is a fortnight?' his son demanded.

'Fourteen days,' Hamid told him with a laugh.

'And fourteen nights,' said his wife as she drew into
the kerb below the sign for Turkish Airways. She
touched a button on the dashboard and the boot flicked
up. Hamid jumped out of the car, grabbed his luggage
from the boot, and put it on the pavement before climb-
ing into the back of the car. He hugged his daughter

137

first, and then his son. May was crying – not because he was going away, but because she always cried when the car came to a sudden halt. He allowed her to stroke his bushy moustache, which usually stopped the flow of tears.

'Fourteen days,' repeated his son. Hamid hugged his wife, and felt the small swelling of a third child between them.

'We'll be here waiting to pick you up,' Shereen called out as her husband tipped the skycap on the kerb.

Once his six empty cases had been checked in, Hamid disappeared into the terminal, and made his way to the Turkish Airlines desk. As he took the same flight twice a year, he didn't need to ask the girl at the ticket counter for directions.

After he had checked in and been presented with his boarding pass, Hamid still had an hour to wait before they would call his flight. He began the slow trek to Gate B27. It was always the same – the Turkish Airlines plane would be parked halfway back to Manhattan. As he passed the Pan Am check-in desk on B5 he observed that they would be taking off an hour earlier than him, a privilege for those who were willing to pay an extra sixty-three dollars.

When he reached the check-in area, a Turkish Airlines stewardess was slipping the sign for Flight 014, New York–London–Istanbul, onto a board. Estimated time of departure, 10.10.

The seats were beginning to fill up with the usual

cosmopolitan group of passengers: Turks going home to visit their families, those Americans taking a holiday who cared about saving sixty-three dollars, and businessmen whose bottom line was closely watched by tight-fisted accountants.

Hamid strolled over to the restaurant bar and ordered coffee and two eggs sunnyside up, with a side order of hash browns. It was the little things that reminded him daily of his new-found freedom, and of just how much he owed to America.

'Would those passengers travelling to Istanbul with young children please board the plane now,' said the stewardess over the loudspeaker.

Hamid swallowed the last mouthful of his hash browns – he hadn't yet become accustomed to the American habit of covering everything in ketchup – and took a final swig of the weak, tasteless coffee. He couldn't wait to be reunited with the thick Turkish coffee served in small bone china cups. But that was a tiny sacrifice when weighed against the privilege of living in a free land. He settled his bill and left a dollar in the little tin tray.

'Would those passengers seated in rows 35 to 41 please board the aircraft now.'

Hamid picked up his briefcase and headed for the passageway that led to Flight 014. An official from Turkish Airlines checked his boarding pass and ushered him through.

He had been allocated an aisle seat near the back of economy. Ten more trips, he told himself, and he would

fly Pan Am Business Class. By then he would be able
to afford it.

Whenever the wheels of his plane left the ground,
Hamid would look out of the little window and watch
his adopted country as it disappeared out of sight, the
same thoughts always going through his mind.

It had been nearly five years since Saddam Hussein
had dismissed him from the Iraqi Cabinet, after he had
held the post of Minister of Agriculture for only two
years. The wheat crops had been poor that autumn, and
after the People's Army had taken their share, and the
middlemen their cut, the Iraqi people ended up with
short rations. Someone had to take the blame, and the
obvious scapegoat was the Minister of Agriculture.
Hamid's father, a carpet dealer, had always wanted him
to join the family business, and had even warned him
before he died not to accept Agriculture, the last three
holders of that office having first been sacked, and later
disappeared – and everyone in Iraq knew what 'disappeared' meant. But Hamid did accept the post. The
first year's crop had been abundant, and after all, he
convinced himself, Agriculture was only a stepping stone
to greater things. In any case, had not Saddam described
him in front of the whole Revolutionary Command
Council as 'my good and close friend'? At thirty-two
you still believe you are immortal.

Hamid's father was proved right, and Hamid's only
real friend – friends melted away like snow in the morning sun when this particular president sacked you –
helped him to escape.

The only precaution Hamid had taken during his days as a Cabinet Minister was to withdraw from his bank account each week a little more cash than he actually needed. He would then change the extra money into American dollars with a street trader, using a different dealer each time, and never exchanging enough to arouse suspicion. In Iraq everyone is a spy.

The day he was sacked, he checked how much was hidden under his mattress. It amounted to eleven thousand two hundred and twenty-one American dollars.

The following Thursday, the day on which the weekend begins in Baghdad, he and his pregnant wife took the bus to Erbil. He left his Mercedes conspicuously parked in the front drive of his large home in the suburbs, and they carried no luggage with them – just two passports, the roll of dollars secreted in his wife's baggy clothing, and some Iraqi dinars to get them as far as the border.

No one would be looking for them on a bus to Erbil.

Once they arrived in Erbil, Hamid and his wife took a taxi to Sulaimania, using most of the remaining dinars to pay the driver. They spent the night in a small hotel far from the city centre. Neither slept as they waited for the morning sun to come shining through the curtainless window.

Next day, another bus took them high into the hills of Kurdistan, arriving in Zakho in the early evening.

The final part of the journey was the slowest of all. They were taken up through the hills on mules, at a cost of two hundred dollars – the young Kurdish smuggler showed no interest in Iraqi dinars. He delivered the former Cabinet Minister and his wife safely over the border in the early hours of the morning, leaving them to make their way on foot to the nearest village on Turkish soil. They reached Kirmizi Renga that evening, and spent another sleepless night at the local station, waiting for the first train for Istanbul.

Hamid and Shereen slept all the way through the long train journey to the Turkish capital, and woke up the following morning as refugees. The first visit Hamid made in the city was to the Iz Bank, where he deposited ten thousand eight hundred dollars. The next was to the American Embassy, where he produced his diplomatic passport and requested political asylum. His father had once told him that a recently sacked Cabinet Minister from Iraq was always a good catch for the Americans.

The Embassy arranged accommodation for Hamid and his wife in a first-class hotel, and immediately informed Washington of their little coup. They promised Hamid that they would get back to him as quickly as possible, but gave him no clue as to how long that might take. He decided to use the time to visit the carpet bazaars on the south side of the city, so often frequented by his father.

Many of the dealers remembered Hamid's father – an honest man who liked to bargain and drink gallons of coffee, and who had often talked about his son going into politics. They were pleased to make his acquaintance, especially when they learned of what he planned to do once he had settled in the States.

The Zebaris were granted American visas within the week and flown to Washington at the government's expense, which included a charge for excess baggage of twenty-three Turkish carpets.

After five days of intensive questioning by the CIA, Hamid was thanked for his co-operation and the useful information he had supplied. He was then released to begin his new life in America. He, his pregnant wife and the twenty-three carpets boarded a train for New York.

It took Hamid six weeks to find the right shop, on the Lower East Side of Manhattan, from which to sell his carpets. Once he had signed the five-year lease, Shereen immediately set about painting their new Americanised name above the door.

Hamid didn't sell his first carpet for nearly three months, by which time his meagre savings had all but disappeared. But by the end of the first year, sixteen of the twenty-three carpets had been sold, and he realised he would soon have to travel back to Istanbul to buy more stock.

Four years had passed since then, and the Zebaris had recently moved to a larger establishment on the West Side, with a small apartment above the shop. Hamid kept telling his wife that this was only the beginning, that anything was possible in the United States. He now considered himself a fully-fledged American citizen, and not just because of the treasured blue passport that confirmed his status. He accepted that he could never return to his birthplace while Saddam remained its ruler. His home and possessions had long ago been requisitioned by the Iraqi state, and the death sentence had been passed on him in his absence. He doubted if he would ever see Baghdad again.

After the stopover in London, the plane landed at Istanbul's Ataturk Airport a few minutes ahead of schedule. Hamid booked into his usual small hotel, and planned how best to allocate his time over the next two weeks. He was happy to be back among the hustle and bustle of the Turkish capital.

There were thirty-one dealers he wanted to visit, because this time he hoped to return to New York with at least sixty carpets. That would require fourteen days of drinking thick Turkish coffee, and many hours of bargaining, as a dealer's opening price would be three times as much as Hamid was willing to pay – or what the dealer really expected to receive. But there was no short cut in the bartering process, which – like his father – Hamid secretly enjoyed.

By the end of the fortnight, Hamid had purchased fifty-seven carpets, at a cost of a little over twenty-one thousand dollars. He had been careful to select only those carpets that would be sought after by the most discerning New Yorkers, and he was confident that this latest batch would fetch almost a hundred thousand dollars in America. It had been such a successful trip that Hamid felt he would indulge himself by taking the earlier Pan Am flight back to New York. After all, he had undoubtedly earned himself the extra sixty-three dollars many times over in the course of his trip.

He was looking forward to seeing Shereen and the

children even before the plane had taken off, and the American flight attendant with her pronounced New York accent and friendly smile only added to the feeling that he was already home. After lunch had been served, and having decided he didn't want to watch the in-flight movie, Hamid dozed off and dreamt about what he could achieve in America, given time. Perhaps his son would go into politics. Would the United States be ready for an Iraqi President by the year 2025? He smiled at the thought, and fell contentedly into a deep sleep.

'Ladies and gentlemen,' a deep Southern voice boomed out over the intercom, 'this is your captain. I'm sorry to interrupt the movie, or to wake those of you who've been resting, but we've developed a small problem in an engine on our starboard wing. Nothing to worry about, folks, but Federal Aviation Authority rulings insist that we land at the nearest airport and have the problem dealt with before we continue with our journey. It shouldn't take us more than an hour at the most, and then we'll be on our way again. You can be sure that we'll try to make up as much of the lost time as possible, folks.'

Hamid was suddenly wide awake.

'We won't be disembarking from the aircraft at any time, as this is an unscheduled stop. However, you'll be able to tell the folks back home that you've visited Baghdad.'

Hamid felt his whole body go limp, and then his head rocked forward. The flight attendant rushed up to his side.

'Are you feeling all right, sir?' she asked.

He looked up and stared into her eyes. 'I must see the captain immediately. Immediately.'

The flight attendant was in no doubt of the passenger's anxiety, and quickly led him forward, up the spiral staircase into the first-class lounge and onto the flight deck.

She tapped on the door of the cockpit, opened it and said, 'Captain, one of the passengers needs to speak to you urgently.'

'Show him in,' said the Southern voice. The captain turned to face Hamid, who was now trembling uncontrollably. 'How can I be of help, sir?' he asked.

'My name is Hamid Zebari. I am an American citizen,' he began. 'If you land in Baghdad, I will be arrested, tortured and then executed.' The words tumbled out. 'I am a political refugee, and you must understand that the regime will not hesitate to kill me.'

The captain only needed to take one look at Hamid to realise he wasn't exaggerating.

'Take over, Jim,' he said to his co-pilot, 'while I have a word with Mr Zebari. Call me the moment we've been given clearance to land.'

The captain unfastened his seatbelt, and led Hamid to an empty corner of the first-class lounge.

'Take me through it slowly,' he said.

During the next few minutes Hamid explained why he had had to leave Baghdad, and how he came to be living in America. When he had reached the end of his story the captain shook his head and smiled. 'No need to panic, sir,' he assured Hamid. 'No one is going to have to leave the aircraft at any time, so the passengers' passports won't even be checked. Once the engine has been attended to, we'll be back up and on our way immediately. Why don't you just stay here in first class, then you'll be able to speak to me at any time, should you feel at all anxious.'

How anxious can you feel? Hamid wondered, as the captain left him to have a word with the co-pilot. He started to tremble once more.

'It's the captain once again, folks, just bringing you up to date. We've been given clearance by Baghdad, so we've begun our descent and expect to land in about twenty minutes. We'll then be taxiing to the far end of the runway, where we'll await the engineers. Just as soon as they've dealt with our little problem, we'll be back up and on our way again.'

A collective sigh went up, while Hamid gripped the armrest and wished he hadn't eaten any lunch. He didn't stop shaking for the next twenty minutes, and almost fainted when the wheels touched down on the land of his birth.

He stared out of the porthole as the aircraft taxied past the terminal he knew so well. He could see the armed guards stationed on the roof and at the doors leading onto the tarmac. He prayed to Allah, he prayed to Jesus, he even prayed to President Reagan.

For the next fifteen minutes the silence was broken only by the sound of a van driving across the tarmac and coming to a halt under the starboard wing of the aircraft.

Hamid watched as two engineers carrying bulky

toolbags got out of the van, stepped onto a small crane and were hoisted up until they were level with the wing. They began unscrewing the outer plates of one of the engines. Forty minutes later they screwed the plates back on and were lowered to the ground. The van then headed off towards the terminal.

Hamid felt relieved, if not exactly relaxed. He fastened his seatbelt hopefully. His heartbeat fell from 180 a minute to around 110, but he knew it wouldn't return to normal until the plane lifted off and he could be sure they wouldn't turn back. Nothing happened for the next few minutes, and Hamid became anxious again. Then the door of the cockpit opened, and he saw the captain heading towards him, a grim expression on his face.

'You'd better join us on the flight deck,' the captain said in a whisper. Hamid undid his seatbelt and somehow managed to stand. He unsteadily followed the captain into the cockpit, his legs feeling like jelly. The door was closed behind them.

The captain didn't waste any words. 'The engineers can't locate the problem. The chief engineer won't be free for another hour, so we've been ordered to disembark and wait in the transit area until he's completed the job.'

'I'd rather die in a plane crash,' Hamid blurted out.

'Don't worry, Mr Zebari, we've thought of a way round your problem. We're going to put you in a spare uniform. That will make it possible for you to stay with us the whole time, and use the crew's facilities. No one will ask to see your passport.'

'But if someone recognises me . . .' began Hamid.

'Once you've got rid of that moustache, and you're wearing a flight officer's uniform, dark glasses and a peaked hat, your own mother wouldn't know you.'

With the help of scissors, followed by shaving foam, followed by a razor, Hamid removed the bushy moustache that he had been so proud of, to leave an upper lip that looked as pale as a blob of vanilla ice cream. The senior flight attendant applied some of her make-up to his skin, until the white patch blended in with the rest of his face. Hamid still wasn't convinced, but after he had changed into the co-pilot's spare uniform and studied himself in the toilet mirror, he had to admit that it would indeed be remarkable if anyone recognised him.

The passengers were the first to leave the plane, and were ferried by an airport bus to the main terminal. A smart transit van then came out to collect the crew, who left as a group and sheltered Hamid by making sure that he was surrounded at all times. Hamid became more and more nervous with each yard the van travelled towards the terminal.

The security guard showed no particular interest in the air crew as they entered the building, and they were left to find themselves seats on wooden benches in the white-walled hall. The only decoration was a massive portrait of Saddam Hussein in full uniform carrying a kalashnikov rifle. Hamid couldn't bring himself to look at the picture of his 'good and close friend'.

Another crew was also sitting around waiting to board

their aircraft, but Hamid was too frightened to start up a conversation with any of them.

'They're French,' he was informed by the senior flight attendant. 'I'm about to find out if my night classes were worth all the expense.' She took the spare place next to the captain of the French aircraft, and tried a simple opening question.

The French captain was telling her that they were bound for Singapore via New Delhi, when Hamid saw him: Saad al-Takriti, once a member of Saddam's personal guard, marched into the hall. From the insignia on his shoulder, he now appeared to be in charge of airport security.

Hamid prayed that he wouldn't look in his direction. Al-Takriti sauntered through the room, glancing at the French and American crews, his eyes lingering on the stewardesses' black-stockinged legs.

The captain touched Hamid on the shoulder, and he nearly leapt out of his skin.

'It's OK, it's OK. I just thought you'd like to know that the chief engineer is on his way out to the aircraft, so it shouldn't be too long now.'

Hamid looked beyond the Air France plane, and watched a van come to a halt under the starboard wing of the Pan Am aircraft. A man in blue overalls stepped out of the vehicle and onto the little crane.

Hamid stood up to take a closer look, and as he did so Saad al-Takriti walked back into the hall. He came to a sudden halt, and the two men stared briefly at each other, before Hamid quickly resumed his place next to the captain. Al-Takriti disappeared into a side room marked 'Do Not Enter'.

'I think he's spotted me,' said Hamid. The make-up started to run down onto his lips.

The captain leant across to his chief flight attendant and interrupted her parley with the French captain. She listened to her boss's instructions, and then tried a tougher question on the Frenchman.

Saad al-Takriti marched back out of the office and began striding towards the American captain. Hamid thought he would surely faint.

Without even glancing at Hamid, al-Takriti barked, 'Captain, I require you to show me your manifest, the number of crew you are carrying, and their passports.'

'My co-pilot has all the passports,' the captain replied. 'I'll see you get them.'

'Thank you,' said al-Takriti. 'When you have collected them, you will bring them to my office so that I can check each one. Meanwhile, please ask your crew to remain here. They are not, under any circumstances, to leave the building without my permission.'

The captain rose from his place, walked slowly over to the co-pilot, and asked for the passports. Then he issued an order which took him by surprise. The captain took the passports into the security office just as a bus drew up outside the transit area to take the French crew back to their plane.

Saad al-Takriti placed the fourteen passports in front of him on his desk. He seemed to take pleasure in checking each one of them slowly. When he had finished the task, he announced in mock surprise, 'I do believe, captain, that I counted fifteen crew wearing Pan Am uniforms.'

'You must have been mistaken,' said the captain. 'There are only fourteen of us.'

'Then I will have to make a more detailed check, won't I, captain? Please return these documents to their rightful owners. Should there happen to be anyone not in possession of a passport, they will naturally have to report to me.'

'But that is against international regulations,' said the captain, 'as I'm sure you know. We are in transit, and therefore, under UN Resolution 238, not legally in your country.'

'Save your breath, captain. We have no use for UN resolutions in Iraq. And, as you correctly point out, as far as we are concerned, you are not legally even in our country.'

The captain realised he was wasting his time, and could bluff no longer. He gathered up the passports as slowly as he could and allowed al-Takriti to lead him back into the hall. As they entered the room the Pan Am crew members who were scattered around the benches suddenly rose from their places and began walking about, continually changing direction, while at the same time talking at the top of their voices.

'Tell them to sit down,' hissed al-Takriti, as the crew zig-zagged backwards and forwards across the hall.

'What's that you're saying?' asked the captain, cupping his ear.

. 'Tell them to sit down!' shouted al-Takriti.

The captain gave a half-hearted order, and within a few moments everyone was seated. But they still continued talking at the top of their voices.

'And tell them to shut up!'

The captain moved slowly round the room, asking his crew one by one to lower their voices.

Al-Takriti's eyes raked the benches of the transit hall, as the captain glanced out onto the tarmac and watched the French aircraft taxiing towards the far runway.

Al-Takriti began counting, and was annoyed to discover that there were only fourteen Pan Am crew members in the hall. He stared angrily around the room, and quickly checked once again.

'All fourteen seem to be present,' said the captain after he had finished handing back the passports to his crew.

'Where is the man who was sitting next to you?' al-Takriti demanded, jabbing a finger at the captain.

'You mean my first officer?'

'No. The one who looked like an Arab.'

'There are no Arabs on my crew,' the captain assured him.

Al-Takriti strode over to the senior flight attendant. 'He was sitting next to you. His upper lip had make-up on it that was beginning to run.'

'The captain of the French plane was sitting next to me,' the senior flight attendant said. She immediately realised her mistake.

Saad al-Takriti turned and looked out of the window

to see the Air France plane at the end of the runway preparing for take-off. He jabbed a button on his hand phone as the thrust of the jet engines started up, and barked out some orders in his native tongue. The captain didn't need to speak Arabic to get the gist of what he was saying.

By now the American crew were all staring at the French aircraft, willing it to move, while al-Takriti's voice was rising with every word he uttered.

The Air France 747 eased forward and slowly began to gather momentum. Saad al-Takriti cursed loudly, then ran out of the building and jumped into a waiting jeep. He pointed towards the plane and ordered the driver to chase after it. The jeep shot off, accelerating as it weaved its way in and out of the parked aircraft. By the time it reached the runway it must have been doing ninety miles an hour, and for the next hundred yards it sped along parallel to the French aircraft, with al-Takriti standing on the front seat, clinging onto the windscreen and waving his fist at the cockpit.

The French captain acknowledged him with a crisp salute, and as the 747's wheels lifted off, a loud cheer went up in the transit lounge.

The American captain smiled and turned to his chief flight attendant. 'That only proves my theory that the French will go to any lengths to get an extra passenger.'

Hamid Zebari landed in New Delhi six hours later, and immediately phoned his wife to let her know what had happened. Early the next morning Pan Am flew him back to New York – first class. When Hamid emerged from the airport terminal, his wife jumped out of the car and threw her arms around him.

Nadim wound the window down and declared, 'You were wrong, Papa. A fortnight turns out to be fifteen days.' Hamid grinned at his son, but his daughter burst into tears, and not because their car had come to a sudden halt. It was just that she was horrified to see her mother hugging a strange man.

CHUNNEL VISION

WHENEVER I'M IN NEW YORK, I ALWAYS try to have dinner with an old friend of mine called Duncan McPherson. We are opposites, and so naturally we attract. In fact, Duncan and I have only one thing in common: we are both writers. But even then there's a difference, because Duncan specialises in screenplays, which he writes in the intervals between his occasional articles for *Newsweek* and the *New Yorker*, whereas I prefer novels and short stories.

One of the other differences between us is the fact that I have been married to the same woman for twenty-eight years, while Duncan seems to have a different girlfriend every time I visit New York – not bad going, as I average at least a couple of trips a year. The girls are always attractive, lively and bright, and there are various levels of intensity – depending on what stage the relationship is at. In the past I've been around at the beginning (very physical) and in the middle (starting to cool off), but this trip was to be the first time I experienced an ending.

I phoned Duncan from my hotel on Fifth Avenue to let him know I was in town to promote my new novel, and he immediately asked me over for dinner the following evening. I assumed, as in the past, that it would be at his apartment. Another opposite: unlike me, he's a quite superlative cook.

'I can't wait to see you,' he said. 'I've come up with an idea for a novel at last, and I want to try the plot out on you.'

'Delighted,' I replied. 'Look forward to hearing all about it tomorrow night. And may I ask . . .' I hesitated.

'Christabel,' he said.

'Christabel . . .' I repeated, trying to recall if I had ever met her.

'But there's no need for you to remember anything about her,' he added. 'Because she's about to be given the heave-ho, to use one of your English expressions. I've just met a new one – Karen. She's absolutely sensational. You'll adore her.'

I didn't feel this was the appropriate moment to point out to Duncan that I had adored them all. I merely asked which one was likely to be joining us for dinner.

'Depends if Christabel has finished packing,' Duncan replied. 'If she has, it will be Karen. We haven't slept together yet, and I'd been planning on that for tomorrow night. But as you're in town, it will have to be postponed.'

I laughed. 'I could wait,' I assured him. 'After all, I'm here for at least a week.'

'No, no. In any case, I must tell you about my idea for a novel. That's far more important. So why don't you come to my place tomorrow evening. Shall we say around seven thirty?'

Before I left the hotel, I wrapped up a copy of my latest book, and wrote 'Hope you enjoy it' on the outside.

Duncan lives in one of those apartment blocks on 72nd and Park, and though I've been there many times, it always takes me a few minutes to locate the entrance to the building. And, like Duncan's girlfriends, the door-man seems to change with every trip.

The new doorman grunted when I gave my name, and directed me to the elevator on the far side of the hall. I slid the grille doors across and pressed the button for the fourteenth floor. It was one of those top floors that could not be described as a penthouse even by the most imaginative of estate agents.

I pulled back the doors and stepped out onto the land-ing, rehearsing the appropriate smiles for Christabel (goodbye) and Karen (hello). As I walked towards Duncan's front door I could hear raised voices – a very British expression, born of understatement; let's be frank and admit that they were screaming at each other at the tops of their voices. I concluded that this had to be the end of Christabel, rather than the beginning of Karen.

I was already a few minutes late, so there was no turning back. I pressed the doorbell, and to my relief the voices immediately fell silent. Duncan opened the door, and although his cheeks were scarlet with rage, he still managed a casual grin. Which reminds me that I forgot to tell you about a few more opposites – the damn man has a mop of boyish dark curly hair, the rugged features of his Irish ancestors, and the build of a champion tennis player.

'Come on in,' he said. 'This is Christabel, by the way – if you hadn't already guessed.'

I'm not by nature a man who likes other people's cast-offs, but I'm bound to confess I would have been happy to make Christabel the exception. She had an oval face, deep blue eyes, and an angelic smile. She was also graced with that fine fair hair that only the Nordic races are born with, and the type of figure that slimming advertisements make their profits out of. She wore a cashmere sweater and tapered white jeans that left little to the imagination.

Christabel shook me by the hand, and apologised for looking a little scruffy. 'I've been packing all afternoon,' she explained.

The proof of her labours was there for all to see – three large suitcases and two cardboard boxes full of books standing by the door. On the top of one of the boxes lay a copy of a Dorothy L. Sayers murder mystery with a torn red dustjacket.

I was becoming acutely aware that I couldn't have chosen a worse evening for a reunion with my old friend. 'I'm afraid we're going to have to eat out for a change,' Duncan said. 'It's been' – he paused – 'a busy day. I haven't had a chance to visit the local store. Good thing, actually,' he added. 'It'll give me more time to take you through the plot of my novel.'

'Congratulations,' Christabel said.

I turned to face her.

'*Your* novel,' she said. 'Number one on the *New York Times* bestseller list, isn't it?'

'Yes, congratulations,' said Duncan. 'I haven't got round to reading it yet, so don't tell me anything about it. It wasn't on sale in Bosnia,' he added with a laugh.

I handed him my little gift.

'Thank you,' he said, and placed it on the hall table. 'I'll look forward to it.'

'I've read it,' said Christabel.

Duncan bit his lip. 'Let's go,' he said, and was about to turn and say goodbye to Christabel when she asked me, 'Would you mind if I joined you? I'm starving, and as Duncan said, there's absolutely nothing in the icebox.'

I could see that Duncan was about to protest, but by then Christabel had passed him, and was already in the corridor and heading for the elevator.

'We can walk to the restaurant,' Duncan said as we trundled down to the ground floor. 'It's only Californians who need a car to take them one block.'

As we strolled west on 72nd Street Duncan told me that he had chosen a fancy new French restaurant to take me to.

I began to protest, not just because I've never really cared for ornate French food, but I was also aware of Duncan's unpredictable pecuniary circumstances. Sometimes he was flush with money, at other times stony broke. I just hoped that he'd had an advance on the novel.

'No, like you, I normally wouldn't bother,' he said. 'But it's only just opened, and the *New York Times* gave it a rave review. In any case, whenever I'm in London, you always entertain me "right royally",' he added, in what he imagined was an English accent.

It was one of those cool evenings that make walking in New York so pleasant, and I enjoyed the stroll, as Duncan began to tell me about his recent trip to Bosnia.

'You were lucky to catch me in New York,' he was saying. 'I've only just got back after being holed up in the damned place for three months.'

'Yes, I know. I read your article in *Newsweek* on the plane coming over,' I said, and went on to tell him how fascinated I had been by his evidence that a group of UN soldiers had set up their own underground network, and felt no scruples about operating an illegal black market in whatever country they were stationed.

'Yes, that's caused quite a stir at the UN,' said Duncan. 'The *New York Times* and the *Washington Post* have both followed the story up with features on the main culprits – but without bothering to give me any credit for the original research, of course.'

I turned round to see if Christabel was still with us. She seemed to be deep in thought, and was lagging a few paces behind. I smiled a smile that I hoped said I think Duncan's a fool and you're fantastic, but I received no response.

After a few more yards I spotted a red and gold awning flapping in the breeze outside something called 'Le Manoir'. My heart sank. I've always preferred simple food, and have long considered pretentious French cuisine to be one of the major cons of the eighties, and one that should have been passé, if not part of culinary history, by the nineties.

Duncan led us down a short crazy-paving path through a heavy oak door and into a brightly lit restaurant. One look around the large, over-decorated room and my worst fears were confirmed. The maître d' stepped forward and said, 'Good evening, monsieur.'

'Good evening,' replied Duncan. 'I have a table reserved in the name of McPherson.'

The maître d' checked down a long list of bookings. 'Ah, yes, a table for two.' Christabel pouted, but looked no less beautiful.

'Can we make it three?' my host asked rather half-heartedly.

'Of course, sir. Allow me to show you to your table.'

We were guided through a crowded room to a little alcove in the corner which had only been set for two.

One look at the tablecloth, the massive flowered plates with 'Le Manoir' painted in crimson all over them, and the arrangement of lilies on the centre of the table, made me feel even more guilty about what I had let Duncan in for. A waiter dressed in a white open-neck shirt, black trousers and black waistcoat with 'Le Manoir' sewn in red on the breast pocket hurriedly supplied Christabel with a chair, while another deftly laid a place for her.

A third waiter appeared at Duncan's side and enquired if we would care for an aperitif. Christabel smiled sweetly and asked if she might have a glass of champagne. I requested some Evian water, and Duncan nodded that he would have the same.

For the next few minutes, while we waited for the menus to appear, we continued to discuss Duncan's trip to Bosnia, and the contrast between scraping one's food out of a billycan in a cold dugout accompanied by the sound of bullets, and dining off china plates in a warm restaurant, with a string quartet playing Schubert in the background.

Another waiter appeared at Duncan's side and handed us three pink menus the size of small posters. As I glanced down the list of dishes, Christabel whispered something to the waiter, who nodded and slipped quietly away.

I began to study the menu more carefully, unhappy to discover that this was one of those restaurants which allows only the host to have the bill of fare with the prices attached. I was trying to work out which would be the cheapest dishes, when another glass of champagne was placed at Christabel's side.

I decided that the clear soup was likely to be the least expensive starter, and that it would also help my feeble efforts to lose weight. The main courses had me more perplexed, and with my limited knowledge of French I finally settled on duck, as I couldn't find any sign of 'poulet'.

When the waiter returned moments later, he immediately spotted Christabel's empty glass, and asked, 'Would you care for another glass of champagne, madame?'

'Yes, please,' she replied sweetly, as the maître d' arrived to take our order. But first we had to suffer an ordeal that nowadays can be expected at every French restaurant in the world.

'Today our specialities are,' he began, in an accent that would not have impressed central casting, 'for hors d'oeuvres *Gelée de saumon sauvage et caviar impérial en aigre doux*, which is wild salmon slivers and imperial caviar in a delicate jelly with sour cream and courgettes soused in dill vinegar. Also we have *Cuisses de grenouilles à la purée d'herbes à soupe, fricassée de chanterelles et racines de persil*, which are pan-fried frogs' legs in a parsley purée, fricassee of chanterelles and parsley roots. For the main course we have *Escalope de turbot*, which is a poached fillet of turbot on a watercress purée, lemon sabayon and a Gewürztraminer sauce. And, of course, everything that is on the menu can be recommended.'

I felt full even before he had finished the descriptions.

Christabel appeared to be studying the menu with due diligence. She pointed to one of the dishes, and the maître d' smiled approvingly.

Duncan leaned across and asked if I had selected anything yet.

'Consommé and the duck will suit me just fine,' I said without hesitation.

'Thank you, sir,' said the maître d'. 'How would you like the duck? Crispy, or perhaps a little underdone?'

'Crispy,' I replied, to his evident disapproval.

'And monsieur?' he asked, turning to Duncan.

'Caesar salad and a rare steak.'

The maître d' retrieved the menus and was turning to go as Duncan said, 'Now, let me tell you all about my idea for a novel.'

'Would you care to order some wine, sir?' asked another waiter, who was carrying a large red leather book with golden grapes embossed on its cover.

'Should I do that for you?' suggested Christabel. 'Then there'll be no need to interrupt your story.'

Duncan nodded his agreement, and the waiter handed the wine list over to Christabel. She opened the red leather cover with as much eagerness as if she was about to begin a bestselling novel.

'You may be surprised,' Duncan was saying, 'that my book is set in Britain. Let me start by explaining that the timing for its publication is absolutely vital. As you know, a British and French consortium is currently building a tunnel between Folkestone and Sangatte, which is scheduled to be opened by Queen Elizabeth on 6 May 1994. In fact, *Chunnel* will be the title of my book.'

I was horrified. Another glass of champagne was placed in front of Christabel.

'The story begins in four separate locations, with four different sets of characters. Although they are all from diverse age groups, social backgrounds and countries, they have one thing in common: they have all booked on the first passenger train to travel from London to Paris via the Channel Tunnel.'

I felt a sudden pang of guilt, and wondered if I should say something, but at this point a waiter returned with a bottle of white wine, the label of which Christabel studied intently. She nodded, and the sommelier extracted the cork and poured a little into her empty glass. A sip brought the smile back to her lips. The waiter then filled our glasses.

Duncan continued: 'There will be an American family – mother, father, two teenage children – on their first visit to England; a young English couple who have just got married that morning and are about to begin their honeymoon; a Greek self-made millionaire and his French wife who booked their tickets a year before, but are now considering a divorce; and three students.'

Duncan paused as a Caesar salad was placed in front of him and a second waiter presented me with a bowl of consommé. I glanced at the dish Christabel had chosen. A plate of thinly cut smoked gravadlax with a blob of caviar in the centre. She was happily squeezing half a lemon, protected by muslin, all over it.

'Now,' said Duncan, 'in the first chapter it's important that the reader doesn't realise that the students are connected in any way, as that later becomes central to the plot. We pick up all four groups in the second chapter as they're preparing for the journey. The reader discovers their motivations for wanting to be on the train, and I build a little on the background of each of the characters involved.'

'What period of time will the plot cover?' I asked anxiously, between spoonfuls of consommé.

'Probably three days,' replied Duncan. 'The day before the journey, the day of the journey, and the day after.

But I'm still not certain – by the final draft it might all happen on the same day.'

Christabel grabbed the wine bottle from the ice-bucket and refilled her glass before the wine waiter had a chance to assist her.

'Around chapter three,' continued Duncan, 'we find the various groups arriving at Waterloo station to board "le shuttle". The Greek millionaire and his French wife will be shown to their first-class seats by a black crew member, while the others are directed to second class. Once they are all on board, some sort of ceremony to commemorate the inauguration of the tunnel will take place on the platform. Big band, fireworks, cutting of tape by royalty etc. That should prove quite adequate to cover another chapter at least.'

While I was visualising the scene and sipping my soup – the restaurant may have been pretentious, but the food was excellent – the wine waiter filled my glass and then Duncan's. I don't normally care for white wine, but I had to admit that this one was quite exceptional.

Duncan paused to eat, and I turned my attention to Christabel, who was being served a second dollop of caviar that appeared even bigger than the first.

'Chapter five,' said Duncan, 'opens as the train moves out of the station. Now the real action begins. The American family are enjoying every moment. The young bride and groom make love in the rest room. The millionaire is having another row with his wife about her continual extravagance, and the three students have met up for the first time at the bar. By now you should begin to suspect that they're not ordinary students, and that they may have known each other before they got on the train.' Duncan smiled and continued with his salad. I frowned.

Christabel winked at me, to show she knew exactly what was going on. I felt guilty at being made a part of her conspiracy, and wanted to tell Duncan what she was up to.

'It's certainly a strong plot,' I ventured as the wine waiter filled our glasses for a third time and, having managed to empty the bottle, looked towards Madame. She nodded sweetly.

'Have you started on the research yet?' I asked.

'Yes. Research is going to be the key to this project, and I'm well into it already,' said Duncan. 'I wrote to Sir Alastair Morton, the Chairman of Eurotunnel, on *Newsweek* headed paper, and his office sent me back a caseload of material. I can tell you the length of the rolling stock, the number of carriages, the diameter of the wheels, why the train can go faster on the French side than the British, even why it's necessary for them to have a different-gauge track on either side of the Channel . . .'

The pop of a cork startled me, and the wine waiter began pouring from a second bottle. Should I tell him now?

'During chapter six the plot begins to unfold,' said Duncan, warming to his theme, as one of the waiters whipped away the empty plates and another brushed a few breadcrumbs off the tablecloth into a little silver scoop. 'The trick is to keep the reader interested in all four groups at the same time.'

I nodded.

'Now we come to the point in the story when the reader discovers that the students are not really students, but terrorists, who plan to hijack the train.'

Three dishes topped by domed silver salvers were placed in front of us. On a nod from the maître d', all three domes were lifted in unison by the waiters. It would be churlish of me not to admit that the food looked quite magnificent. I turned to see what Christabel had selected: truffles with foie gras. They reminded me of a Miró painting, until she quickly smudged the canvas.

'What do you think the terrorists' motive for hijacking the train should be?' Duncan asked.

This was surely the moment to tell him – but once again I funked it. I tried to remember what point in the story we had reached. 'That would depend on whether you eventually wanted them to escape,' I suggested. 'Which might prove quite difficult, if they're stuck in the middle of a tunnel, with a police force waiting for them at either end.' The wine waiter presented Christabel with the bottle of claret she had chosen. After no more than a sniff of the cork she indicated that it was acceptable.

'I don't think they should be interested in financial reward,' said Duncan. 'They ought to be IRA, Islamic fundamentalists, Basque separatists, or whatever the latest terrorist group catching the headlines happens to be.'

I sipped the wine. It was like velvet. I had only tasted such a vintage once before, in the home of a friend who possessed a cellar of old wine put down with new money. It was a taste that had remained etched in my memory.

'In chapter seven I've come up against a block,' continued Duncan, intent on his theme. 'One of the terrorists must somehow come into contact with the newly-married couple, or at least with the bridegroom.' He paused. 'I should have told you earlier that in the character-building at the beginning of the book, one of the students turns out to be a loner, while the other two, a man and a woman, have been living together for some time.' He began digging into his steak. 'It's how I bring the loner and the bridegroom together that worries me. Any ideas?'

'That shouldn't be too hard,' I said, 'what with restaurant cars, snack bars, carriages, a corridor, not to mention a black crew member, railway staff and rest rooms.'

'Yes, but it must appear natural,' Duncan said, sounding as if he was in deep thought.

My heart sank as I noticed Christabel's empty plate being whisked away, despite the fact that Duncan and I had hardly begun our main courses.

'The chapter ends with the train suddenly coming to a halt about halfway through the tunnel,' said Duncan, staring into the distance.

'But how? And why?' I asked.

'That's the whole point. It's a false alarm. Quite innocent. The youngest child of the American family – his name's Ben – pulls the communication cord while he's sitting on the lavatory. It's such a hi-tech lavatory that he mistakes it for the chain.'

I was considering if this was plausible when a breast of quail on fondant potatoes with a garnish of smoked bacon was placed in front of Christabel. She wasted no time in attacking the fowl.

Duncan paused to take a sip of wine. Now, I felt, I had to let him know, but before I had a chance to say anything he was off again. 'Right,' he said. 'Chapter eight. The train has come to a halt several miles inside the tunnel, but not quite halfway.'

'Is that significant?' I asked feebly.

'Sure is,' said Duncan. 'The French and British have agreed the exact point inside the tunnel where French jurisdiction begins and British ends. As you'll discover, this becomes relevant later in the plot.'

The waiter began moving round the table, topping up our glasses once again with claret. I placed a hand over mine – not because the wine wasn't pure nectar, but simply because I didn't wish to give Christabel the opportunity to order another bottle. She made no attempt to exercise the same restraint, but drank her wine in generous gulps, while toying with her quail. Duncan continued with his story.

'So, the hold-up,' said Duncan, 'turns out to be nothing more than a diversion, and it's sorted out fairly quickly. Child in tears, family apologises, explanation given by the guard over the train's intercom, which relieves any anxieties the passengers might have had. A few minutes later, the train starts up again, and this time it does cross the halfway point.'

Three waiters removed our empty plates. Christabel touched the side of her lips with a napkin, and gave me a huge grin.

'So then what happens?' I asked, avoiding her eye.

'When the train stopped, the terrorists were afraid that there might be a rival group on board, with the same purpose as them. But as soon as they find out what has actually happened, they take advantage of the commotion caused by young Ben to get themselves into the cabin next to the driver's.'

'Would you care for anything from the dessert trolley, madame?' the maître d' asked Christabel. I looked on aghast as she was helped to what looked like a large spoonful of everything on offer.

'It's gripping, isn't it?' said Duncan, misunderstanding my expression for one of deep concern for those on the train. 'But there's still more to come.'

'Monsieur?'

'I'm full, thank you,' I told the maitre d'. 'Perhaps a coffee later.'

'No, nothing, thank you,' said Duncan, trying not to lose his thread. 'By the start of chapter nine the terrorists have got themselves into the driver's cabin. At gunpoint they force the chef de train and his co-driver to bring the engine to a halt for a second time. But what they don't realise is that they are now on French territory. The passengers are told by the loner over the train's intercom that this time it's not a false alarm, but the train has been taken over by whichever gang I settle on, and is going to be blown up in fifteen minutes. He tells them to get themselves off the train, into the tunnel, and as far away as they possibly can before the explosion. Naturally, some of the passengers begin to panic. Several of them leap out into the dimly lit tunnel. Many are looking frantically for their husbands, wives, children, whatever, while others begin running towards the British or French side, according to their nationality.'

I became distracted when the maître d' began wheeling yet another trolley towards our table. He paused, bowed to Christabel, and then lit a small burner. He poured some brandy into a shallow copper-bottomed pan and set about preparing a crêpe suzette.

'This is the point in the story, probably chapter ten, where the father of the American family decides to remain on the train,' said Duncan, becoming more excited than ever. 'He tells the rest of his tribe to jump off and get the hell out of it. The only other passengers who stay on board are the millionaire, his wife, and the young newly-married man. All will have strong personal reasons for wanting to remain behind, which will have been set up earlier in the plot.'

The maître d' struck a match and set light to the crêpe. A blue flame licked around the pan and shot into the air. He scooped his *pièce de résistance* onto a warm platter in one movement, and placed it in front of Christabel.

I feared we had now passed the point at which I could tell Duncan the truth.

'Right, now I have three terrorists in the cab with the chef de train. They've killed the co-driver, and there are just four passengers still left on the train, plus the black ticket collector – who may turn out to be SAS in disguise, I haven't decided yet.'

'Coffee, madame?' the maître d' asked when Duncan paused for a moment.

'Irish,' said Christabel.

'Regular, please,' I said.

'Decaff for me,' said Duncan.

'Any liqueurs or cigars?'

Only Christabel reacted.

'So, at the start of chapter eleven the terrorists open negotiations with the British police. But they say they can't deal with them because the train is no longer under their jurisdiction. This throws the terrorists completely, because none of them speaks French, and in any case their quarrel is with the British government. One of them searches the train for someone who can speak French, and comes across the Greek millionaire's wife.

'Meanwhile, the police on either side of the Channel stop all the trains going in either direction. So, our train is now stranded in the tunnel on its own – there would normally be twenty trains travelling in either direction between London and Paris at any one time.' He paused to sip his coffee.

'Is that so?' I asked, knowing the answer perfectly well.

'It certainly is,' Duncan said. 'I've done my research thoroughly.'

A glass of deep red port was being poured for Christabel. I glanced at the label: Taylor's '55. This was something I had never had the privilege of tasting. Christabel indicated that the bottle should be left on the table. The waiter nodded, and Christabel immediately poured me a glass, without asking if I wanted it. Meanwhile, the maître d' clipped a cigar for Duncan that he hadn't requested.

'In chapter twelve we discover the terrorists' purpose,' continued Duncan. 'Namely, blowing up the train as a publicity stunt, guaranteed to get their cause onto every front page in the world. But the passengers who have remained on the train, led by the American father, are planning a counter-offensive.'

The maître d' lit a match and Duncan automatically picked up the cigar and put it in his mouth. It silenced him . . .

'The self-made millionaire might feel he's the natural leader,' I suggested.

. . . but only for a moment. 'He's a Greek. If I'm going to make any money out of this project, it's the American market I have to aim for. And don't forget the film rights,' Duncan said, jabbing the air with his cigar.

I couldn't fault his logic.

'Can I have the check?' Duncan asked as the maître d' passed by our table.

'Certainly, sir,' he replied, not even breaking his stride.

'Now, my trouble is going to be the ending . . .'

began Duncan as Christabel suddenly, if somewhat unsteadily, rose from her chair.

She turned to face me and said, 'I'm afraid the time has come for me to leave. It's been a pleasure meeting you, although I have a feeling we won't be seeing each other again. I'd just like to say how much I enjoyed your latest novel. Such an original idea. It deserved to be number one.'

I stood, kissed her hand and thanked her, feeling more guilty than ever.

'Goodbye, Duncan,' she said, turning to face her former lover, but he didn't even bother to look up. 'Don't worry yourself,' she added. 'I'll be out of the apartment by the time you get back.'

She proceeded to negotiate a rather wobbly route across the restaurant, eventually reaching the door that led out onto the street. The maître d' held it open for her and bowed low.

'I can't pretend I'm sorry to see her go,' said Duncan, puffing away on his cigar. 'Fantastic body, great between the sheets, but she's totally lacking in imagination.'

The maître d' reappeared by Duncan's side, this time to place a small black leather folder in front of him.

'Well, the critics were certainly right about this place,' I commented. Duncan nodded his agreement.

The maître d' bowed, but not quite as low as before.

'Now, my trouble, as I was trying to explain before Christabel decided to make her exit,' continued Duncan, 'is that I've done the outline, completed the research, but I still don't have an ending. Any ideas?' he asked, as a middle-aged woman rose from a nearby table and began walking determinedly towards us.

Duncan flicked open the leather cover, and stared in disbelief at the bill.

The woman came to a halt beside our table. 'I just wanted to tell you how much I enjoyed your new book,' she said in a loud voice.

Other diners turned round to see what was going on.

'Thank you,' I said somewhat curtly, hoping to prevent her from adding to my discomfort.

Duncan's eyes were still fixed on the bill.

'And the ending,' she said. 'So clever! I would never have guessed how you were going to get the American family out of the tunnel alive . . .'

SHOESHINE BOY

TED BARKER WAS ONE OF THOSE MEMBERS of Parliament who never sought high office. He'd had what was described by his fellow officers as a 'good war' – in which he was awarded the Military Cross and reached the rank of major. After being demobbed in November 1945 he was happy to return to his wife Hazel and their home in Suffolk.

The family engineering business had also had a good war, under the diligent management of Ted's elder brother Ken. As soon as he arrived home, Ted was offered his old place on the board, which he happily accepted. But as the weeks passed by, the distinguished warrior became first bored and then disenchanted. There was no job for him at the factory which even remotely resembled active service.

It was around this time that he was approached by Ethel Thompson, the works convenor and – more important for the advancement of this tale – Chairman of the Wedmore branch of the North Suffolk Conservative Association. The incumbent MP, Sir Dingle Lightfoot, known in the constituency as 'Tiptoe', had made it clear that once the war was over they must look for someone to replace him.

'We don't want some clever clogs from London coming up here and telling us how to run this division,' pronounced Mrs Thompson. 'We need someone who knows the district and understands the problems of the local people.' Ted, she suggested, might be just the ticket.

Ted confessed that he had never given such an idea a moment's thought, but promised Mrs Thompson that he would take her proposal seriously, only asking for a week in which to consider his decision. He discussed the suggestion with his wife, and having received her enthusiastic support, he paid a visit to Mrs Thompson at her home the following Sunday afternoon. She was delighted to hear that Mr Barker would be pleased to allow his name to go forward for consideration as the prospective parliamentary candidate for the division of North Suffolk.

The final shortlist included two clever clogs from London – one of whom later served in a Macmillan Cabinet – and the local boy, Ted Barker. When the chairman announced the committee's decision to the local press, he said that it would be improper to reveal the number of votes each candidate had polled. In fact, Ted had comfortably outscored his two rivals put together.

Six months later the Prime Minister called a general election, and after a lively three-week campaign, Ted was returned as the Member of Parliament for North Suffolk with a majority of over seven thousand. He quickly became respected and popular with colleagues on both sides of the House, though he never pretended to be anything other than, in his own words, 'an amateur politician'.

As the years passed, Ted's popularity with his constituents grew, and he increased his majority with each succeeding general election. After fourteen years of diligent service to the party nationally and locally, the Prime Minister of the day, Harold Macmillan, recommended to the Queen that Ted should receive a knighthood.

By the end of the 1960s, Sir Ted (he was never known as Sir Edward) felt that the time was fast approaching when the division should start looking for a younger candidate, and he made it clear to the local chairman that he did not intend to stand at the next election. He and Hazel quietly prepared for a peaceful retirement in their beloved East Anglia.

Shortly after the election, Ted was surprised to receive a call from 10 Downing Street: 'The Prime Minister would like to see Sir Ted at 11.30 tomorrow morning.'

Ted couldn't imagine why Edward Heath should want to see him. Although he had of course visited Number 10 on several occasions when he was a Member of Parliament, those visits had only been for cocktail parties, receptions, and the occasional dinner for a visiting head of state. He admitted to Hazel that he was a little nervous.

Ted presented himself at the front door of Number 10 at 11.17 the next day. The duty clerk accompanied him down the long corridor on the ground floor, and asked him to take a seat in the small waiting area that adjoins the Cabinet Room. By now Ted's nervousness was turning to apprehension. He felt like an errant schoolboy about to come face to face with his head-master.

After a few minutes a private secretary appeared. 'Good morning, Sir Ted. The Prime Minister will see you now.' He accompanied Ted into the Cabinet Room, where Mr Heath stood to greet him. 'How kind of you to come at such short notice, Ted.' Ted had to suppress a smile, because he knew the Prime Minister knew that it would have taken the scurvy or a localised hurricane to stop him from answering such a summons.

'I'm hoping you can help me with a delicate matter, Ted,' continued the Prime Minister, a man not known for wasting time on small-talk. 'I'm about to appoint the next Governor of St George's, and I can't think of anyone better qualified for the job than you.'

Ted recalled the day when Mrs Thompson had asked him to think about standing for Parliament. But on this occasion he didn't require a week to consider his reply – even if he couldn't quite bring himself to admit that although he'd heard of St George's, he certainly couldn't have located it on a map. Once he'd caught his breath, he simply said, 'Thank you, Prime Minister. I'd be honoured.'

During the weeks that followed Sir Ted paid several visits to the Foreign and Colonial Office to receive briefings on various aspects of his appointment. Thereafter he assiduously read every book, pamphlet and government paper the mandarins supplied.

After a few weeks of boning up on his new subject, the Governor-in-waiting had discovered that St George's was a tiny group of islands in the middle of the North Atlantic. It had been colonised by the British in 1643, and thereafter had a long history of imperial rule, the islanders having scorned every offer of independence. They were one of Her Majesty's sovereign colonies, and that was how they wished to remain.

Even before he set out on his adventure, Ted had become used to being addressed as 'Your Excellency'. But after being fitted up by Alan Bennett of Savile Row with two different full dress uniforms, Ted feared that he looked – what was that modern expression? – O.T.T. In winter he was expected to wear an outfit of dark blue doeskin with scarlet collar and cuffs embroidered with silver oakleaves, while in the summer he was to be adorned in white cotton drill with a gold-embroidered collar and gold shoulder cords. The sight of him in either uniform caused Hazel to laugh out loud.

Ted didn't laugh when the tailors sent him the bill, especially after he learned that he would be unlikely to wear either uniform more than twice a year. 'Still, think what a hit you'll be at fancy dress parties once you've retired,' was Hazel's only comment.

The newly-appointed Governor and Commander-in-Chief of St George's and his lady flew out to take up their post on 12 January 1971. They were greeted by the Prime Minister, as the colony's first citizen, and the

Chief Justice, as the legal representative of the Queen. After the new Governor had taken the salute from six off-duty policemen standing vaguely to attention, the town band gave a rendering of the national anthem. The Union Jack was raised on the roof of the airport terminal and a light splattering of applause broke out from the assembled gathering of twenty or thirty local dignitaries.

Sir Ted and Lady Barker were then driven to the official residence in a spacious but ageing Rover that had already served the two previous Governors. When they reached Government House, the driver brought the car to a halt and leaped out to open the gates. As they continued up the drive, Ted and Hazel saw their new home for the first time.

The colonial mansion was magnificent by any standards. Obviously built at the height of the British Empire, it was vastly out of proportion to either the importance of the island or Britain's current position in the real world. But size, as the Governor and his wife were quickly to discover, didn't necessarily equate with efficiency or comfort.

The air conditioning didn't work, the plumbing was unreliable, Mrs Rogers, the daily help, was regularly off sick, and the only thing Ted's predecessor had left behind was an elderly black labrador. Worse, the Foreign Office had no funds available to deal with any of these problems, and whenever Ted mentioned them in dispatches, he was met only with suggestions for cutbacks.

After a few weeks, Ted and Hazel began to think of St George's as being rather like a great big parliamentary constituency, split into several islands, the two largest being Suffolk and Edward Island. This heartened Ted, who even wondered if that was what had given the Prime Minister the idea of offering him the post in the first place.

The Governor's duties could hardly have been described as onerous: he and Hazel spent most of their time visiting hospitals, delivering speeches at school prize-givings and judging flower shows. The highlight of the year was undoubtedly the Queen's official birthday in June, when the Governor held a garden party for local dignitaries at Government House and Suffolk played Edward Island at cricket – an opportunity for most of the colony's citizens to spend two days getting thoroughly drunk.

Ted and Hazel accepted the local *realpolitik* and settled down for five years of relaxed diplomacy among delightful people in a heavenly climate, seeing no cloud on the horizon that could disturb their blissful existence.

Until the phone call came.

It was a Thursday morning, and the Governor was in his study with that Monday's *Times*. He was putting off reading a long article on the summit meeting taking place in Washington until he had finished the crossword, and was just about to fill in the answer to 12 across – Erring herd twists to create this diversion (3,7) – when his private secretary, Charles Roberts, came rushing into his office without knocking.

Ted realised it had to be something important, because he had never known Charles to rush anywhere, and certainly he had never known him to enter the study without the courtesy of a knock.

'It's Mountbatten on the line,' Charles blurted out. He could hardly have looked more anxious had he been reporting that the Germans were about to land on the north shore of the island. The Governor raised an eyebrow. 'Admiral of the Fleet Earl Mountbatten of Burma,' said Charles, as if Ted hadn't understood.

'Then put him through,' said Ted quietly, folding up his copy of *The Times* and placing it on the desk in front of him. He had met Mountbatten three times over the past twenty years, but doubted if the great man would recall any of these encounters. Indeed, on the third occasion Ted had found it necessary to slip out of the function the Admiral was addressing, as he was feeling a little queasy. He couldn't imagine what Mountbatten would want to speak to him about, and he had no time to consider the problem, as the phone on his desk was already ringing.

As Ted picked up the receiver he was still wondering whether to call Mountbatten 'My Lord' as he was an Earl, 'Commander-in-Chief', as he was a former Chief of the Defence Staff, or 'Admiral', as Admiral of the Fleet is a life appointment. He settled for 'Good morning, sir.'

'Good morning, Your Excellency. I hope I find you well?'

'Yes, thank you, sir,' replied Ted.

'Because if I remember correctly, when we last met you were suffering from a tummy bug.'

'That's right, sir,' said the surprised Governor. He

was reasonably confident that the purpose of Mountbatten's call wasn't to enquire about his health after all these years.

'Governor, you must be curious to know why I am calling.'

'Yes, sir.'

'I am presently in Washington attending the summit, and I had originally planned to return to London tomorrow morning.'

'I understand, sir,' said Ted, not understanding at all.

'But I thought I might make a slight detour and drop in to see you. I do enjoy visiting our colonies whenever I get the chance. It gives me the opportunity to brief Her Majesty on what's happening. I hope that such a visit would not be inconvenient.'

'Not at all, sir,' said Ted. 'We would be delighted to welcome you.'

'Good,' said Mountbatten. 'Then I would be obliged if you could warn the airport authorities to expect my aircraft around four tomorrow afternoon. I would like to stay overnight, but if I'm to keep to my schedule I will need to leave you fairly early the following morning.'

'Of course, sir. Nothing could be easier. My wife and I will be at the airport to welcome you at four o'clock tomorrow afternoon.'

'That's kind of you, Governor. By the way, I'd rather things were left fairly informal. Please don't put yourself to any trouble.' The line went dead.

Once he had replaced the receiver, it was Ted's turn to run for the first time in several months. He found

Charles striding down the long corridor towards him, having obviously listened in on the extension.

'Find my wife and get yourself a notepad – and then both of you join me in my office immediately. Immediately,' Ted repeated as he scuttled back into his study.

Hazel arrived a few minutes later, clutching a bunch of dahlias, followed by the breathless private secretary.

'Why the rush, Ted? What's the panic?'

'Mountbatten's coming.'

'When?' Hazel asked quietly.

'Tomorrow afternoon. Four o'clock.'

'That *is* a good reason to panic,' Hazel admitted. She dumped the flowers in a vase on the windowsill and took a seat opposite her husband on the other side of his desk. 'Perhaps this isn't the best time to let you know that Mrs Rogers is off sick.'

'You have to admire her timing,' said Ted. 'Right, we'll just have to bluff it.'

'What *do* you mean, "bluff it"?' asked Hazel.

'Well, don't let's forget that Mountbatten's a member of the Royal Family, a former Chief of the Defence Staff and an Admiral of the Fleet. The last colonial post he held was Viceroy of India with three regiments under his command and a personal staff of over a thousand. So I can't imagine what he'll expect to find when he turns up here.'

'Then let's begin by making a list of things that will have to be done,' said Hazel briskly.

Charles removed a pen from his inside pocket, turned

over the cover of his pad, and waited to write down his master's instructions.

'If he's arriving at the airport, the first thing he will expect is a red carpet,' said Hazel.

'But we don't have a red carpet,' said Ted.

'Yes we do. There's the one that leads from the dining room to the drawing room. We'll have to use that, and hope we can get it back in place before he visits that part of the house. Charles, you will have to roll it up and take it to the airport' – she paused – 'and then bring it back.'

Charles scowled, but began writing furiously.

'And Charles, can you also see that it's cleaned by tomorrow?' interjected the Governor. 'I hadn't even realised it was red. Now, what about a guard of honour?'

'We haven't got a guard of honour,' said Hazel. 'If you remember, when we arrived on the island we were met by the Prime Minister, the Chief Justice and six off-duty policemen.'

'True,' said Ted. 'Then we'll just have to rely on the Territorial Army.'

'You mean Colonel Hodges and his band of hopeful warriors? They don't even all have matching uniforms. And as for their rifles . . .'

'Hodges will just have to get them into some sort of shape by four o'clock tomorrow afternoon. Leave that one to me,' said Ted, making a note on his pad. 'I'll phone him later this morning. Now, what about a band?'

'Well there's the town band,' said Charles. 'And, of course, the police band.'

'On this occasion they'll have to combine,' said Hazel, 'so we don't offend either of them.'

'But they only know three tunes between them,' said Ted.

'They only need to know one,' said Hazel. 'The national anthem.'

'Right,' said the Governor. 'As there are sure to be a lot of musical feathers that will need unruffling, I'll leave you to deal with them, Hazel. Our next problem is how we transport him from the airport to Government House.'

'Certainly not in the old Rover,' said Hazel. 'It's broken down three times in the last month, and it smells like a kennel.'

'Henry Bendall has a Rolls-Royce,' said Ted. 'We'll just have to commandeer that.'

'As long as no one tells Mountbatten that it's owned by the local undertaker, and what it was used for the morning before he arrived.'

'Mick Flaherty also has an old Rolls,' piped up Charles. 'A Silver Shadow, if I remember correctly.'

'But he loathes the British,' said Hazel.

'Agreed,' said Ted, 'but he'll still want to have dinner at Government House when he discovers the guest of honour is a member of the Royal Family.'

'Dinner?' said Hazel, her voice rising in horror.

'Of course we will have to give a dinner in his honour,' said Ted. 'And, worse, everyone who is anyone will expect to be invited. How many can the dining room hold?' He and Hazel turned to the private secretary.

'Sixty if pushed,' replied Charles, looking up from his notes.

'We're pushed,' said Ted.

'We certainly are,' said Hazel. 'Because we don't have sixty plates, let alone sixty coffee cups, sixty teaspoons, sixty . . .'

'We still have that Royal Worcester service presented by the late King after his visit in 1947,' said Ted. 'How many pieces of that are fit for use?'

'Enough for about fourteen settings, at the last count,' said Hazel.

'Right, then that's dealt with how many people will be at the top table.'

'What about the menu?' asked Charles.

'And, more important, who is going to cook it?' added Ted.

'We'll have to ask Dotty Cuthbert if she can spare Mrs Travis for the evening,' said Hazel. 'No one on the island is a better cook.'

'And we'll also need her butler, not to mention the rest of her staff,' added Ted.

By now Charles was onto his third page.

'You'd better deal with Lady Cuthbert, my dear,' said Ted. 'I'll try to square Mick Flaherty.'

'Our next problem will be the drink,' said Hazel. 'Don't forget, the last Governor emptied the cellar a few days before he left.'

'And the Foreign Office refuses to restock it,' Ted reminded her. 'Jonathan Fletcher has the best cellar on the island . . .'

'And, God bless him, he won't expect to be at the top table,' said Hazel.

'If we're limited to fourteen places, the top table's looking awfully crowded already,' said Ted.

'Dotty Cuthbert, the Bendalls, the Flahertys, the Hodges,' said Hazel, writing down the names. 'Not to mention the Prime Minister, the Chief Justice, the Mayor, the Chief of Police, plus their wives . . . Let's hope that some of them are indisposed or abroad.' She was beginning to sound desperate.

'Where's he going to sleep?' asked Charles innocently.

'God, I hadn't thought of him sleeping,' said Ted.

'He'll have to take our bedroom. It's the only one with a bed that doesn't sink in the middle,' said Hazel.

'We'll move into the Nelson Room for the night, and suffer those dreadful woodwormed beds and their ancient horsehair mattresses.'

'Agreed,' said Hazel. 'I'll make sure all our things are out of the Queen Victoria Room by this evening.'

'And, Charles,' said the Governor, 'phone the Foreign Office, would you, and find out Mountbatten's likes and dislikes. Food, drink, eccentric habits – anything you can discover. They're sure to have a file on him, and this is one gentleman I don't want to catch me out.'

The private secretary turned over yet another page of his pad, and continued scribbling.

For the next hour, the three of them went over any and every problem that might arise during the visit, and after a self-made sandwich lunch, departed in their different directions to spend the afternoon making begging calls all round the island.

It was Charles's idea that the Governor should appear on the local television station's early-evening news programme, to let the citizens know that a member of the Royal Family would be visiting the island the following day. Sir Ted ended his broadcast by saying that he hoped as many people as possible would be at the airport to welcome 'the great war leader' when his plane touched down at four the following afternoon.

While Hazel spent the evening cleaning every room that the great war leader might conceivably enter, Charles, with the aid of a torch, tended to the flowerbeds that lined the driveway, and Ted supervised the shuttling of plates, cutlery, food and wine from different parts of the island to Government House.

'Now, what have we forgotten?' said Ted, as he climbed into bed at two o'clock that morning.

'Heaven only knows,' Hazel said wearily before turning out the light. 'But whatever it is, let's hope Mountbatten never finds out.'

The Governor, dressed in his summer uniform, with gold piping down the sides of his white trousers, decorations and campaign medals across his chest, and a Wolsey helmet with a plume of red-over-white swan's feathers on his head, walked out onto the landing to join his wife. Hazel was wearing the green summer frock she had bought for the Governor's garden party two years before, and was checking the flowers in the entrance hall.

'Too late for that,' said Ted, as she rearranged a sprig that had strayed half an inch. 'It's time we left for the airport.'

They descended the steps of Government House to find two Rolls-Royces, one black, one white, and their old Rover standing in line. Charles followed closely behind them, carrying the red carpet, which he dropped into the boot of the Rover as his master stepped into the back of the leading Rolls-Royce.

The first thing the Governor needed to check was the chauffeur's name.

'Bill Simmons,' he was informed.

'All you have to remember, Bill, is to look as if you've been doing this job all your life.'

'Right, Guv.'

'No,' said Ted firmly. 'In front of the Admiral, you must address me as "Your Excellency", and Lord Mountbatten as "My Lord". If in any doubt, say nothing.'

'Right, Guv, Your Excellency.'

Bill started up the car and drove towards the gates at what he evidently considered was a stately pace, before turning right and taking the road to the airport. When they reached the terminal fifteen minutes later a policeman ushered the tiny motorcade out onto the tarmac, where the combined bands were playing a medley from *West Side Story* – at least, that was what Ted charitably thought it might be.

As he stepped out of the car Ted came face to face

with three ranks of soldiers from the Territorial Army standing at ease, sixty-one of them, aged from seventeen to seventy. Ted had to admit that although they weren't the Grenadier Guards, they weren't 'Dad's Army' either. And they had two advantages: a real-live Colonel in full dress uniform, and a genuine Sergeant Major, with a voice to match.

Charles had already begun rolling out the red carpet when the Governor turned his attention to the hastily-erected barriers, where he was delighted to see a larger crowd than he had ever witnessed on the island, even at the annual football derby between Suffolk and Edward Island.

Many of the islanders were waving Union Jacks, and some were holding up pictures of the Queen. Ted smiled and checked his watch. The plane was due in seventeen minutes.

The Prime Minister, the local Mayor, the Chief Justice, the Commissioner of Police and their wives were lining up at the end of the red carpet. The sun beat down from a cloudless sky. As Ted turned in a slow circle to take in the scene, he could see for himself that everyone had made a special effort.

Suddenly the sound of engines could be heard, and the crowd began to cheer. Ted looked up, shielded his eyes, and saw an Andover of the Queen's Flight descending towards the airport. It touched down on the far end of the runway at three minutes before the hour, and taxied up to the red carpet as four chimes struck on the clock above the flight control tower.

The door of the plane opened, and there stood Admiral of the Fleet the Earl Mountbatten of Burma, KG, PC, GCB, OM, GCSI, GCIE, GCVO, DSO, FRS, DCL (Hon), LLD (Hon), attired in the full dress uniform of an Admiral of the Fleet (summer wear).

'If that's what he means by "fairly informal", I suppose we should be thankful that he didn't ask us to lay on an official visit,' murmured Hazel as she and Ted walked to the bottom of the steps that had been quickly wheeled into place.

As Mountbatten slowly descended the stairway, the crowd cheered even louder. Once he stepped onto the red carpet the Governor took a pace forward, removed his plumed hat, and bowed. The Admiral saluted, and at that moment the combined bands of town and police struck up the national anthem. The crowd sang 'God Save the Queen' so lustily that the occasional uncertain note was smothered by their exuberance.

When the anthem came to an end the Governor said, 'Welcome to St George's, sir.'

'Thank you, Governor,' replied Mountbatten.

'May I present my wife, Hazel.' The Governor's wife took a pace forward, did a full curtsey, and shook hands with the Admiral.

'How good to see you again, Lady Barker. This is indeed a pleasure.'

The Governor guided his guest to the end of the red carpet and introduced him to the Prime Minister and his wife Sheila, the local mayor and his wife Caroline, the Chief Justice and his wife Janet, and the Commissioner of Police and his latest wife, whose name he couldn't remember.

'Perhaps you'd care to inspect the guard of honour before we leave for Government House,' suggested Ted, steering Mountbatten in the direction of Colonel Hodges and his men.

'Absolutely delighted,' said the Admiral, waving to the crowd as the two of them proceeded across the tarmac towards the waiting guard. When they still had some twenty yards to go, the Colonel sprang to attention, took three paces forward, saluted and said crisply, 'Guard of Honour ready for inspection, sir.'

Mountbatten came to a halt and returned a naval salute, which was a sign for the Sergeant Major, standing at attention six paces behind his Colonel, to bellow out the words, 'Commanding officer on parade! General salute, pre—sent arms!'

The front row, who were in possession of the unit's entire supply of weapons, presented arms, while the second and third rows came rigidly to attention.

Mountbatten marched dutifully up and down the ranks, as gravely as if he were inspecting a full brigade of Life Guards. When he had passed the last soldier in the back row, the Colonel came to attention and saluted once again. Mountbatten returned the salute and said, 'Thank you, Colonel. First-class effort. Well done.'

The Governor then guided Mountbatten towards the white Rolls-Royce, where Bill was standing at what he imagined was attention, while at the same time holding open the back door. Mountbatten stepped in as the Governor hurried round to the other side, opened the door for himself, and joined his guest on the back seat. Hazel and the Admiral's ADC took their places in the black Rolls-Royce, while Charles and the Admiral's secretary had to make do with the Rover. The Governor only hoped that Mountbatten hadn't seen two members of the airport staff rolling up the red carpet and placing it in the Rover's boot. Hazel was only praying that they had enough sheets left over for the bed in the Green Room. If not, the ADC would be wondering about their sleeping habits.

The island's two police motorcycles, with white-uniformed outriders, preceded the three cars as they made their way towards the exit. The crowd waved and cheered lustily as the motorcade began its short journey to Government House. So successful had Ted's television appearance the previous evening been that the ten-mile route was lined with well-wishers.

As they approached the open gates two policemen sprang to attention and saluted as the leading car passed through. In the distance Ted could see a butler, two under-butlers and several maids, all smartly clad, standing on the steps awaiting their arrival. 'Damn it,' he almost said aloud as the car came to a halt at the bottom of the steps. 'I don't know the butler's name.'

The car door was smartly opened by one of the under-butlers while the second supervised the unloading of the luggage from the boot.

The butler took a pace forward as Mountbatten stepped out of the car. 'Carruthers, m'lord,' he said, bowing. 'Welcome to the residence. If you would be kind enough to follow me, I will direct you to your quarters.' The Admiral, accompanied by the Governor and Lady Barker, climbed the steps into Government House and followed Carruthers up the main staircase.

'Magnificent, these old government residences,' said Mountbatten as they reached the top of the stairs. Carruthers opened the door to the Queen Victoria Room and stood to one side, as if he had done so a thousand times before.

'How charming,' said the Admiral, taking in the Governor's private suite. He walked over to the window and looked out onto the newly-mown lawn. 'How very pleasant. It reminds me of Broadlands, my home in Hampshire.'

Lady Barker smiled at the compliment, but didn't allow herself to relax.

'Is there anything you require, m'lord?' asked Carruthers, as an under-butler began to supervise the unpacking of the cases.

Hazel held her breath.

'No, I don't think so,' said Mountbatten. 'Everything looks just perfect.'

'Perhaps you'd care to join Hazel and me for tea in the drawing room when you're ready, sir,' suggested Ted.

'How thoughtful of you,' said the Admiral. 'I'll be down in about thirty minutes, if I may.'

The Governor and his wife left the room, closing the door quietly behind them.

'I think he suspects something,' whispered Hazel as they tiptoed down the staircase.

'You may be right,' said Ted, placing his plumed hat on the stand in the hall, 'but that's all the more reason to check we haven't forgotten anything. I'll start with the dining room. You ought to go and see how Mrs Travis is getting on in the kitchen.'

When Hazel entered the kitchen she found Mrs Travis preparing the vegetables, and one of the maids peeling a mound of potatoes. She thanked Mrs Travis for taking over at such short notice, and admitted she had never seen the kitchen so full of exotic foods, or the surfaces so immaculately clean. Even the floor was spotless. Realising that her presence was superfluous, Hazel joined her husband in the dining room, where she found him admiring the expertise of the second under-butler, who was laying out the place settings for that evening, as a maid folded napkins to look like swans.

'So far, so good,' said Hazel. They left the dining room and entered the drawing room, where Ted paced up and down, trying to think if there was anything he had forgotten while they waited for the great man to join them for tea.

A few minutes later, Mountbatten walked in. He was no longer dressed in his Admiral's uniform, but had changed into a dark grey double-breasted suit.

'Damn it,' thought Ted, immediately aware of what he'd forgotten to do.

Hazel rose to greet her guest, and guided him to a large, comfortable chair.

'I must say, Lady Barker, your butler is a splendid chap,' said Mountbatten. 'He even knew the brand of whisky I prefer. How long have you had him?'

'Not very long,' admitted Hazel.

'Well, if he ever wants a job in England, don't hesitate to let me know – though I'm bound to say, you'd be a fool to part with him,' he added, as a maid came in carrying a beautiful Wedgwood tea service that Hazel had never set eyes on before.

'Earl Grey, if I remember correctly,' said Hazel.

'What a memory you have, Lady Barker,' said the Admiral, as the maid began to pour.

'Thank God for the Foreign Office briefing,' Hazel thought, as she accepted the compliment with a smile.

'And how did the Conference go, sir?' asked Ted, as he dropped a lump of sugar – the one thing he felt might be their own – into his cup of tea.

'For the British, quite well,' said Mountbatten. 'But it would have gone better if the French hadn't been up to their usual tricks. Giscard seems to regard himself as a cross between Charlemagne and Joan of Arc.' His hosts laughed politely. 'No, the real problem we're facing at the moment, Ted, is quite simply . . .'

By the time Mountbatten had dealt with the outcome of the summit, given his undiluted views of James Callaghan and Ted Heath, covered the problem of finding a wife for Prince Charles and mulled over the long-term repercussions of Watergate, it was almost time for him to change.

'Are we dressing for dinner?'

'Yes, sir – if that meets with your approval.'

'Full decorations?' Mountbatten asked, sounding hopeful.

'I thought that would be appropriate, sir,' replied Ted, remembering the Foreign Office's advice about the Admiral's liking for dressing up at the slightest opportunity.

Mountbatten smiled as Carruthers appeared silently at the door. Ted raised an eyebrow.

'I have laid out the full dress uniform, m'lord. I took the liberty of pressing the trousers. The bedroom maid is drawing a bath for you.'

Mountbatten smiled. 'Thank you,' he said as he rose from his chair. 'Such a splendid tea,' he added turning to face his hostess. 'And such wonderful staff. Hazel, I don't know how you do it.'

'Thank you, sir,' said Hazel, trying not to blush.

'What time would you like me to come down for dinner, Ted?' Mountbatten asked.

'The first guests should be arriving for drinks at about 7.30, sir. We were hoping to serve dinner at eight, if that's convenient for you.'

'Couldn't be better,' declared Mountbatten. 'How many are you expecting?'

'Around sixty, sir. You'll find a guest list on your bedside table. Perhaps Hazel and I could come and fetch you at 7.50?'

'You run a tight ship, Ted,' said Mountbatten with approval. 'You'll find me ready the moment you appear,' he added as he followed Carruthers out of the room.

Once the door was closed behind him, Hazel said to the maid, 'Molly, can you clear away the tea things, please?' She hesitated for a moment. 'It is Molly, isn't it?'

'Yes, ma'am,' said the girl.

'I think he knows,' said Ted, looking a little anxious.

'Maybe, but we haven't time to worry about that now,' said Hazel, already on her way to carry out a further inspection of the kitchen.

The mound of potatoes had diminished to a peeled heap. Mrs Travis, who was preparing the sauces, was calling for more pepper and for some spices to be fetched from a shop in town. Aware once again that she wasn't needed in the kitchen, Hazel moved on to the dining room, where she found Ted. The top table was now fully laid with the King's dinner service, three sets of wine glasses, crested linen napkins, and a glorious centrepiece of a silver pheasant, which gave added sparkle.

'Who lent us that?' she asked.

'I have no idea,' replied Ted. 'But one thing's for certain – it will have flown home by the morning.'

'If we keep the lighting low enough,' whispered Hazel, 'he might not notice that the other tables all have different cutlery.'

'Heavens, just look at the time,' said Ted.

They left the dining room and walked quickly up the

stairs. Ted nearly barged straight into Mountbatten's room, but remembered just in time.

The Governor rather liked his dark blue doeskin uniform with the scarlet collar and cuffs. He was admiring the ensemble in the mirror when Hazel entered the room in a pink Hardy Amies outfit, which she had originally thought a waste of money because she never expected it to be given a proper outing.

'Men are so vain,' she remarked as her husband continued to inspect himself in the mirror. 'You do realise you're only meant to wear that in winter.'

'I am well aware of that,' said Ted peevishly, 'but it's the only other uniform I've got. In any case, I bet Mountbatten will outdo us both.' He flicked a piece of fluff from his trousers, which he had just finished pressing.

The Governor and his wife left the Nelson Room and walked down the main staircase just before 7.20, to find yet another under-butler stationed by the front door, and two more maids standing opposite him carrying silver trays laden with glasses of champagne. Hazel introduced herself to the three of them, and again checked the flowers in the entrance hall.

As 7.30 struck on the long-case clock in the lobby the first guest walked in.

'Henry,' said the Governor. 'Lovely to see you. Thank you so much for the use of the Rolls. And Bill, come to that,' he added in a stage whisper.

'My pleasure, Your Excellency,' Henry Bendall replied. 'I must say, I like the uniform.'

Lady Cuthbert came bustling through the front door. 'Can't stop,' she said. 'Ignore me. Just pretend I'm not here.'

'Dotty, I simply don't know what we would have done without you,' Hazel said, chasing after her across the hall.

'Delighted to lend a hand,' said Lady Cuthbert. 'I thought I'd come bang on time, so I could spend a few minutes in the kitchen with Mrs Travis. By the way, Benson is standing out in the drive, ready to rush home if you find you're still short of anything.'

'You are a saint, Dotty. I'll take you through . . .'

'No, don't worry,' said Lady Cuthbert. 'I know my way around. You just carry on greeting your guests.'

'Good evening, Mr Mayor,' said Ted, as Lady Cuthbert disappeared in the direction of the kitchen.

'Good evening, Your Excellency. How kind of you to invite us to such an auspicious occasion.'

'And what a lovely dress, Mrs Janson,' said the Governor.

'Thank you, Your Excellency,' said the Mayor's wife.

'Would you care for a glass of champagne?' said Hazel as she arrived back at her husband's side.

By 7.45 most of the guests had arrived, and Ted was chatting to Mick Flaherty when Hazel touched him on the elbow. He glanced towards her.

'I think we should go and fetch him now,' she whispered.

Ted nodded, and asked the Chief Justice to take over the welcoming of the guests. They wove a path through the chattering throng, and climbed the great staircase. When they reached the door of the Queen Victoria Room, they paused and looked at each other.

Ted checked his watch – 7.50. He leaned forward and gave a gentle tap. Carruthers immediately opened the door to reveal Mountbatten attired in his third outfit of the day: full ceremonial uniform of an Admiral of the Fleet, three stars, a gold and blue sash and eight rows of campaign decorations.

'Good evening, Your Excellency,' said Mountbatten.

'Good evening, sir,' said the Governor, star struck.

The Admiral took three paces forward and came to a halt at the top of the staircase. He stood to attention. Ted and Hazel waited on either side of him. As he didn't move, they didn't.

Carruthers proceeded slowly down the stairs in front of them, stopping on the third step. He cleared his throat and waited for the assembled guests to fall silent.

'Your Excellency, Prime Minister, Mr Mayor, ladies and gentlemen,' he announced. 'The Right Honourable the Earl Mountbatten of Burma.'

Mountbatten descended the stairs slowly as the waiting guests applauded politely. As he passed Carruthers, the butler gave a deep bow. The Governor, with Hazel on his arm, followed two paces behind.

'He must know,' whispered Hazel.

'You may be right. But does he know we know?' said Ted.

Mountbatten moved deftly around the room, as Ted introduced him to each of the guests in turn. They bowed and curtsied, listening attentively to the few words the Admiral had to say to them. The one exception was Mick Flaherty, who didn't stop talking, and remained more upright than Ted had ever seen him before.

At eight o'clock one of the under-butlers banged a gong, which until then neither the Governor nor his wife had even realised existed. As the sound died away, Carruthers announced, 'My Lord, Your Excellency, Prime Minister, Mr Mayor, ladies and gentlemen, dinner is served.'

If there was a better cook on St George's than Mrs Travis, no one at the top table had ever been fed by her, and that evening she had excelled herself.

Mountbatten chatted and smiled, making no secret of how much he was enjoying himself. He spent a long time talking to Lady Cuthbert, whose husband had served under him at Portsmouth, and to Mick Flaherty, to whom he listened with polite interest.

Each course surpassed the one before: soufflé, followed by lamb cutlets, and an apricot hazelnut meringue to complete the feast. Mountbatten remarked on every one of the wines, and even called for a second glass of port.

After dinner, he joined the guests for coffee in the drawing room, and managed to have a word with everyone, even though Colonel Hodges tried to buttonhole him about defence cuts.

The guests began to leave a few minutes before midnight, and Ted was amused to see that when Mick Flaherty bade farewell to the Admiral, he bowed low and said, 'Good night, My Lord. It has been an honour to meet you.'

Dotty was among the last to depart, and she curtsied low to the guest of honour. 'You've helped to make this such a pleasant evening, Lady Cuthbert,' Mountbatten told her.

'If you only knew just how much,' thought Hazel.

After the under-butler had closed the door on the last guest, Mountbatten turned to his hostess and said, 'Hazel, I must thank you for a truly memorable occasion. The head chef at the Savoy couldn't have produced a finer banquet. Perfect in every part.'

'You are very kind, sir. I will pass your thanks on to the staff.' She just stopped herself from saying 'my staff'. 'Is there anything else we can do for you before you retire?'

'No, thank you,' Mountbatten replied. 'It has been a long day, and with your permission, I'll turn in now.'

'And at what time would you like breakfast, sir?' asked the Governor.

'Would 7.30 be convenient?' Mountbatten asked. 'That will give me time to fly out at nine.'

'Certainly,' said Ted. 'I'll see that Carruthers brings a light breakfast up to your room at 7.30 – unless you'd like something cooked.'

'A light breakfast will be just the thing,' Mountbatten said. 'A perfect evening. Your staff could not have done more, Hazel. Good night, and thank you, my dear.'

The Governor bowed and his lady curtsied as the great

man ascended the staircase two paces behind Carruthers. When the butler closed the door of the Queen Victoria Room, Ted put his arm around his wife and said, 'He knows we know.'

'You may be right,' said Hazel. 'But does he know we know he knows?'

'I'll have to think about that,' said Ted.

Arm in arm, they returned to the kitchen, where they found Mrs Travis packing dishes into a crate under the supervision of Lady Cuthbert, the long lace sleeves of whose evening dress were now firmly rolled up.

'How did you get back in, Dotty?' asked Hazel.

'Just walked round to the back yard and came in the servants' entrance,' replied Lady Cuthbert.

'Did you spot anything that went badly wrong?' Hazel asked anxiously.

'I don't think so,' replied Lady Cuthbert. 'Not unless you count Mick Flaherty failing to get a fourth glass of Muscat de Venise.'

'Mrs Travis,' said Ted, 'the head chef at the Savoy couldn't have produced a finer banquet. Perfect in every part. I do no more than repeat Lord Mountbatten's exact words.'

'Thank you, Your Excellency,' said Mrs Travis. 'He's got a big appetite, hasn't he?' she added with a smile.

A moment later, Carruthers entered the kitchen. He checked round the room, which was spotless once again, then turned to Ted and said, 'With your permission, sir, we will take our leave.'

'Of course,' said the Governor. 'And may I thank you, Carruthers, for the role you and your amazing team have played. You all did a superb job. Lord Mountbatten never stopped remarking on it.'

'His Lordship is most kind, sir. At what time would you like us to return in the morning to prepare and serve his breakfast?'

'Well, he asked for a light breakfast in his room at 7.30.'

'Then we will be back by 6.30,' said Carruthers.

Hazel opened the kitchen door to let them all out, and they humped crates full of crockery and baskets full of food to the waiting cars. The last person to leave was Dotty, who was clutching the silver pheasant. Hazel kissed her on both cheeks as she departed.

'I don't know how you feel, but I'm exhausted,' said Ted, bolting the kitchen door.

Hazel checked her watch. It was seventeen minutes past one.

'Shattered,' she admitted. 'So, let's try and grab some sleep, because *we'll* also have to be up by seven to make sure everything is ready before he leaves for the airport.'

Ted put his arm back around his wife's waist. 'A personal triumph for you, my dear.'

They strolled into the hall and wearily began to climb the stairs, but didn't utter another word, for fear of disturbing their guest's repose. When they reached the landing, they came to an abrupt halt, and stared down in horror at the sight that greeted them. Three pairs of black leather shoes had been placed neatly in line outside the Queen Victoria Room.

'Now I'm certain he knows,' said Hazel.

Ted nodded and, turning to his wife, whispered, 'You or me?'

Hazel pointed a finger firmly at her husband. 'Definitely you, my dear,' she said sweetly, before disappearing in the direction of the Nelson Room.

Ted shrugged his shoulders, picked up the Admiral's shoes, and returned downstairs to the kitchen.

His Excellency the Governor and Commander-in-Chief of St George's spent a considerable time polishing those three pairs of shoes, as he realised that not only must they pass inspection by an Admiral of the Fleet, but they must look as if the job had been carried out by Carruthers.

When Mountbatten returned to the Admiralty in Whitehall the following Monday, he made a full written report on his visit to St George's. Copies were sent to the Queen and the Foreign Secretary.

The Admiral told the story of his visit at a family gathering that Saturday evening at Windsor Castle, and once the laughter had died down, the Queen asked him, 'When did you first become suspicious?'

'It was Carruthers who gave it away. He knew everything about Sir Ted, except which regiment he had served in. That's just not possible for an old soldier.'

The Queen had one further question: 'Do you think the Governor knew you knew?'

'I can't be certain, Lillibet,' replied Mountbatten after some thought. 'But I intend to leave him in no doubt that I did.'

The Foreign Secretary laughed uproariously when he read Mountbatten's report, and appended a note to the last sheet asking for clarification on two points:

(a) How can you be certain that the staff who served
    dinner were not part of the Governor's
    entourage?

(b) Do you think Sir Ted knew that you knew?

The Admiral replied by return:

(a) After dinner, one of the maids asked Lady Barker
    if she took sugar in her coffee, but a moment
    later she gave Lady Cuthbert two lumps,
    without needing to ask.

(b) Possibly not. But he certainly will on Christmas
    Day.

Sir Ted was pleased to receive a Christmas card from Lord Mountbatten, signed, 'Best wishes, Dickie. Thank you for a memorable stay.' It was accompanied by a gift.

Hazel unwrapped the little parcel to discover a tin of Cherry Blossom shoe polish (black). Her only comment was, 'So now we know he knew.'

'Agreed,' said Ted with a grin. 'But did he know we knew he knew? That's what I'd like to know.'

YOU'LL NEVER LIVE
TO REGRET IT

AND SO IT WAS AGREED: DAVID WOULD leave everything to Pat. If one of them had to die, at least the other would be financially secure for the rest of their life. David felt it was the least he could do for someone who'd stood by him for so many years, especially as he was the one who had been unfaithful.

They had known each other almost all their lives, because their parents had been close friends for as long as either of them could remember. Both families had hoped David might end up marrying Pat's sister Ruth, and they were unable to hide their surprise – and in Pat's father's case his disapproval – when the two of them started living together, especially as Pat was three years older than David.

For some time David had been putting it off and hoping for a miracle cure, despite a pushy insurance broker from Geneva Life called Marvin Roebuck who had been pressing him to 'take a meeting' for the past nine months. On the first Monday of the tenth month he phoned again, and this time David reluctantly agreed to see him. He chose a date when he knew Pat would be on night duty at the hotel, and asked Roebuck to come round to their apartment – that way, he felt, it would look as if it was the broker who had done the chasing.

David was watering the scarlet *clupea harengus* on the hall table when Marvin Roebuck pressed the buzzer on the front door. Once he had poured his visitor a Budweiser, David told him he had every type of insurance he could possibly need: theft, accident, car, property, health, even holiday.

'But what about life?' asked Marvin, licking his lips.

'That's one I don't need,' said David. 'I earn a good salary, I have more than enough security, and on top of that, my parents will leave everything to me.'

'But wouldn't it be prudent to have a lump sum that comes to you automatically on your sixtieth or sixty-fifth birthday?' asked Marvin, as he continued to push at a door that he had no way of knowing was already wide open. 'After all, you can never be sure what disaster might lie around the corner.'

David knew exactly what disaster lay around the corner, but he still innocently asked, 'What sort of figure are you talking about?'

'Well, that would depend on how much you are currently earning,' said Marvin.

'$120,000 a year,' said David, trying to sound casual, as it was almost double his real income. Marvin was obviously impressed, and David remained silent as he carried out some rapid calculations in his head.

'Well,' said Marvin eventually, 'I'd suggest half a million dollars – as a ballpark figure. After all,' he added, quickly running a finger down a page of actuarial tables he had extracted from his aluminium briefcase, 'you're only twenty-seven, so the payments would be well within your means. In fact, you might even consider a larger sum if you're confident your income will continue to rise over the next few years.'

'It has done every year for the past seven,' said David, this time truthfully.

'What kind of business are you in, my friend?' asked Marvin.

'Stocks and bonds,' replied David, not offering any details of the small firm he worked for, or the junior position he held.

Marvin licked his lips again, even though they had told him not to do so on countless refresher courses, especially when going in for the kill.

'So, what amount do you think I should go for?' asked David, continuing to make sure it was always Marvin who took the lead.

'Well, a million is comfortably within your credit range,' said Marvin, once again checking his little book of tables. 'The monthly payments might seem a bit steep to begin with, but as the years go by, what with inflation and your continual salary increases, you can expect that in time they will become almost insignificant.'

'How much would I have to pay each month to end up getting a million?' asked David, attempting to give the impression he might have been hooked.

'Assuming we select your sixtieth birthday for terminating the contract, a little over a thousand dollars a month,' said Marvin, trying to make it sound a mere pittance. 'And don't forget, sixty per cent of it is tax deductible, so in real terms you'll only be paying around fifteen dollars a day, while you end up getting a million, just at the time when you most need it. And by the way, that one thousand is constant, it never goes up. In fact it's inflation-proof.' He let out a dreadful shrill laugh.

'But would I still receive the full sum, whatever happens to the market?'

'One million dollars on your sixtieth birthday,' confirmed Marvin, 'whatever happens, short of the world coming to an end. Even I can't write a policy for that,' he said, letting out another shrill laugh. 'However, my friend, if unhappily you were to die before your sixtieth birthday – which God forbid – your dependants would receive the full amount immediately.'

'I don't have any dependants,' said David, trying to look bored.

'There must be someone you care about,' said Marvin. 'A good-looking guy like you.'

'Why don't you leave the forms with me, Mr Roebuck, and I'll think about it over the weekend. I promise I'll get back to you.'

Marvin looked disappointed. He didn't need a refresher course to be told that you're supposed to nail the client to the wall at the first meeting, not let them get away, because that only gave them time to think things over. His lips felt dry.

Pat returned from the evening shift in the early hours of the morning, but David had stayed awake so he could go over what had happened at the meeting with Marvin. Pat was apprehensive and uncertain about the plan. David had always taken care of any problems they had had in the past, especially financial ones, and Pat wasn't sure how it would all work out once David was no longer around to give his advice. Thank God it was David who'd had to deal with Marvin — Pat couldn't even say no to a door-to-door brush salesman.

'So, what do we do next?' asked Pat.

'Wait.'

'But you promised Marvin you'd get back to him.'

'I know, but I have absolutely no intention of doing so,' said David, placing his arm round Pat's shoulder. 'I'd bet a hundred dollars on Marvin phoning me first thing on Monday morning. And don't forget, I still need it to look as if he's the one who's doing the pushing.'

As they climbed into bed, Pat felt an attack of asthma coming on, and decided now was not the time to ask David to go over the details again. After all, as David had explained again and again, there would never be any need for Pat to meet Marvin.

Marvin phoned at 8.30 on Monday morning.

'Hoped to catch you before you went off to sell those stocks and bonds,' he said. 'Have you come to a decision?'

'Yes, I have,' said David. 'I discussed the whole idea with my mother over the weekend, and she thinks I should go for the million, because five hundred thousand may not turn out to be such a large sum of money by the time I reach sixty.'

Marvin was glad that David couldn't see him licking his lips. 'Your mother's obviously a shrewd woman,' was his only comment.

'Can I leave you to handle all the paperwork?' asked David, trying to sound as if he didn't want to deal with any of the details.

'You bet,' said Marvin. 'Don't even think about it, my friend. Just leave all that hassle to me. I know you've made the right decision, David. I promise you, you'll never live to regret it.'

The following day, Marvin phoned again to say that the paperwork had been completed, and all that was now required was for David to have a medical – 'routine' was the word he kept repeating. But because of the size of the sum insured, it would have to be with the company's doctor in New York.

David made a fuss about having to travel to New York, adding that perhaps he'd made the wrong decision, but after more pleading from Marvin, mixed with some unctuous persuasion, he finally gave in.

Marvin brought all the forms round to the apartment the following evening after Pat had left for work.

David scribbled his signature on three separate documents between two pencilled crosses. His final act was to print Pat's name in a little box Marvin had indicated with his stubby finger. 'As your sole dependant,' the broker explained, 'should you pass away before 1 September 2027 – God forbid. Are you married to Pat?'

'No, we just live together,' replied David.

After a few more 'my friends' and even more 'you'll

never live to regret it's, Marvin left the apartment, clutching the forms.

'All you have to do now is keep your nerve,' David told Pat once he had confirmed that the paperwork had been completed. 'Just remember, no one knows me as well as you do, and once it's all over, you'll collect a million dollars.'

When they eventually went to bed that night, Pat desperately wanted to make love to David, but they both accepted it was no longer possible.

The two of them travelled down to New York together the following Monday to keep the appointment David had made with Geneva Life's senior medical consultant. They parted a block away from the insurance company's head office, as they didn't want to run the risk of being seen together. They hugged each other once again, but as they parted David was still worried about whether Pat would be able to go through with it.

A couple of minutes before twelve, he arrived at the surgery. A young woman in a long white coat smiled up at him from behind her desk.

'Good morning,' he said. 'My name is David Kravits. I have an appointment with Dr Royston.'

'Oh, yes, Mr Kravits,' said the nurse. 'Dr Royston is expecting you. Please follow me.' She led him down a long, bleak corridor to the last room on the left. A small brass plaque read 'Dr Royston'. She knocked, opened the door and said, 'Mr Kravits, doctor.'

Dr Royston turned out to be a short, elderly man with only a few strands of hair left on his shiny sunburnt head. He wore horn-rimmed spectacles, and had a look on his face which suggested that his own life insurance policy might not be far from reaching maturity. He rose from his chair, shook his patient by the hand and said, 'It's for a life insurance policy, if I remember correctly.'

'Yes, that's right.'

'Shouldn't take us too long, Mr Kravits. Fairly routine, but the company does like to be sure you're fit and well if they're going to be liable for such a large amount of money. Do have a seat,' he said, pointing to the other side of his desk.

'I thought the sum was far too high myself. I would have been happy to settle for half a million, but the broker was very persuasive . . .'

'Any serious illness during the past ten years?' the doctor asked, obviously not interested in the broker's views.

'No. The occasional cold, but nothing I'd describe as serious,' he replied.

'Good. And in your immediate family, any history of heart attacks, cancer, liver complaints?'

'Not that I'm aware of.'

'Father still alive?'

'Very much so.'

'And he's fit and well?'

'Jogs every morning, and pumps weights in the local gym at the weekend.'

'And your mother?'

'Doesn't do either, but I wouldn't be surprised if she outlives him comfortably.'

The doctor laughed. 'Any of your grandparents still living?'

'All except one. My dad's father died two years ago.'

'Do you know the cause of death?'

'He just passed away, I think. At least, that was how the priest described it at his funeral.'

'And how old was he?' the doctor asked. 'Do you remember?'

'Eighty-one, eighty-two.'

'Good,' repeated Dr Royston, ticking another little box on the form in front of him. 'Have you ever suffered from any of these?' he asked, holding up a clipboard in front of him. The list began with arthritis, and ended eighteen lines later with tuberculosis.

He ran an eye slowly down the long list before replying. 'No, none of them,' was all he said, not admitting to asthma on this occasion.

'Do you smoke?'

'Never.'

'Drink?'

'Socially – I enjoy the occasional glass of wine with dinner, but I never drink spirits.'

'Excellent,' said the doctor and ticked the last of the little boxes. 'Now, let's check your height and weight. Come over here, please, Mr Kravits, and climb onto these scales.'

The doctor had to stand on his toes in order to push the wooden marker up until it was flat across his patient's head. 'Six feet one inch,' he declared, then looked down at the weighing machine, and flicked the little weight across until it just balanced. 'A hundred and seventy-nine pounds. Not bad.' He filled in two more lines of his report. 'Perhaps just a little overweight.

'Now I need a urine sample, Mr Kravits. If you would be kind enough to take this plastic container next door, fill it about halfway up, leave it on the ledge when you've finished, and then come back to me.'

The doctor wrote out some more notes while his patient left the room. He returned a few moments later.

'I've left the container on the ledge,' was all he said.

'Good. The next thing I need is a blood sample. Could you roll up your right sleeve?' The doctor placed a rubber pad around his right bicep and pumped until the veins stood out clearly. 'A tiny prick,' he said. 'You'll hardly feel a thing.' The needle went in, and he turned away as the doctor drew his blood. Dr Royston cleaned the wound and fixed a small circular plaster over the broken skin. The doctor then bent over and placed a cold stethoscope on different parts of the patient's chest, occasionally asking him to breathe in and out.

'Good,' he kept repeating. Finally he said, 'That just about wraps it up, Mr Kravits. You'll need to spend a few minutes down the corridor with Dr Harvey, so she can take a chest x-ray, and have some fun with her electric pads, but after that you'll be through, and you can go home to' – he checked his pad – 'New Jersey. The company will be in touch in a few days, as soon as we've had the results.'

'Thank you, Dr Royston,' he said as he buttoned up his shirt. The doctor pressed a buzzer on his desk and the nurse reappeared and led him to another room, with a plaque on the door that read 'Dr Mary Harvey'. Dr Harvey, a smartly-dressed middle-aged woman with her grey hair cropped short, was waiting for him. She smiled at the tall, handsome man and asked him to take off his shirt again and to step up onto the platform and stand in front of the x-ray unit.

'Place your arms behind your back and breathe in. Thank you.' Next she asked him to lie down on the bed in the corner of the room. She leaned over his chest, smeared blodges of paste on his skin and fixed little pads to them. While he stared up at the white ceiling she flicked a switch and concentrated on a tiny television screen on the corner of her desk. Her expression gave nothing away.

After she had removed the paste with a damp flannel she said, 'You can put your shirt back on, Mr Kravits. You are now free to leave.'

Once he was fully dressed, the young man hurried out of the building and down the steps, and ran all the way to the corner where they had parted. They hugged each other again.

'Everything go all right?'

'I think so,' he said. 'They told me I'd be hearing from them in the next few days, once they've had the results of all their tests.'

'Thank God it hasn't been a problem for you.'

'I only wish it wasn't for you.'

'Don't let's even think about it,' said David, holding tightly onto the one person he loved.

Marvin rang a week later to let David know that Dr Royston had given him a clean bill of health. All he had to do now was send the first instalment of $1100 to the insurance company. David posted a cheque off to Geneva Life the following morning. Thereafter his payments were made by wire transfer on the first day of each month.

Nineteen days after the seventh payment had been cleared, David Kravits died of AIDS.

Pat tried to remember the first thing he was meant to do once the will had been read. He was to contact a Mr Levy, David's lawyer, and leave everything in his hands. David had warned him not to become involved in any way himself. Let Levy, as his executor, make the claim from the insurance company, he had said, and then pass the money on to him. If in any doubt, say nothing, was the last piece of advice David had given Pat before he died.

Ten days later, Pat received a letter from a claims representative at Geneva Life requesting an interview with the beneficiary of the policy. Pat passed the letter straight to David's lawyer. Mr Levy wrote back agreeing to an interview, which would take place, at his client's request, at the offices of Levy, Goldberg and Levy in Manhattan.

'Is there anything you haven't told me, Patrick?' Levy asked him a few minutes before the insurance company's claims representative was due to arrive. 'Because if there is, you'd better tell me now.'

'No, Mr Levy, there's nothing more to tell you,' Pat replied, carrying out David's instructions to the letter.

From the moment the meeting began, the representative of Geneva Life, his eyes continually boring into Pat's bowed head, left Mr Levy in no doubt that he was not happy about paying out on this particular claim. But the lawyer stonewalled every question, strengthened by the knowledge that eight months before, when rigorous tests had been taken, Geneva Life's doctors had found no sign of David's being HIV positive.

Levy kept repeating, 'However much noise you make, your company will have to pay up in the end.' He added for good measure, 'If I have not received the full amount due to my client within thirty days, I will immediately instigate proceedings against Geneva Life.' The claims representative asked Levy if he would consider a deal. Levy glanced at Pat, who bowed his head even lower, and replied, 'Certainly not.'

Pat arrived back at the apartment two hours later, exhausted and depressed, fearing that an attack of asthma might be coming on. He tried to prepare some supper before he went to work, but everything seemed so pointless without David. He was already wondering if he should have agreed to a settlement.

The phone rang only once during the evening. Pat rushed to pick it up, hoping it might be either his mother or his sister Ruth. It turned out to be Marvin, who bleated, 'I'm in real trouble, Pat. I'm probably going to lose my job over that policy I made out for your friend David.'

Pat said how sorry he was, but felt there was nothing he could do to help.

'Yes, there is,' insisted Marvin. 'For a start, you could take out a policy yourself. That might just save my skin.'

'I don't think that would be wise,' said Pat, wondering what David would have advised.

'Surely David wouldn't have wanted to see me fired,' Marvin pleaded. 'Have mercy on me, my friend. I just can't afford another divorce.'

'How much would it cost me?' asked Pat, desperate to find some way of getting Marvin off the line.

'You're going to get a million dollars in cash,' Marvin almost shouted, 'and you're asking me what it's going to cost? What's a thousand dollars a month to someone as rich as you?'

'But I can't be sure that I am going to get the million,' Pat protested.

'That's all been settled,' Marvin told him, his voice falling by several decibels. 'I'm not meant to let you know this, but you'll be receiving the cheque on the thirtieth of the month. The company know that your lawyer's got them by the balls . . . You wouldn't even have to make the first payment until after you'd received the million.'

'All right,' said Pat, desperate to be rid of him. 'I'll do it, but not until I've received the cheque.'

'Thank you, my friend. I'll drop round with the paper-work tomorrow night.'

'No, that's not possible,' said Pat. 'I'm working nights this month. You'd better make it tomorrow afternoon.'

'You won't be working nights once you've received that cheque, my friend,' said Marvin, letting out one of his dreadful shrill laughs. 'Lucky man,' he added before he put the phone down.

By the time Marvin came round to the apartment the following afternoon, Pat was already having second thoughts. If he had to visit Dr Royston again, they would immediately realise the truth. But once Marvin had assured him that the medical could be with any doctor of his choice, and that the first payment would be post-dated, he caved in and signed all the forms between the pencilled crosses, making Ruth his sole beneficiary. He hoped David would have approved of that decision, at least.

'Thank you, my friend. I won't be bothering you again,' promised Marvin. His final words as he closed the door behind him were, 'I promise you, you'll never live to regret it.'

Pat saw his doctor a week later. The examination didn't take long, as Pat had recently had a complete check-up. On that occasion, as the doctor recalled, Pat had appeared quite nervous, and couldn't hide his relief when he'd phoned to give him the all-clear. 'Not much wrong with you, Patrick,' he said, 'apart from the asthma, which doesn't seem to be getting any worse.'

Marvin called a week later to let Pat know that the doctor had given him a clean bill of health, and that he had held on to his job with Geneva Life.

'I'm pleased for you,' said Pat. 'But what about my cheque?'

'It will be paid out on the last day of the month. Only a matter of processing it now. Should be with you twenty-four hours before the first payment is due on your policy. Just like I said, you win both ways.'

Pat rang David's lawyer on the last day of the month to ask if he had received the cheque from Geneva Life.

'There was nothing in this morning's post,' Levy told him, 'but I'll phone the other side right now, in case it's already been issued and is on its way. If not, I'll start proceedings against them immediately.'

Pat wondered if he should tell Levy that he had signed a cheque for $1100 which was due to be cleared the following day, and that he only just had sufficient funds in his account to cover it – certainly not enough to see him through until his next pay packet. All his surplus cash had gone to help with David's monthly payments to Geneva Life. He decided not to mention it. David had repeatedly told him that if he was in any doubt, he should say nothing.

'I'll phone you at close of business tonight and let you know exactly what the position is,' said Levy.

'No, that won't be possible,' said Pat. 'I'm on night duty all this week. In fact I have to leave for work right now. Perhaps you could call me first thing tomorrow morning?'

'Will do,' promised the lawyer.

When Pat returned home from work in the early hours, he couldn't get to sleep. He tossed and turned, worrying how he would survive for the rest of the month if his cheque was presented to the bank that morning, and he still hadn't received the million dollars from Geneva Life.

His phone rang at 9.31. Pat grabbed it, and was relieved to hear Mr Levy's voice on the other end of the line.

'Patrick, I had a call from Geneva Life yesterday evening while you were at work, and I must tell you that you've broken Levy's golden rule.'

'Levy's golden rule?' asked Pat, mystified.

'Yes, Levy's golden rule. It's quite simple really, Patrick. By all means drop anything you like, on anyone you like, but don't *ever* drop it all over your own lawyer.'

'I don't understand,' said Pat.

'Your doctor has supplied Geneva Life with a sample of your blood and urine, and they just happen to be identical to the ones Dr Royston has in his laboratory in the name of David Kravits.'

Pat felt the blood draining from his head as he realised the trick Marvin must have played on him. His heart began beating faster and faster. Suddenly his legs gave way, and he collapsed on the floor, gasping for breath.

'Did you hear me, Patrick?' asked Levy. 'Are you still there?'

A paramedic team broke into the apartment twenty minutes later, but, moments before they reached him, Pat had died of a heart attack brought on by a suffocating bout of asthma.

Mr Levy did nothing until he was able to confirm with

Pat's bankers that his client's cheque for $1100 had been cleared by the insurance company.

Nineteen months later Pat's sister Ruth received a payment of one million dollars from Geneva Life, but not until they had gone through a lengthy court battle with Levy, Goldberg and Levy.

The jury finally accepted that Pat had died of natural causes, and that the insurance policy was in existence at the time of his death.

I promise you, Marvin Roebuck lived to regret it.

NEVER STOP
ON THE MOTORWAY

DIANA HAD BEEN HOPING TO GET AWAY by five, so she could be at the farm in time for dinner. She tried not to show her true feelings when at 4.37 her deputy, Phil Haskins, presented her with a complex twelve-page document that required the signature of a director before it could be sent out to the client. Haskins didn't hesitate to remind her that they had lost two similar contracts that week.

It was always the same on a Friday. The phones would go quiet in the middle of the afternoon and then, just as she thought she could slip away, an authorisation would land on her desk. One glance at this particular document and Diana knew there would be no chance of escaping before six.

The demands of being a single parent as well as a director of a small but thriving City company meant there were few moments left in any day to relax, so when it came to the one weekend in four that James and Caroline spent with her ex-husband, Diana would try to leave the office a little earlier than usual to avoid getting snarled up in the weekend traffic.

She read through the first page slowly and made a

couple of emendations, aware that any mistake made hastily on a Friday night could be regretted in the weeks to come. She glanced at the clock on her desk as she signed the final page of the document. It was just flicking over to 5.51.

Diana gathered up her bag and walked purposefully towards the door, dropping the contract on Phil's desk without bothering to suggest that he have a good weekend. She suspected that the paperwork had been on his desk since nine o'clock that morning, but that holding it until 4.37 was his only means of revenge now that she had been made head of department. Once she was safely in the lift, she pressed the button for the basement carpark, calculating that the delay would probably add an extra hour to her journey.

She stepped out of the lift, walked over to her Audi estate, unlocked the door and threw her bag onto the back seat. When she drove up onto the street the stream of twilight traffic was just about keeping pace with the pinstriped pedestrians who, like worker ants, were hurrying towards the nearest hole in the ground.

She flicked on the six o'clock news. The chimes of Big Ben rang out, before spokesmen from each of the three main political parties gave their views on the European election results. John Major was refusing to comment on his future. The Conservative Party's explanation for its poor showing was that only thirty-six per cent of the country had bothered to go to the polls. Diana felt guilty – she was among the sixty-four per cent who had failed to register their vote.

The newscaster moved on to say that the situation in Bosnia remained desperate, and that the UN was threatening dire consequences if Radovan Karadzik and the Serbs didn't come to an agreement with the other warring parties. Diana's mind began to drift – such a threat was hardly news any longer. She suspected that if she turned on the radio in a year's time they would probably be repeating it word for word.

As her car crawled round Russell Square, she began to think about the weekend ahead. It had been over a year since John had told her that he had met another woman and wanted a divorce. She still wondered why, after seven years of marriage, she hadn't been more shocked – or at least angry – at his betrayal. Since her appointment as a director, she had to admit they had spent less and less time together. And perhaps she had become anaesthetised by the fact that a third of the married couples in Britain were now divorced or separated. Her parents had been unable to hide their disappointment, but then they had been married for forty-two years.

The divorce had been amicable enough, as John, who earned less than she did – one of their problems, perhaps – had given in to most of her demands. She had kept the flat in Putney, the Audi estate and the children, to whom John was allowed access one weekend in four. He would have picked them up from school earlier that afternoon, and, as usual, he'd return them to the flat in Putney around seven on Sunday evening.

Diana would go to almost any lengths to avoid being

left on her own in Putney when they weren't around, and although she regularly grumbled about being landed with the responsibility of bringing up two children without a father, she missed them desperately the moment they were out of sight.

She hadn't taken a lover and she didn't sleep around. None of the senior staff at the office had ever gone further than asking her out to lunch. Perhaps because only three of them were unmarried – and not without reason. The one person she might have considered having a relationship with had made it abundantly clear that he only wanted to spend the night with her, not the days.

In any case, Diana had decided long ago that if she was to be taken seriously as the company's first woman director, an office affair, however casual or short-lived, could only end in tears. Men are so vain, she thought. A woman only had to make one mistake and she was immediately labelled as promiscuous. Then every other man on the premises either smirks behind your back, or treats your thigh as an extension of the arm on his chair.

Diana groaned as she came to a halt at yet another red light. In twenty minutes she hadn't covered more than a couple of miles. She opened the glove box on the passenger side and fumbled in the dark for a cassette. She found one and pressed it into the slot, hoping it would be Pavarotti, only to be greeted by the strident tones of Gloria Gaynor assuring her 'I will survive'. She smiled and thought about Daniel, as the light changed to green.

She and Daniel had read Economics at Bristol University in the early 1980s, friends but never lovers. Then Daniel met Rachael, who had come up a year after them, and from that moment he had never looked at another woman. They married the day he graduated, and after they returned from their honeymoon Daniel took over the management of his father's farm in Bedfordshire. Three children had followed in quick succession, and Diana had been proud when she was asked to be godmother to Sophie, the eldest. Daniel and Rachael had now been married for twelve years, and Diana felt confident that they wouldn't be disappointing *their* parents with any suggestion of a divorce. Although they were convinced she led an exciting and fulfilling life, Diana often envied their gentle and uncomplicated existence.

She was regularly asked to spend the weekend with them in the country, but for every two or three invitations Daniel issued, she only accepted one – not because she wouldn't have liked to join them more often, but because since her divorce she had no desire to take advantage of their hospitality.

Although she enjoyed her work, it had been a bloody week. Two contracts had fallen through, James had been dropped from the school football team, and Caroline had never stopped telling her that her father didn't mind her watching television when she ought to be doing her prep.

Another traffic light changed to red.

It took Diana nearly an hour to travel the seven miles out of the city, and when she reached the first dual carriageway, she glanced up at the A1 sign, more out of habit than to seek guidance, because she knew every yard of the road from her office to the farm. She tried to increase her speed, but it was quite impossible, as both lanes remained obstinately crowded.

'Damn.' She had forgotten to get them a present, even a decent bottle of claret. 'Damn,' she repeated: Daniel and Rachael always did the giving. She began to wonder if she could pick something up on the way, then remembered there was nothing but service stations between here and the farm. She couldn't turn up with yet another box of chocolates they'd never eat. When she reached the roundabout that led onto the A1, she managed to push the car over fifty for the first time. She began to relax, allowing her mind to drift with the music.

There was no warning. Although she immediately slammed her foot on the brakes, it was already too late. There was a dull thump from the front bumper, and a slight shudder rocked the car.

A small black creature had shot across her path, and despite her quick reactions, she hadn't been able to avoid hitting it. Diana swung onto the hard shoulder and screeched to a halt, wondering if the animal could possibly have survived. She reversed slowly back to the spot where she thought she had hit it as the traffic roared past her.

And then she saw it, lying on the grass verge — a cat that had crossed the road for the tenth time. She stepped out of the car, and walked towards the lifeless body. Suddenly Diana felt sick. She had two cats of her own, and she knew she would never be able to tell the children what she had done. She picked up the dead animal and laid it gently in the ditch by the roadside.

'I'm so sorry,' she said, feeling a little silly. She gave it one last look before walking back to her car. Ironically, she had chosen the Audi for its safety features.

She climbed back into the car and switched on the ignition to find Gloria Gaynor was still belting out her opinion of men. She turned her off, and tried to stop thinking about the cat as she waited for a gap in the traffic large enough to allow her to ease her way back into the slow lane. She eventually succeeded, but was still unable to erase the dead cat from her mind.

Diana had accelerated up to fifty again when she suddenly became aware of a pair of headlights shining through her rear windscreen. She put up her arm and waved in her rear-view mirror, but the lights continued to dazzle her. She slowed down to allow the vehicle to pass, but the driver showed no interest in doing so. Diana began to wonder if there was something wrong with her car. Was one of her lights not working? Was the exhaust billowing smoke? Was . . .

She decided to speed up and put some distance between herself and the vehicle behind, but it remained within a few yards of her bumper. She tried to snatch a look at the driver in her rear-view mirror, but it was hard to see much in the harshness of the lights. As her eyes became more accustomed to the glare, she could make out the silhouette of a large black van bearing down on her, and what looked like a young man behind the wheel. He seemed to be waving at her.

Diana slowed down again as she approached the next roundabout, giving him every chance to overtake her on the outside lane, but once again he didn't take the opportunity, and just sat on her bumper, his headlights still undimmed. She waited for a small gap in the traffic coming from her right. When one appeared she slammed her foot on the accelerator, shot across the roundabout and sped on up the A1.

She was rid of him at last. She was just beginning to relax and to think about Sophie, who always waited up so that she could read to her, when suddenly those high-beam headlights were glaring through her rear wind-screen and blinding her once again. If anything, they were even closer to her than before.

She slowed down, he slowed down. She accelerated, he accelerated. She tried to think what she could do next, and began waving frantically at passing motorists as they sped by, but they remained oblivious to her predicament. She tried to think of other ways she might alert some-one, and suddenly recalled that when she had joined the board of the company they had suggested she have a car phone fitted. Diana had decided it could wait until the car went in for its next service, which should have been a fortnight ago.

She brushed her hand across her forehead and removed a film of perspiration, thought for a moment, then manoeuvred her car into the fast lane. The van swung across after her, and hovered so close to her bumper that she became fearful that if she so much as touched her brakes she might unwittingly cause an enormous pile-up.

Diana took the car up to ninety, but the van wouldn't be shaken off. She pushed her foot further down on the accelerator and touched a hundred, but it still remained less than a car's length behind.

She flicked her headlights onto high-beam, turned on her hazard lights and blasted her horn at anyone who dared to remain in her path. She could only hope that the police might see her, wave her onto the hard shoulder and book her for speeding. A fine would be infinitely preferable to a crash with a young tearaway, she thought, as the Audi estate passed a hundred and ten for the first time in its life. But the black van couldn't be shaken off.

Without warning, she swerved back into the middle lane and took her foot off the accelerator, causing the van to draw level with her, which gave her a chance to look at the driver for the first time. He was wearing a black leather jacket and pointing menacingly at her. She shook her fist at him and accelerated away, but he simply swung across behind her like an Olympic runner determined not to allow his rival to break clear.

And then she remembered, and felt sick for a second time that night. 'Oh my God,' she shouted aloud in terror. In a flood, the details of the murder that had taken place on the same road a few months before came rushing back to her. A woman had been raped before having her throat cut with a knife with a serrated edge and dumped in a ditch. For weeks there had been signs posted on the A1 appealing to passing motorists to phone a certain number if they had any information that might assist the police with their enquiries. The signs had now disappeared, but the police were still searching for the killer. Diana began to tremble as she remembered their warning to all woman drivers: 'Never stop on the motorway'.

A few seconds later she saw a road sign she knew well. She had reached it far sooner than she had anticipated. In three miles she would have to leave the motorway for the sliproad that led to the farm. She began to pray that if she took her usual turning, the black-jacketed man would continue on up the A1 and she would finally be rid of him.

Diana decided that the time had come for her to speed him on his way. She swung back into the fast lane and once again put her foot down on the accelerator. She reached a hundred miles per hour for the second time as she sped past the two-mile sign. Her body was now covered in sweat, and the speedometer touched a hundred and ten. She checked her rear-view mirror, but he was still right behind her. She would have to pick the exact moment if she was to execute her plan successfully. With a mile to go, she began to look to her left, so as to be sure her timing would be perfect. She no longer needed to check in her mirror to know that he would still be there.

The next signpost showed three diagonal white lines, warning her that she ought to be on the inside lane if she intended to leave the motorway at the next junction. She kept the car in the outside lane at a hundred miles per hour until she spotted a large enough gap. Two white lines appeared by the roadside: Diana knew she would have only one chance to make her escape. As she passed the sign with a single white line on it she suddenly swung across the road at ninety miles per hour, causing cars in the middle and inside lanes to throw on their brakes and blast out their angry opinions. But Diana didn't care what they thought of her, because she was now travelling down the sliproad to safety, and the black van was speeding on up the A1.

She laughed out loud with relief. To her right, she could see the steady flow of traffic on the motorway. But then her laugh turned to a scream as she saw the black van cut sharply across the motorway in front of a lorry, mount the grass verge and career onto the slip-road, swinging from side to side. It nearly drove over the edge and into a ditch, but somehow managed to steady itself, ending up a few yards behind her, its lights once again glaring through her rear windscreen.

When she reached the top of the sliproad, Diana turned left in the direction of the farm, frantically trying to work out what she should do next. The nearest town was about twelve miles away on the main road, and the farm was only seven, but five of those miles were down a winding, unlit country lane. She checked her petrol gauge. It was nearing empty, but there should still be enough in the tank for her to consider either option. There was less than a mile to go before she reached the turning, so she had only a minute in which to make up her mind.

With a hundred yards to go, she settled on the farm. Despite the unlit lane, she knew every twist and turn, and she felt confident that her pursuer wouldn't. Once she reached the farm she could be out of the car and inside the house long before he could catch her. In any case, once he saw the farmhouse, surely he would flee.

The minute was up. Diana touched the brakes and skidded into a country road illuminated only by the moon.

Diana banged the palms of her hands on the steering wheel. Had she made the wrong decision? She glanced up at her rear-view mirror. Had he given up? Of course he hadn't. The back of a Land Rover loomed up in front of her. Diana slowed down, waiting for a corner she knew well, where the road widened slightly. She held her breath, crashed into third gear, and overtook. Would a head-on collision be preferable to a cut throat? She rounded the bend and saw an empty road ahead of her. Once again she pressed her foot down, this time managing to put a clear seventy, perhaps even a hundred, yards between her and her pursuer, but this only offered her a few moments' respite. Before long the familiar headlights came bearing down on her once again.

With each bend Diana was able to gain a little time as the van continued to lurch from side to side, unfamiliar with the road, but she never managed a clear break of more than a few seconds. She checked the mileometer. From the turn-off on the main road to the farm it was just over five miles, and she must have covered about two by now. She began to watch each tenth of a mile clicking up, terrified at the thought of the van overtaking her and forcing her into the ditch. She stuck determinedly to the centre of the road.

Another mile passed, and still he clung on to her. Suddenly she saw a car coming towards her. She switched her headlights to full beam and pressed on the horn. The other car retaliated by mimicking her actions, which caused her to slow down and brush against the hedgerow as they shot past each other. She checked the mileometer once again. Only two miles to go.

Diana would slow down and then speed up at each familiar bend in the road, making sure the van was never given enough room to pull level with her. She tried to concentrate on what she should do once the farmhouse came into sight. She reckoned that the drive leading up to the house must be about half a mile long. It was full of potholes and bumps which Daniel had often explained he couldn't afford to have repaired. But at least it was only wide enough for one car.

The gate to the driveway was usually left open for her, though on the odd rare occasion Daniel had forgotten, and she'd had to get out of the car and open it for herself. She couldn't risk that tonight. If the gate was closed, she would have to travel on to the next town and stop outside the Crimson Kipper, which was always crowded at this time on a Friday night, or, if she could find it, on the steps of the local police station. She checked her petrol gauge again. It was now touching red. 'Oh my God,' she said, realising she might not have enough petrol to reach the town.

She could only pray that Daniel had remembered to leave the gate open.

She swerved out of the next bend and speeded up, but once again she managed to gain only a few yards, and she knew that within seconds he would be back in place. He was. For the next few hundred yards they remained within feet of each other, and she felt certain he must run into the back of her. She didn't once dare to touch her brakes – if they crashed in that lane, far from any help, she would have no hope of getting away from him.

She checked her mileometer. A mile to go.

'The gate must be open. It must be open,' she prayed. As she swung round the next bend, she could make out the outline of the farmhouse in the distance. She almost screamed with relief when she saw that the lights were on in the downstairs rooms.

She shouted, 'Thank God!' then remembered the gate again, and changed her plea to 'Dear God, let it be open.' She would know what needed to be done as soon as she came round the last bend. 'Let it be open, just this once,' she pleaded. 'I'll never ask for anything again, ever.' She swung round the final bend only inches ahead of the black van. 'Please, please, please.' And then she saw the gate.

It was open.

Her clothes were now drenched in sweat. She slowed down, wrenched the gearbox into second, and threw the car between the gap and into the bumpy driveway, hitting the gatepost on her right-hand side as she careered on up towards the house. The van didn't hesitate to follow her, and was still only inches behind as she straightened up. Diana kept her hand pressed down on the horn as the car bounced and lurched over the mounds and potholes.

Flocks of startled crows flapped out of overhanging branches, screeching as they shot into the air. Diana began screaming, 'Daniel! Daniel!' Two hundred yards ahead of her, the porch light went on.

Her headlights were now shining onto the front of the house, and her hand was still pressed on the horn. With a hundred yards to go, she spotted Daniel coming out of the front door, but she didn't slow down, and neither did the van behind her. With fifty yards to go she began flashing her lights at Daniel. She could now make out the puzzled, anxious expression on his face.

With thirty yards to go she threw on her brakes. The heavy estate car skidded across the gravel in front of the house, coming to a halt in the flowerbed just below the kitchen window. She heard the screech of brakes behind her. The leather-jacketed man, unfamiliar with the terrain, had been unable to react quickly enough, and as soon as his wheels touched the gravelled forecourt he began to skid out of control. A second later the van came crashing into the back of her car, slamming it against the wall of the house and shattering the glass in the kitchen window.

Diana leapt out of the car, screaming, 'Daniel! Get a gun, get a gun!' She pointed back at the van. 'That bastard's been chasing me for the last twenty miles!'

The man jumped out of the van and began limping towards them. Diana ran into the house. Daniel followed and grabbed a shotgun, normally reserved for rabbits, that was leaning against the wall. He ran back outside to face the unwelcome visitor, who had come to a halt by the back of Diana's Audi.

Daniel raised the shotgun to his shoulder and stared straight at him. 'Don't move or I'll shoot,' he said calmly. And then he remembered the gun wasn't loaded. Diana ducked back out of the house, but remained several yards behind him.

'Not me! Not me!' shouted the leather-jacketed youth, as Rachael appeared in the doorway.

'What's going on?' she asked nervously.

'Ring for the police,' was all Daniel said, and his wife quickly disappeared back into the house.

Daniel advanced towards the terrified-looking young man, the gun aimed squarely at his chest.

'Not me! Not me!' he shouted again, pointing at the Audi. 'He's in the car!' He quickly turned to face Diana. 'I saw him get in when you were parked on the hard shoulder. What else could I have done? You just wouldn't pull over.'

Daniel advanced cautiously towards the rear door of the car and ordered the young man to open it slowly, while he kept the gun aimed at his chest.

The youth opened the door, and quickly took a pace backwards. The three of them stared down at a man crouched on the floor of the car. In his right hand he held a long-bladed knife with a serrated edge. Daniel swung the barrel of the gun down to point at him, but said nothing.

The sound of a police siren could just be heard in the distance.

NOT FOR SALE

SALLY SUMMERS WON HER SCHOOL'S
senior art prize at the age of fourteen. In her last four
years at St Bride's the only serious competition was for
second place. When, in her final year, she was awarded
the top scholarship to the Slade School of Fine Art none
of her contemporaries was at all surprised. The head-
mistress told the assembled parents on Speech Day that
she was confident Sally had a distinguished career ahead
of her, and that her work would soon be exhibited in
one of London's major galleries. Sally was flattered by
all this unqualified praise, but still wasn't sure if she had
any real talent.

By the end of her first year at the Slade, the staff and
senior students were already becoming aware of Sally's
work. Her drawing technique was regarded as quite
exceptional, and her brushwork became bolder with each
term. But, above all, it was the originality of her ideas
that caused other students to stop and stare at her
canvases.

In her final year, Sally won both the Mary Rischgitz
Prize for oil painting and the Henry Tonks Prize for
drawing: a rare double. They were presented to her by

Sir Roger de Grey, the President of the Royal Academy, and Sally was among that tiny group who were spoken of as 'having a future'. But surely, she told her parents, that could be said of the top student in any year – and most of them ended up working in the creative departments of advertising agencies, or teaching art to bored schoolchildren in far-flung parts of the kingdom.

Once she had graduated, Sally had to decide whether she too would apply for a job with an advertising agency, take up a teaching appointment, or risk everything and try to put together enough original work for a London gallery to consider her for a one-woman show.

Her parents were convinced that their daughter had real talent, but what do parents know when you're their only child? thought Sally. Especially when one of them was a music teacher and the other an accountant who were the first to admit that they didn't know much about art, but they knew what they liked. Still, they seemed quite willing to support her for another year if she wanted (to use an expression of the young) to go for it.

Sally was painfully aware that, although her parents were fairly comfortably off, another year in which she produced no income could only be a burden for them. After much soul-searching she told them, 'One year, and one year only. After that, if the paintings aren't good enough, or if no one shows any interest in exhibiting them, I'll be realistic and look for a proper job.'

For the next six months Sally worked hours that she hadn't realised existed when she'd been a student.

During that time she produced a dozen canvases. She allowed no one to see them, for fear that her parents and friends would not be frank with her. She was determined to finish her portfolio and then listen only to the toughest opinions possible, those of the professional gallery owners, and, tougher still, those of the buying public.

Sally had always been a voracious reader, and she continued to devour books and monographs on artists from Bellini to Hockney. The more she read, the more she became aware that however talented an artist might be, it was industry and dedication that ultimately marked out the few who succeeded from the many who failed. This inspired her to work still harder, and she began to turn down invitations to parties, dances, even weekends with old friends, making use of every spare moment to visit art galleries or to attend lectures on the great masters.

By the eleventh month, Sally had completed twenty-seven works, but she still wasn't sure whether they displayed any real talent. Nevertheless, she felt the time had finally come to allow others to pass judgement on them.

She looked long and hard at each of the twenty-seven paintings, and the following morning she packed six of them in a large canvas folder her parents had given her the previous Christmas, and joined the early-morning commuters on their journey from Sevenoaks into London.

Sally began her quest in Cork Street, where she came across galleries exhibiting works by Bacon, Freud,

Hockney, Dunston and Chadwick. She felt overawed at the prospect of even entering their portals, let alone submitting her own humble work to the appraisal of their proprietors. She humped her canvas folder a couple of blocks north to Conduit Street, and in the windows she recognised the works of Jones, Campbell, Wczenski, Frink and Paolozzi. She became even more discouraged and unwilling to push open any of the galleries' front doors.

Sally returned home that night exhausted, her canvas folder unopened. She understood for the first time how an author must feel after receiving a string of rejection slips. She was unable to sleep that night. But as she lay awake she came to the conclusion that she must know the truth about her work, even if it meant being humiliated.

She joined the commuters again the following morning, and this time headed for Duke Street, St James's. She didn't bother with the galleries exhibiting old masters, Dutch still lifes or English landscapes, and therefore walked straight past Johnny van Haeften and Rafael Valls. Halfway down the street she turned right, and finally came to a halt outside the Simon Bouchier Gallery, which was exhibiting the sculptures of the late Sydney Harpley and the paintings of Muriel Pemberton, whose obituary Sally had read in the *Independent* only a few days before.

It was the thought of death that made Sally settle on the Bouchier Gallery. Perhaps they would be looking for someone young, she tried to convince herself, someone who had a long career ahead of them.

She stepped inside the gallery and found herself in a large, empty room, surrounded by Muriel Pemberton's watercolours. 'Can I help you?' asked a young woman who was sitting behind a desk near the window.

'No, thank you,' Sally replied. 'I was just looking.'

The girl eyed Sally's canvas folder, but said nothing. Sally decided she would do one circuit of the room, and then make good her escape. She began to circle the gallery, studying the pictures carefully. They were good, very good – but Sally believed she could do just as well, given time. She would have liked to see Muriel Pemberton's work when *she* was her age.

When Sally reached the far end of the gallery, she became aware of an office in which a short, balding man, wearing an old tweed jacket and corduroy trousers, was closely examining a picture. He looked about the same age as her father. Also studying the picture was another man, who caused Sally to stop in her tracks. He must have been a little over six foot, with those dark Italian looks that people normally only come across in glossy magazines; and *he* was old enough to be her brother.

Was he Mr Bouchier? she wondered. She hoped so, because if he owned the gallery she might be able to summon up the courage to introduce herself to him, once the little man in the scruffy jacket had left. At that moment the young man looked up and gave her a huge grin. Sally turned quickly away and began to study the pictures on the far wall.

She was wondering if it was worth hanging around any longer when the two men suddenly strolled out of the office and began walking towards the door.

She froze, pretending to concentrate on a portrait of a young girl in pastel blues and yellows, a picture that had a Matisse-like quality about it.

'What's in there?' asked a cheeky voice. Sally turned round and came face to face with the two men. The smaller one was pointing at her canvas bag.

'Just a few pictures,' Sally stammered. 'I'm an artist.'

'Let's have a look,' said the man, 'and perhaps *I* can decide if you're an artist or not.'

Sally hesitated.

'Come on, come on,' he teased. 'I haven't got all day. As you can see, I have an important client to take to lunch,' he added, indicating the tall, well-dressed young man, who still hadn't spoken.

'Oh, are *you* Mr Bouchier?' she asked, unable to hide her disappointment.

'Yes. Now, am I going to be allowed to look at your pictures or not?'

Sally quickly unzipped her canvas bag and laid out the six paintings on the floor. Both of the men bent down and studied them for some time before either offered an opinion.

'Not bad,' said Bouchier eventually. 'Not bad at all. Leave them with me for a few days, and then let's meet again next week.' He paused. 'Say Monday, 11.30. And if you have any more examples of your recent work, bring them with you.' Sally was speechless. 'Can't see you before Monday,' he continued, 'because the RA's Summer Exhibition opens tomorrow. So for the next few days I won't have a moment to spare. Now, if you'll excuse me . . .'

The younger man was still examining Sally's pictures closely. At last he looked up at her. 'I'd like to buy the one of the interior with the black cat on the windowsill. How much is it?'

'Well,' said Sally, 'I'm not sure . . .'

'N.F.S.,' said Mr Bouchier firmly, guiding his client towards the door.

'By the way,' the taller man said, turning back, 'I am Antonio Flavelli. My friends call me Tony.' But Mr Bouchier was already pushing him out onto the street.

Sally returned home that afternoon with an empty canvas folder, and was prepared to admit to her parents that a London dealer had shown an interest in her work. But it was, she insisted, no more than an interest.

The following morning Sally decided to go to the opening day of the Royal Academy Summer Exhibition, which would give her the chance to find out just how good her rivals were. For over an hour she stood in the long queue that stretched from the front door, right across the carpark and out onto the pavement. When she eventually reached the top of the wide staircase, she wished she was six feet six tall, so that she could see over the tops of the heads of the mass of people who were crowding every room. After a couple of hours strolling round the many galleries, Sally was confident that she was already good enough to enter a couple of her pictures for next year's exhibition.

She stopped to admire a Craigie Aitchison of Christ

on the cross, and checked in her little blue catalogue to find out the price: ten thousand pounds, more than she could hope to earn if she were to sell every one of her canvases. Suddenly her concentration was broken, as a soft Italian voice behind her said, 'Hello, Sally.' She swung round to find Tony Flavelli smiling down at her.

'Mr Flavelli,' she said.

'Tony, please. You like Craigie Aitchison?'

'He's superb,' Sally replied. 'I know his work well — I had the privilege of being taught by him when I was at the Slade.'

'I can remember, not so long ago, when you could pick up an Aitchison for two, three hundred pounds at the most. Perhaps the same thing will happen to you one day. Have you seen anything else you think I ought to look at?'

Sally was flattered to have her advice sought by a serious collector, and said, 'Yes, I think the sculpture of "Books on a Chair" by Julie Major is very striking. She has talent, and I'm sure she has a future.'

'So do you,' said Tony.

'Do you think so?' asked Sally.

'It's not important what I think,' said Tony. 'But Simon Bouchier is convinced.'

'Are you teasing me?' asked Sally.

'No, I'm not, as you'll find out for yourself when you see him next Monday. He talked of little else over lunch yesterday — "The daring brushwork, the unusual use of colour, the originality of ideas." I thought he was never

268

going to stop. Still, he's promised I can have "The Sleeping Cat that Never Moved" once you've both settled on a price.'

Sally was speechless.

'Good luck,' Tony said, turning to leave. 'Not that I think you need it.' He hesitated for a moment before swinging back to face her. 'By the way, are you going to the Hockney exhibition?'

'I didn't even know there was one,' Sally confessed.

'There's a private view this evening. Six to eight.' Looking straight into her eyes he said, 'Would you like to join me?'

She hesitated, but only for a moment. 'That would be nice.'

'Good, then why don't we meet in the Ritz Palm Court at 6.30.' Before Sally could tell him that she didn't know where the Ritz was, let alone its Palm Court, the tall, elegant man had disappeared into the crowd.

Sally suddenly felt gauche and scruffy, but then, she hadn't dressed that morning with the Ritz in mind. She looked at her watch – 12.45 – and began to wonder if she had enough time to return home, change, and be back at the Ritz by 6.30. She decided that she didn't have much choice, as she doubted if they would let her into such a grand hotel dressed in jeans and a T-shirt of Munch's 'The Scream'. She ran down the wide staircase, out onto Piccadilly, and all the way to the nearest tube station.

When she arrived back home in Sevenoaks – far earlier than her mother had expected – she rushed into the kitchen and explained that she would be going out again shortly.

'Was the Summer Exhibition any good?' her mother asked.

'Not bad,' Sally replied as she ran upstairs. But once she was out of earshot she muttered under her breath, 'Certainly didn't see a lot that worried me.'

'Will you be in for supper?' asked her mother, sticking her head out from behind the kitchen door.

'I don't think so,' shouted Sally. She disappeared into her bedroom and began flinging off her clothes before heading for the bathroom.

She crept back downstairs an hour later, having tried on and rejected several outfits. She checked her dress in the hall mirror – a little too short, perhaps, but at least it showed her legs to best advantage. She could still remember those art students who during life classes had spent more time staring at her legs than at the model they were supposed to be drawing. She only hoped Tony would be similarly captivated.

' 'Bye, Mum,' she shouted, and quickly closed the door behind her before her mother could see what she was wearing.

Sally took the next train back to Charing Cross. She stepped on to the platform unwilling to admit to any passer-by that she had no idea where the Ritz was, so she hailed a taxi, praying she could get to the hotel for four pounds, because that was all she had on her. Her eyes remained fixed on the meter as it clicked past two pounds, and then three – far too quickly, she thought –

three pounds twenty, forty, sixty, eighty . . . She was just about to ask the cabbie to stop, so she could jump out and walk the rest of the way, when he drew in to the kerb.

The door was immediately opened by a statuesque man dressed in a heavy blue trenchcoat who raised his top hat to her. Sally handed over her four pounds to the cabbie, feeling guilty about the measly twenty pence tip. She ran up the steps, through the revolving door and into the hotel foyer. She checked her watch: 6.10. She decided she had better go back outside, walk slowly around the block, and return a little later. But just as she reached the door, an elegant man in a long black coat approached her and asked, 'Can I help you, madam?'

'I'm meeting Mr Tony Flavelli,' Sally stammered, hoping he would recognise the name.

'Mr Flavelli. Of course, madam. Allow me to show you to his table in the Palm Court.'

She followed the black-coated man down the wide, deeply carpeted corridor, then up three steps to a large open area full of small circular tables, almost all of which were occupied.

Sally was directed to a table at the side, and once she was seated a waiter asked, 'Can I get you something to drink, madam? A glass of champagne, perhaps?'

'Oh, no,' said Sally. 'A coke will be just fine.'

The waiter bowed and left her. Sally gazed nervously around the beautifully furnished room. Everyone seemed so relaxed and sophisticated. The waiter returned a few moments later and placed a fine cut-glass tumbler with Coca-Cola, ice and lemon in front of her. She thanked him and began sipping her drink, checking her watch every few minutes. She pulled her dress down as far as it would go, wishing she had chosen something longer. She was becoming anxious about what would happen if Tony didn't turn up, because she didn't have any money left to pay for her drink. And then suddenly she saw him, dressed in a loose double-breasted suit and an open-neck cream shirt. He had stopped to chat to an elegant young woman on the steps. After a couple of minutes he kissed her on the cheek, and made his way over to Sally.

'I am so sorry,' he said. 'I didn't mean to keep you waiting. I do hope I'm not late.'

'No, no you're not. I arrived a few minutes early,' Sally said, flustered, as he bent down and kissed her hand.

'What did you think of the Summer Exhibition?' he asked as the waiter appeared by his side.

'Your usual, sir?' he asked.

'Yes, thank you, Michael,' he replied.

'I enjoyed it,' said Sally. 'But . . .'

'But you felt you could have done just as well yourself,' he suggested.

'I didn't mean to imply that,' she said, looking up to see if he was teasing. But the expression on his face remained serious. 'I'm sure I will enjoy the Hockney more,' she added as a glass of champagne was placed on the table.

'Then I'll have to come clean,' said Tony.

Sally put down her drink and stared at him, not knowing what he meant.

'There isn't a Hockney exhibition on at the moment,' he said. 'Unless you want to fly to Glasgow.'

Sally looked puzzled. 'But you said . . .'

'I just wanted an excuse to see you again.'

Sally felt bemused and flattered, and was uncertain how to respond.

'I'll leave the choice to you,' he said. 'We could have dinner together, or you could simply take the train back to Sevenoaks.'

'How did you know I live in Sevenoaks?'

'It was inscribed in big bold letters on the side of your canvas folder,' said Tony with a smile.

Sally laughed. 'I'll settle for dinner,' she said. Tony paid for the drinks, then guided Sally out of the hotel and a few yards down the road to a restaurant on the corner of Arlington Street.

This time Sally did try a glass of champagne, and allowed Tony to select for her from the menu. He could not have been more attentive, and seemed to know so much about so many things, even if she didn't manage to find out exactly what he did.

After Tony had called for the bill, he asked her if she would like to have coffee at 'my place'.

'I'm afraid I can't,' she said, looking at her watch. 'I'd miss the last train home.'

'Then I'll drive you to the station. We wouldn't want you to miss the last train home, would we?' he said, scrawling his signature across the bill.

This time she knew he was teasing her, and she blushed.

When Tony dropped her off at Charing Cross he asked, 'When can I see you again?'

'I have an appointment with Mr Bouchier at 11.30 . . .'

'. . . next Monday morning, if I remember correctly. So why don't we have a celebration lunch together after he's signed you up? I'll come to the gallery at about 12.30. Goodbye.' He leaned over and kissed her gently on the lips.

Sitting in a cold, smelly carriage on the last train back to Sevenoaks, Sally couldn't help wondering what coffee at Tony's place might have been like.

Sally walked into the gallery a few minutes before 11.30 the following Monday to find Simon Bouchier kneeling on the carpet, head down, studying some paintings. They weren't hers, and she hoped he felt the same way about them as she did.

Simon looked up. 'Good morning, Sally. Dreadful, aren't they? You have to look through an awful lot of rubbish before you come across someone who shows any real talent.' He rose to his feet. 'Mind you, Natasha Krasnoselyodkina does have one advantage over you.'

'What's that?' asked Sally.

'She would draw the crowds for any opening.'

'Why?'

'Because she claims to be a Russian countess. Hints

she's a direct descendant of the last tsar. Frankly, I think the Pearly Queen is about the nearest she's been to royalty, but still, she's the "in" face at the moment – a sort of "Minah Bird" of the nineties. What did Andy Warhol say – "In the future, everyone will be famous for fifteen minutes." By that standard, Natasha looks good for about thirty. I see this morning's tabloids are even hinting she's the new love in Prince Andrew's life. My bet is they've never met. But if he were to turn up at the opening, we'd be packed out, that's for sure. We wouldn't sell a picture, of course, but we'd be packed out.'

'Why wouldn't you sell anything?' asked Sally.

'Because the public are not that stupid when it comes to buying paintings. A picture is a large investment for most people, and they want to believe that they have a good eye, and that they've invested wisely. Natasha's pictures won't satisfy them on either count. With you, though, Sally, I'm beginning to feel they might be convinced on both. But first, let me see the rest of your portfolio.'

Sally unzipped her bulging folder, and laid out twenty-one paintings on the carpet.

Simon dropped to his knees, and didn't speak again for some time. When he eventually did offer an opinion, it was only to repeat the single word 'Consistent.'

'But I'll need even more, and of the same quality,' he said after he had risen to his feet. 'Another dozen canvases at least, and by October. I want you to concentrate on interiors – you're good at interiors. And they'll have to be better than good if you expect me to invest my time, expertise, and a great deal of money in you, young lady. Do you think you can manage another dozen pictures by October, Miss Summers?'

'Yes, of course,' said Sally, giving little thought to the fact that October was only five months away.

'That's good, because if you deliver, and I only say *if*, I'll risk the expense of launching you on an unsuspecting public this autumn.' He walked into his office, flicked through his diary and said, 'October the seventeenth, to be precise.'

Sally was speechless.

'I don't suppose you could manage an affair with Prince Charles lasting, say, from the end of September to the beginning of November? That would knock the Russian Countess from the Mile End Road off the front pages and guarantee us a full house on opening night.'

'I'm afraid not,' said Sally, 'especially if you expect me to produce another dozen canvases by then.'

'Pity,' said Simon, 'because if we can attract the punters to the opening, I'm confident they'll want to buy your work. The problem is always getting them to come for an unknown.' He suddenly looked over Sally's shoulder and said, 'Hello, Tony. I wasn't expecting to see you today.'

'Perhaps that's because you're not seeing me,' Tony replied. 'I've just come to whisk Sally off to what I was rather hoping might be a celebratory lunch.'

'"The Summers Exhibition",' Simon said, grinning

at his little play on words, 'will open not in June at the Royal Academy, but in October at the Bouchier Gallery. October the seventeenth is to be Sally's day of reckoning.'

'Congratulations,' said Tony, turning to Sally. 'I'll bring all my friends.'

'I'm only interested in the rich ones,' said Simon, as someone else entered the Gallery.

'Natasha,' said Simon, turning to face a slim, dark-haired woman. Sally's first reaction was that she should have been an artists' model, not an artist.

'Thanks for coming back so quickly, Natasha. Have a nice lunch, you two,' he added, smiling at Tony, who couldn't take his eyes off the new arrival.

Natasha didn't notice, as her only interest seemed to be in Sally's pictures. She was unable to conceal her envy as Tony and Sally walked out of the gallery.

'Wasn't she stunning?' said Sally.

'Was she?' said Tony. 'I didn't notice.'

'I wouldn't blame Prince Andrew if he was having an affair with her.'

'Damn,' said Tony placing a hand in his inside pocket. 'I forgot to give Simon a cheque I promised him. Don't move, I'll be back in a minute.'

Tony sprinted off in the direction of the gallery, and Sally waited on the corner for what seemed like an awfully long minute before he reappeared back on the street.

'Sorry. Simon was on the phone,' Tony explained. He took Sally's arm and led her across the road to a small Italian restaurant, where once again he seemed to have his own table.

He ordered a bottle of champagne, 'To celebrate your great triumph.' As Sally raised her glass in response, she realised for the first time just how much work she would have to do before October if she was going to keep her promise to Simon.

When Tony poured her a second glass, Sally smiled. 'It's been a memorable day. I ought to phone my parents and let them know, but I don't think they'd believe me.'

When a third glass had been filled and Sally still hadn't finished her salad, Tony took her hand, leaned across and kissed it. 'I've never met anyone as beautiful as you,' he said. 'And certainly no one as talented.'

Sally quickly took a gulp of the champagne, to hide her embarrassment. She still wasn't sure whether to believe him, but a glass of white wine, followed by two glasses of red, helped to convince her that she should.

After Tony had signed the bill, he asked her again if she would like to come back to his place for coffee. Sally had already decided that she wasn't going to be able to do any work that day, so she nodded her agreement. In any case, she felt she had earned an afternoon off.

In the taxi on the way to Chelsea, she rested her head on Tony's shoulder, and he began to kiss her gently.

When they arrived at his town house in Bywater Street, he helped her out of the taxi, up the steps and through the front door. He led her along a dimly lit corridor and into the drawing room. She curled up in a corner of the sofa, as Tony disappeared into another room. Most of the furniture, and the pictures that covered every inch of the walls, were a blur to her. Tony returned a moment later, carrying another bottle of champagne and two glasses. Sally didn't notice that he was no longer wearing his jacket, tie or shoes.

He poured her a drink, which she sipped as he sat down next to her on the sofa. His arm slipped round her shoulder and he drew her close to him. When he kissed her again, she felt a little silly dangling an empty glass in mid-air. He took it from her and placed it on a side table, then held her in his arms and began to kiss her more passionately. As she fell back, his hand slipped onto the inside of her thigh, and began moving slowly up her leg.

Every time Sally was about to stop him going any further, Tony seemed to know exactly what to do next. She had always felt in control in the past whenever an over-enthusiastic art student had started to go a little too far in the back row of a cinema, but she had never experienced anyone as subtle as Tony. When her dress fell off her shoulders, she hadn't even noticed that he had undone the twelve little buttons down the back.

They broke away for a second. Sally felt she ought to make a move to go, before it was too late. Tony smiled, and undid the buttons of his own shirt before taking her back in his arms. She felt the warmth of his chest, and he was so gentle that she did not complain when she realised that the clasp of her bra had come loose. She sank back, enjoying every second, knowing that until that moment she had never experienced what it was like to be properly seduced.

Tony finally lay back and said, 'Yes, it has been a memorable day. But I don't think I'll phone my parents to let them know.' He laughed, and Sally felt slightly ashamed. Tony was only the fourth man who had made love to her, and she had known the other three for months beforehand – in one case, years.

For the next hour they talked about many things, but all Sally really wanted to know was how Tony felt about her. He gave her no clue.

Then, once again, he took her in his arms, but this time he pulled her onto the floor and made love to her with such passion that afterwards Sally wondered if she had ever made love before.

She was just in time to catch the last train home, but she couldn't help wishing she had missed it.

Over the next few months Sally devoted herself to getting her latest ideas onto canvas. When each new painting was finished, she would take it up to London for Simon to comment on. The smile on his face became broader and broader with each new picture he saw, and the word he kept repeating now was 'Original.' Sally would tell him about her ideas for the next one, and he would bring her up to date with his plans for the opening in October.

Tony would often meet her for lunch, and afterwards they would go back to his house, where they would make love until it was time for her to catch the last train home.

Sally often wished she could spend more time with Tony. But she was always conscious of the deadline set by Simon, who warned her that the printers were already proof-reading the catalogue, and that the invitations for the opening were waiting to be sent out. Tony seemed almost as busy as she was, and lately he hadn't always been able to fit in with her expeditions to London. Sally had taken to staying overnight, and catching an early train home the following morning. Tony occasionally hinted that she might consider moving in with him. When she thought about it – and she often did – she reflected that his attic could easily be converted into a studio. But she decided that before such a move could even be contemplated, the exhibition had to be a success. Then, if the hint became an offer, she would have her answer ready.

Just two days before the exhibition was due to open, Sally completed her final canvas and handed it over to Simon. As she pulled it out of the canvas folder he threw his arms in the air, and shouted, 'Hallelujah! It's your best yet. As long as we're sensible about our prices, I think that, with a touch of luck, we should sell at least half of your pictures before the exhibition closes.'

'Only half?' said Sally, unable to hide her disappointment.

'That wouldn't be at all bad for your first attempt, young lady,' said Simon. 'I only sold one Leslie Anne

Ivory at her first exhibition, and now she sells everything in the first week.'

Sally still looked crestfallen, and Simon realised he
had perhaps been a little tactless.

'Don't worry. Any unsold ones will be put into stock,
and they'll be snapped up the moment you start getting
good reviews.'

Sally continued to pout.

'How do you feel about the frames and mounts?'
Simon asked, trying to change the subject.

Sally studied the deep golden frames and light-grey
mounts. The smile returned to her face.

'They're good, aren't they?' said Simon. 'They bring
out the colour in the canvases wonderfully.'

Sally nodded her agreement, but was now beginning
to worry about how much they must have cost, and
whether she would ever be given a second exhibition if
the first one wasn't a success.

'By the way,' Simon said, 'I have a friend at the P.A.
called Mike Sallis who . . .'

'P.A.?' said Sally.

'Press Association. Mike's a photographer – always
on the lookout for a good story. He says he'll come
round and take a picture of you standing next to one of
the pictures. Then he'll hawk the photo around Fleet
Street, and we'll just have to cross our fingers, and pray
that Natasha has taken the day off. I don't want to get
your hopes up, but someone just might bite. Our only
line at present is that it's your first exhibition since
leaving the Slade. Hardly a front-page splash.' Simon

paused, as once again Sally looked discouraged. 'It's not too late for you to have a fling with Prince Charles, you know. That would solve all our problems.'

Sally smiled. 'I don't think Tony would like that.'

Simon decided against making another tactless remark.

Sally spent that evening with Tony at his home in Chelsea. He seemed a little distracted, but she blamed herself — she was unable to hide her disappointment at Simon's estimate of how few of her pictures might be sold. After they had made love, Sally tried to raise the topic of what would happen to them once the exhibition was over, but Tony deftly changed the subject back to how much he was looking forward to the opening.

That night Sally went home on the last train from Charing Cross.

The following morning she woke up with a terrible feeling of anti-climax. Her room was bereft of canvases, and all she could do now was wait. Her mood wasn't helped by the fact that Tony had told her he would be out of London on business until the day of her opening. She lay in the bath thinking about him.

'But I'll be your first customer on the night,' he had promised. 'Don't forget, I still want to buy "The Sleeping Cat that Never Moved".'

The phone was ringing, but someone answered it before Sally could get out of the bath.

'It's for you,' shouted her mother from the bottom of the stairs.

Sally wrapped a towel around her and grabbed the phone, hoping it would be Tony.

'Hi, Sally, it's Simon. I've got some good news. Mike Sallis has just called from the P.A. He's coming round to the gallery at midday tomorrow. All the pictures should be framed by then, and he'll be the first person from the press to see them. They all want to be first. I'm trying to think up some wheeze to convince him that it's an exclusive. By the way, the catalogues have arrived, and they look fantastic.'

Sally thanked him, and was about to ring Tony to suggest that she stay overnight with him, so that they could go to the gallery together the following day, when she remembered that he was out of town. She spent the day pacing anxiously around the house, occasionally talking to her most compliant model, the sleeping cat that never moved.

The following morning Sally caught an early commuter train from Sevenoaks, so she could spend a little time checking the pictures against their catalogue entries. When she walked into the gallery, her eyes lit up: half a dozen of the paintings had already been hung, and she actually felt, for the first time, that they really weren't bad. She glanced in the direction of the office, and saw that Simon was occupied on the phone. He smiled and waved to indicate that he would be with her in a moment.

She had another look at the pictures, and then spotted a copy of the catalogue lying on the table. The cover read 'The Summers Exhibition', above a picture of an interior looking from her parents' drawing room through an open window and out onto a garden overgrown with weeds. A black cat lay asleep on the windowsill, ignoring the rain.

Sally opened the catalogue and read the introduction on the first page.

> Sometimes judges feel it necessary to say: It's been hard to pick this year's winner. But from the moment one set eyes on Sally Summers' work, the task was made easy. Real talent is obvious for all to see, and Sally has achieved the rare feat of winning both the Slade's major prizes, for oils and for drawing, in the same year. I much look forward to watching her career develop over the coming years.

It was an extract from Sir Roger de Grey's speech when he had presented Sally with the Mary Rischgitz and the Henry Tonks Prizes at the Slade two years before.

Sally turned the pages, seeing her works reproduced in colour for the first time. Simon's attention to detail and layout was evident on every page.

She looked back towards the office, and saw that Simon was still on the phone. She decided to go downstairs and check on the rest of her pictures, now that they had all been framed. The lower gallery was a mass of colour, and the newly framed paintings were so skilfully hung that even Sally saw them in a new light.

Once she had circled the room Sally suppressed a smile of satisfaction before turning to make her way back upstairs. As she passed a table in the centre of the gallery, she noticed a folder with the initials 'N.K.' printed on it. She idly lifted the cover, to discover a pile of undistinguished watercolours.

As she leafed through her rival's never-to-be-exhibited efforts, Sally had to admit that the nude self-portraits didn't do Natasha justice. She was just about to close the folder and join Simon upstairs when she came to a sudden halt.

Although it was clumsily executed, there was no doubt who the man was that the half-clad Natasha was clinging on to.

Sally felt sick. She slammed the folder shut, walked quickly across the room and back up the stairs to the ground floor. In the corner of the large gallery Simon was chatting to a man who had several cameras slung over his shoulder.

'Sally,' he said, coming towards her, 'this is Mike . . .'

But Sally ignored them both, and started running towards the open door, tears flooding down her cheeks. She turned right into St James's, determined to get as far away from the gallery as possible. But then she came to an abrupt halt. Tony and Natasha were walking towards her, arm in arm.

Sally stepped off the pavement and began to cross the road, hoping to reach the other side before they spotted her.

The screech of tyres and the sudden swerve of the van came just a moment too late, and she was thrown headlong into the middle of the road.

When Sally came to, she felt awful. She blinked her eyes, and thought she could hear voices. She blinked again, but it was several moments before she was able to focus on anything.

She was lying in a bed, but it was not her own. Her right leg was covered in plaster, and was raised high in the air, suspended from a pulley. Her other leg was under the sheet, and it felt all right. She wiggled the toes of her left foot: yes, they were fine. Then she began to try to move her arms. A nurse came up to the side of the bed.

'Welcome back to the world, Sally.'

'How long have I been like this?' she asked.

'A couple of days,' said the nurse, checking Sally's pulse. 'But you're making a remarkably quick recovery. Before you ask, it's only a broken leg, and the black eyes will have gone long before we let you out. By the way,' she added, as she moved on to the next patient, 'I loved that picture of you in the morning papers. And what about those flattering remarks your friend made? So what's it like to be famous?'

Sally wanted to ask what she was talking about, but the nurse was already taking the pulse of the person in the next bed.

'Come back,' Sally wanted to say, but a second nurse

had appeared by her bedside with a mug of orange juice, which she thrust into her hand.

'Let's get you started on this,' she said. Sally obeyed, and tried to suck the liquid through a bent plastic straw.

'You've got a visitor,' the nurse told her once she'd emptied the contents of the mug. 'He's been waiting for some time. Do you think you're up to seeing him?'

'Sure,' said Sally, not particularly wanting to face Tony, but desperate to find out what had happened.

She looked towards the swing doors at the end of the ward, but had to wait for some time before Simon came bouncing through them. He walked straight up to her bed, clutching what might just about have been described as a bunch of flowers. He gave her plaster cast a big kiss.

'I'm so sorry, Simon,' Sally said, before he had even said hello. 'I know just how much trouble and expense you've been to on my behalf. And now I've let you down so badly.'

'You certainly have,' said Simon. 'It's always a let-down when you sell everything off the walls on the first night. Then you haven't got anything left for your old customers, and they start grumbling.'

Sally's mouth opened wide.

'Mind you, it was a rather good photo of Natasha, even if it was an awful one of you.'

'What are you talking about, Simon?'

'Mike Sallis got his exclusive, and you got your break,' he said, patting her suspended leg. 'When Natasha bent over your body in the street, Mike began clicking away for dear life. And I couldn't have scripted her quotes better myself: "The most outstanding young artist of our generation. If the world were to lose such a talent . . ."'

Sally laughed at Simon's wicked imitation of Natasha's Russian accent.

'You hit most of the next morning's front pages,' he continued. '"Brush with Death" in the *Mail*; "Still Life in St James's" in the *Express*. And you even managed "Splat!" in the *Sun*. The punters flocked into the gallery that evening. Natasha was wearing a black see-through dress and proceeded to give the press soundbite after soundbite about your genius. Not that it made any difference. We'd already sold every canvas long before their second editions hit the street. But, more important, the serious critics in the broadsheets are already acknowledging that you might actually have some talent.'

Sally smiled. 'I may have failed to have an affair with Prince Charles, but at least it seems I got something right.'

'Well, not exactly,' said Simon.

'What do you mean?' asked Sally, suddenly anxious. 'You said all the pictures have been sold.'

'True, but if you'd arranged to have the accident a few days earlier, I could have jacked up the prices by at least fifty per cent. Still, there's always next time.'

'Did Tony buy "The Sleeping Cat that Never Moved"?' Sally asked quietly.

'No, he was late as usual, I'm afraid. It was snapped up in the first half hour, by a serious collector. Which reminds me,' Simon added, as Sally's parents came through the swing doors into the ward, 'I'll need another forty canvases if we're going to hold your second show in the spring. So you'd better get back to work right away.'

'But look at me, you silly man,' Sally said, laughing. 'How do you expect me to –'

'Don't be so feeble,' said Simon, tapping her plaster cast. 'It's your leg that's out of action, not your arm.'

Sally grinned and looked up to see her parents standing at the end of the bed.

'Is this Tony?' her mother asked.

'Good heavens no, Mother,' laughed Sally. 'This is Simon. He's far more important. Mind you,' she confessed, 'I made the same mistake the first time I met him.'

TIMEO DANAOS...

Aʀɴᴏʟᴅ ʙᴀᴄᴏɴ ᴡᴏᴜʟᴅ ʜᴀᴠᴇ ᴍᴀᴅᴇ ᴀ
fortune if he hadn't taken his father's advice.

Arnold's occupation, as described in his passport, was
'banker'. For those of you who are pedantic about such
matters, he was the branch manager of Barclays Bank
in St Albans, Hertfordshire, which in banking circles is
about the equivalent of being a captain in the Royal
Army Pay Corps.

His passport also stated that he was born in 1937,
was five feet nine inches tall, with sandy hair and no
distinguishing marks – although in fact he had several
lines on his forehead, which served only to prove that
he frowned a great deal.

He was a member of the local Rotary Club (Hon.
Treasurer), the Conservative Party (Branch Vice-
Chairman), and was a past Secretary of the St Albans
Festival. He had also played rugby for the Old Albanians
2nd XV in the 1960s and cricket for St Albans C.C. in
the 1970s. His only exercise for the past two decades,
however, had been the occasional round of golf with
his opposite number from the National Westminster.
Arnold did not boast a handicap.

During these excursions round the golf course Arnold
would often browbeat his opponent with his conviction
that he should never have been a banker in the first
place. After years of handing out loans to customers
who wanted to start up their own businesses, he had
become painfully aware that he himself was really one
of nature's born entrepreneurs. If only he hadn't listened
to his father's advice and followed him into the bank,
heaven knows what heights he might have reached by
now.

His colleague nodded wearily, then holed a seven-foot
putt, ensuring that the drinks would not be on him.

'How's Deirdre?' he asked as the two men strolled
towards the clubhouse.

'Wants to buy a new dinner service,' said Arnold,
which slightly puzzled his companion. 'Not that I can
see what's wrong with our old Coronation set.'

When they reached the bar, Arnold checked his watch
before ordering half a pint of lager for himself and a gin
and tonic for the victor, as Deirdre wouldn't be expecting
him back for at least an hour. He stopped pontificating
only when another member began telling them the latest
rumours about the club captain's wife.

Deirdre Bacon, Arnold's long-suffering wife, had
come to accept that her husband was now too set in his
ways for her to hope for any improvement. Although
she had her own opinions on what would have happened
to Arnold if he hadn't followed his father's advice, she
no longer voiced them. At the time of their engagement
she had considered Arnold Bacon 'quite a catch'. But as

the years passed, she had become more realistic about her expectations, and after two children, one of each sex, she had settled into the life of a housewife and mother – not that anything else had ever been seriously contemplated.

The children had now grown up, Justin to become a solicitor's clerk in Chelmsford, and Virginia to marry a local boy whom Arnold described as an official with British Rail. Deirdre, more accurately, told her friends at the hairdresser's that Keith was a train driver.

For the first ten years of their marriage, the Bacons had holidayed in Bournemouth, because Arnold's parents had always done so. They only graduated to the Costa del Sol after Arnold read in the *Daily Telegraph*'s 'Sun Supplement' that that was where most bank managers were to be found during the month of August.

For many years Arnold had promised his wife that they would do 'something special' when it came to celebrating their twenty-fifth wedding anniversary, though he had never actually committed himself to defining what 'special' meant.

It was only when he read in the bank's quarterly staff magazine that Andrew Buxton, the Chairman of Barclays, would be spending his summer sailing around the Greek islands on a private yacht that Arnold began writing off to numerous cruise companies and travel agents, requesting copies of their brochures. After having studied hundreds of glossy pages, he settled on a seven-day cruise aboard the *Princess Corina*, starting out from Piraeus to sail around the Greek islands, ending up at

Mykonos. Deirdre's only contribution to the discussion was that she would rather go back to the Costa del Sol, and spend the money they saved on a new dinner service. She was delighted, however, to read in one of the brochures that the Greeks were famous for their pottery.

By the time they boarded the coach to Heathrow, Arnold's junior staff, fellow members of the Rotary Club, and even a few of his more select customers were becoming tired of being reminded of how Arnold would be spending his summer break. 'I shall be sailing around the Greek islands on a liner,' he would tell them. 'Not unlike the bank's Chairman, Andrew Buxton, you know.' If anyone asked Deirdre what she and Arnold were doing for their holidays, she said that they were going on a seven-day package tour, and that the one thing she hoped to come home with was a new dinner service.

The old 'Coronation' service that had been given to them by Deirdre's parents as a wedding gift some twenty-five years before was now sadly depleted. Several of the plates were chipped or broken, while the pattern of crowns and sceptres on the pieces that were still serviceable had almost faded away.

'I can't see what's wrong with it myself,' said Arnold when his wife raised the subject once more as they waited in the departure lounge at Heathrow. Deirdre made no effort to list its defects again.

Arnold spent most of the flight to Athens complaining that the aircraft was full of Greeks. Deirdre didn't feel it was worth pointing out to him that, if one booked a passage with Olympic Airways, that was likely to be the outcome. She also knew his reply would be, 'But it saved us twenty-four pounds.'

Once they had landed at Hellenikon International Airport, the two holidaymakers climbed aboard a bus. Arnold doubted whether it would have passed its MOT in St Albans, but nevertheless it somehow managed to transport them into the centre of Athens, where Arnold had booked them overnight into a two-star hotel (two Greek stars). Arnold quickly found the local branch of Barclays and cashed one of his travellers' cheques, explaining to his wife that there was no point in changing more, as once they were on board the liner everything had already been paid for. He was sure that was how entrepreneurs conducted themselves.

The Bacons rose early the following morning, mainly because they hadn't been able to get a great deal of sleep. Their bodies had continually rolled to the centre of the lumpy concave mattress, and their ears ached after a night resting on the brick-hard convex pillows. Even before the sun had risen, Arnold jumped out of bed and threw open the little window that looked out onto a back yard. He stretched his arms and declared he had never felt better. Deirdre didn't comment, as she was already busy packing their clothes.

Over breakfast – a meal consisting of a croissant, which Arnold felt was too sticky, and which in any case fell apart in his fingers, feta cheese, which he didn't care for the smell of, and an obstinately empty cup, because the management refused to serve tea – a long debate developed between them as to whether they should hire a taxi or take a bus to the liner. They both came to the conclusion that a taxi would be more sensible, Deirdre because she didn't want to be crammed into a hot bus with a lot of sweaty Athenians, and Arnold because he wanted to be seen arriving at the gangplank in a car.

Once Arnold had settled their bill – having checked the little row of figures presented to him three times before he was willing to part with another travellers' cheque – he hailed a taxi and instructed the driver to take them to the quayside. The longer than expected journey, in an ancient car with no air conditioning, did not put Arnold into a good humour.

When he first set eyes on the *Princess Corina*, Arnold was unable to mask his disappointment. The ship was neither as large nor as modern as it had appeared in the glossy brochure. He had a feeling his Chairman would not be experiencing the same problem.

Mr and Mrs Bacon ascended the gangplank and were escorted to their cabin, which to Arnold's dismay consisted of two bunks, a washbasin, a shower and a porthole, without even enough room between the bunks for both of them to be able to undress at the same time. Arnold pointed out to his wife that this particular cabin had certainly not been illustrated in the brochure, even if it had been described on the tariff by the encomium 'De Luxe'. The brochure must have been put together by an out-of-work estate agent, he concluded.

Arnold set out to take a turn around the deck – not a particularly lengthy excursion. On the way he bumped

into a solicitor from Chester who had been innocently
strolling with his wife in the opposite direction. After
Arnold had established that Malcolm Jackson was a
senior partner in his firm, and his wife Joan was a magistrate, he suggested they should join up for lunch.

Once they had selected their meal from the buffet,
Arnold lost no time in telling his new-found friends that
he was a born entrepreneur, explaining, for example,
the immediate changes he would make to improve
efficiency on the *Princess Corina* had he been the chairman of this particular shipping line. (The list, I fear,
turned out to be far too long to include in a short story.)

The solicitor, who had not had to suffer any of
Arnold's opinions before, seemed quite content to listen,
while Deirdre chatted away to Joan about how she was
hoping to find a new dinner service on one of the islands.
'The Greeks are famous for their pottery, you know,'
she kept saying.

The conversation didn't vary a great deal when the
two couples reunited over dinner that evening.

Although the Bacons were tired after their first day
on board, neither of them slept for more than a few
moments that night. But Arnold was unwilling to admit,
as they bobbed across the Aegean in their little cabin,
that given the choice he would have preferred the two-
star hotel (two Greek stars), with its lumpy mattress and
brick-hard pillows, to the bunks on which they were
now being tossed from side to side.

After two days at sea the ship docked at Rhodes, and
by then even Arnold had stopped describing it as a

'liner'. Most of the passengers piled off down the gangway, only too delighted to have the chance of spending
a few hours on land.

Arnold and Malcolm beat a path to the nearest Barclays Bank to cash a travellers' cheque each, while
Deirdre and Joan set off in the opposite direction in
search of a dinner service. At the bank, Arnold immediately informed the manager who he was, ensuring that
both he and Malcolm received a tiny improvement on
the advertised rate of exchange.

Arnold smiled as they stepped out of the bank, and
onto the hot, dusty, cobbled street. 'I should have gone
into futures trading, you know,' he told Malcolm as
they sauntered off down the hill. 'I would have made a
fortune.'

Deirdre's quest for a dinner service didn't turn out to
be quite so straightforward. The shops were numerous
and varied in quality, and she quickly discovered that
Rhodes boasted a great many potters. It was therefore
necessary for her to establish which of them was the
most highly regarded by the locals, and then find the
shop that sold his work. This information was gained
by talking to the old women dressed in black who could
be found sitting silently on the street corners, about one
in ten of whom, she discovered, had some broken English. While her husband was at the bank saving a few
drachmas, Deirdre managed to find out all the inside
information she required.

The four of them met up at a small taverna in the
centre of the town for lunch. Over a plate of souvlakia

Arnold tried to convince Deirdre that as they were visiting five islands in the course of the trip, it might perhaps be wise to wait until their final port of call, so they could purchase the dinner service at the last possible moment.

'Prices will undoubtedly fall,' declared Arnold, 'the closer we get to Athens.' He spoke with the air of a true entrepreneur.

Although Deirdre had already seen a thirty-two-piece set she liked, at a price well within their budget, she reluctantly agreed to Arnold's suggestion. Her acquiescence was largely brought about by the fact that it was her husband who was in possession of all the travellers' cheques.

By the time the ship had docked at Heraklion on Crete, Arnold had vetted all the British nationals on board, and had permitted a Major (Territorial Reserve) and his spouse to join their table for lunch – but only after discovering that the fellow held an account at Barclays. A dinner invitation followed once it had been established that the Major occasionally played bridge with Arnold's area manager.

From that moment Arnold spent many happy hours at the bar explaining to the Major or to Malcolm – neither of whom actually listened any longer – why he should never have taken his father's advice and followed him into the bank, as he was after all one of nature's born entrepreneurs.

By the time the ship had weighed anchor and sailed from Santorini, Deirdre knew exactly the type of dinner service she wanted, and how to establish quickly which potter she should trade with as soon as they set foot in a new port. But Arnold continued to insist that they should wait for the bigger market as they approached Athens – 'More competition, forces prices down,' he explained for the umpteenth time. Deirdre knew there was no point in telling him that prices seemed to be rising with each sea-mile they covered on their journey back towards the Greek capital.

Páros only served as further proof of Deirdre's suspicions – if proof were still needed – as the prices there were noticeably steeper than they had been on Santorini. As the *Princess Corina* steamed on towards Mykonos, Deirdre felt that although their final port of call would probably be able to supply her with a satisfactory dinner service, it would surely no longer be at a price they could afford.

Arnold kept assuring her, with the confidence of a man who knows about such things, that all would be well. He even tapped the side of his nose with his forefinger. The Major and Malcolm had reached the stage of simply nodding at him to indicate that they were still awake.

Deirdre was among the first down the gangplank when they docked at Mykonos that Friday morning. She had told her husband that she would carry out a recce of the pottery shops while he did the same with the banks. Joan and the Major's wife were happy to accompany Deirdre, as by now she had become something of an expert on the subject of Greek pottery.

The three ladies began their search at the north end of the town, and Deirdre was relieved to find that there was a greater variety of shops in Mykonos than there had been on any of the other islands. She was also able to discover, with the help of several black-clad ladies, that the town boasted a potter of genuine fame, whose work could only be purchased from one shop, The House of Pétros.

Once Deirdre had located this establishment, she spent the rest of the morning inspecting all the dinner services they had to offer. After a couple of hours she came to the conclusion that the 'Delphi' set which was prominently displayed in the centre of the shop would be a prized possession for any housewife in St Albans. But as it was double the cost of anything she had seen on any of the other islands, she knew that Arnold would dismiss it as being out of their price range.

As the three ladies finally left the shop to join their husbands for lunch, a good-looking young man in a grubby T-shirt and torn jeans, with a couple of days' stubble on his chin, jumped out in front of them and asked, 'You English?'

Deirdre stopped and stared into his deep blue eyes for a moment, but said nothing. Her companions stepped out into the cobbled road and quickened their pace, pretending it was not them to whom the stranger had spoken. Deirdre smiled at him as he stood to one side, allowing her to continue on her way. Arnold had warned her never to engage in conversation with the natives.

When they reached ρεγγα κοκκινη, the restaurant at

which they'd arranged to meet up for lunch, the three ladies found their husbands drinking imported lager at the bar. Arnold was explaining to the Major and Malcolm why he had refused to pay his subscription to the Conservative Party that year. 'Not a penny will I part with,' he insisted, 'while they can't get their own house in order.' Deirdre suspected that his unwillingness to pay had rather more to do with his recent defeat when he had stood as Chairman of the local branch.

Arnold passed the next hour offering his views on everything from defence cuts to New Age travellers to single-parent families, all of which he was resolutely against. When the bill for lunch was finally presented, he spent some considerable time working out what each of them had eaten, and therefore how much they should contribute towards the total.

Arnold had already resigned himself to the fact that he would have to allocate part of his afternoon to bargaining on Deirdre's behalf, now that she had finally found the dinner service she had set her heart on. Everyone else had agreed to come along and watch the born entrepreneur at work.

When Arnold entered The House of Pétros, he had to admit that Deirdre seemed to have 'located the correct establishment'. He kept repeating this observation, as if to prove that he had been right all along to insist that she wait until their final port of call before the big decision was taken. He seemed blissfully unaware of how the price of pottery had increased from island to island, and Deirdre made no attempt to enlighten him.

She simply guided him over to the 'Delphi' service displayed on a large table in the centre of the room, and prayed. They all agreed it was quite magnificent, but when Arnold was told the price, he shook his head sadly. Deirdre would have protested, but she, like so many of the bank's customers over the years, had seen that look on her husband's face before. She therefore resigned herself to settling for the 'Pharos' set – excellent, but unquestionably second best, and far more expensive than comparable sets had been on any of the other four islands.

The three wives began selecting the pieces they would like to buy, while their husbands gravely reminded them how much they could afford. The choices having been made, Arnold spent a considerable time haggling with the shopkeeper. He finally managed to get a twenty per cent discount on the total. Once the figure had been established, Arnold was dispatched to find an English bank at which he could change the necessary travellers' cheques. With passports and signed cheques in hand, he left the shop to carry out his mission.

As he stepped onto the pavement, the young man who had approached Deirdre leaped into his path and asked, 'You English?'

'Naturally,' replied Arnold, sidestepping him and marching on briskly in order to avoid any further conversation with such a scruffy individual. As he had told the Major over lunch, '*Timeo Danaos et dona ferentis.*' It was the one snippet of Latin he could still recall from his schooldays.

When he had selected a bank, Arnold marched straight into the manager's office and changed everyone's cheques at a minutely better rate than the one displayed on the board in the window. Pleased with his saving of fifty drachmas, he headed back to The House of Pétros.

He was displeased to find the young man was still loitering on the pavement outside the shop. Arnold refused to favour the unshaven ruffian with even a glance, but he did catch the words, 'You want to save money, Englishman?'

Arnold stopped in his tracks, as any born entrepreneur would, and turned to study more closely the loutish youth who had addressed him. He was about to continue on his way when the young man said, 'I know where pottery is everything half price.'

Arnold hesitated once again, and looked through the shop window to see his companions standing around waiting for his return; on the counter stood six large packages, already wrapped up and awaiting payment.

Arnold turned back to take a closer look at the inarticulate foreigner.

'Potter comes from village called Kalafatis,' he said. 'Bus journey only half hour, then everything half price.'

While Arnold was digesting this piece of information, the young Greek's hand shot out hopefully. Arnold extracted a fifty-drachma note from the roll of money he had obtained at the bank, willing to speculate with the profit he had made on that particular transaction in exchange for the information he had just acquired – the act of a true entrepreneur, he thought as he marched triumphantly into the shop.

'I have made an important discovery,' he announced, and beckoned them all into a corner to impart his inside information.

Deirdre did not seem at all convinced, until Arnold suggested, 'Perhaps we might even be able to afford the "Delphi" set you hankered after, my dear. In any case, why pay double, when the only sacrifice you need to make is a half-hour bus journey.'

Malcolm nodded his agreement, as if listening to sage advice from senior counsel, and even the Major, though grumbling a little, finally fell into line.

'As we set sail for Athens early this evening,' declared the Major, 'we ought to take the next bus to Kalafatis.' Arnold nodded, and without another word led his little band out of the shop, not even glancing towards the packages that were left behind on the counter.

When they stepped out onto the street, Arnold was relieved to find that the young man who had given him the tip-off was no longer to be seen.

They came to a halt at the bus stop, where Arnold was a little disappointed to discover several passengers from the ship already standing in the queue, but he persuaded himself that they would not be heading for the same destination. They waited in the hot sun for another forty minutes before a bus eventually pulled up. When Arnold first saw the vehicle, his heart sank. 'Just think of how much money we'll be saving,' he said when he noticed the looks of despair on the faces of his companions.

The journey across the island to the east coast might well have taken thirty minutes had it been in a Range Rover with no reason to slow down. But as the bus driver picked up everybody he saw along the way, without regard to official stops, they eventually arrived in Kalafatis an hour and twenty minutes later. Long before they had clambered off the ancient vehicle Deirdre was exhausted, Joan was exasperated, and the Major's wife was developing a migraine.

'Bus goes no further,' said the driver as Arnold and his companions filed off. 'Leave for return journey to Khóra one hour. Last bus of the day.'

The little band gazed up at the narrow, winding track that led to the potter's workplace.

'The journey was worth it for the view alone,' gasped Arnold, as he came to a halt halfway along the path and gazed out over the Aegean. His companions didn't even bother to stop and look, let alone offer an opinion. It took them another ten minutes of determined walking before they reached their destination, and by then even Arnold had fallen silent.

As the six weary tourists finally entered the pottery, what breath they had left was taken away. They stood mesmerised by shelf after shelf of beautiful objects. Arnold felt a warm glow of triumph.

Deirdre immediately went about her business, and quickly located the 'Delphi' dinner service. It looked even more magnificent than she remembered, but

when she checked a little label that hung from a soup
tureen's handle she was horrified to discover that the cost
was only a little less than it had been at The House of
Pétros.

Deirdre came to a decision. She turned to face her
husband, who was toying with a pipe stand, and declared
in a clarion voice that all could hear, 'As everything is
at half price, Arnold, presumably I can go ahead and buy
the "Delphi"?'

The other four swung round to see how the great
entrepreneur would react. Arnold seemed to hesitate for
a moment before he placed the pipe stand back on the
shelf and said, 'Of course, my dear. Isn't that why we
came all this way in the first place?'

The three women immediately began selecting items
from the shelves, finally gathering between them one
dinner service, two tea sets, one coffee set, three vases,
five ashtrays, two jugs and a toast rack. Arnold abandoned the pipe stand.

When the bill for Deirdre's purchases was presented
to her husband he hesitated once again, but he was painfully aware that all five of his shipmates were glaring
at him. He reluctantly cashed his remaining travellers'
cheques, unwilling to bring himself even to glance at
the disadvantageous exchange rate that was displayed
in the window. Deirdre made no comment. Malcolm
and the Major silently signed away their own travellers'
cheques, with little appearance of triumph showing on
either of their faces.

The goods having been paid for, the six tourists

emerged from the workshop, laden down with carrier bags. As they began to retrace their steps back down the winding track, the door of the pottery was closed behind them.

'We'll have to get a move on if we're not going to miss the last bus,' shouted Arnold as he stepped into the centre of the path, avoiding a large cream Mercedes that was parked outside the workshop. 'But what a worthwhile excursion,' he added as they trundled off down the track. 'You have to admit, I saved you all a fortune.'

Deirdre was the last to leave the shop. She paused to rearrange her numerous bags, and was surprised to see a number of the pottery's staff forming a queue at a table by the side of the shop. A handsome young man in a grubby T-shirt and torn jeans was presenting each of them in turn with a small brown envelope.

Deirdre couldn't take her eyes off the young man. Where had she seen him before? He looked up, and for a moment she stared into those deep blue eyes. And then she remembered. The young man shrugged his shoulders and smiled. Deirdre returned the smile, picked up her bags and set off down the path after her companions.

As they clambered onto the bus, Deirdre was just in time to hear Arnold declare: 'You know, Major, I should never have taken my father's advice and settled for the life of a banker. You see, I'm one of nature's born entre . . .'

Deirdre smiled again as she looked out of the window

and watched the good-looking young man speed past them in his large cream Mercedes.

He smiled and waved to her as the last bus began its slow journey back to Mykonos.

AN EYE FOR AN EYE

SIR MATTHEW ROBERTS QC CLOSED THE
file and placed it on the desk in front of him. He was
not a happy man. He was quite willing to defend Mary
Banks, but he was not at all confident about her plea of
not guilty.

Sir Matthew leaned back in his deep leather chair to
consider the case while he awaited the arrival of the
instructing solicitor who had briefed him, and the junior
counsel he had selected for the case. As he gazed out
over the Middle Temple courtyard, he only hoped he
had made the right decision.

On the face of it, the case of Regina v. Banks was a
simple one of murder; but after what Bruce Banks
had subjected his wife to during the eleven years of
their marriage, Sir Matthew was confident not only
that he could get the charge reduced to manslaughter,
but that if the jury was packed with women, he might
even secure an acquittal. There was, however, a
complication.

He lit a cigarette and inhaled deeply, something his
wife had always chided him for. He looked at Victoria's
photograph on the desk in front of him. It reminded

him of his youth: but then, Victoria would always be young – death had ensured that.

Reluctantly, he forced his mind back to his client and her plea of mitigation. He reopened the file. Mary Banks was claiming that she couldn't possibly have chopped her husband up with an axe and buried him under the pigsty, because at the time of his death she was not only a patient in the local hospital, but was also blind. As Sir Matthew inhaled deeply once again, there was a knock on the door.

'Come in,' he bellowed – not because he liked the sound of his own voice, but because the doors of his chambers were so thick that if he didn't holler, no one would ever hear him.

Sir Matthew's clerk opened the door and announced Mr Bernard Casson and Mr Hugh Witherington. Two very different men, thought Sir Matthew as they entered the room, but each would serve the purpose he had planned for them in this particular case.

Bernard Casson was a solicitor of the old school – formal, punctilious, and always painstakingly correct. His conservatively tailored herringbone suit never seemed to change from one year to the next; Matthew often wondered if he had purchased half a dozen such suits in a closing-down sale and wore a different one every day of the week. He peered up at Casson over his half-moon spectacles. The solicitor's thin moustache and neatly parted hair gave him an old-fashioned look that had fooled many an opponent into thinking he had a second-class mind. Sir Matthew regularly gave thanks that his friend was no orator, because if Bernard had been a barrister, Matthew would not have relished the prospect of opposing him in court.

A pace behind Casson stood his junior counsel for this brief, Hugh Witherington. The Lord must have been feeling particularly ungenerous on the day Witherington entered the world, as He had given him neither looks nor brains. If He had bestowed any other talents on him, they were yet to be revealed. After several attempts Witherington had finally been called to the Bar, but for the number of briefs he was offered, he would have had a more regular income had he signed on for the dole. Sir Matthew's clerk had raised an eyebrow when the name of Witherington had been mooted as junior counsel in the case, but Sir Matthew just smiled, and had not offered an explanation.

Sir Matthew rose, stubbed out his cigarette, and ushered the two men towards the vacant chairs on the other side of his desk. He waited for both of them to settle before he proceeded.

'Kind of you to attend chambers, Mr Casson,' he said, although they both knew that the solicitor was doing no more than holding with the traditions of the Bar.

'My pleasure, Sir Matthew,' replied the elderly solicitor, bowing slightly to show that he still appreciated the old courtesies.

'I don't think you know Hugh Witherington, my junior in this case,' said Sir Matthew, gesturing towards the undistinguished young barrister.

Witherington nervously touched the silk handkerchief in his breast pocket.

'No, I hadn't had the pleasure of Mr Witherington's acquaintance until we met in the corridor a few moments ago,' said Casson. 'May I say how delighted I am that you have been willing to take on this case, Sir Matthew?'

Matthew smiled at his friend's formality. He knew Bernard would never dream of calling him by his Christian name while junior counsel was present. 'I'm only too happy to be working with you again, Mr Casson. Even if you have presented me on this occasion with something of a challenge.'

The conventional pleasantries over, the elderly solicitor removed a brown file from his battered Gladstone bag. 'I have had a further consultation with my client since I last saw you,' he said as he opened the file, 'and I took the opportunity to pass on your opinion. But I fear Mrs Banks remains determined to plead not guilty.'

'So she is still protesting her innocence?'

'Yes, Sir Matthew. Mrs Banks emphatically claims that she couldn't have committed the murder because she had been blinded by her husband some days before he died, and in any case, at the time of his death she was registered as a patient at the local hospital.'

'The pathologist's report is singularly vague about the time of death,' Sir Matthew reminded his old friend. 'After all, they didn't discover the body for at least a couple of weeks. As I understand it, the police feel the murder could have been committed twenty-four or even forty-eight hours before Mrs Banks was taken to the hospital.'

'I have also read their report, Sir Matthew,' Casson replied, 'and informed Mrs Banks of its contents. But she remains adamant that she is innocent, and that the jury will be persuaded of it. "Especially with Sir Matthew Roberts as my defender," were the exact words she used, if I remember correctly,' he added with a smile.

'I am not seduced, Mr Casson,' said Sir Matthew, lighting another cigarette.

'You did promise Victoria –' interjected the solicitor, lowering his shield, but only for a moment.

'So, I have one last chance to convince her,' said Sir Matthew, ignoring his friend's comment.

'And Mrs Banks has one last chance to convince you,' said Mr Casson.

'Touché,' said Sir Matthew, nodding his appreciation of the solicitor's neat riposte as he stubbed out his almost untouched cigarette. He felt he was losing this fencing match with his old friend, and that the time had come to go on the attack.

He returned to the open file on his desk. 'First,' he said, looking straight at Casson, as if his colleague were in the witness box, 'when the body was dug up, there were traces of your client's blood on the collar of the dead man's shirt.'

'My client accepts that,' said Casson, calmly checking his own notes. 'But . . .'

'Second,' said Sir Matthew before Casson had a chance to reply, 'when the instrument that had been used to chop up the body, an axe, was found the following day, a hair from Mrs Banks's head was discovered lodged in its handle.'

'We won't be denying that,' said Casson.

'We don't have a lot of choice,' said Sir Matthew, rising from his seat and beginning to pace around the room. 'And third, when the spade that was used to dig the victim's grave was finally discovered, your client's fingerprints were found all over it.'

'We can explain that as well,' said Casson.

'But will the jury accept our explanation,' asked Sir Matthew, his voice rising, 'when they learn that the murdered man had a long history of violence, that your client was regularly seen in the local village either bruised, or with a black eye, sometimes bleeding from cuts around the head – once even nursing a broken arm?'

'She has always stated that those injuries were sustained when working on the farm where her husband was manager.'

'That places a strain on my credulity which it's quite unable to withstand,' said Sir Matthew, as he finished circling the room and returned to his chair. 'And we are not helped by the fact that the only person known to have visited the farm regularly was the postman. Apparently everyone else in the village refused to venture beyond the front gate.' He flicked over another page of his notes.

'That might have made it easier for someone to come in and kill Banks,' suggested Witherington.

Sir Matthew was unable to hide his surprise as he

looked across at his junior, having almost forgotten that he was in the room. 'Interesting point,' he said, unwilling to stamp on Witherington while he still had it in his power to play the one trump card in this case.

'The next problem we face,' he went on, 'is that your client claims that she went blind after her husband struck her with a hot frying pan. Rather convenient, Mr Casson, wouldn't you say?'

'The scar can still be seen clearly on the side of my client's face,' said Casson. 'And the doctor remains convinced that she is indeed blind.'

'Doctors are easier to convince than prosecuting counsels and world-weary judges, Mr Casson,' said Sir Matthew, turning another page of his file. 'Next, when samples from the body were examined – and God knows who was willing to carry out that particular task – the quantity of strychnine found in the blood would have felled a bull elephant.'

'That was only the opinion of the Crown's pathologists,' said Mr Casson.

'And one I will find hard to refute in court,' said Sir Matthew, 'because counsel for the prosecution will undoubtedly ask Mrs Banks to explain why she purchased four grams of strychnine from an agricultural supplier in Reading shortly before her husband's death. If I were in his position, I would repeat that question over and over again.'

'Possibly,' said Casson, checking his notes, 'but she has explained that they had been having a problem with rats, which had been killing the chickens, and she feared

321

for the other animals on the farm, not to mention their nine-year-old son.'

'Ah, yes, Rupert. But he was away at boarding school at the time, was he not?' Sir Matthew paused. 'You see, Mr Casson, my problem is a simple one.' He closed his file. 'I don't believe her.'

Casson raised an eyebrow.

'Unlike her husband, Mrs Banks is a very clever woman. Witness the fact that she has already fooled several people into believing this incredible story. But I can tell you, Mr Casson, that she isn't going to fool me.'

'But what can we do, Sir Matthew, if Mrs Banks insists that this is her case, and asks us to defend her accordingly?' asked Casson.

Sir Matthew rose again and paced around the room silently, coming to a halt in front of the solicitor. 'Not a lot, I agree,' he said, reverting to a more conciliatory tone. 'But I do wish I could convince the dear lady to plead guilty to manslaughter. We'd be certain to gain the sympathy of any jury, after what she's been put through. And we can always rely on some women's group or other to picket the court throughout the hearing. Any judge who passed a harsh sentence on Mary Banks would be described as chauvinistic and sexually discriminatory by every newspaper leader writer in the land. I'd have her out of prison in a matter of weeks. No, Mr Casson, we *must* get her to change her plea.'

'But how can we hope to do that, when she remains so adamant that she is innocent?' asked Casson.

A smile flickered across Sir Matthew's face. 'Mr Witherington and I have a plan, don't we, Hugh?' he said, turning to Witherington for a second time.

'Yes, Sir Matthew,' replied the young barrister, sounding pleased to at last have his opinion sought, even in this rudimentary way. As Sir Matthew volunteered no clue as to the plan, Casson did not press the point.

'So, when do I come face to face with our client?' asked Sir Matthew, turning his attention back to the solicitor.

'Would eleven o'clock on Monday morning be convenient?' asked Casson.

'Where is she at the moment?' asked Sir Matthew, thumbing through his diary.

'Holloway,' replied Casson.

'Then we will be at Holloway at eleven on Monday morning,' said Sir Matthew. 'And to be honest with you, I can't wait to meet Mrs Mary Banks. That woman must have real guts, not to mention imagination. Mark my words, Mr Casson, she'll prove a worthy opponent for any counsel.'

When Sir Matthew entered the interviewing room of Holloway Prison and saw Mary Banks for the first time, he was momentarily taken aback. He knew from his file on the case that she was thirty-seven, but the frail, grey-haired woman who sat with her hands resting in her lap looked nearer fifty. Only when he studied her fine cheekbones and slim figure did he see that she might once have been a beautiful woman.

Sir Matthew allowed Casson to take the seat opposite her at a plain formica table in the centre of an otherwise empty, cream-painted brick room. There was a small, barred window halfway up the wall that threw a shaft of light onto their client. Sir Matthew and his junior took their places on either side of the instructing solicitor. Leading counsel noisily poured himself a cup of coffee.

'Good morning, Mrs Banks,' said Casson.

'Good morning, Mr Casson,' she replied, turning slightly to face the direction from which the voice had come. 'You have brought someone with you.'

'Yes, Mrs Banks, I am accompanied by Sir Matthew Roberts QC, who will be acting as your defence counsel.'

She gave a slight bow of the head as Sir Matthew rose from his chair, took a pace forward and said, 'Good morning, Mrs Banks,' then suddenly thrust out his right hand.

'Good morning, Sir Matthew,' she replied, without moving a muscle, still looking in Casson's direction. 'I'm delighted that you will be representing me.'

'Sir Matthew would like to ask you a few questions, Mrs Banks,' said Casson, 'so that he can decide what might be the best approach in your case. He will assume the role of counsel for the prosecution, so that you can get used to what it will be like when you go into the witness box.'

'I understand,' replied Mrs Banks. 'I shall be happy to answer any of Sir Matthew's questions. I'm sure it won't prove difficult for someone of his eminence to show that a frail, blind woman would be incapable of chopping up a vicious sixteen-stone man.'

'Not if that vicious sixteen-stone man was poisoned before he was chopped up,' said Sir Matthew quietly.

'Which would be quite an achievement for someone lying in a hospital bed five miles from where the crime was committed,' replied Mrs Banks.

'If indeed that *was* when the crime was committed,' responded Sir Matthew. 'You claim your blindness was caused by a blow to the side of your head.'

'Yes, Sir Matthew. My husband picked up the frying pan from the stove while I was cooking breakfast, and struck me with it. I ducked, but the edge of the pan caught me on the left side of my face.' She touched a scar above her left eye that looked as if it would remain with her for the rest of her life.

'And then what happened?'

'I passed out and collapsed onto the kitchen floor. When I came to I could sense someone else was in the room. But I had no idea who it was until he spoke, when I recognised the voice of Jack Pembridge, our postman. He carried me to his van and drove me to the local hospital.'

'And it was while you were in hospital that the police discovered your husband's body?'

'That is correct, Sir Matthew. After I had been in Parkmead for nearly two weeks, I asked the vicar, who had been to visit me every day, to try and find out how Bruce was coping without me.'

'Did you not think it surprising that your husband

hadn't been to see you once during the time you were in hospital?' asked Sir Matthew, who began slowly pushing his cup of coffee towards the edge of the table.

'No. I had threatened to leave him on several occasions, and I don't think . . .' The cup fell off the table and shattered noisily on the stone floor. Sir Matthew's eyes never left Mrs Banks.

She jumped nervously, but did not turn to look in the direction of the broken cup.

'Are you all right, Mr Casson?' she asked.

'My fault,' said Sir Matthew. 'How clumsy of me.'

Casson suppressed a smile. Witherington remained unmoved.

'Please continue,' said Sir Matthew as he bent down and began picking up the pieces of china scattered across the floor. 'You were saying, "I don't think . . ."'

'Oh, yes,' said Mrs Banks. 'I don't think Bruce would have cared whether I returned to the farm or not.'

'Quite so,' said Sir Matthew after he had placed the broken pieces on the table. 'But can you explain to me why the police found one of your hairs on the handle of the axe that was used to dismember your husband's body?'

'Yes, Sir Matthew, I can. I was chopping up some wood for the stove before I prepared his breakfast.'

'Then I am bound to ask why there were no finger-prints on the handle of the axe, Mrs Banks.'

'Because I was wearing gloves, Sir Matthew. If you had ever worked on a farm in mid-October, you would know only too well how cold it can be at five in the morning.'

This time Casson did allow himself to smile.

'But what about the blood found on your husband's collar? Blood that was shown by the Crown's forensic scientist to match your own.'

'You will find my blood on many things in that house, should you care to look closely, Sir Matthew.'

'And the spade, the one with your fingerprints all over it? Had you also been doing some digging before breakfast that morning?'

'No, but I would have had cause to use it every day the previous week.'

'I see,' said Sir Matthew. 'Let us now turn our attention to something I suspect you didn't do every day, namely the purchase of strychnine. First, Mrs Banks, why did you need such a large amount? And second, why did you have to travel twenty-seven miles to Reading to purchase it?'

'I shop in Reading every other Thursday,' Mrs Banks explained. 'There isn't an agricultural supplier any nearer.'

Sir Matthew frowned and rose from his chair. He began slowly to circle Mrs Banks, while Casson watched her eyes. They never moved.

When Sir Matthew was directly behind his client, he checked his watch. It was 11.17. He knew his timing had to be exact, because he had become uncomfortably aware that he was dealing not only with a clever woman, but also an extremely cunning one. Mind you, he reflected, anyone who had lived for eleven years with such a man as Bruce Banks would have had to be cunning simply to survive.

'You still haven't explained why you needed such a large amount of strychnine,' he said, remaining behind his client.

'We had been losing a lot of chickens,' Mrs Banks replied, still not moving her head. 'My husband thought it was rats, so he told me to get a large quantity of strychnine to finish them off. "Once and for all" were his exact words.'

'But as it turned out, it was he who was finished off, once and for all – and undoubtedly with the same poison,' said Sir Matthew quietly.

'I also feared for Rupert's safety,' said Mrs Banks, ignoring her counsel's sarcasm.

'But your son was away at school at the time, am I not correct?'

'Yes, you are, Sir Matthew, but he was due back for half term that weekend.'

'Have you ever used that supplier before?'

'Regularly,' said Mrs Banks, as Sir Matthew completed his circle and returned to face her once again. 'I go there at least once a month, as I'm sure the manager will confirm.' She turned her head and faced a foot or so to his right.

Sir Matthew remained silent, resisting the temptation to look at his watch. He knew it could only be a matter of seconds. A few moments later the door on the far side of the interview room swung open and a boy of about nine years of age entered. The three of them watched their client closely as the child walked silently towards her. Rupert Banks came to a halt in front of his mother and smiled, but received no response. He waited for a further ten seconds, then turned and walked back out, exactly as he had been instructed to do. Mrs Banks's eyes remained fixed somewhere between Sir Matthew and Mr Casson.

The smile on Casson's face was now almost one of triumph.

'Is there someone else in the room?' asked Mrs Banks. 'I thought I heard the door open.'

'No,' said Sir Matthew. 'Only Mr Casson and I are in the room.' Witherington still hadn't moved a muscle.

Sir Matthew began to circle Mrs Banks for what he knew had to be the last time. He had almost come to believe that he might have misjudged her. When he was directly behind her once again, he nodded to his junior, who remained seated in front of her.

Witherington removed the silk handkerchief from his breast pocket, slowly unfolded it, and laid it out flat on the table in front of him. Mrs Banks showed no reaction. Witherington stretched out the fingers of his right hand, bowed his head slightly, and paused before placing his right hand over his left eye. Without warning he plucked the eye out of its socket and placed it in the middle of the silk handkerchief. He left it on the table for a full thirty seconds, then began to polish it. Sir Matthew completed his circle, and observed beads of perspiration appearing on Mrs Banks's forehead as he sat down.

When Witherington had finished cleaning the almond-shaped glass object, he slowly raised his head until he was staring directly at her, then eased the eye back into its socket. Mrs Banks momentarily turned away. She quickly tried to compose herself, but it was too late.

Sir Matthew rose from his chair and smiled at his client. She returned the smile.

'I must confess, Mrs Banks,' he said, 'I would feel much more confident about a plea of guilty to manslaughter.'

ONE MAN'S MEAT...

COULD ANYONE BE THAT BEAUTIFUL?

I was driving round the Aldwych on my way to work when I first saw her. She was walking up the steps of the Aldwych Theatre. If I'd stared a moment longer I would have driven into the back of the car in front of me, but before I could confirm my fleeting impression she had disappeared into the throng of theatregoers.

I spotted a parking space on my left-hand side and swung into it at the last possible moment, without indicating, causing the vehicle behind me to let out several appreciative blasts. I leapt out of my car and ran back towards the theatre, realising how unlikely it was that I'd be able to find her in such a mêlée, and that even if I did, she was probably meeting a boyfriend or husband who would turn out to be about six feet tall and closely to resemble Harrison Ford.

Once I reached the foyer I scanned the chattering crowd. I slowly turned 360 degrees, but could see no sign of her. Should I try to buy a ticket? I wondered. But she could be seated anywhere – the stalls, the dress circle, even the upper circle. Perhaps I should walk up and down the aisles until I spotted her. But I realised I wouldn't be allowed into any part of the theatre unless I could produce a ticket.

And then I saw her. She was standing in a queue in front of the window marked 'Tonight's Performance', and was just one away from being attended to. There were two other customers, a young woman and a middle-aged man, waiting in line behind her. I quickly joined the queue, by which time she had reached the front. I leant forward and tried to overhear what she was saying, but I could only catch the box office manager's reply: 'Not much chance with the curtain going up in a few minutes' time, madam,' he was saying. 'But if you leave it with me, I'll see what I can do.'

She thanked him and walked off in the direction of the stalls. My first impression was confirmed. It didn't matter if you looked from the ankles up or from the head down – she was perfection. I couldn't take my eyes off her, and I noticed that she was having exactly the same effect on several other men in the foyer. I wanted to tell them all not to bother. Didn't they realise she was with me? Or rather, that she would be by the end of the evening.

After she had disappeared from view, I craned my neck to look into the booth. Her ticket had been placed to one side. I sighed with relief as the young woman two places ahead of me presented her credit card and picked up four tickets for the dress circle.

I began to pray that the man in front of me wasn't looking for a single.

ONE MAN'S MEAT . . .

'Do you have one ticket for tonight's performance?' he asked hopefully, as the three-minute bell sounded. The man in the booth smiled.

I scowled. Should I knife him in the back, kick him in the groin, or simply scream abuse at him?

'Where would you prefer to sit, sir? The dress circle or the stalls?'

'Don't say stalls,' I willed. 'Say Circle . . . Circle . . . Circle . . .'

'Stalls,' he said.

'I have one on the aisle in row H,' said the man in the box, checking the computer screen in front of him. I uttered a silent cheer as I realised that the theatre would be trying to sell off its remaining tickets before it bothered with returns handed in by members of the public. But then, I thought, how would I get around that problem?

By the time the man in front of me had bought the ticket on the end of row H, I had my lines well rehearsed, and just hoped I wouldn't need a prompt.

'Thank goodness. I thought I wasn't going to make it,' I began, trying to sound out of breath. The man in the ticket booth looked up at me, but didn't seem all that impressed by my opening line. 'It was the traffic. And then I couldn't find a parking space. My girlfriend may have given up on me. Did she by any chance hand in my ticket for resale?'

He looked unconvinced. My dialogue obviously wasn't gripping him. 'Can you describe her?' he asked suspiciously.

'Short-cropped dark hair, hazel eyes, wearing a red silk dress that . . .'

'Ah, yes. I remember her,' he said, almost sighing. He picked up the ticket by his side and handed it to me.

'Thank you,' I said, trying not to show my relief that he had come in so neatly on cue with the closing line from my first scene. As I hurried off in the direction of the stalls, I grabbed an envelope from a pile on the ledge beside the booth.

I checked the price of the ticket: twenty pounds. I extracted two ten-pound notes from my wallet, put them in the envelope, licked the flap and stuck it down.

The girl at the entrance to the stalls checked my ticket. 'F-11. Six rows from the front, on the right-hand side.'

I walked slowly down the aisle until I spotted her. She was sitting next to an empty place in the middle of the row. As I made my way over the feet of those who were already seated, she turned and smiled, obviously pleased to see that someone had purchased her spare ticket.

I returned the smile, handed over the envelope containing my twenty pounds, and sat down beside her. 'The man in the box office asked me to give you this.'

'Thank you.' She slipped the envelope into her evening bag. I was about to try the first line of my second scene on her, when the house lights faded and the curtain rose for Act One of the real performance. I suddenly realised that I had no idea what play I was

about to see. I glanced across at the programme on her
lap and read the words 'An Inspector Calls, by J.B.
Priestley'.

I remembered that the critics had been full of praise
for the production when it had originally opened at the
National Theatre, and had particularly singled out the
performance of Kenneth Cranham. I tried to concentrate
on what was taking place on stage.

The eponymous inspector was staring into a house in
which an Edwardian family were preparing for a dinner
to celebrate their daughter's engagement. 'I was thinking
of getting a new car,' the father was saying to his prospective son-in-law as he puffed away on his cigar.

At the mention of the word 'car', I suddenly
remembered that I had abandoned mine outside the
theatre. Was it on a double yellow line? Or worse? To
hell with it. They could have it in part-exchange for the
model sitting next to me. The audience laughed, so I
joined in, if only to give the impression that I was following the plot. But what about my original plans for the
evening? By now everyone would be wondering why I
hadn't turned up. I realised that I wouldn't be able to
leave the theatre during the interval, either to check on
my car or to make a phone call to explain my absence,
as that would be my one chance of developing my own
plot.

The play had the rest of the audience enthralled, but
I had already begun rehearsing the lines from my own
script, which would have to be performed during the
interval between Acts One and Two. I was painfully

aware that I would be restricted to fifteen minutes, and
that there would be no second night.

By the time the curtain came down at the end of the
first act, I was confident of my draft text. I waited for
the applause to die down before I turned towards her.

'What an original production,' I began. 'Quite mod-
ernistic.' I vaguely remembered that one of the critics
had followed that line. 'I was lucky to get a seat at the
last moment.'

'I was just as lucky,' she replied. I felt encouraged. 'I
mean, to find someone who was looking for a single
ticket at such short notice.'

I nodded. 'My name's Michael Whitaker.'

'Anna Townsend,' she said, giving me a warm smile.

'Would you like a drink?' I asked.

'Thank you,' she replied, 'that would be nice.' I stood
up and led her through the packed scrum that was heading towards the stalls bar, occasionally glancing back to
make sure she was still following me. I was somehow
expecting her no longer to be there, but each time I
turned to look she greeted me with the same radiant
smile.

'What would you like?' I asked, once I could make
out the bar through the crowd.

'A dry martini, please.'

'Stay here, and I'll be back in a moment,' I promised,
wondering just how many precious minutes would be
wasted while I had to wait at the bar. I took out a five-
pound note and held it up conspicuously, in the hope
that the prospect of a large tip might influence the bar-

man's sense of direction. He spotted the money, but I still had to wait for another four customers to be served before I managed to secure the dry martini and a Scotch on the rocks for myself. The barman didn't deserve the tip I left him, but I hadn't any more time to waste waiting for the change.

I carried the drinks back to the far corner of the foyer, where Anna stood studying her programme. She was silhouetted against a window, and in that stylish red silk dress, the light emphasised her slim, elegant figure.

I handed her the dry martini, aware that my limited time had almost run out.

'Thank you,' she said, giving me another disarming smile.

'How did you come to have a spare ticket?' I asked as she took a sip from her drink.

'My partner was held up on an emergency case at the last minute,' she explained. 'Just one of the problems of being a doctor.'

'Pity. They missed a quite remarkable production,' I prompted, hoping to tease out of her whether her partner was male or female.

'Yes,' said Anna. 'I tried to book seats when it was still at the National Theatre, but they were sold out for any performances I was able to make, so when a friend offered me two tickets at the last minute, I jumped at them. After all, it's coming off in a few weeks.' She took another sip from her martini. 'What about you?' she asked as the three-minute bell sounded.

There was no such line in my script.

'Me?'

'Yes, Michael,' she said, a hint of teasing in her voice. 'How did you come to be looking for a spare seat at the last moment?'

'Sharon Stone was tied up for the evening, and at the last second Princess Diana told me that she would have loved to have come, but she was trying to keep a low profile.' Anna laughed. 'Actually, I read some of the crits, and I dropped in on the off-chance of picking up a spare ticket.'

'And you picked up a spare woman as well,' said Anna, as the two-minute bell went. I wouldn't have dared to include such a bold line in her script – or was there a hint of mockery in those hazel eyes?

'I certainly did,' I replied lightly. 'So, are you a doctor as well?'

'As well as what?' asked Anna.

'As well as your partner,' I said, not sure if she was still teasing.

'Yes. I'm a GP in Fulham. There are three of us in the practice, but I was the only one who could escape tonight. And what do you do when you're not chatting up Sharon Stone or escorting Princess Diana to the theatre?'

'I'm in the restaurant business,' I told her.

'That must be one of the few jobs with worse hours and tougher working conditions than mine,' Anna said as the one-minute bell sounded.

I looked into those hazel eyes and wanted to say – Anna, let's forget the second act: I realise the play's superb, but all I want to do is spend the rest of the evening alone with you, not jammed into a crowded auditorium with eight hundred other people.

'Wouldn't you agree?'

I tried to recall what she had just said. 'I expect we get more customer complaints than you do,' was the best I could manage.

'I doubt it,' Anna said, quite sharply. 'If you're a woman in the medical profession and you don't cure your patients within a couple of days, they immediately want to know if you're fully qualified.'

I laughed, and finished my drink as a voice boomed over the Tannoy, 'Would the audience please take their seats for the second act. The curtain is about to rise.'

'We ought to be getting back,' Anna said, placing her empty glass on the nearest window ledge.

'I suppose so,' I said reluctantly, and led her in the opposite direction to the one in which I really wanted to take her.

'Thanks for the drink,' she said as we returned to our seats.

'Small recompense,' I replied. She glanced up at me questioningly. 'For such a good ticket,' I explained.

She smiled as we made our way along the row, stepping awkwardly over more toes. I was just about to risk a further remark when the house lights dimmed.

During the second act I turned to smile in Anna's direction whenever there was laughter, and was occasionally rewarded with a warm response. But my supreme moment of triumph came towards the end of

the act, when the detective showed the daughter a photograph of the dead woman. She gave a piercing scream,
and the stage lights were suddenly switched off.

Anna grabbed my hand, but quickly released it and
apologised.

'Not at all,' I whispered. 'I only just stopped myself
from doing the same thing.' In the darkened theatre, I
couldn't tell how she responded.

A moment later the phone on the stage rang. Everyone in the audience knew it must be the detective on
the other end of the line, even if they couldn't be sure
what he was going to say. That final scene had the whole
house gripped.

After the lights dimmed for the last time, the cast
returned to the stage and deservedly received a long
ovation, taking several curtain calls.

When the curtain was finally lowered, Anna turned
to me and said, 'What a remarkable production. I'm so
glad I didn't miss it. And I'm even more pleased that I
didn't have to see it alone.'

'Me too,' I told her, ignoring the fact that I'd never
planned to spend the evening at the theatre in the first
place.

We made our way up the aisle together as the audience
flowed out of the theatre like a slow-moving river. I
wasted those few precious moments discussing the
merits of the cast, the power of the director's interpret-
ation, the originality of the macabre set and even the
Edwardian costumes, before we reached the double doors
that led back out into the real world.

'Goodbye, Michael,' Anna said. 'Thank you for adding to my enjoyment of the evening.' She shook me by the hand.

'Goodbye,' I said, gazing once again into those hazel eyes.

She turned to go, and I wondered if I would ever see her again.

'Anna,' I said.

She glanced back in my direction.

'If you're not doing anything in particular, would you care to join me for dinner . . .'

Author's Note

At this point in the story, the reader is offered the choice of four different endings.

You might decide to read all four of them, or simply select one, and consider that your own particular ending. If you do choose to read all four, they should be taken in the order in which they have been written:

1 RARE

2 BURNT

3 OVERDONE

4 À POINT

Rare

'THANK YOU, MICHAEL. I'D LIKE THAT.'

I smiled, unable to mask my delight. 'Good. I know a little restaurant just down the road that I think you might enjoy.'

'That sounds fun,' Anna said, linking her arm in mine. I guided her through the departing throng.

As we strolled together down the Aldwych, Anna continued to chat about the play, comparing it favourably with a production she had seen at the Haymarket some years before.

When we reached the Strand I pointed to a large grey double door on the other side of the road. 'That's it,' I said. We took advantage of a red light to weave our way through the temporarily stationary traffic, and after we'd reached the far pavement I pushed one of the grey doors open to allow Anna through. It began to rain just as we stepped inside. I led her down a flight of stairs into a basement restaurant buzzing with the talk of people who had just come out of theatres, and waiters dashing, plates in both hands, from table to table.

'I'll be impressed if you can get a table here,' Anna said, eyeing a group of would-be customers who were clustered round the bar, impatiently waiting for someone to leave.

I strolled across to the reservations desk. The head waiter, who until that moment had been taking a customer's order, rushed over. 'Good evening, Mr Whitaker,' he said. 'How many are you?'

'Just the two of us.'

'Follow me, please, sir,' Mario said, leading us to my usual table in the far corner of the room.

'Another dry martini?' I asked her as we sat down.

'No, thank you,' she replied. 'I think I'll just have a glass of wine with the meal.'

I nodded my agreement, as Mario handed us our menus. Anna studied hers for a few moments before I asked if she had spotted anything she fancied.

'Yes,' she said, looking straight at me. 'But for now I think I'll settle for the fettucini, and a glass of red wine.'

'Good idea,' I said. 'I'll join you. But are you sure you won't have a starter?'

'No, thank you, Michael. I've reached that age when I can no longer order everything I'm tempted by.'

'Me too,' I confessed. 'I have to play squash three times a week to keep in shape,' I told her as Mario reappeared.

'Two fettucini,' I began, 'and a bottle of . . .'

'Half a bottle, please,' said Anna. 'I'll only have one glass. I've got an early start tomorrow morning, so I shouldn't overdo things.'

I nodded, and Mario scurried away.

I looked across the table and into Anna's eyes. 'I've always wondered about women doctors,' I said, immediately realising that the line was a bit feeble.

'You mean, you wondered if we're normal?'

'Something like that, I suppose.'

'Yes, we're normal enough, except every day we have to see a lot of men in the nude. I can assure you, Michael, most of them are overweight and fairly unattractive.'

I suddenly wished I were half a stone lighter. 'But are there many men who are brave enough to consider a woman doctor in the first place?'

'Quite a few,' said Anna, 'though most of my patients are female. But there are just about enough intelligent, sensible, uninhibited males around who can accept that a woman doctor might be just as likely to cure them as a man.'

I smiled as two bowls of fettucini were placed in front of us. Mario then showed me the label on the half-bottle he had selected. I nodded my approval. He had chosen a vintage to match Anna's pedigree.

'And what about you?' asked Anna. 'What does being "in the restaurant business" actually mean?'

'I'm on the management side,' I said, before sampling the wine. I nodded again, and Mario poured a glass for Anna and then topped up mine.

'Or at least, that's what I do nowadays. I started life as a waiter,' I said, as Anna began to sip her wine.

'What a magnificent wine,' she remarked. 'It's so good I may end up having a second glass.'

'I'm glad you like it,' I said. 'It's a Barolo.'

'You were saying, Michael? You started life as a waiter . . .'

'Yes, then I moved into the kitchens for about five years, and finally ended up on the management side. How's the fettucini?'

'It's delicious. Almost melts in your mouth.' She took another sip of her wine. 'So, if you're not cooking, and no longer a waiter, what do you do now?'

'Well, at the moment I'm running three restaurants in the West End, which means I never stop dashing from one to the other, depending on which is facing the biggest crisis on that particular day.'

'Sounds a bit like ward duty to me,' said Anna. 'So who turned out to have the biggest crisis today?'

'Today, thank heaven, was not typical,' I told her with feeling.

'That bad?' said Anna.

'Yes, I'm afraid so. We lost a chef this morning who cut off the top of his finger, and won't be back at work for at least a fortnight. My head waiter in our second restaurant is off, claiming he has 'flu, and I've just had to sack the barman in the third for fiddling the books. Barmen always fiddle the books, of course, but in this case even the customers began to notice what he was up to.' I paused. 'But I still wouldn't want to be in any other business.'

'In the circumstances, I'm amazed you were able to take the evening off.'

'I shouldn't have, really, and I wouldn't have,

except . . .' I trailed off as I leaned over and topped up Anna's glass.

'Except what?' she said.

'Do you want to hear the truth?' I asked as I poured the remains of the wine into my own glass.

'I'll try that for starters,' she said.

I placed the empty bottle on the side of the table, and hesitated, but only for a moment. 'I was driving to one of my restaurants earlier this evening, when I spotted you going into the theatre. I stared at you for so long that I nearly crashed into the back of the car in front of me. Then I swerved across the road into the nearest parking space, and the car behind almost crashed into me. I leapt out, ran all the way to the theatre, and searched everywhere until I saw you standing in the queue for the box office. I joined the line and watched you hand over your spare ticket. Once you were safely out of sight, I told the box office manager that you hadn't expected me to make it in time, and that you might have put my ticket up for resale. After I'd described you, which I was able to do in great detail, he handed it over without so much as a murmur.'

Anna put down her glass of wine and stared across at me with a look of incredulity. 'I'm glad he fell for your story,' she said. 'But should I?'

'Yes, you should. Because then I put two ten-pound notes into a theatre envelope and took the place next to you. The rest you already know.' I waited to see how she would react.

She didn't speak for some time. 'I'm flattered,' she

eventually said, and touched my hand. 'I didn't realise there were any old-fashioned romantics left in the world.' She squeezed my fingers and looked me in the eyes. 'Am I allowed to ask what you have planned for the rest of the evening?'

'Nothing has been planned so far,' I admitted. 'Which is why it's all been so refreshing.'

'You make me sound like an After Eight mint,' said Anna with a laugh.

'I can think of at least three replies to that,' I told her as Mario reappeared, looking a little disappointed at the sight of the half-empty plates.

'Was everything all right, sir?' he asked, sounding anxious.

'Couldn't have been better,' said Anna, who hadn't stopped looking at me.

'Would you like some coffee?' I asked.

'Yes,' said Anna. 'But perhaps we could have it somewhere a little less crowded.'

I was so taken by surprise that it was several moments before I recovered. I was beginning to feel that I was no longer in control. Anna rose from her place and said, 'Shall we go?' I nodded to Mario, who just smiled.

Once we were back out on the street, she linked her arm with mine as we retraced our steps along the Aldwych and past the theatre.

'It's been a wonderful evening,' she was saying as we reached the spot where I had left my car. 'Until you arrived on the scene it had been a rather dull day, but you've changed all that.'

'It hasn't actually been the best of days for me either,' I admitted. 'But I've rarely enjoyed an evening more. Where would you like to have coffee? Annabels? Or why don't we try the new Dorchester Club?'

'If you don't have a wife, your place. If you do . . .'

'I don't,' I told her simply.

'Then that's settled,' she said as I opened the door of my BMW for her. Once she was safely in I walked round to take my seat behind the wheel, and discovered that I had left my sidelights on and the keys in the ignition.

I turned the key, and the engine immediately purred into life. 'This has to be my day,' I said to myself.

'Sorry?' Anna said, turning in my direction.

'We were lucky to miss the rain,' I replied, as a few drops landed on the windscreen. I flicked on the wipers.

On our way to Pimlico, Anna told me about her childhood in the south of France, where her father had taught English at a boys' school. Her account of being the only girl among a couple of hundred teenage French boys made me laugh again and again. I found myself becoming more and more enchanted with her company.

'Whatever made you come back to England?' I asked.

'An English mother who divorced my French father, and the chance to study medicine at St Thomas's.'

'But don't you miss the south of France, especially on nights like this?' I asked as a clap of thunder crackled above us.

'Oh, I don't know,' she said. I was about to respond when she added, 'In any case, now the English have learnt how to cook, the place has become almost civilised.' I smiled to myself, wondering if she was teasing me again.

I found out immediately. 'By the way,' she said, 'I assume that was one of your restaurants we had dinner at.'

'Yes, it was,' I said sheepishly.

'That explains how you got a table so easily when it was packed out, why the waiter knew it was a Barolo you wanted without your having to ask, and how you could leave without paying the bill.'

I was beginning to wonder if I would always be a yard behind her.

'Was it the missing waiter, the four-and-a-half-fingered chef, or the crooked bartender?'

'The crooked bartender,' I replied, laughing. 'But I sacked him this afternoon, and I'm afraid his deputy didn't look as if he was coping all that well,' I explained as I turned right off Millbank, and began to search for a parking space.

'And I thought you only had eyes for me,' sighed Anna, 'when all the time you were looking over my shoulder and checking on what the deputy barman was up to.'

'Not *all* the time,' I said as I manoeuvred the car into the only space left in the mews where I lived. I got out of the car and walked round to Anna's side, opened the door and guided her to the house.

As I closed the door behind us, Anna put her arms around my neck and looked up into my eyes. I leaned down and kissed her for the first time. When she broke away, all she said was, 'Don't let's bother with coffee, Michael.' I slipped off my jacket, and led her upstairs and into my bedroom, praying that it hadn't been the housekeeper's day off. When I opened the door I was relieved to find that the bed had been made and the room was tidy.

'I'll just be a moment,' I said, and disappeared into the bathroom. As I cleaned my teeth, I began to wonder if it was all a dream. When I returned to the bedroom, would I discover she didn't exist? I dropped the toothbrush into its mug and went back to the bedroom. Where was she? My eyes followed a trail of discarded clothes that led all the way to the bed. Her head was propped up on the pillow. Only a sheet covered her body.

I quickly took off my clothes, dropping them where they fell, and switched off the main lights, so that only the one by the bed remained aglow. I slid under the sheets to join her. I looked at her for several seconds before I took her in my arms. I slowly explored every part of her body, as she began to kiss me again. I couldn't believe that anyone could be that exciting, and at the same time so tender. When we finally made love, I knew I never wanted this woman to leave me.

She lay in my arms for some time before either of us spoke. Then I began talking about anything that came into my head. I confided my hopes, my dreams, even my worst anxieties, with a freedom I had never experienced with anyone before. I wanted to share everything with her.

And then she leaned across and began kissing me once again, first on the lips, then the neck and chest, and as she slowly continued down my body I thought I would explode. The last thing I remember was turning off the light by my bed as the clock on the hall table chimed one.

When I woke the following morning, the first rays of sunlight were already shining through the lace curtains, and the glorious memory of the night before was instantly revived. I turned lazily to take her in my arms, but she was no longer there.

'Anna?' I cried out, sitting bolt upright. There was no reply. I flicked on the light by the side of the bed, and glanced across at the bedside clock. It was 7.29. I was about to jump out of bed and go in search of her when I noticed a scribbled note wedged under a corner of the clock.

I picked it up, read it slowly, and smiled.

'So will I,' I said, and lay back on the pillow, thinking about what I should do next. I decided to send her a dozen roses later that morning, eleven white and one red. Then I would have a red one delivered to her on the hour, every hour, until I saw her again.

After I had showered and dressed, I roamed aimlessly around the house. I wondered how quickly I could persuade Anna to move in, and what changes she would want to make. Heaven knows, I thought as I walked through to the kitchen, clutching her note, the place could do with a woman's touch.

As I ate breakfast I looked up her number in the telephone directory, instead of reading the morning paper. There it was, just as she had said. Dr Townsend, listing a surgery number in Parsons Green Lane where she could be contacted between nine and six. There was a second number, but deep black lettering requested that it should only be used in case of emergencies.

Although I considered my state of health to be an emergency, I dialled the first number, and waited impatiently. All I wanted to say was, 'Good morning, darling. I got your note, and can we make last night the first of many?'

A matronly voice answered the phone. 'Dr Townsend's surgery.'

'Dr Townsend, please,' I said.

'Which one?' she asked. 'There are three Dr Townsends in the practice – Dr Jonathan, Dr Anna and Dr Elizabeth.'

'Dr Anna,' I replied.

'Oh, Mrs Townsend,' she said. 'I'm sorry, but she's not available at the moment. She's just taken the children off to school, and after that she has to go to the airport to pick up her husband, Dr Jonathan, who's returning this morning from a medical conference in Minneapolis. I'm not expecting her back for at least a couple of hours. Would you like to leave a message?'

There was a long silence before the matronly voice asked, 'Are you still there?' I placed the receiver back on the hook without replying, and looked sadly down at the hand-written note by the side of the phone.

Dear Michael,
I will remember tonight for the rest of my life.
Thank you.
Anna

Burnt

'THANK YOU, MICHAEL. I'D LIKE THAT.'
I smiled, unable to mask my delight.

'Hi, Anna. I thought I might have missed you.'

I turned and stared at a tall man with a mop of fair hair, who seemed unaffected by the steady flow of people trying to pass him on either side.

Anna gave him a smile that I hadn't seen until that moment.

'Hello, darling,' she said. 'This is Michael Whitaker. You're lucky – he bought your ticket, and if you hadn't turned up I was just about to accept his kind invitation to dinner. Michael, this is my husband, Jonathan – the one who was held up at the hospital. As you can see, he's now escaped.'

I couldn't think of a suitable reply.

Jonathan shook me warmly by the hand. 'Thank you for keeping my wife company,' he said. 'Won't you join us for dinner?'

'That's very kind of you,' I replied, 'but I've just remembered that I'm meant to be somewhere else right now. I'd better run.'

'That's a pity,' said Anna. 'I was rather looking

forward to finding out all about the restaurant business. Perhaps we'll meet again sometime, whenever my husband next leaves me in the lurch. Goodbye, Michael.'

'Goodbye, Anna.'

I watched them climb into the back of a taxi together, and wished Jonathan would drop dead in front of me. He didn't, so I began to retrace my steps back to the spot where I had abandoned my car. 'You're a lucky man, Jonathan Townsend,' was the only observation I made. But no one was listening.

The next word that came to my lips was 'Damn!' I repeated it several times, as there was a distressingly large space where I was certain I'd left my car.

I walked up and down the street in case I'd forgotten where I'd parked it, cursed again, then marched off in search of a phone box, unsure if my car had been stolen or towed away. There was a pay phone just around the corner in Kingsway. I picked up the handset and jabbed three nines into it.

'Which service do you require? Fire, Police or Ambulance,' a voice asked.

'Police,' I said, and was immediately put through to another voice.

'Charing Cross Police Station. What is the nature of your enquiry?'

'I think my car has been stolen.'

'Can you tell me the make, colour and registration number please, sir.'

'It's a red Ford Fiesta, registration H107 SHV.'

There was a long pause, during which I could hear other voices talking in the background.

'No, it hasn't been stolen, sir,' said the officer when he came back on the line. 'The car was illegally parked on a double yellow line. It's been removed and taken to the Vauxhall Bridge Pound.'

'Can I pick it up now?' I asked sulkily.

'Certainly, sir. How will you be getting there?'

'I'll take a taxi.'

'Then just ask the driver for the Vauxhall Bridge Pound. Once you get there, you'll need some form of identification, and a cheque for £105 with a banker's card – that is if you don't have the full amount in cash.'

'£105?' I repeated in disbelief.

'That's correct, sir.'

I slammed the phone down just as it started to rain. I scurried back to the corner of the Aldwych in search of a taxi, only to find that they were all being commandeered by the hordes of people still hanging around outside the theatre.

I put my collar up and nipped across the road, dodging between the slow-moving traffic. Once I had reached the far side, I continued running until I found an overhanging ledge broad enough to shield me from the blustery rain.

I shivered, and sneezed several times before an empty cab eventually came to my rescue.

'Vauxhall Bridge Pound,' I told the driver as I jumped in.

'Bad luck, mate,' said the cabbie. 'You're my second this evening.'

I frowned.

As the taxi manoeuvred its way slowly through the rainswept post-theatre traffic and across Waterloo Bridge, the driver began chattering away. I just about managed monosyllabic replies to his opinions on the weather, John Major, the England cricket team and foreign tourists. With each new topic, his forecast became ever more gloomy.

When we reached the car pound I passed him a ten-pound note and waited in the rain for my change. Then I dashed off in the direction of a little Portakabin, where I was faced by my second queue that evening. This one was considerably longer than the first, and I knew that when I eventually reached the front of it and paid for my ticket, I wouldn't be rewarded with any memorable entertainment. When my turn finally came, a burly policeman pointed to a form sellotaped to the counter.

I followed its instructions to the letter, first producing my driving licence, then writing out a cheque for £105, payable to the Metropolitan Police. I handed them both over, with my cheque card, to the policeman, who towered over me. The man's sheer bulk was the only reason I didn't suggest that perhaps he ought to have more important things to do with his time, like catching drug dealers. Or even car thieves.

'Your vehicle is in the far corner,' said the officer, pointing into the distance, over row upon row of cars.

'Of course it is,' I replied. I stepped out of the Portakabin and back into the rain, dodging puddles as I ran between the lines of cars. I didn't stop until I reached the farthest corner of the pound. It still took me several more minutes to locate my red Ford Fiesta – one disadvantage, I thought, of owning the most popular car in Britain.

I unlocked the door, squelched down onto the front seat, and sneezed again. I turned the key in the ignition, but the engine barely turned over, letting out only the occasional splutter before giving up altogether. Then I remembered I hadn't switched the sidelights off when I made my unscheduled dash for the theatre. I uttered a string of expletives that only partly expressed my true feelings.

I watched as another figure came running across the pound towards a Range Rover parked in the row in front of me. I quickly wound down my window, but he had driven off before I could shout the magic words 'jump leads'. I got out and retrieved my jump leads from the boot, walked to the front of the car, raised the bonnet, and attached the leads to the battery. I began to shiver once again as I settled down for another wait.

I couldn't get Anna out of my mind, but accepted that the only thing I'd succeeded in picking up that evening was the 'flu.

In the following forty rain-drenched minutes, three people passed by before a young black man asked, 'So what's the trouble, man?' Once I had explained my problem he manoeuvred his old van alongside my car, then raised his bonnet and attached the jump leads to his battery. When he switched on his ignition, my engine began to turn over.

'Thanks,' I shouted, rather inadequately, once I'd revved the engine several times.

'My pleasure, man,' he replied, and disappeared into the night.

As I drove out of the car pound I switched on my radio, to hear Big Ben striking twelve. It reminded me that I hadn't turned up for work that night. The first thing I needed to do, if I wanted to keep my job, was to come up with a good excuse. I sneezed again, and decided on the 'flu. Although they'd probably taken the last orders by now, Gerald wouldn't have closed the kitchens yet.

I peered through the rain, searching the pavements for a pay phone, and eventually spotted a row of three outside a post office. I stopped the car and jumped out, but a cursory inspection revealed that they'd all been vandalised. I climbed back into the car and continued my search. After dashing in and out of the rain several times, I finally spotted a single phone box on the corner of Warwick Way that looked as if it might just be in working order.

I dialled the restaurant, and waited a long time for someone to answer.

'Laguna 50,' said an Italian-sounding young girl.

'Janice, is that you? It's Mike.'

'Yes, it's me, Mike,' she whispered, reverting to her Lambeth accent. 'I'd better warn you that every time your name's been mentioned this evening, Gerald picks up the nearest meat-axe.'

'Why?' I asked. 'You've still got Nick in the kitchen to see you through.'

'Nick chopped the top off one of his fingers earlier this evening, and Gerald had to take him to hospital. I was left in charge. He's not best pleased.'

'Oh, hell,' I said. 'But I've got . . .'

'The sack,' said another voice, and this one wasn't whispering.

'Gerald, I can explain . . .'

'Why you didn't turn up for work this evening?'

I sneezed, then held my nose. 'I've got the 'flu. If I'd come in tonight I would have given it to half the customers.'

'Would you?' said Gerald. 'Well, I suppose that might have been marginally worse than giving it to the girl who was sitting next to you in the theatre.'

'What do you mean?' I asked, letting go of my nose.

'Exactly what I said, Mike. You see, unfortunately for you, a couple of our regulars were two rows behind you at the Aldwych. They enjoyed the show almost as much as you seemed to, and one of them added, for good measure, that he thought your date was "absolutely stunning".'

'He must have mistaken me for someone else,' I said, trying not to sound desperate.

'He may have done, Mike, but I haven't. You're sacked, and don't even think about coming in to collect your pay packet, because there isn't one for a head waiter who'd rather take some bimbo to the theatre than do a night's work.' The line went dead.

I hung up the phone and started muttering obscenities under my breath as I walked slowly back towards my car. I was only a dozen paces away from it when a young lad jumped into the front seat, switched on the ignition, and lurched hesitatingly into the centre of the road in what sounded horribly like third gear. I chased after the retreating car, but once the youth began to accelerate, I knew I had no hope of catching him.

I ran all the way back to the phone box, and dialled 999 once again.

'Fire, Police or Ambulance?' I was asked for a second time that night.

'Police,' I said, and a moment later I was put through to another voice.

'Belgravia Police Station. What is the nature of your enquiry?'

'I've just had my car stolen!' I shouted.

'Make, model and registration number please, sir.'

'It's a red Ford Fiesta, registration H107 SHV.'

I waited impatiently.

'It hasn't been stolen, sir. It was illegally parked on a double . . .'

'No it wasn't!' I shouted even more loudly. 'I paid £105 to get the damn thing out of the Vauxhall Bridge Pound less than half an hour ago, and I've just seen it being driven off by a joyrider while I was making a phone call.'

'Where are you, sir?'

'In a phone box on the corner of Vauxhall Bridge Road and Warwick Way.'

'And in which direction was the car travelling when you last saw it?' asked the voice.

'North up Vauxhall Bridge Road.'

'And what is your home telephone number, sir?'

'081 290 4820.'

'And at work?'

'Like the car, I don't have a job any longer.'

'Right, I'll get straight onto it, sir. We'll be in touch with you the moment we have any news.'

I put the phone down and thought about what I should do next. I hadn't been left with a great deal of choice. I hailed a taxi and asked to be taken to Victoria, and was relieved to find that this driver showed no desire to offer any opinions on anything during the short journey to the station. When he dropped me I passed him my last note, and patiently waited while he handed over every last penny of my change. He also muttered an expletive or two. I bought a ticket for Bromley with my few remaining coins, and went in search of the platform.

'You've just about made it, mate,' the ticket collector told me. 'The last train's due in at any minute.' But I still had to wait for another twenty minutes on the cold, empty platform before the last train eventually pulled into the station. By then I had memorised every advertisement in sight, from Guinness to Mates, while continuing to sneeze at regular intervals.

When the train came to a halt and the doors squelched open I took a seat in a carriage near the front. It was another ten minutes before the engine lurched into action, and another forty before it finally pulled into Bromley station.

I emerged into the Kent night a few minutes before one o'clock, and set off in the direction of my little terraced house.

Twenty-five minutes later, I staggered up the short path to my front door. I began to search for my keys, then remembered that I'd left them in the car ignition. I didn't have the energy even to swear, and began to grovel around in the dark for the spare front-door key that was always hidden under a particular stone. But which one? At last I found it, put it in the lock, turned it and pushed the door open. No sooner had I stepped inside than the phone on the hall table began to ring.

I grabbed the receiver.

'Mr Whitaker?'

'Speaking.'

'This is the Belgravia police. We've located your car, sir, and . . .'

'Thank God for that,' I said, before the officer had a chance to finish the sentence. 'Where is it?'

'At this precise moment, sir, it's on the back of a pick-up lorry somewhere in Chelsea. It seems the lad who nicked it only managed to travel a mile or so before he hit the kerb at seventy, and bounced straight into a wall. I'm sorry to have to inform you, sir, that your car's a total write-off.'

'A total write-off?' I said in disbelief.

'Yes, sir. The garage who towed it away has been given your number, and they'll be in touch with you first thing in the morning.'

I couldn't think of any comment worth making.

'The good news is we've caught the lad who nicked it,' continued the police officer. 'The bad news is that he's only fifteen, doesn't have a driver's licence, and, of course, he isn't insured.'

'That's not a problem,' I said. 'I'm fully insured myself.'

'As a matter of interest, sir, did you leave your keys in the ignition?'

'Yes, I did. I was just making a quick phone call, and thought I'd only be away from the car for a couple of minutes.'

'Then I think it's unlikely you'll be covered by your insurance, sir.'

'Not covered by my insurance? What are you talking about?'

'It's standard policy nowadays not to pay out if you leave your keys in the ignition. You'd better check, sir,' were the officer's final words before ringing off.

I put the phone down and wondered what else could possibly go wrong. I slipped off my jacket and began to climb the stairs, but came to a sudden halt when I saw my wife waiting for me on the landing.

'Maureen . . .' I began.

'You can tell me later why the car is a total write-off,' she said, 'but not until you've explained why you didn't turn up for work this evening, and just who this "classy tart" is that Gerald said you were seen with at the theatre.'

Overdone

'No, I'm not doing anything in particular,' said Anna.

I smiled, unable to mask my delight.

'Good. I know a little restaurant just down the road that I think you might enjoy.'

'That sounds just fine,' said Anna as she made her way through the dense theatre crowd. I quickly followed, having to hurry just to keep up with her.

'Which way?' she asked. I pointed towards the Strand. She began walking at a brisk pace, and we continued to talk about the play.

When we reached the Strand I pointed to a large grey double door on the other side of the road. 'That's it,' I said. I would have taken her hand as she began to cross, but she stepped off the pavement ahead of me, dodged between the stationary traffic, and waited for me on the far side.

She pushed the grey doors open, and once again I followed in her wake. We descended a flight of steps into a basement restaurant buzzing with the talk of people who had just come out of theatres, and waiters dashing, plates in both hands, from table to table.

'I don't expect you'll be able to get a table here if you haven't booked,' said Anna, eyeing a group of would-be customers who were clustered round the bar, impatiently waiting for someone to leave.

'Don't worry about that,' I said with bravado, and strode across to the reservations desk. I waved a hand imperiously at the head waiter, who was taking a customer's order. I only hoped he would recognise me.

I turned round to smile at Anna, but she didn't look too impressed.

After the waiter had taken the order, he walked slowly over to me. 'How may I help you, sir?' he asked.

'Can you manage a table for two, Victor?'

'Victor's off tonight, sir. Have you booked?'

'No, I haven't, but . . .'

The head waiter checked the list of reservations and then looked at his watch. 'I might be able to fit you in around 11.15 – 11.30 at the latest,' he said, not sounding too hopeful.

'No sooner?' I pleaded. 'I don't think we can wait that long.' Anna nodded her agreement.

'I'm afraid not, sir,' said the head waiter. 'We are fully booked until then.'

'As I expected,' said Anna, turning to leave.

Once again I had to hurry to keep up with her. As we stepped out onto the pavement I said, 'There's a little Italian restaurant I know not far from here, where I can always get a table. Shall we risk it?'

'Can't see that we've got a lot of choice,' replied Anna. 'Which direction this time?'

'Just up the road to the right,' I said as a clap of thunder heralded an imminent downpour.

'Damn,' said Anna, placing her handbag over her head for protection.

'I'm sorry,' I said, looking up at the black clouds. 'It's my fault. I should have . . .'

'Stop apologising all the time, Michael. It isn't your fault if it starts to rain.'

I took a deep breath and tried again. 'We'd better make a dash for it,' I said desperately. 'I don't expect we'll be able to pick up a taxi in this weather.'

This at least secured her ringing endorsement. I began running up the road, and Anna followed closely behind. The rain was getting heavier and heavier, and although we couldn't have had more than seventy yards to cover, we were both soaked by the time we reached the restaurant.

I sighed with relief when I opened the door and found the dining room was half-empty, although I suppose I should have been annoyed. I turned and smiled hopefully at Anna, but she was still frowning.

'Everything all right?' I asked.

'Fine. It's just that my father had a theory about restaurants that were half-empty at this time of night.'

I looked quizzically at my guest, but decided not to make any comment about her eye make-up, which was beginning to run, or her hair, which had come loose at the edges.

'I'd better carry out some repair work. I'll only be a

couple of minutes,' she said, heading for a door marked 'Signorinas'.

I waved at Mario, who was serving no one in particular. He hurried over to me.

'There was a call for you earlier, Mr Whitaker,' Mario said as he guided me across the restaurant to my usual table. 'If you came in, I was to ask you to phone Gerald urgently. He sounded pretty desperate.'

'I'm sure it can wait. But if he rings again, let me know immediately.' At that moment Anna walked over to join us. The make-up had been restored, but the hair could have done with further attention.

I rose to greet her.

'You don't have to do that,' she said, taking her seat.

'Would you like a drink?' I asked, once we were both settled.

'No, I don't think so. I have an early start tomorrow morning, so I shouldn't overdo things. I'll just have a glass of wine with my meal.'

Another waiter appeared by her side. 'And what would madam care for this evening?' he asked politely.

'I haven't had time to look at the menu yet,' Anna replied, not even bothering to look up at him.

'I can recommend the fettucini, madam,' the waiter said, pointing to a dish halfway down the list of entrées. 'It's our speciality of the day.'

'Then I suppose I might as well have that,' said Anna, handing him the menu.

I nodded, indicating 'Me too,' and asked for a half-bottle of the house red. The waiter scooped up my menu and left us.

'Do you . . . ?'

'Can I . . . ?'

'You first,' I said, attempting a smile.

'Do you always order half a bottle of the house wine on a first date?' she asked.

'I think you'll find it's pretty good,' I said, rather plaintively.

'I was only teasing, Michael. Don't take yourself so seriously.'

I took a closer look at my companion, and began to wonder if I'd made a terrible mistake. Despite her efforts in the washroom, Anna wasn't quite the same girl I'd first seen – admittedly at a distance – when I'd nearly crashed my car earlier in the evening.

Oh my God, the car. I suddenly remembered where I'd left it, and stole a glance at my watch.

'Am I boring you already, Michael?' Anna asked. 'Or is this table on a time share?'

'Yes. I mean no. I'm sorry, I've just remembered something I should have checked on before we came to dinner. Sorry,' I repeated.

Anna frowned, which stopped me saying sorry yet again.

'Is it too late?' she asked.

'Too late for what?'

'To do something about whatever it is you should have checked on before we came to dinner?'

I looked out of the window, and wasn't pleased to see

that it had stopped raining. Now my only hope was that the late-night traffic wardens might not be too vigilant.

'No, I'm sure it will be all right,' I said, trying to sound relaxed.

'Well, that's a relief,' said Anna, in a tone that bordered on the sarcastic.

'So. What's it like being a doctor?' I asked, trying to change the subject.

'Michael, it's my evening off. I'd rather not talk about my work, if you don't mind.'

For the next few moments neither of us spoke. I tried again. 'Do you have many male patients in your practice?' I asked, as the waiter reappeared with our fettucini.

'I can hardly believe I'm hearing this,' Anna said, unable to disguise the weariness in her voice. 'When are people like you going to accept that one or two of us are capable of a little more than spending our lives waiting hand and foot on the male sex.'

The waiter poured some wine into my glass.

'Yes. Of course. Absolutely. No. I didn't mean it to sound like that . . .' I sipped the wine and nodded to the waiter, who filled Anna's glass.

'Then what did you mean it to sound like?' demanded Anna as she stuck her fork firmly into the fettucini.

'Well, isn't it unusual for a man to go to a woman doctor?' I said, realising the moment I had uttered the words that I was only getting myself into even deeper water.

'Good heavens, no, Michael. We live in an enlightened age. I've probably seen more naked men than you have

— and it's not an attractive sight, I can assure you.' I laughed, in the hope that it would ease the tension. 'In any case,' she added, 'quite a few men are confident enough to accept the existence of women doctors, you know.'

'I'm sure that's true,' I said. 'I just thought . . .'

'You didn't think, Michael. That's the problem with so many men like you. I bet you've never even considered consulting a woman doctor.'

'No, but . . . Yes, but . . .'

' "No but, yes but" — Let's change the subject before I get really angry,' Anna said, putting her fork down. 'What do you do for a living, Michael? It doesn't sound as if you're in a profession where women are treated as equals.'

'I'm in the restaurant business,' I told her, wishing the fettucini was a little lighter.

'Ah, yes, you told me in the interval,' she said. 'But what does being "in the restaurant business" actually mean?'

'I'm on the management side. Or at least, that's what I do nowadays. I started life as a waiter, then I moved into the kitchens for about five years, and finally . . .'

'. . . found you weren't very good at either, so you took up managing everyone else.'

'Something like that,' I said, trying to make light of it. But Anna's words only reminded me that one of my other restaurants was without a chef that night, and that that was where I'd been heading before I'd allowed myself to become infatuated by Anna.

'I've lost you again,' Anna said, beginning to sound exasperated. 'You were going to tell me all about restaurant management.'

'Yes, I was, wasn't I? By the way, how's your fettucini?'

'Not bad, considering.'

'Considering?'

'Considering this place was your second choice.'

I was silenced once again.

'It's not that bad,' she said, taking another reluctant forkful.

'Perhaps you'd like something else instead? I can always . . .'

'No, thank you, Michael. After all, this was the one dish the waiter felt confident enough to recommend.'

I couldn't think of a suitable response, so I remained silent.

'Come on, Michael, you still haven't explained what restaurant management actually involves,' said Anna.

'Well, at the moment I'm running three restaurants in the West End, which means I never stop dashing from one to the other, depending on which is facing the biggest crisis on that particular day.'

'Sounds a bit like ward duty to me,' said Anna. 'So who turned out to have the biggest crisis today?'

'Today, thank heaven, was not typical,' I told her with feeling.

'That bad?' said Anna.

'Yes, I'm afraid so. We lost a chef this morning who cut off the top of his finger, and won't be back at work for at least a fortnight. My head waiter in our second restaurant is off, claiming he has 'flu, and I've just had to sack the barman in the third for fiddling the books. Barmen always fiddle the books, of course, but in this case even the customers began to notice what he was up to.' I paused, wondering if I should risk another mouthful of fettucini. 'But I still wouldn't want to be in any other business.'

'In the circumstances, I'm frankly amazed you were able to take the evening off.'

'I shouldn't have, really, and wouldn't have, except . . .' I trailed off as I leaned over and topped up Anna's wine glass.

'Except what?' she said.

'Do you want to hear the truth?' I asked as I poured the remains of the wine into my own glass.

'I'll try that for starters,' she said.

I placed the empty bottle on the side of the table, and hesitated, but only for a moment. 'I was driving to one of my restaurants earlier this evening, when I spotted you going into the theatre. I stared at you for so long that I nearly crashed into the back of the car in front of me. Then I swerved across the road into the nearest parking space, and the car behind almost crashed into me. I leapt out, ran all the way to the theatre, and searched everywhere until I saw you standing in the queue for the box office. I joined the line and watched you hand over your spare ticket. Once you were safely out of sight, I told the box office manager that you hadn't expected me to make it in time, and that you might have put my ticket up for resale. Once I'd described you, which I was able to do in great detail, he handed it over without so much as a murmur.'

'More fool him,' said Anna, putting down her glass and staring at me as if I'd just been released from a lunatic asylum.

'Then I put two ten-pound notes into a theatre envelope and took the place next to you,' I continued. 'The rest you already know.' I waited, with some trepidation, to see how she would react.

'I suppose I ought to be flattered,' Anna said after a moment's consideration. 'But I don't know whether to laugh or cry. One thing's for certain; the woman I've been living with for the past ten years will think it's highly amusing, especially as you paid for her ticket.'

The waiter returned to remove the half-finished plates. 'Was everything all right, sir?' he asked, sounding anxious.

'Fine, just fine,' I said unconvincingly. Anna grimaced, but made no comment.

'Would you care for coffee, madam?'

'No, I don't think I'll risk it,' she said, looking at her watch. 'In any case, I ought to be getting back. Elizabeth will be wondering where I've got to.'

She stood up and walked towards the door. I followed a yard behind. She was just about to step onto the pavement when she turned to me and asked, 'Don't you think you ought to settle the bill?'

'That won't be necessary.'

'Why?' she asked, laughing. 'Do you own the place?'

'No. But it is one of the three restaurants I manage.'

Anna turned scarlet. 'I'm so sorry, Michael,' she said. 'That was tactless of me.' She paused for a moment before adding, 'But I'm sure you'll agree that the food wasn't exactly memorable.'

'Would you like me to drive you home?' I asked, trying not to sound too enthusiastic.

Anna looked up at the black clouds. 'That would be useful,' she replied, 'if it's not miles out of your way. Where's your car?' she said before I had a chance to ask where she lived.

'I left it just up the road.'

'Oh, yes, I remember,' said Anna. 'When you jumped out of it because you couldn't take your eyes off me. I'm afraid you picked the wrong girl this time.'

At last we had found something on which we could agree, but I made no comment as we walked towards the spot where I had abandoned my car. Anna limited her conversation to whether it was about to rain again, and how good she had thought the wine was. I was relieved to find my Volvo parked exactly where I had left it.

I was searching for my keys when I spotted a large sticker glued to the windscreen. I looked down at the front offside wheel, and saw the yellow clamp.

'It just isn't your night, is it?' said Anna. 'But don't worry about me, I'll just grab a cab.'

She raised her hand and a taxi skidded to a halt. She turned back to face me. 'Thanks for dinner,' she managed, not altogether convincingly, and added, even less convincingly, 'Perhaps we'll meet again.' Before I could respond, she had slammed the taxi door closed.

As I watched her being driven away, it started to rain.

I took one more look at my immovable car, and decided I would deal with the problem in the morning.

I was about to rush for the nearest shelter when another taxi came around the corner, its yellow light indicating that it was for hire. I waved frantically and it drew up beside my clamped car.

'Bad luck, mate,' said the cabbie, looking down at my front wheel. 'My third tonight.'

I attempted a smile.

'So, where to, guv?'

I gave him my address in Lambeth and climbed into the back.

As the taxi manoeuvred its way slowly through the rainswept post-theatre traffic and across Waterloo Bridge, the driver began chattering away. I just about managed monosyllabic replies to his opinions on the weather, John Major, the England cricket team and foreign tourists. With each new topic, his forecast became ever more gloomy.

He only stopped offering his opinions when he came to a halt outside my house in Fentiman Road. I paid him, and smiled ruefully at the thought that this would be the first time in weeks that I'd managed to get home before midnight. I walked slowly up the short path to the front door.

I turned the key in the lock and opened the door quietly, so as not to wake my wife. Once inside I went through my nightly ritual of slipping off my jacket and shoes before creeping quietly up the stairs.

Before I had reached the bedroom I began to get undressed. After years of coming in at one or two in the morning, I was able to take off all my clothes, fold and stack them, and slide under the sheets next to Judy without waking her. But just as I pulled back the cover she said drowsily, 'I didn't think you'd be home so early, with all the problems you were facing tonight.' I wondered if she was talking in her sleep. 'How much damage did the fire do?'

'The fire?' I said, standing in the nude.

'In Davies Street. Gerald phoned a few moments after you'd left to say a fire had started in the kitchen and had spread to the restaurant. He was just checking to make certain you were on your way. He'd cancelled all the bookings for the next two weeks, but he didn't think they'd be able to open again for at least a month. I told him that as you'd left just after six you'd be with him at any minute. So, just how bad is the damage?'

I was already dressed by the time Judy was awake enough to ask why I had never turned up at the restaurant. I shot down the stairs and out onto the street in search of another cab. It had started raining again.

A taxi swung round and came to a halt in front of me.

'Where to this time, guv?'

À Point

'THANK YOU, MICHAEL. I'D LIKE THAT.'

I smiled, unable to mask my delight.

'Hi, Pipsqueak. I thought I might have missed you.'

I turned and stared at a tall man with a mop of fair hair, who seemed unaffected by the steady flow of people trying to pass him on either side.

Anna gave him a smile that I hadn't seen until that moment.

'Hello, Jonathan,' she said. 'This is Michael Whitaker. You're lucky – he bought your ticket, and if you hadn't turned up I was just about to accept his kind invitation to dinner. Michael, this is my brother, Jonathan – the one who was held up at the hospital. As you can see, he's now escaped.'

I couldn't think of a suitable reply.

Jonathan shook me warmly by the hand. 'Thank you for keeping my sister company,' he said. 'Won't you join us for dinner?'

'That's kind of you,' I replied, 'but I've just remembered that I'm meant to be somewhere else right now. I'd better . . .'

'You're not meant to be anywhere else right now,'

interrupted Anna, giving me the same smile. 'Don't be so feeble.' She linked her arm in mine. 'In any case, we'd *both* like you to join us.'

'Thank you,' I said.

'There's a restaurant just down the road that I've been told is rather good,' said Jonathan, as the three of us began walking off in the direction of the Strand.

'Great. I'm famished,' said Anna.

'So, tell me all about the play,' Jonathan said as Anna linked her other arm in his.

'Every bit as good as the critics promised,' said Anna.

'You were unlucky to miss it,' I said.

'But I'm rather glad you did,' said Anna as we reached the corner of the Strand.

'I think that's the place I'm looking for,' said Jonathan, pointing to a large grey double door on the far side of the road. The three of us weaved our way through the temporarily stationary traffic.

Once we reached the other side of the road Jonathan pushed open one of the grey doors to allow us through. It started to rain just as we stepped inside. He led Anna and me down a flight of stairs into a basement restaurant buzzing with the talk of people who had just come out of theatres, and waiters dashing, plates in both hands, from table to table.

'I'll be impressed if you can get a table here,' Anna said to her brother, eyeing a group of would-be customers who were clustered round the bar, impatiently waiting for someone to leave. 'You should have booked,' she added as he began waving at the head waiter, who was fully occupied taking a customer's order.

I remained a yard or two behind them, and as Mario came across, I put a finger to my lips and nodded to him.

'I don't suppose you have a table for three?' asked Jonathan.

'Yes, of course, sir. Please follow me,' said Mario, leading us to a quiet table in the corner of the room.

'That was a bit of luck,' said Jonathan.

'It certainly was,' Anna agreed. Jonathan suggested that I take the far chair, so his sister could sit between us.

Once we had settled, Jonathan asked what I would like to drink.

'How about you?' I said, turning to Anna. 'Another dry martini?'

Jonathan looked surprised. 'You haven't had a dry martini since . . .'

Anna scowled at him and said quickly, 'I'll just have a glass of wine with the meal.'

Since when? I wondered, but only said, 'I'll have the same.'

Mario reappeared, and handed us our menus. Jonathan and Anna studied theirs in silence for some time before Jonathan asked, 'Any ideas?'

'It all looks so tempting,' Anna said. 'But I think I'll settle for the fettucini and a glass of red wine.'

'What about a starter?' asked Jonathan.

'No. I'm on first call tomorrow, if you remember – unless of course you're volunteering to take my place.'

'Not after what I've been through this evening, Pipsqueak. I'd rather go without a starter too,' he said. 'How about you, Michael? Don't let our domestic problems get in your way.'

'Fettucini and a glass of red wine would suit me just fine.'

'Three fettucini and a bottle of your best Chianti,' said Jonathan when Mario returned.

Anna leaned over to me and whispered conspiratorially, 'It's the only Italian wine he can pronounce correctly.'

'What would have happened if we'd chosen fish?' I asked her.

'He's also heard of Frascati, but he's never quite sure what he's meant to do when someone orders duck.'

'What are you two whispering about?' asked Jonathan as he handed his menu back to Mario.

'I was asking your sister about the third partner in the practice.'

'Not bad, Michael,' Anna said. 'You should have gone into politics.'

'My wife, Elizabeth, is the third partner,' Jonathan said, unaware of what Anna had been getting at. 'She, poor darling, is on call tonight.'

'You note, two women and one man,' said Anna as the wine waiter appeared by Jonathan's side.

'Yes. There used to be four of us,' said Jonathan, without explanation. He studied the label on the bottle before nodding sagely.

'You're not fooling anyone, Jonathan. Michael has

already worked out that you're no sommelier,' said Anna, sounding as if she was trying to change the subject. The waiter extracted the cork and poured a little wine into Jonathan's glass for him to taste.

'So, what do you do, Michael?' asked Jonathan after he had given a second nod to the wine waiter. 'Don't tell me you're a doctor, because I'm not looking for another man to join the practice.'

'No, he's in the restaurant business,' said Anna, as three bowls of fettucini were placed in front of us.

'I see. You two obviously swapped life histories during the interval,' said Jonathan. 'But what does being "in the restaurant business" actually mean?'

'I'm on the management side,' I explained. 'Or at least, that's what I do nowadays. I started life as a waiter, then I moved into the kitchens for about five years, and finally ended up in management.'

'But what does a restaurant manager actually do?' asked Anna.

'Obviously the interval wasn't long enough for you to go into any great detail,' said Jonathan as he jabbed his fork into some fettucini.

'Well, at the moment I'm running three restaurants in the West End, which means I never stop dashing from one to the other, depending on which is facing the biggest crisis on that particular day.'

'Sounds a bit like ward duty to me,' said Anna. 'So who turned out to have the biggest crisis today?'

'Today, thank heaven, was not typical,' I said with feeling.

'That bad?' said Jonathan.

'Yes, I'm afraid so. We lost a chef this morning who cut off the top of his finger, and won't be back at work for at least a fortnight. My head waiter in our second restaurant is off, claiming he has 'flu, and I've just had to sack the barman in the third for fiddling the books. Barmen always fiddle the books, of course, but in this case even the customers began to notice what he was up to.' I paused. 'But I still wouldn't want to be in any other . . .'

A shrill ring interrupted me. I couldn't tell where the sound was coming from until Jonathan removed a tiny cellular phone from his jacket pocket.

'Sorry about this,' he said. 'Hazard of the job.' He pressed a button and put the phone to his ear. He listened for a few seconds, and a frown appeared on his face. 'Yes, I suppose so. I'll be there as quickly as I can.' He flicked the phone closed and put it back into his pocket.

'Sorry,' he repeated. 'One of my patients has chosen this particular moment to have a relapse. I'm afraid I'm going to have to leave you.' He stood up and turned to his sister. 'How will you get home, Pipsqueak?'

'I'm a big girl now,' said Anna, 'so I'll just look around for one of those black objects on four wheels with a sign on the top that reads T-A-X-I, and then I'll wave at it.'

'Don't worry, Jonathan,' I said. 'I'll drive her home.'

'That's very kind of you,' said Jonathan, 'because if it's still pouring by the time you leave, she may not be able to find one of those black objects to wave at.'

'In any case, it's the least I can do, after I ended up getting your ticket, your dinner and your sister.'

396

'Fair exchange,' said Jonathan as Mario came rushing up.

'Is everything all right, sir?' he asked.

'No, it isn't. I'm on call, and have to go.' He handed over an American Express card. 'If you'd be kind enough to put this through your machine, I'll sign for it and you can fill in the amount later. And please add fifteen per cent.'

'Thank you, sir,' said Mario, and rushed away.

'Hope to see you again,' said Jonathan. I rose to shake him by the hand.

'I hope so too,' I said.

Jonathan left us, headed for the bar and signed a slip of paper. Mario handed him back his American Express card.

As Anna waved to her brother, I looked towards the bar and shook my head slightly. Mario tore up the little slip of paper and dropped the pieces into a waste-paper basket.

'It hasn't been a wonderful day for Jonathan, either,' said Anna, turning back to face me. 'And what with your problems, I'm amazed you were able to take the evening off.'

'I shouldn't have, really, and wouldn't have, except . . .' I trailed off as I leaned over and topped up Anna's glass.

'Except what?' she asked.

'Do you want to hear the truth?' I asked as I poured the remains of the wine into my own glass.

'I'll try that for starters,' she said.

I placed the empty bottle on the side of the table, and hesitated, but only for a moment. 'I was driving to one of my restaurants earlier this evening, when I spotted you going into the theatre. I stared at you for so long that I nearly crashed into the back of the car in front of me. Then I swerved across the road into the nearest parking space, and the car behind almost crashed into me. I leapt out, ran all the way to the theatre, and searched everywhere until I saw you standing in the queue for the box office. I joined the line and watched you hand over your spare ticket. Once you were safely out of sight, I told the box office manager that you hadn't expected me to make it in time, and that you might have put my ticket up for resale. After I'd described you, which I was able to do in great detail, he handed it over without so much as a murmur.'

Anna put down her glass of wine and stared across at me with a look of incredulity. 'I'm glad he fell for your story,' she said. 'But should I?'

'Yes, you should. Because then I put two ten-pound notes into a theatre envelope and took the place next to you,' I continued. 'The rest you already know.' I waited to see how she would react. She didn't speak for some time.

'I'm flattered,' she said eventually. 'I didn't realise there were any old-fashioned romantics left in the world.' She lowered her head slightly. 'Am I allowed to ask what you have planned for the rest of the evening?'

'Nothing has been planned so far,' I admitted. 'Which is why it's all been so refreshing.'

'You make me sound like an After Eight mint,' said Anna with a laugh.

'I can think of at least three replies to that,' I told her as Mario reappeared, looking a little disappointed at the sight of the half-empty plates.

'Is everything all right, sir?' he asked, sounding anxious.

'Couldn't have been better,' said Anna, who hadn't stopped looking at me.

'Would you like a coffee, madam?' Mario asked her.

'No, thank you,' said Anna firmly. 'We have to go in search of a marooned car.'

'Heaven knows if it will still be there after all this time,' I said as she rose from her place.

I took Anna's hand, led her towards the entrance, back up the stairs and out onto the street. Then I began to retrace my steps to the spot where I'd abandoned my car. As we strolled up the Aldwych and chatted away, I felt as if I was with an old friend.

'You don't have to give me a lift, Michael,' Anna was saying. 'It's probably miles out of your way, and in any case it's stopped raining, so I'll just hail a taxi.'

'I want to give you a lift,' I told her. 'That way I'll have your company for a little longer.' She smiled as we reached a distressingly large space where I had left the car.

'Damn,' I said. I quickly checked up and down the road, and returned to find Anna laughing.

'Is this another of your schemes to have more of my company?' she teased. She opened her bag and took out a mobile phone, dialled 999, and passed it over to me.

'Which service do you require? Fire, Police or Ambulance?' a voice asked.

'Police,' I said, and was immediately put through to another voice.

'Charing Cross Police Station. What is the nature of your enquiry?'

'I think my car has been stolen.'

'Can you tell me the make, colour and registration number please, sir.'

'It's a blue Rover 600, registration K857 SHV.'

There was a long pause, during which I could hear other voices talking in the background.

'No, it hasn't been stolen, sir,' said the officer who had been dealing with me when he came back on the line. 'The vehicle was illegally parked on a double yellow line. It's been removed and taken to the Vauxhall Bridge Pound.'

'Can I pick it up now?' I asked.

'Certainly, sir. How will you be getting there?'

'I'll take a taxi.'

'Then just ask the driver for the Vauxhall Bridge Pound. Once you get there, you'll need some form of identification, and a cheque for £105 with a banker's card – that is if you don't have the full amount in cash.'

'£105?' I said quietly.

'That's correct, sir.'

Anna frowned for the first time that evening.

'Worth every penny.'

'I beg your pardon, sir?'

400

'Nothing, officer. Goodnight.'

I handed the phone back to Anna, and said, 'The next thing I'm going to do is find you a taxi.'

'You certainly are not, Michael, because I'm staying with you. In any case, you promised my brother you'd take me home.'

I took her hand and hailed a taxi, which swung across the road and came to a halt beside us.

'Vauxhall Bridge Pound, please.'

'Bad luck, mate,' said the cabbie. 'You're my fourth this evening.'

I gave him a broad grin.

'I expect the other three also chased you into the theatre, but luckily they were behind me in the queue,' I said to Anna as I joined her on the back seat.

As the taxi manoeuvred its way slowly through the rainswept post-theatre traffic and across Waterloo Bridge, Anna said, 'Don't you think I should have been given the chance to choose between the four of you? After all, one of them might have been driving a Rolls-Royce.'

'Not possible.'

'And why not, pray?' asked Anna.

'Because you couldn't have parked a Rolls-Royce in that space.'

'But if he'd had a chauffeur, that would have solved all my problems.'

'In that case, I would simply have run him over.'

The taxi had travelled some distance before either of us spoke again.

'Can I ask you a personal question?' Anna eventually said.

'If it's what I think it is, I was about to ask you the same thing.'

'Then you go first.'

'No – I'm not married,' I said. 'Nearly, once, but she escaped.' Anna laughed. 'And you?'

'I was married,' she said quietly. 'He was the fourth doctor in the practice. He died three years ago. I spent nine months nursing him, but in the end I failed.'

'I'm so sorry,' I said, feeling a little ashamed. 'That was tactless of me. I shouldn't have raised the subject.'

'I raised it, Michael, not you. It's me who should apologise.'

Neither of us spoke again for several minutes, until Anna said, 'For the past three years, since Andrew's death, I've immersed myself in work, and I seem to spend most of my spare time boring Jonathan and Elizabeth to distraction. They couldn't have been more understanding, but they must be heartily sick of it by now. I wouldn't be surprised if Jonathan hadn't arranged an emergency for tonight, so someone else could take me to the theatre for a change. It might even give me the confidence to go out again. Heaven knows,' she added as we drove into the car pound, 'enough people have been kind enough to ask me.'

I passed the cabbie a ten-pound note and we dashed through the rain in the direction of a little Portakabin.

I walked up to the counter and read the form sellotaped

to it. I took out my wallet, extracted my driving licence, and began counting.

I only had eighty pounds in cash, and I never carry a chequebook.

Anna grinned, and took the envelope I'd presented to her earlier in the evening from her bag. She tore it open and extracted the two ten-pound notes, added a five-pound note of her own, and handed them over to me.

'Thank you,' I said, once again feeling embarrassed.

'Worth every penny,' she replied with a grin.

The policeman counted the notes slowly, placed them in a tin box, and gave me a receipt.

'It's right there, in the front row,' he said, pointing out of the window. 'And if I may say so, sir, it was perhaps unwise of you to leave your keys in the ignition. If the vehicle had been stolen, your insurance company would not have been liable to cover the claim.' He passed me my keys.

'It was my fault, officer,' said Anna. 'I should have sent him back for them, but I didn't realise what he was up to. I'll make sure he doesn't do it again.'

The officer looked up at me. I shrugged my shoulders and led Anna out of the cabin and across to my car. I opened the door to let her in, then nipped round to the driver's side as she leant over and pushed my door open. I took my place behind the wheel and turned to face her. 'I'm sorry,' I said. 'The rain has ruined your dress.' A drop of water fell off the end of her nose. 'But, you know, you're just as beautiful wet or dry.'

'Thank you, Michael,' she smiled. 'But if you don't have any objection, on balance I'd prefer to be dry.'

I laughed. 'So, where shall I take you?' I asked, suddenly aware that I didn't know where she lived.

'Fulham, please. 49 Parsons Green Lane. It's not too far.'

I pushed the key into the ignition, not caring how far it was. I turned the key and took a deep breath. The engine spluttered, but refused to start. Then I realised I had left the sidelights on.

'Don't do this to me,' I begged, as Anna began laughing again. I turned the key a second time, and the motor caught. I let out a sigh of relief.

'That was a close one,' Anna said. 'If it hadn't started, we might have ended up spending the rest of the night together. Or was that all part of your dastardly plan?'

'Nothing's gone to plan so far,' I admitted as I drove out of the pound. I paused before adding, 'Still, I suppose things might have turned out differently.'

'You mean if I hadn't been the sort of girl you were looking for?'

'Something like that.'

'I wonder what those other three men would have thought of me,' said Anna wistfully.

'Who cares? They're not going to have the chance to find out.'

'You sound very sure of yourself, Mr Whitaker.'

'If you only knew,' I said. 'But I would like to see you again, Anna. If you're willing to risk it.'

She seemed to take an eternity to reply. 'Yes, I'd like

that,' she said eventually. 'But only on condition that you pick me up at my place, so I can be certain you park your car legally, and remember to switch your lights off.'

'I accept your terms,' I told her. 'And I won't even add any conditions of my own if we can begin the agreement tomorrow evening.'

Once again Anna didn't reply immediately. 'I'm not sure I know what I'm doing tomorrow evening.'

'Neither do I,' I said. 'But I'll cancel it, whatever it is.'

'Then so will I,' said Anna as I drove into Parsons Green Lane, and began searching for number forty-nine.

'It's about a hundred yards down, on the left,' she said.

I drew up and parked outside her front door.

'Don't let's bother with the theatre this time,' said Anna. 'Come round at about eight, and I'll cook you some supper.' She leant over and kissed me on the cheek before turning back to open the car door. I jumped out and walked quickly round to her side of the car as she stepped onto the pavement.

'So, I'll see you around eight tomorrow evening,' she said.

'I'll look forward to that.' I hesitated, and then took her in my arms. 'Goodnight, Anna.'

'Goodnight, Michael,' she said as I released her. 'And thank you for buying my ticket, not to mention dinner. I'm glad my other three would-be suitors only made it as far as the car pound.'

I smiled as she pushed the key into the lock of her front door.

She turned back. 'By the way, Michael, was that the restaurant with the missing waiter, the four-and-a-half-fingered chef, or the crooked bartender?'

'The crooked bartender,' I replied with a smile.

She closed the door behind her as the clock on a nearby church struck one.

OTHER PAN BOOKS
AVAILABLE FROM PAN MACMILLAN